DARK HOLLOW

BRIAN KEENE

deadite
press

deadite
press

DEADITE PRESS
205 NE BRYANT
PORTLAND, OR 97211
www.DEADITEPRESS.com

AN ERASERHEAD PRESS COMPANY
www.ERASERHEADPRESS.com

ISBN: 1-62105-030-0

Originally published as The Rutting Season

Printed in the USA.

Acknowledgements

For this new edition of Dark Hollow, my thanks to everyone at Deadite Press; Alex McVey; Mary SanGiovanni; and my sons. Thanks also to Larry Roberts, Cassandra, Sam, the Shrewsbury Fire Department, Elizabeth, Lindsey, Don, Uta, Mike, Doug, Jason, Paul, Shannon, Toni, Michael, and Steve Pattee.

DEADITE PRESS BOOKS BY BRIAN KEENE

Urban Gothic
Jack's Magic Beans
Take The Long Way Home
A Gathering of Crows
Darkness On the Edge of Town
Tequila's Sunrise
Dead Sea
Kill Whitey
Castaways
Ghoul
The Cage
Dark Hollow
Ghost Walk
Clickers II (with J. F. Gonzalez)
Clickers III (with J. F. Gonzalez – ebook only)

Author's Note: Although many of the Central Pennsylvanian locations in this novel are real, I have taken certain fictional liberties with them. So if you live there, don't look for your woods or hollow. You wouldn't recognize it—and if you go searching for it, you might hear the shepherd's pipe and end up dancing in the firelight...

For Tim Lebbon,

You bring the bourbon. I'll save a seat in the backyard.
Cheers and chairs, logger and lager.

To watch thy wantonness weeping through
The tangled grove, the gnarled bole
Of the living tree that is spirit and soul
I am thy mate, I am thy man,
Goat of thy flock, I am gold, I am god
With hoofs of steel I race on the rocks
Through solstice stubborn to equinox
And I rave; and I rape and I rip and I rend
Everlasting, world without end . . .

—Aleister Crowley
"Hymn To Pan"

ONE

It was on the first day of spring that Big Steve and I saw Shelly Carpenter giving head to the hairy man.

Winter had been a hard one. Two books to write in five-month's time. It's not something I recommend doing, if you can help it. There was a lot of pressure involved. The sales of my first novel, *Heart of the Matter*, caught my critics, my publisher, and even myself by surprise. It did very well—something a book of its kind isn't supposed to do, especially a mid-list, mass-market mystery paperback with no promotional campaign behind it other than a quarter-page advertisement in one lone trade magazine. Publishers don't buy a lot of advertising for mid-list authors.

Suffice to say, I beat the odds. Flush with success, I quit my day job—only to learn that I wouldn't be getting a royalty check for at least another year. We'd already blown through the advance; mortgage payments, credit card payments, car and truck payments, new living room furniture for my wife, Tara, and a new laptop for me. Plus, I'd spent quite a bit of my own cash traveling to book signings. Publishers don't pay for mid-list book signing tours either.

If I'd had an agent, maybe they would have explained the pay schedule to me. Or then again, maybe they wouldn't have. Personally, I'm glad I don't have an agent. They require fifteen percent of your earnings, and I was broke. Fifteen percent of shit is still shit.

I could have gone back to work part time at the paper mill in Spring Grove, but I figured that if I applied myself to the writing, I'd be making about as much money as I would at the mill anyway, so I decided to follow what I love doing.

Tara still worked, insisting that she pay the bills while I stayed home and wrote. We needed the health insurance her company provided, but we couldn't survive on just one income. Thus—two more books for two different publishers in five-month's time, written just for the advance money, which would see us through the winter. Don't get me wrong. It was a nice chunk of change, but when you totaled up the hours I spent writing, the advance for the next two novels came out to about a buck eighty an hour. And to make matters worse, they weren't really stories that I wanted to write. They didn't speak to me. I wasn't passionate about them, and had lost my sense of wonder.

But we needed the money. Some people call that being a hack. I call it necessity.

The pressure got to me. I started smoking again—two packs a day—and drank coffee nonstop. I'd get up at five, make the daily commute from the bed to the coffee pot to the computer, and start writing. I'd work on one novel until noon, take a break for lunch, and then work on the second novel until late evening. After a full day of that, I'd take care of business; reading contracts, responding to fan mail, checking my message board, giving interviews—all the other things that constitute writing but don't actually involve putting words on paper—and go to bed around midnight. Then I'd get up the next morning and do it all over again. Seven days a week. The glamorous life of a writer.

During those rough months, I'd have gone insane if not for Big Steve. Tara brought him home from the pound to keep me company during the day. Big Steve was a mixed breed mutt—part Beagle, part Rottweiler, part Black Lab, and one hundred percent pussy. Despite his formidable size and bark, Big Steve was scared of his own shadow. He ran from butterflies and squirrels, fled from birds and wind-tossed leaves, and cowered when the mailwoman came to the door. When Tara first brought him home, he hid in the corner of the kitchen for half a day, shaking, with his tail between his legs. He warmed up to us fairly quick, but he was still frightened by anything else. Not that he let it show. When something—it didn't matter what, a groundhog or Seth Ferguson, the kid from across the street—stepped onto our property, the Rottweiler inside him came out. He was all bark and no bite, but a robber would have had a hard time believing that.

Big Steve became my best friend. He listened while I read manuscript pages out loud to him. He'd lie on the couch and watch television with me when I took a break from writing. We liked the same beer, and the same food (because dog food just didn't do it for Big Steve; he preferred a nice, juicy steak or some cheese-dripping pizza). Most importantly, Big Steve knew when it was time to drag my ass away from the computer. That was how we started our daily walks, and now they were a scheduled routine. Two per day—one at dawn, shortly after Tara left for work, and the second at sundown, before I started making dinner, when she was on her way home. Tara commutes to Baltimore everyday, and it was at those times—when she first left and when she was due home—that the house seemed especially lonely. Big Steve had impeccable timing. He'd get me outside and that always cheered me up.

Which brings us back to Shelly Carpenter and the hairy man.

When Tara left for work that Monday, the first day of spring, Big Steve stood at the door and barked; once—short and to the point.

Behold, I stand at the door and bark; therefore I need to pee.

"You ready to go outside?" I asked.

He thumped his tail in affirmation, and his ears perked up. His big, brown eyes shone with excitement. It didn't take much to make Big Steve happy.

I clipped his leash to his collar (despite his fear of anything that moves, there is enough Beagle in Big Steve to inspire a love of running off into the woods with his nose to the ground, and not coming home until after dark). We stepped outside. The sun was shining, and it felt good on my face. It was unseasonably warm, almost like summer. Tara and I had planted a lilac bush the year before, and the flowers bloomed, their scent fragrant and sweet. Birds chirped and sang to each other in the big oak tree in our backyard. A squirrel ran along the roof of my garage, chattering at Big Steve. The dog shrank away from it.

The long, cold winter had come and gone, and somehow, I'd made it through and finished both manuscripts, *Cold As Ice* and *When the Rain Comes*. Now, I could finally focus on the novel that I *wanted* to write, something other than a mid-list mystery. Something big, with enough crossover potential to really get me noticed, maybe a novel about the Civil War. I felt good. Better than I had in months. The weather probably had something to do with that. Now it was spring, the season of rebirth and renewal and all that jazz. The time when nature lets the animal kingdom know that it's time to make lots of babies. Spring, the season of sex and happiness. .

Big Steve celebrated the first day of spring by pissing on the lilac bush, pissing on the garage, pissing on the sidewalk, and pissing twice on the big oak tree—which further infuriated the squirrel. The tree limbs shook as it expressed its displeasure. Big Steve barked at his aggressor, but only after he was safely behind me.

Our house is sandwiched between Main Street and a narrow back alley separating us from the community Fire Hall. The Fire Hall borders a grassy vacant lot and a neighborhood park, the kind with swings and monkey bars and deep piles of mulch to keep kids from skinning their knees when they come down the sliding boards. Beyond the playground lies the forest—roughly thirty square miles of protected Pennsylvanian woodland, zoned to prevent farmers and realtors from cutting it all down and planting crops or building subdivisions. The forest is surrounded on all sides by our town, and the towns of Seven Valleys, New Freedom, Spring Grove and New Salem. They all have video stores and grocery outlets and pizza shops (and our town even has a Wal-Mart), but you wouldn't know it while standing inside the forest. Stepping through that tree line is like traveling through time to a Pennsylvania where the Susquehanna Indians still roamed free and the Germans, Quakers, and Amish were yet to come. At the center, at the dark heart of the forest, was LeHorn's Hollow, source of central Pennsylvanian ghost stories and legends. Every region has such a place, and LeHorn's Hollow was ours.

An artist friend of mine once visited us from California. Tara and I took him for a walk through those same woods, maybe half a mile inside, and he said something that has always stuck with me. He said that our woods felt different. I'd scoffed at the time, reminding him that his own state had the majestic Redwood forests (Tara and I had spent part of our honeymoon walking amongst the coastal Redwoods, and I'd wanted to live there ever since). But he'd insisted that our small patch of forest was different.

He said it felt primordial.

After Big Steve finished watering the yard, he tugged me toward the alley, his ears perked up and tongue lolling in hopeful anticipation.

"You want to go for a walk in the woods? You want to sniff for some bunnies?"

He wagged his tail with enthusiastic confirmation and tilted his head to the side.

"Come on, then." I grinned. His mood was infectious. It was impossible to feel anything other than good that morning.

He put his nose to the ground and led me forward. Shelly Carpenter jogged by on her regular morning run just as we reached the edge of the alley. Her red hair jiggled with each step. So did the rest of her. I didn't know Shelly well, but we usually made small talk every morning as we passed by each other.

"Hey Adam," she panted, running in place. "Hi Stevie!"

Big Steve wagged the tip of his tail and darted between my legs.

"Oh, come on, Stevie." She turned off her iPod and removed her headphones. "Don't be shy! You know me."

Big Steve's tail thumped harder, confirming that yes, he did indeed know her, but he shrank away farther.

Shelly laughed. "God, he's such a 'fraidy cat."

"Yeah, he is. Runs from his own shadow. We got him from the pound, and we think that his previous owner may have beat him or something."

Her brow creased. “That’s so sad. What’s wrong with some people?”

I nodded. “Yeah, people like that should be shot. You out for your morning jog?”

“You know it. Isn’t it beautiful today?”

“It sure is. Spring is finally here.”

She looked up at the sun and squinted. “Spring is my favorite time of year.”

Her thin t-shirt was damp with sweat, and it clung to her bouncing breasts, revealing perfection. Her pert, dime-sized nipples strained against the fabric, hinting at the dark areolas beneath. Before she could catch me leering, I looked down. Big mistake. Her gray sweatpants had ridden up, hugging her crotch like a second skin. They too were wet with perspiration.

I quickly glanced back up. Shelly was staring at me with an odd expression.

“You okay, Adam?” She arched her eyebrows.

I cleared my throat. “Yeah. Sure. I was just thinking about my deadline.”

“Seems like you’re always daydreaming.”

“That’s the way it is with writers.”

“How’s the next book coming?”

“Good.” I smiled, and bent down to pet Big Steve. Mistake number two. My face was inches from her groin. I imagined that I could smell her sweat—and something else. Something intoxicating. The scent of a woman.

What the hell was wrong with me? It was like spring fever had turned me into a horn dog or something. My reactions were uncharacteristic, and I felt embarrassed.

Shelly placed a hand on her hip and arched her back. “What’s it going to be?”

I jumped. “W-what?”

“The book.” Her breasts bounced up and down as she began jogging in place again. “What’s it going to be about? Another mystery?”

“I’m not sure yet, actually. Maybe a Civil War novel, but I don’t know. Still working it out in my head. Whatever it turns out to be, it’s going to be big.”

"Big is good." She licked her lips. Her glistening tongue looked so inviting.

I found myself wondering if she was aware that she was doing it. Her eyes seemed to glaze over, and she moved closer to me. Big Steve shifted nervously between my legs.

I cleared my throat again, breaking the spell.

"Well," Shelly said, "I'd better let you get back to work, then. See you. Tell Tara that I said hi."

"Okay. Will do. See you later."

Shelly put her headphones back on, raised her hand and waved, and then blew Big Steve a kiss. We stared after her as she jogged down the alley and crossed over into the park. I watched her perfect ass moving beneath her sweatpants. Then she vanished from sight. The next time I saw that ass was when she was on her knees in front of the hairy man.

Big Steve panted heavily, then turned around and licked his balls.

I knew how he felt. My own erection strained uncomfortably against my jeans. Shuffling from one foot to another, I made sure nobody was watching. Then I reached down inside my pants and readjusted.

I took a deep breath, trying to stave off the guilt that welled up inside me. I'd never cheated on Tara, but the opportunities were there. The bigger my career got, the more of them there seemed to be. Not dozens of them, at least, not yet. But there were several women who'd brought bourbon and crotchless panties to my book signings, or asked me to sign their breasts with magic marker. They sent me emails telling me how much my writing turned them on. Genre groupies. It was flattering and tempting and great for selling books. But it was surprising too, especially considering my modest success. I often wondered if it would get worse, the bigger I got.

The thing I was most afraid of was myself—my own libido. Tara's moratorium on sex affected me more than I let on. Yes, I loved her, but it was also a huge factor in our lives. I worried sometimes about cheating on her, was afraid that one day my traitorous libido would push me into it.

But I'd never done anything. And my erotic overreaction

to Shelly's workout attire left me feeling puzzled and guilty, as did her uncharacteristic flirting—if that's what it was. Had she really flirted, or was it my imagination?

I was pretty sure I'd read the situation correctly.

At the time, I dismissed it all. Just something in the air. Spring fever, maybe.

But now I know just how right I was. There was something in the air—music and magic—and it affected us both.

Big Steve strained against his leash, urging me forward. We crossed the alley and walked into the field, heading in the same general direction that Shelly had gone. The grass was wet with dew. Steve put his nose to the ground, catching a scent. He started tracking.

In the oak tree's branches, two squirrels began humping away, celebrating the season by making babies.

I wondered if Tara and I would ever have a baby. Then I thought of the last miscarriage. Sadness welled up inside me, and I fought back sudden and surprising tears.

Steve tugged at the leash, chasing the bad memories away like the good dog that he was.

We walked on. The wet grass soaked my shoes and his paws. I took us around the playground. It wouldn't do to have the neighborhood children come flying down the slide and land in a pile of dog shit. As if reading my mind, Big Steve dutifully dropped a pile in the grass. Wincing at the smell, I turned my nose away. The dog wagged his tail, and it seemed like he was grinning. Then we moved along.

The neighborhood came to life around us. Paul Legerski's black Chevy Suburban roared down the alley, with Flotsam and Jetsam's "Liquid Noose" blasting from the speakers. An oldie but a goodie. Paul had the bass turned up loud, just like the high school kids that did the same thing with their hip-hop. He blew the horn and waved, and I waved back. Paul and his wife, Shannon, were good people. One of my next-door neighbors, Merle, tried to start his lawnmower. It sputtered, stalled, and then sputtered again. Merle's curses were loud and clear, and I chuckled. Then I heard the hiss of running water as another of my neighbors, Dale Haubner, a retiree, turned on his garden hose. A flock of geese flew overhead, honking out their springtime return from southern climates. Honeybees buzzed in the clover growing next to the seesaw.

But beneath all of these familiar noises was another sound. At first, I thought I'd imagined it. But Big Steve's ears were up and his head cocked. He'd heard it too.

As we stood there, it came again—a high, melodic piping. It sounded like a flute. Just a few short, random notes, and then they faded away on the breeze and weren't repeated. I looked around to see if Shelly had heard it, but she was gone, as if the woods had swallowed her up.

In a way, I guess that's what happened.

The musical piping drifted towards us again, faint but clear. I became aroused again, and dimly wondered why. Shelly was gone, and there was nobody else in sight. I hadn't been thinking about sex. It was weird.

Big Steve planted his feet, raised his hackles, and growled. I tugged the leash, but he refused to budge. His growl grew louder, more intense. I noticed that he had another hard on as well.

"Come on," I said. "It's nothing. Just some kid practicing for the school band."

Big Steve flicked his eyes toward me, then turned back to the woods and growled again.

The music abruptly stopped. There was no gradual fading away—it was as if someone had flipped a switch.

It occurred to me that it was Monday morning, and all the kids were in school, so it couldn't have been a kid practicing. Then Steve's haunches sagged and he returned to normal, his nose to the ground and his tail wagging with excitement over every new scent.

The narrow trail leading into the woods was hidden between two big maple trees. I don't know who made the path; kids or deer, but Big Steve and I used it every day. Dead leaves crunched under our feet as we slipped into the forest, while new leaves budded on the branches above us. Flowers burst from the dark soil, lining the trail with different colors and fragrances.

I stopped to light a cigarette while Big Steve nosed around a mossy stump. I inhaled, stared up into the leafy canopy over our heads, and noticed how much darker it was, even just inside the tree line.

Primordial, I thought.

I shivered. The sun's rays didn't reach here. There was no warmth inside the forest—only shadows.

The woods were quiet at first, but gradually came to life. Birds sang and squirrels played in the boughs above us. A plane passed overhead, invisible beyond the treetops. Probably heading to the airports in Baltimore or Harrisburg. The sun returned, peeking through the limbs. But I couldn't feel its warmth, and the rays seemed sparse.

Big Steve pulled at the leash, and we continued on. The winding path sloped steadily downward. We picked our way through clinging vines and thorns, and I spotted some raspberry bushes, which gave me something to look forward to when summer arrived. If I picked them, Tara would bake me a pie. Blue and green moss clung to squat, gray stones thrusting up from the forest floor like half-uncovered dinosaur skeletons. And then there were the trees, standing tall and stern.

I shivered again. The air was growing chillier, more like the normal temperature for this time of year. Stepping over a fallen log, I wondered again who'd made the path, and who used it other than Big Steve and myself. The most we'd ever gone was a mile into the forest, but the trail continued on well past that. How deep did it run? All the way out to the other side? Did it intersect with other, less-used pathways? Did it go all the way to LeHorn's Hollow?

I mentioned the hollow earlier. I'd only been there once, when I was in high school and was looking for a secluded spot to get inside Becky Schrum's pants. It was our first date, and I remember it well. 1987—my senior year. We saw a *Friday the 13th* flick (I can't remember which one), and when it was over, we cruised around in my '81 Mustang hatchback, listening to Ratt's *Out Of The Cellar* and talking about school and stuff.

Eventually, we found ourselves on the dirt road that led to the LeHorn farm. The farmhouse and buildings had stood vacant for three years. Nelson LeHorn had killed his wife, Patricia, in 1985, and then disappeared. He hadn't been seen since, and his children were scattered across the country. His son, Matty, was doing time for armed robbery in the Cresson state penitentiary up north. His daughter, Claudia, was married and living in Idaho. And his youngest daughter, Gina, was teaching school in New York. None of them had ever returned home, as far as I knew. Because the old man was legally still alive, the children were unable to sell the property, and Pennsylvania law prevented the county or the state from seizing it. So it sat, boarded up and abandoned, providing a haven for rats and groundhogs.

The LeHorn place sat in the middle of miles of woodlands, untouched by the explosive development that had marred other parts of the state, and surrounded by a vast expanse of barren cornfields, the rolling hills not worked since the murder and LeHorn's disappearance. In the center of the fields, like an island, was the hollow.

I'd parked the car near the house, and Becky and I had talked about whether or not it was haunted. And like clockwork, she was snuggled up against me, afraid of the dark.

I remember glancing towards the hollow as we made out. Even in the darkness, I could see the bright, yellow NO TRESPASSING and POSTED signs, hanging from a few of the outer tree trunks.

Becky let me slip my hand into her jeans, and her breathing quickened as I delved into her wetness with my fingers and rubbed her hard nipples beneath my palms. But then she cut me off. Not wanting to show my annoyance and disappointment, I'd suggested we walk to the hollow. I hoped that if her level of fright increased, her chastity might crumble.

The hollow was a massive dark spot at the bottom of the intersection of four wide, sloping hills. It was choked with old growth trees that had never known a chainsaw or an axe. A shallow, serpentine creek wound through its center. We heard the trickling water, but never made it far enough inside to see the stream.

Because something moved in the black space between the trees . . .

Something big. It crashed towards us, branches snapping like gunshots beneath its feet. Becky screamed, and gripped my hand tight enough to bruise it. We got the hell out of there. We never saw the thing, whatever it was, but we heard it snort—a primal sound, and I can still hear that sound today. A deer, probably, or maybe even a black bear. All I know is it scared the shit out of me, and I've never been back to the hollow since.

Big Steve brought me back to the present by stopping suddenly in the middle of the trail. He stood stiff as a board, legs locked and his tail tucked between them. The growl started as a low rumble deep down inside him, and got louder and louder as it spilled out. I'd never heard him make a sound like this, and wondered if I'd mistakenly clipped someone else's dog to the leash. He'd never gotten this worked up over something. He sounded vicious. Brave.

Or terrified.

Suddenly, as if summoned from my memories, something crashed through the bushes towards us. Big Steve's hair stood on end, and his growl turned into a rumbling bark.

"Come on, Steve. Let's go!" My heart raced in my chest. I tugged the leash, but he refused to budge. He barked again.

The noise drew closer. Twigs snapped. Leaves rustled.

The branches parted.

I screamed.

The deer, a spotted fawn, leaped over a fallen tree, darted across the path, and vanished again into the undergrowth, its white tail flashing. It looked about as scared as we were.

"Jesus fucking Christ!" I gasped for breath, trying to get my racing pulse under control.

Big Steve, meanwhile, had ducked behind me as soon as the fawn emerged. I glanced down at him. He looked back up at me with those soft, brown eyes, and then thumped the tip of his tail, as if embarrassed.

"You *should* be embarrassed," I told him, and he lowered

his ears and looked away.

My heart still hammered in my chest and my temples throbbed. I felt half sick from the adrenalin surge.

Big Steve whined.

I shrugged. "Okay, maybe we both should be embarrassed. Is that better?"

Big Steve flipped his tail in agreement and then sulked out from between my legs. He sniffed around where the deer had been. Then his tail wagged steadily as he got his courage back. Deciding that it was all right to continue on our way, he pulled me forward.

I laughed. The brave mid-list mystery writer and his faithful canine companion, scared shitless by a deer. Not just any deer, but a *baby* deer, at that.

A baby. . .

Unbidden, thoughts of Tara's last miscarriage came to me again. My stomach ached, and I blinked away tears.

The woods seemed even colder.

TWO

When Tara had her first miscarriage, we weren't even sure that's what it was at the time. It happened a year after we were married. We'd been trying to have a baby since our honeymoon, but weren't having much luck. I can tell you that it wasn't for a lack of trying. You know the old adage about rabbits? That applied to us— morning, noon, and night, and triple that when she was ovulating. Maybe we were trying too hard, because despite the frequency, we couldn't conceive.

Then, one month, her period was a few days late. Tara was usually regular as clockwork, so we both figured she was finally pregnant. Before we could take one of those home pregnancy tests, Tara began experiencing sharp pains, cramps, and a heavy flow. Heavier than normal. There was a lot of blood, but then it was all over, and we chalked the whole thing up to just an unusually strong period. It wasn't until Tara's second miscarriage that we learned that's what that first experience had most likely been.

The second miscarriage was a lot worse. It happened a little over a year ago. That time, we knew she was pregnant. There were no doubts. Tara took the first home pregnancy test about a week before her period was due. It showed positive, but the bar indicating the results was faint, so we waited. After trying for so long, we tried not to get our hopes up, promised each other that we wouldn't, and then, of course, we did anyway. Finally, we took the second test and it was also positive, and the following exam at the doctor's office confirmed what we'd prayed for. We were finally going to have a baby.

Tara started planning on what color to paint the baby's room, and I started planning how to ask my publisher for more money so that I wouldn't have to get a full-time job again just to pay the bills. (Back then, I was working part-time at the paper mill and writing the rest of the day.) Knowing that we were about to become parents was weird and scary and exciting, all at the same time. We started thinking about names. If it turned out to be a boy, Tara wanted to name him John or Paul. That was her latent Catholic heritage shining through. I didn't think much of those. I was partial to Hunter, after Hunter S. Thompson, my literary hero. She didn't think much of that. For a girl, we were in agreement and narrowed the choices down to Abigail, Amanda, or Emily. We bought an infant's car seat, and a family-friendly new car to go with it. We also got a crib, infant swing, high chair, and a closet full of baby clothes. Tara finally decided on light purple for the baby's room, complete with Eeyore wall borders. I spent a long, tiring weekend painting it, so she wouldn't have to breathe the paint fumes.

Tara went to her first pre-natal care class, and began researching maternity stuff on the net. We discussed the merits of breastfeeding versus a bottle. I'd catch her looking in the full-length mirror in our bedroom, trying to figure out if she was showing yet. She asked me if I thought she'd be a good mother. I told her she'd be the best. We held hands a lot, and talked more often, and spent more time together. In many ways, it was like we fell in love all over again. I don't know if either of us had ever been happier in our entire lives.

Then, six weeks later, Tara started bleeding.

We were scared, of course. Neither of us knew what it was. It happened so suddenly. One morning, she sat down to pee, and when she wiped, there was blood on the toilet paper. Not a lot of blood, like the first time. Just a smear. But it was bright red smear.

I remember her saying that, the shocked disbelief in her voice. "It's so *bright*. It shouldn't look like that."

Immediately, the specter of a miscarriage reared its ugly head, along with the possibility that it was cancer or some other horrible thing. We made an appointment and went to the doctor, and the ride there was silent and terrifying. I drove very slowly.

The doctor told us it could be a miscarriage but it could also just be spotting. According to her, a quarter of all pregnant women spotted during the early stages of pregnancy. Tara's own mother had bled so much when she was pregnant with Tara, that she thought she was having her period. They checked Tara's HCG count, and while it wasn't rising, it hadn't dropped either. I didn't understand a lot of what they said, but I understood that if her count began to drop, that was bad.

So we waited, and the blood continued to flow and our fears multiplied. The cramps started early the next morning—mild and sporadic at first, but then stronger, more insistent. I made Tara lay down in bed, and I lay next to her. We stayed there for the entire day. We didn't talk much, but we both cried a lot. I held her while she trembled, and she did the same for me. Once in a while, she'd go pee, or check her pad, and there would be more of that bright, shiny blood. Tara tried to sound hopeful, but I saw the apprehension in her eyes. She said that maybe the blood was just pooling inside of her because she was laying down, and that's why there seemed to be more of it when she went to the bathroom. I smiled and nodded and agreed that's probably what it was. She smiled back.

Then we both started crying again.

I tried to distract her. We played *Scrabble* and *Uno* in bed, but neither one of us could concentrate. I called the doctor's office again, and the nurse, in very sympathetic tones, told me to keep waiting. I wanted to holler at her, tell her we were sick of waiting, but I bit my tongue instead. We tried watching television, but every channel had a reminder; the characters on the soaps and sitcoms were pregnant or thought they were. I switched over to the news. It was full of stories about abducted children found murdered, and abandoned babies left in garbage dumpsters. It felt like the entire world was conspiring against us.

Eventually, Tara cried herself to sleep. I lay there, feeling afraid. I thought about getting up and trying to write, but at the time, I didn't own a laptop, and my computer was downstairs in my office. I didn't want to leave Tara's side. In truth, I probably couldn't have written anyway. I was numb.

The worst part was the waiting, the certainty of knowing what was happening, that we were losing the baby, and the realization that I was powerless to do anything about it. I felt so fucking helpless. Tara was my wife and this was our child. I should have been able to fix things. That's what good husbands do. We take the vow on our wedding day. That's our job. We make everything better; keep our loved ones safe from the bad things in life. But I couldn't protect her. I couldn't do shit.

The hours ticked away. I pulled the new *Repairman Jack* novel off my nightstand and tried losing myself in the story, but gave up when I found myself reading the same sentence six times in a row and still not comprehending it. The words blurred together. I couldn't help my family, couldn't write, couldn't read, and couldn't sleep. All I could do was curl up next to Tara and hold her while she slept, and try not to weep. Try not to wake her up. I listened to her breathing, felt her chest rise and fall.

Listened to her cry in her sleep.

She cried and bled and slept, while I wondered what to do next.

I was desperate and grasping at figurative straws. I prayed to God for the first time in a very long while. I wasn't particularly religious. Tara went to Mass on Sunday sometimes, while I stayed home and wrote. My parents took me to church when I was a kid— Methodist. It never did much for me. I didn't feel God inside the church. Didn't feel much of anything, except boredom. Each week, we sang a hymn, read something in unison from the bulletin, listened to a sermon (during which, I'd watch the old men nodding off around me), put our offering envelopes in the plate, and then mingled after the service, drinking coffee and discussing football. None of that filled me with the urge to talk to God, but I talked to Him then, that night, when I needed Him the most. I guess it's that way for everyone, whether they believe or not. When you've got nowhere else to turn, you turn to God. I pleaded with Him, asked Him to help us out, to make everything okay. I begged

Him to keep my wife and unborn child safe from harm, and promised Him the world if He came through for me.

I prayed silently for a long time. Eventually, I fell asleep. My dreams were dark, and I tossed and turned a lot.

Halfway through the night, a particularly strong cramp woke Tara from her own troubled sleep. She got up to pee, and that was when it happened. Her screams woke me. I ran to the bathroom. Tara was doubled over on the toilet, sobbing uncontrollably. I helped her up, and put her back to bed. She curled into a ball and shrieked. I called the doctor's office. While I was explaining the situation to the answering service, I walked back into the bathroom and glanced down at the toilet.

The water in the bowl was dark blue from one of those disinfectant tablets, and it made the blood look like green slime. There was a lot of blood—too much. And there in the middle of the dark blue water and clumps of toilet paper, was our child. Sexless, not yet formed. It was about the size of a dime, really nothing more than a blob.

When we'd started pre-natal care, the doctor gave us a calendar with little factoids that allowed you to follow along with your child's development as the pregnancy progressed. According to the calendar, between the sixth and seventh weeks, the embryo's eyes, ears, and mouth were just beginning to form, as were the major internal organs, such as the heart, liver, and lungs.

An embryo. That's what they called it. Not a baby; just an embryo.

But the blob floating in the toilet wasn't our embryo. It was our child. Our baby. Our hopes and dreams.

And it was dead.

Standing over the toilet, I thought then, and still do to this day, that I saw eyes staring back up at me. Pleading.

Two little eyes, begging me to make things better—to not let this happen.

As I watched, it slid off the little island of bloody toilet paper and sank to the bottom of the toilet bowl.

And I screamed.

I clutched the phone, my fingers tightening around it

hard enough that my knuckles popped. The woman from the doctor's answering service was still on the line, asking me if everything was all right, wondering if I was still there. I could barely hear her over my own screams. My prayers had been ineffective or ignored. I cursed God, and had He been there at that moment, I would have cheerfully put a bullet right between His fucking eyes.

After that, well—we were both basket cases for a few weeks. I was angry and Tara was comatose. She missed work, I couldn't write for shit, and acted like a zombie at the paper mill, sleepwalking through my shift. Neither of us ate much. We cried a lot. I tried to hold it together for both of us, and didn't do a real good job. We'd told people she was pregnant; Tara's parents, her co-workers and some of my fellow authors. As we told each of them what had happened, it was like going through the miscarriage all over again.

Eventually, we moved on, I guess—if you can ever really recover from something like that. There was a deep, unspoken sadness between us for a long time. We never discussed trying to have another child. Not that we'd have had much luck. Tara's sex drive became zero after the miscarriage, and hadn't improved much in the year since then. I guess I can understand that. Making love was now just another dark reminder of what had happened, because that was how you made babies. And children can break your heart in ways nothing else ever will.

But a few months later, she came home with Big Steve, and he brightened up both our lives. And really, having him around was just like having a kid.

Sort of . . .

Sometimes at night, when I close my eyes, I still see our child staring up at me from the toilet bowl. See the baby floating in that bloody water. I feel the silent accusations in those tiny eyes, and the commode handle beneath my fingertips. I hear the sound of the toilet flushing—the sound of our baby, our hopes and dreams, going down the drain.

In those moments, I still hate God and I still want to scream. But I'm afraid that if I start, I won't be able to stop again. Each time, my heart breaks all over again.

We married later in life. Tara is thirty-five years old, and I am almost forty. No, we're not old yet, but we're not getting any younger either. Our chances of having a child lessen with each passing year. I will probably never have a happy Father's Day. I don't think God should be allowed to have one either.

THREE

Big Steve came to a sudden stop in the middle of the trail, bringing me back to the present again. Momentum still carried me forward a few more steps, and I tripped over him. The dog yelped in surprise. My arms pinwheeled. I fell, sprawling in a thicket of blooming poison ivy. Luckily, I wasn't allergic to it. When I was a kid, my great-grandmother told me to eat a poison ivy leaf. She said I'd be immune to it from then on, and she'd been right.

I'd managed to keep hold of the dog's leash during the tumble, but he scuttled away from me. I picked myself back up and brushed dead leaves from my shirt and pants.

"Damn it, Big Steve—" I tugged the leash, trying to get him to come back.

He whined uneasily, and stared down the trail.

I froze. The forest was strangely silent. No birds or squirrels in the treetops; not even a breeze. The unmoving air was damp and chilly, and the musty scent of rotting flora hung over it all. I didn't recognize any landmarks. Lost in my thoughts, I'd taken us further inside the woods than we'd ever been before. The unfamiliar trees seemed taller—almost sinister. I got the impression they were watching us. I tried to laugh, and found I couldn't. They reminded me of the Ents from Tolkien's *Lord of the Rings*, but with dark personalities, rather than beings of light and goodness. I felt on some subtle level that whatever souls these trees possessed had gone bad and curdled like spoiled milk. Their bark was black and gray, rather than brown, and sickly, yellow moss clung to some of the gnarled trunks. Dark sap seeped from one, looking very much like blood. The trees clustered together in dense rows, forming a wall alongside the trail. Thick, snaking vines with blood-red thorns grew between them. It was as if Mother Nature were warning us not to stray from the path. Overhead, skeletal limbs stretched over the trail, forming a leafy archway. It was a tunnel made of foliage, and the path we were on led directly into its center.

Big Steve stared into the tunnel and refused to budge. His tail was tucked firmly between his legs. He whined again.

"What's the matter, buddy?" I was worried that maybe I'd hurt him when I tripped over him. He didn't seem to be limping or anything, but I couldn't be sure.

Slowly, Big Steve turned his eyes away from the path and stared at me. He whined a third time.

He wasn't hurt. He was afraid.

"Come on." I tugged on his leash again. I was nervous, and the most unnerving part of it was that I didn't understand why. "Let's go home. Daddy's got writing to do, and I think you've had enough excitement for one day. Especially after that deer spooked us."

But Big Steve held firm. His ears flattened against his head, and he started growling again. His nails dug into the dirt. Then he began to bark. The woods rang with the echo. Dogs can hear sounds octaves above what humans can hear, but they sure as hell bark on our level. "Come on!" I raised my voice, insistent. "Move, Big St—"

That reedy, musical piping started up again, cutting me off in mid-sentence. It was louder now, and seemed to be all around us. I held my breath in apprehension, and scanned the forest, but I couldn't see anything through the thick foliage.

"What the hell?" I asked the dog. "You hear that?"

Big Steve stopped barking, but kept growling.

The music continued. My unease doubled, but I felt a twinge of curiosity as well. Beneath my jeans, my penis inexplicably stirred again. Big Steve stopped growling, sat down on his haunches, and began licking himself. Whatever was turning me on had affected him as well.

Then we heard something else. A woman's voice, moaning. From pain or ecstasy, I couldn't tell which. But she was nearby. Curiosity overcame my fears, and I started forward, as if in a trance. Big Steve followed along behind me.

We entered the tunnel, and as the leaves closed over our heads, the air grew even colder. The stench of rotting vegetation grew stronger, yet I couldn't find a source. No sunlight reached us now, not even a hint of it from overhead. The darkness between the tree trunks seemed like a solid thing. Big Steve pulled at his leash, hesitant to continue. Goosebumps crawled up my arms, and I was about to agree with him, when the woman moaned again.

We crept forward, and I realized that I was holding my breath again.

The woman giggled, and then murmured something. I couldn't make out the words, but her voice sounded familiar. I'd heard that laugh earlier, when Shelly Carpenter had giggled at Big Steve. I was positive it was her.

The trail ended at a vine-covered deadfall. Big Steve sat down at my side, panting hard. I reached out and brushed the sinewy vines out of the way. Something else caught my eye. On the ground, sandwiched between the dead branches, was a white stone marker, like a gravestone. Miraculously, the fallen tree hadn't smashed it. I cleared more foliage away from the stone, bent over, and tried to read the writing. Moss and dirt clung between the letters. I brushed it away and traced the lettering with my fingertips. The surface was cool, and seemed to throb beneath my touch. I yanked my hand away as if I'd been shocked. When I touched the marker again, the throbbing continued. I tried to read what was carved.

DEVOMLABYRINTHI
NLEHORNPOSSVIT
PROPTERNVPTIAS
QUASVIDITSVBVMRA

The words—their form and cadence—seemed vaguely familiar. It looked like Latin, written by somebody who didn't even know the basics of the language. I studied them some more, but couldn't make heads or tails of it. The stone itself didn't seem that old. It wasn't severely cracked or worn; didn't have that weather beaten look I'd expect it to have.

Before I could consider it any further, Shelly's laughter—if it was Shelly—came again, almost as if it were right in front of us. Despite his unease, Big Steve clambered onto the fallen tree. I followed him. The stench of rotten vegetation seemed to swell, but I still couldn't find its location. Climbing over the deadfall, I pushed the vines aside with my hand, got pricked by several thorns, and peered through the greenery.

On the other side of the deadfall was a small hollow, bordered on all four sides by thick trees. The clearing was carpeted with long blades of lush, green grass, and a small stream trickled through its center. The sound of the flowing water was soothing. The sun shined brightly overhead, and after the darkness of the forest, the dazzling brilliance blinded me for a moment. When my eyesight returned, I stared in disbelief.

Shelly Carpenter knelt in the middle of the hollow, completely naked. Her clothes and iPod were strewn about the grass. The sun flashed off her alabaster skin. Her back was to me, and I could see the freckles on her shoulders, and a tiny butterfly tattoo in the small of her back.

Grinning, I thought, *Never knew she had that.*

Big Steve whined, low and mournful—and urgent, but I barely heard him. My attention was focused on Shelly, and the thing she knelt in front of.

It was a stone statue carved in the image of a bearded man. At least, that's what I thought at first, but then I saw that it wasn't human. It was a statue of a satyr, the half-man, and half-goat of Greek mythology. I was close enough to see the blob of bird shit on the stone shoulder, and a vine entwined around its waist. The details were amazingly lifelike. Horns jutted from his head, and his ears were those of a goat. He had a large, hooked nose, and his body was covered with thick, curly hair. One of his hands clutched a seven-reed shepherd's pipe to his lips, and the other was positioned between his legs. The lower half matched his ears—the legs of a goat, and between those frozen legs, a monstrous phallus, easily ten inches in length and thick as a flashlight. Whoever had carved the statue had made the organ obscenely erect. It would have been funny if not for the lascivious attention Shelly was paying to it.

Her lips closed around the stone penis, and her head bobbed up and down. She moaned again, pulled away, and looked lovingly up into the satyr's eyes. The statue stared back down at her, unmoving. Shelly's expression was dazed, her eyes glassy. Giggling, she took the carved member in her mouth again.

"Holy shit," I whispered, reaching out to scratch Big Steve's ears. I'd had no idea my neighbor was so kinky. Even worse, I couldn't believe how turned on the scene made me. I'd never been interested in voyeurism, but I couldn't tear my eyes away. I kept watching, barely aware that I was licking my lips.

Big Steve stiffened beneath my fingers, and growled, loud and menacing. I froze, but if Shelly heard him, she didn't show it. I tried to quiet him, but his growls grew louder.

Then the statue blinked.

I jumped up from my crouch, and the statue blinked again. Its head swiveled toward me, while Shelly continued with her blowjob. The satyr's cold eyes stared directly at our hiding place. Color flowed across its skin. The stone hair turned brown, ruffling in the breeze. The carven leg muscles flexed, and the penis plopped out of Shelly's mouth.

"Holy shit," I said again. There wasn't much else to say. I just stood there gaping. It wasn't in disbelief now, because as impossible as it seemed, it really was happening right in front of me. The statue was coming to life. Not moving like a statue in an old Ray Harryhausen movie, but actually changing from stone into flesh and fur.

Shelly began to work harder.

Big Steve barked, but Shelly ignored him. She wrapped her fingers around the satyr's thick cock and stroked it rapidly. Then her mouth closed over it again. Her cheeks stretched to accommodate the organ, and she made a grunting noise in the back of her throat.

"Shelly," I called. "What are you—"

The satyr opened its mouth and laughed. Its voice was deep and guttural, and the sound vibrated through me. Slowly, the creature raised a hand and pointed at us. Then it brought the shepherd's pipe to its lips and began to play.

The music was louder this time—more real. I don't know how else to describe it. It was almost as if what we'd heard before was just an echo—a psychic recording, perhaps, and now we were hearing the real thing.

My erection was instantaneous and almost painful. So was my fear.

Big Steve howled loud enough to drown it out, and backed away. A quick glance between his back legs showed that the music had affected him as well.

The satyr stopped playing and laughed again. Shelly released the creature's penis and turned towards us. Smiling, she waved her fingers. They were slick with saliva and pre-cum. The monstrous phallus twitched, entwining itself in her hair as if it had a mind of its own. Grunting, the satyr turned Shelly back to his engorged organ. Then he released a stream of urine directly into her willing face. She closed her eyes, and sighed with degenerate bliss. Steaming, yellow fluid ran down her shoulders and back and in the crevice between her breasts. My nose wrinkled. I could smell it, even from where I stood—sharp and musky, overpowering the reeking vegetation. It was a male stench. Hormonal. Animal. I watched in disgust as the creature's erection bobbed upward, and then the stream hit the satyr's own thick beard. Droplets shone in the curly hair like beads of morning dew.

Still pissing, the satyr beckoned to me. "Come. You may bear witness as I sow my seed."

I shook my head and tried to speak, but no sound escaped my lips.

The satyr began to play again, and some unseen force pulled at me, drawing me into the hollow. I stared at Shelly's glistening sex. It was like a magnet and my cock felt like steel. My thoughts were consumed with how she'd feel, how she'd taste. My ears filled with the piping melody, and my cock swelled.

"Come," the satyr said again. "Celebrate the season."

Instead, I turned and ran, dragging Big Steve along behind me. He pulled ahead, tail between his legs, and it was all I could do to keep a hold on his leash. We dashed through the tunnel and back up the trail. I'm not ashamed to admit that I screamed most of the way. What would you have done? It's not everyday you get lost in the woods while walking your dog, and stumble across one of your sexy neighbors giving head to a stone statue—a statue that then comes to life as a result of her attentions.

We raced along the path. Branches whipped my face and grasped at my clothes like clawing fingers. My breath burned in my throat and my heart pounded, keeping time with my feet. I tripped over a root and fell on my face, knocking the air from me. The leash slipped from my hand and Big Steve kept running. He crested the hill and vanished.

Gasping for breath, I crawled to my feet and called after him. "Big Steve! Get back here. Sit! STAY!"

But he was gone, vanished into the shadows between the trees.

Groaning, I started after him. I felt like puking. My sides hurt. There were no sounds of pursuit from behind us, but still I ran. I didn't want to linger in this dark forest for another second. The leaves overhead seemed to draw closer, as if the trees were bending down, reaching for me.

I continued on for about another mile. I shouted for the dog, but he'd disappeared. Despite the temperature, sweat stung my eyes. A cloud of buzzing gnats swarmed after me, darting into my eyes and ears. Swatting at them, I hollered in frustration and kept on. Exhausted, I had slowed down to an erratic jog.

Soon, I stepped over a fallen log that I recognized, and began to get my bearings. This part of the woods was familiar. It felt like home. The sun crept back through the treetops, and the air grew warm again. I paused to catch my breath. Pains shot through my sides, and I was drenched in sweat.

The woods had returned to normal. Birds sang overhead and squirrels clambered through the branches. Spring flowers bloomed through the leaves covering the forest floor. A spider crawled over my feet and hurried away.

I cupped my hands to my mouth. "Steve! Come on, boy! Come here!"

In response, I heard a metallic jingle—the dog tags around his collar.

"Come on, Big Steve." I slapped my hands against my thighs. "Come here, buddy. Good dog."

The brush rustled to my right. Big Steve emerged, looking pitiful. His big, brown eyes were apologetic, and his tail, which was still between his legs, flipped cautiously back and forth. I couldn't scold him. After all, I'd been just as terrified as he was. I should have had the good sense to listen to him earlier, when he'd tried to tell me that something was wrong.

Wrong? I glanced behind us, back into the dark part of the forest. Something wasn't just wrong. Something was terribly fucked up. And despite the sunlight and the warm spring air, I didn't want to stay in those woods a moment longer.

"Come on, buddy. Let's get the hell out of here." I lit a cigarette and that seemed to make things a little better.

Big Steve wagged his tail in eager confirmation, and we headed home.

For a brief second, as we left the tree line and crossed back into the park, I thought I heard the satyr's pipe. But then I realized it was just a bird, singing from its perch high on the monkey bars.

The bird caught sight of Big Steve and flew away. It darted towards the forest, and then veered in mid-air and turned towards the open sky, almost as if it feared the woods more than it did the dog.

FOUR

By the time we made it back to the house, my arms, legs, and hands were tingling as if they'd fallen asleep. My ears rang, and I felt both nauseous and exhausted. Despite the warm weather, I was shivering. Cold sweat beaded on my forehead and under my arms. Then my vision blurred. Delayed shock. I almost fell over right there in the yard. Stumbling for the door, I tried to shake it off.

"We didn't see that," I told Big Steve, and then repeated it to myself. But saying it out loud didn't make it any less real.

I unhooked the dog's leash and he made a beeline for the kitchen. We kept his food and water dishes on the kitchen floor, next to Tara's grandmother's antique china cabinet. While I hung up the leash and lit another cigarette, Big Steve buried his snout in his water bowl and slurped greedily. His fast flicking tongue sloshed water out onto the floor. I wiped it up with a paper towel. Finished drinking, Big Steve ran over to the counter. On top of it was a wicker basket filled with rawhide chews and dog treats. He looked at me expectantly, and wagged his tail.

I laughed, and as I did, I felt some of the tension drain away. Despite everything that had just occurred, Big Steve still had his priorities in order. Every day, after returning from our morning walk, the first thing I did was give him a rawhide to gnaw on. Usually he chewed it underneath my desk while I started the day's work. It kept him busy and out of my hair for the first half hour or so. After that, he'd usually take a nap. If he didn't, I'd then find other ways to distract him.

I grinned. "You want a bone?"

He leapt into the air, slammed back down onto the floor,

and then ran in an excited little circle. It was times like that I wished we'd had him when he was a puppy. I'll bet he was cute back then.

I fished a rawhide out of the basket and surrendered it without making him first run through his gamut of tricks (sit, shake, lay down, roll over, and stand up). After all he'd been through, it didn't seem right making him work for his treat.

Big Steve expertly caught the rawhide chip in his mouth and then trotted away with his head held high. He curled up underneath my desk and chewed away in happy contentment.

I tried to follow his lead, tried to shake off the morning's weird experience. I made a pot of coffee, and while it was brewing, fired up my laptop and turned on the stereo, setting the fifty-disc changer to random play, and keeping the volume low. I like to write to music, but I keep it turned down, almost like background noise. The random play option chose Queensryche, and then followed them up with the Waterboys. I'm pretty eclectic with my musical tastes. By the time I'd poured myself a mug and returned to my office, the computer was ready. I clicked the mouse, created a new document, and stared at the blank, white screen.

A new novel. Anything I wanted to write about. No pre-sold synopsis binding me, so I could do the Civil War book if I wanted to. The sky was the limit. I didn't need to turn it in until mid-July. This would be easy.

I continued with the daily ritual, twisting my head from side to side, popping my neck joints, and then cracking my knuckles. It might sound funny, but that's how I started work every morning. I lit another cigarette, took a sip of coffee, sat the mug down, then took a deep breath and exhaled. My fingers hovered over the keyboard in restless anticipation.

The laptop beeped, and I imagined it sounded like a note from a shepherd's pipe. In the background, the Waterboys sang about the great god Pan still being alive.

Pan. The name wandered around for a moment inside my head, looking for something to connect with. Pan. He was a god from Greek or Roman mythology, if I remembered correctly. A satyr.

"Shit."

My hands started shaking. My lips quivered and the tip of my cigarette trembled.

Like a tidal wave, the visions returned and engulfed me—Shelly on her hands and knees in the middle of the grassy hollow, sucking the dick of a petrified satyr. The statue coming to life, stone turning into flesh. The creature's laughter echoed in my head, along with that haunting pipe melody. And that weird stone marker with the undecipherable words carved on it. It couldn't have all been real, could it?

I ran it over in my mind. The stone marker; I'd touched it, felt it vibrate beneath my fingertips, cleared dirt away from the lettering. I looked at my fingernails. They were black underneath. So I hadn't imagined that part. What it was, who had carved the lettering, and what it was doing out there, I had no clue. But it had been real enough. It wasn't easily explainable, but it was real just the same. Maybe it had just been some kids—a prop for Halloween, or something for a secret clubhouse somewhere in the forest.

I got my mind around that, accepted it, and then moved on to the satyr. That's when my mind begged me to stop, came to a screeching halt, and decided to take a break for a bit until I came back to a more reasonable line of thinking.

This wasn't like my teenage years, when I'd heard something in the woods while trying to get in Becky Schrum's pants. What we'd experienced that night was easily explainable as a deer or a bear, or some drunken redneck trying to scare us.

This was different. Satyrs were mythological creatures. They didn't exist. And yet, despite that pesky little fact, I'd seen one. I'd watched a statue of a satyr come to life in front of me. It couldn't have been real, but it was. That left few possibilities. One, I'd gone insane, or was on my way there. That didn't appeal to me very much. Maybe I'd hallucinated the whole thing, blacked out in the middle of the woods and dreamed it all up. But I didn't believe that, either. It sounded like a cheesy plot device from a novel, the kind my editor would shoot me for if I ever used it. And besides, Big Steve had seen and reacted to the situation as well, and his sanity was beyond reproach.

However, statues didn't just come to life like that, so maybe it hadn't been a statue at all. Maybe it had just been a guy dressed up in a satyr suit. At first, I'd thought he was just a hairy man, until I saw the horns and the ears and the hooves. Perhaps he was just some hairy guy, and he'd been wearing prosthetics. Those were easy enough to make. I'd been a guest at a mystery, science fiction, fantasy, and horror convention the year before, and saw costumes that were just as convincing; people dressed like elves and Klingons and Jedi knights. For a few bucks, you could buy fake Vulcan ears at any novelty store. It seemed plausible. Shelly had a new boyfriend; one who liked to play kinky games outdoors. He was one of those people who like to dress up in stuffed animal costumes and have orgies. Furries, the media called them. They planned ahead of time to meet in the woods. Thought the hollow would be a nice, secluded spot where they could get their freak on without getting caught—except that Big Steve and I accidentally stumbled across them in mid-blow job. Or mid-golden shower, I thought, remembering how he'd pissed directly into Shelly's face, and into his own. Maybe he was bi-sexual or into threesomes, as well. After all, he'd invited me to join them. That was another thing. He'd spoken clear English. As for the stone turning into flesh, that could have easily been some weird trick of the light. A mirage. It had been pretty dark from my vantage point, the sunshine was bright in the hollow, and my eyes could have deceived me. It all made sense.

I told myself that's all it was, just a freak in a suit, but I didn't believe a word of it.

Still, I tried to move on. I had a book to write. U2's *Achtung Baby* was playing on the stereo. I tried to lose myself in the melodies, tried to summon the words, but nothing came. My hands had stopped shaking but my fingers still refused to move. I got another cup of coffee, took a deep breath, and sat back down. The cursor blinked at me like an eye. I gave it the middle finger.

Big Steve finished his rawhide bone, and curled up under the desk. He closed his eyes, and his breathing grew shallow. Sound asleep. Apparently, he'd already made up his mind about what we'd seen.

I cracked my knuckles again and then typed CHAPTER ONE.

"Okay," I said to my muse. "We're off to a good start. What happens next?"

What happened next is that I sat there for fifteen minutes and smoked cigarette after cigarette and stared at the blank screen. I didn't believe in writer's block, a term used by authors to describe days when they can't seem to find the words or the ideas behind the words. Writer's block is nothing more than a convenient excuse for laziness. Get me drunk in a room full of writers or editors and you'd hear me say it time and time again. When you're writing fulltime like I am, writing to pay the bills and keep a roof over your head and food on the table, you can't afford to have writer's block. It's just like any other job. When you show up, and the whistle blows, you start working, whether you feel like it or not. Otherwise, you're just a lazy bum who's relying on his spouse to bring home the bacon all by themselves.

I didn't believe in writer's block, but I sure as shit couldn't write that morning. I tried forcing it, but the words still wouldn't come. Each of those great ideas I'd had regarding the Civil War, the ones I'd mulled over all winter long, had vanished. I couldn't remember a single one, and when I wracked my brain, all I got was a headache. Eventually, after a prolonged period of inactivity, my screen saver popped up.

Resigned to not writing, I logged onto the net and checked my email. There was nothing new. A few readers had dropped me notes about my books. I responded to each, and thanked them for the kind words if they liked it, and apologized if they didn't, and told them I hoped they'd like the next one regardless. My editor had emailed as well, wanting to know how the next book was coming and if she would get first look. I lied and told her it was coming along well, really cooking now, and I'd be happy to send her the first three chapters very soon.

My headache grew worse, to the point where I couldn't even concentrate on email. I sighed in exasperation. Big Steve opened one eye, looked at me, and then went back to sleep.

I reopened the file and tried writing again, but the cursor just kept blinking.

"Fuck this."

I shut the computer off, went outside, and walked down to the gas station on the corner to get a pack of cigarettes. The weather was still nice, but my mood had soured.

The door beeped as I walked in. Leslie Vandercamp was on duty at the register, just like she was every weekday from eight to five. Every month, she dyed her hair a different color. Yesterday it had been auburn. Now it was hot pink.

"Hey, Adam." She smiled, cracking her gum.

"Dig the hair," I said.

"Thanks. Did it last night."

"It's very pink."

She laughed. "Start the new book yet?"

I opened the cooler and grabbed a soda. "Don't ask."

"That bad, huh?" She rang up a customer buying gas and lottery tickets, while I got in line. I liked Leslie. She was a single mom in her early twenties, with a two-year old son at home. She'd met the father at the Maryland Line bar, and never saw him again after that because two days later, he was killed in a car wreck. His blood alcohol level had been the equivalent of a brewery.

Leslie read all my books, and over the years, she'd become my sounding board for story ideas. Plus, she kept me supplied with cigarettes, which made her the third most important woman in my life, after my wife and my editor.

Eventually, the customer left, and Leslie turned her attention back to me. "Writer's block?"

"Yeah." I nodded. "Bad."

She looked surprised. "I thought you didn't believe in writer's block."

"I do now."

She reached above the counter and automatically pulled down two packs of my brand of cigarettes, without me even asking for them. Like I said, she was good. I paid her for the soda and smokes. As she handed me back my change, Leslie frowned.

"You okay, Adam? You don't so look good."

"Think I might be getting sick," I lied. "A cold or something."

She glanced outside. "In this weather? That sucks. It's beautiful outside. Almost feels like summer."

We made small talk for a few more minutes. Leslie was excited. She told me about the big date she had lined up for Wednesday night with some guy named Michael Gitelson, how she'd bought a new outfit and her Mom was going to baby sit for her.

Another regular, an old man named Marvin, walked in. He picked up a newspaper, saw Leslie and I talking, and smiled.

"Watch what you say to this guy, Leslie. He'll put it in his next book!"

He laughed, and I smiled politely and wished death upon him because all writers hear things like that, and it gets really annoying. Then I told Leslie I'd see her same time tomorrow, said goodbye to Marvin, and left.

When I got home, I knew I still wouldn't be able to write, so I decided to mow the lawn instead. It didn't really need cutting yet, but there's something about that first mowing of spring that really makes you feel good, the smell of fresh cut grass and the feel of the mower in your hands, and the neat, symmetrical rows. I thought maybe some time spent doing that would kick-start the idea machine inside my head.

I made sure the mower had enough oil and gas, and then I rolled it out into the driveway. I primed it, pulled the cord, and it started on the second tug. If my neighbor Merle was watching, it would really give him something to curse about, after the trouble he'd had with his earlier that morning.

Remembering Merle's outburst made me think about what had happened in the woods again. Things had seemed so normal at that point. My neighborhood was operating the way it was supposed to. Merle cursing and Paul Legerski flying down the alley with 80's metal blasting from his truck's speakers—these were everyday things. They were safe. Mundane. They weren't supposed to lead to what I'd seen in the forest.

But in hindsight, even at that point, things had been weird.

I'd heard the pipes about the same time as I'd heard Merle and Paul.

I mowed on autopilot, pushing the lawnmower up and down the yard in neat rows. Insects jumped out of my way, and the first dandelions of spring disappeared beneath the blades. The smell of fresh cut grass hung thick in the air, and a cool breeze tickled my face, but I couldn't enjoy either of them. The lawnmower's handle vibrated under my palms, but I barely felt it. My thoughts were elsewhere. I pictured Shelly, naked and on her knees, and then pushed the image from my mind. I was hard again.

I'd completed three loops and was beginning my fourth when I felt a tap on my shoulder. I jumped. My hands slipped off the safety bar, and the lawnmower dutifully turned itself off.

I spun around, heart pounding, and Merle stood behind me. He was laughing, and his beer belly shook like bread dough.

"Sorry, Adam," he apologized when he got his breath back. His meaty face was beet red. "Didn't mean to give you a heart attack."

"Looks like you're about to have one yourself," I said. "Maybe laughter isn't the best medicine for you."

A year earlier, Merle had a stint put into his heart; right after his divorce was finalized. It was his second heart attack in as many years. He'd suffered the first one when his wife, Peggy, told him that she was leaving him for her Tae Kwon Do instructor. The guy was twenty years younger than Merle.

Smiling in spite of the scare he'd given me, I wiped my sweaty brow with the back of my hand.

"If I die now," Merle joked, "then I won't have to pay any more alimony."

Merle Laughman lived two houses to the left of us. He was a big, jovial man in his early fifties. He loved to eat, loved to drink, and especially loved to laugh. Given his last name, that was pretty appropriate. He sold antiques out of his home, which doubled as a store because of the zoning laws on Main Street. Years ago, the borough had decided to turn our tiny downtown section into an antique row, and now many of the homes were also storefronts. Tara and I had considered doing this ourselves, maybe opening a used bookstore, but we'd never seriously followed up on the idea. In addition to his antique store, he had a woodshop out back, where he crafted furniture. A little loud, and always ready with an opinion or a joke, but Merle was a good guy, and a great neighbor.

Between Merle's home and ours was a house that had been converted into apartments, one upstairs and one below. Cory Peters lived in the downstairs apartment. He was a nice enough kid, early twenties, tall and skinny with leftover acne from his teenage years, as well as a fashion penchant for backwards ball caps and letting his jeans fall off his ass. He'd dropped out of college and now worked in the local Wal-Mart's produce department, where he got us all a discount on our groceries. Cory played too many video games and owned all of the James Bond movies on DVD. He also had the worst fake British accent in the history of the world.

Cliff Swanson lived above him. Cliff was a twice-divorced, and now hardcore bachelor in his early forties. He worked at a furniture plant in Baltimore and rode his Harley to work when the weather was nice. Cliff kept the bike in our garage, because his landlord didn't provide storage space on the property. Cliff had a ponytail that made me jealous, a sex life I envied, and a sullen loneliness about him that made me glad for everything I did have. Sometimes I wondered which was better, but I guess it was just subjective.

Then there was Dale Haubner, who lived in the house to the right of us. He was a retired engineer in his early seventies, who was always trying to give me story ideas. Tara and I had pretty much adopted him and his wife, Claudine, as surrogate parents. I mowed Dale's lawn in the summer and shoveled his sidewalk in the winter. Dale and Claudine gave us vegetables from their garden and kept an eye on Tara and Big Steve when I was off on a book signing tour, or in New York on business with my publisher. We had keys to each other's homes, and Tara and I trusted them implicitly.

It was a nice neighborhood and we had good neighbors.

Sure, Merle borrowed movies from me and didn't return them or sometimes took a joke too far, and Cliff liked to get drunk and then race his Harley up and down the alley, or brag about his wild sexual exploits, and Dale went to work on his yard at the crack of dawn every Saturday, making a lot of noise while the rest of us were still trying to sleep, and Cory had a bad habit of telling people that he knew 'Adam Senft the mystery writer' and letting it slip where I lived (Tara and I value our privacy, and a few times, people had knocked on our door and asked me to sign books as a result of Cory's inability to keep his neighbor's identity a secret). And all of them liked to pick on me at election time, since they were all Republicans and I was a Democrat (except for Cory, who, in the last election, had been hard pressed to even name either of the candidates or care about the issues). But these were minor things, and despite them, or maybe because of them, I liked my neighbors very much. These days, you're lucky if you even know the last name of the people who live next door. Maybe you smile and nod when you pass each other, or exchange greetings or small talk, but that's usually all you do. Our neighbors were also our friends, and I enjoyed living between them. We were a happy little community, there on our corner of Main Street.

Merle's laughter tapered off into a sigh. He held up two cans of beer. "Thought you might like one of these."

"You thought right." I accepted a can. It was frosty and wet, and the sound of the tab popping was music to my ears. I drained half in one gulp, and then cooled my forehead with the can. "That hits the spot."

"Nothing like a cold beer on a warm spring day," Merle agreed, taking a sip of his own. "And man, is it warm! Can't remember when it was this hot, this early. Almost feels like summer."

I nodded. "Yeah, it does. I hope it lasts for a while, and doesn't get chilly again."

"Trust me, it's gonna be a weird spring." He took another long sip and belched.

"Is it?" I asked.

"Sure. The *Farmer's Almanac* says so, and it's never wrong."

"You believe that thing, huh?" The *Farmer's Almanac* was an annual collection of folklore, crop reports, and farming tips that was quite popular in rural towns like ours.

"Sure," Merle said. "We had a windy winter so that means we'll have a warm spring. There've been all kinds of other signs, too. That clear, white moon we had last week? That's a sign. The crickets are out early, and cobwebs are showing up in the grass in the mornings. And my Rhododendrons."

"What about them?" I tried to suppress my disbelieving grin.

"They're blooming already, and their leaves are completely open. That's a sure sign of warm weather."

"According to who—the *Farmer's Almanac?*"

He nodded. "Yeah, that and others. The old timers know how to tell these things."

"By what?" I asked. "Doing powwow?"

Merle winked at me. "Yep. My Grandmother did powwow when I was a kid, and she was never wrong."

I knew all about the art of powwow. Central Pennsylvania is a cultural mixing pot, settled primarily by the Germans, English, and Irish. One of the most prominent beliefs among those people was powwowing. It's sort of a rustic hodge-podge of white and black magic, folklore, and the Bible. They call it hoodoo down south (not to be confused with voodoo), but here, it's known as powwow. Earlier, I told you about when my great-grandmother had me eat a poison ivy leaf, and how I'd never contracted poison ivy since. That was an example of minor powwow. I guess it probably sounds like something out of the nineteenth century, but it's still practiced today in some of the more desolate corners of the state.

The original inhabitants of our area, the Susquehannock Indians, had a form of shamanism called pawwaw, and when the German settlers arrived, they brought their own form with them, a magical discipline of braucherei. Over the years, the two mixed, and became known as powwow. The belief had its own rulebook, *The Long Lost Friend* by John George

Hohman. First printed in 1819, this was the primary bible on which powwow was based. I'd seen a copy in a used bookstore once, but it was expensive and behind glass, so I hadn't flipped through it. Supposedly, the book was derived from many different sources, including the Hebrew Cabala, African tribal beliefs, German mysticism, Gypsy lore, Druid ceremonies, and ancient Egyptian teachings. It offered a strange mix of cures, spells, and protections. Powwow doctors, who cured their patients using methods from the book, were common in the area up until the late sixties, and even today, some of the older residents still visited them before going to a medical doctor.

"So powwow practitioners can predict the weather?" I asked.

Merle shrugged his big shoulders. "I guess. I know my grandma sure could."

"Shit." I paused to light a cigarette. "You don't need to know powwow to do that. My Dad got some shrapnel in his leg over in Vietnam, and he used to say that it started to hurt before every thunderstorm."

"Yeah," Merle agreed. "There's always that way, too."

I ran my hand through my hair and blinked the sweat out of my eyes. "Well, you're right about one thing. It is hot out here."

"You're not getting much writing done today, I guess," Merle observed, tilting his can of beer towards the lawnmower. "I should let you get back to work."

"No, it's okay. I'm not going to get shit done today anyway— mowing or writing."

"Why's that?"

I sighed. "It's been a weird morning."

There was one of those uncomfortable pauses where the listener clearly wants to know more and the speaker doesn't want to say anything else. We each filled the silence by drinking our beers.

I prodded the dirt with my shoe. "Merle, can I ask you something?"

"Sure."

"You know Shelly Carpenter, lives over on Forrest Avenue?"

His face brightened. "The girl who jogs by here every morning? The one with the cute ass?"

"That's the one."

Merle belched again. "What about her?"

"Does she—does she have a boyfriend, that you know of?"

His brow furrowed. "A boyfriend? Don't know her that well, Adam. I just watch her butt when she runs by."

"Oh." I finished my beer and crumpled the can.

Merle stared at me with a knowing half-grin on his face. "Why? You interested? You gonna be one of those writers that hits the bestseller lists and then gets himself a young chickadee?"

"No." I bristled. "Don't be a dick. I just thought I saw a guy in the forest with her this morning. Seemed a little odd."

Merle stuck an index finger up his nose and pulled out a prize. He wiped it on his shirt and then looked at me. "What were you doing in the forest? And for that matter, what was she doing in there?"

"I was walking Big Steve, just like I do every morning. I don't know what Shelly was doing. That's why I asked you."

"I don't know, buddy." Merle frowned. "And I don't want to know, either."

"What the hell is that supposed to mean?"

"It means I don't want to know who's sleeping with who on this street. Ain't none of my business, and it only leads to hard feelings."

"Merle . . ." I gritted my teeth. "Knock it off. I'm not having an affair with Shelly Carpenter. Like I said, Big Steve and I saw her with a guy this morning. I was just curious."

"Don't know why you go walking in those woods anyway. They give me the creeps."

I was taken aback. In all the years I'd known Merle, I'd never heard him admit to being afraid of anything other than his ex-wife's lawyers.

He looked around. "Where is Big Steve, anyway?"

I pointed at the house. "Inside. Probably sleeping under my desk. He's a lazy thing."

"Yeah, but he's good dog. Wouldn't hurt a fly."

I remembered Big Steve's reaction in the woods earlier that morning.

"Hey," a voice called across the yard. "You guys need a refill?"

Merle and I both turned around. Dale Haubner walked towards us, carrying three more beers.

"Is this a private party," he asked, "or can anybody join in?"

He handed us each a beer, which we gratefully accepted. I had no desire to get drunk in the middle of the afternoon, but it was the neighborly thing to do. I checked my watch. Tara would be home from work in a few hours, and I resigned myself to the fact that I probably wouldn't get any writing done at all. Merle and Dale could both talk, and when they were together and there was beer involved, it was hard to get away from them.

"So, what's happening?" Dale asked.

"We called a meeting," Merle said, popping the tab on his can. "We're gonna evict you from the neighborhood and then rent your house to a sorority volleyball team."

Dale frowned. "See if I bring you a beer again, you fat bastard."

Since we were in my yard, we moved over to my outdoor patio. I wrote there sometimes, when the weather was nice. It had a grill and a round table with an umbrella and four plastic lawn chairs. Each of us took a seat, and sipped our beers. I flicked cigarette ashes into the yard.

"Hey Dale," Merle said, "you know that piece of ass that jogs up the alley every morning? The Carpenter girl?"

I suppressed a groan. Last thing I wanted was for all the neighbors to know I was asking about Shelly. Something like that would make its way back to Tara and cause all kinds of problems before I convinced her of my intentions.

"Shelly?" Dale propped his feet up on an empty chair. "Sure, I know her. Used to work with her father, as a matter of fact."

"Is she single?" Merle asked.

"I have no idea," Dale said. "But you're a little old for her, aren't you Merle?"

"It ain't for me. It's for Adam. And besides, I could still get it up for a young girl like that. I get it up every time I see Leslie down at the gas station. I don't need Viagra, like some people I could mention, you old fart."

Dale ignored him and turned to me, looking concerned. "Are you and Tara having troubles?"

"No!" I slammed my beer down harder than I'd intended to, and both men jumped in their seats.

"Sorry," Dale apologized.

"No," I said again, softer this time. "I was just curious. Saw her with a strange guy this morning and wondered if it was her boyfriend."

"He was over in the woods," Merle explained, cocking his thumb in the general direction of the forest. "Walking the dog."

"Those woods give me the creeps," Dale said.

Merle nodded in agreement. "I told him the same thing. He ought to take his dog for a walk down Main Street instead."

"Why do you guys keep saying that?" I asked. I didn't tell them about my own scare. "What's so bad about those woods?"

"Well," Merle sighed. "For one thing, if you go in far enough, they hook up with LeHorn's Hollow."

"Yeah," I agreed, "but those woods are over twenty miles wide, and the hollow sits in the center. We're not anywhere near it."

"Don't be so sure," Merle said. "That forest, and the cornfields and everything else surrounding it, takes up five different townships. The land is owned by a lot of different people—farmers, the paper mill over in Spring Grove, the local governments, even the State. But it's all connected, Adam. LeHorn's Hollow is kind of like the heart, and it's got veins running all through those woods."

The writer inside of me was impressed by his analogy, and I told him so. "You should try your hand at writing, Merle."

"And give up my failing antique business? I don't think so. But you're right about one thing. It would make a great book."

"A horror novel," Dale muttered.

I drained my beer. "I don't know about a horror novel, but it would make a good mystery or true crime book. LeHorn murdering his wife and then disappearing—people would eat that shit up."

Dale stared at his beer and Merle found something interesting to look at in the yard.

Their silence confused me, and I wondered what I'd said wrong. "What? It was your idea."

"There's a lot more to it than just the murder," Dale said quietly. "No offense Adam, but you're a lot younger than us. Most of this stuff happened when you were still playing with your G. I. Joes."

"Most of *what* stuff happened? What are you talking about?"

"The stories about the woods," Dale replied. "People say they're haunted."

I wasn't sure if they were kidding with me or not, so I played along. "Haunted? You mean ghosts?"

Dale nodded. "For starters. But that's just the tip of the iceberg. All kinds of weird things happen in there."

"Like what?" Now I was genuinely curious. I'd heard the occasional folk tale, how Patricia LeHorn's ghost wandered the farmhouse at night, and there was my own experience from high school, but that was all.

"Remember earlier, when we were talking about powwow?" Merle asked.

"Yeah."

"Nelson LeHorn was a warlock. Practiced black powwow. Powerful stuff, they say."

Dale's expression was grave. "That forest always had an evil reputation. The Indians thought it was cursed. Called it 'bad ground', and refused to live anywhere near the hollow. There are accounts of them not pursuing wounded game beyond the borders of the forest, because they believed it was infested with demons. They thought there was a portal to another place inside. I've read that they'd banish their criminals and insane to the forest. And apparently, it worked, 'cause none of them were ever seen again."

Merle stirred restlessly. "I always thought none of that stuff happened until after LeHorn murdered his wife."

"Well," Dale said, "The stuff I read about all happened long before Nelson LeHorn's ancestors came to America. Maybe it did, maybe it didn't. That's the thing with legends. The truth and the bullshit mix over the years, and you can't tell the two apart."

"Whatever happened to him?" I asked.

Dale whispered, "They say Nelson LeHorn is still in the woods somewhere, hiding and doing his spells."

I toyed with my lighter, spinning it on the tabletop. "Come on. Do you really think he's still there?"

"Not personally." Dale shook his head. "I figure he's either dead or living in Mexico. You'd have to be pretty stupid to still live near the scene of the crime. But there's other stuff. People see lights in the woods at night. Will o' wisps, they call them. Strange noises—growling, whispers, and things like that. Crop circles."

"Crop circles?" I tried not to snicker. "You mean like flying saucers?"

"I mean crop circles," Dale said. "I don't care to guess what makes them. There's other stuff, too. Back in the nineties, some researchers from Penn State discovered strange pockets of magnetic ground scattered throughout the forest. They never did figure out what caused it. Some New Age nut said it was an intersection of ley lines, whatever those are. And folks tell of a big, black dog with fiery red eyes that roams around the forest at night. They call it a hellhound."

"And the trees move," Merle added. "People go in, following a trail, and when they turn around, the trail is gone and there are trees where there weren't any before."

I remembered having the same impression that morning, the feeling that the trees were sentient—and that they meant Big Steve and I harm.

"Do you guys really believe that stuff?" I asked, trying to sound skeptical. My voice quavered. Both men shrugged. Dale got up from his chair. "I'll go get us more beers."

He crossed the yard slowly. He seemed exhausted, as if talking about the woods had drained him. I chalked it up to arthritis and the unseasonable heat.

When he was gone, Merle said, "It's no bullshit, Adam. People have vanished inside those woods."

"When? How many?"

"Oh, couple of dozen that I know of, over the years. Deer hunters. Hikers. Kids out to get laid. Even a logger for the pulp wood company. Some were found, and some. . .well, some weren't. They pulled one guy out about two years ago, fella by the name of Chalmers. You remember him?"

I searched my memory, and after a moment, it clicked.

"Craig Chalmers? The child molester? The one who kidnapped that little girl in Seven Valleys three days after he'd made parole from Camp Hill?"

Merle nodded. "That's him. They should have never let that son of a bitch out of prison in the first place. Remember how, after he'd kidnapped her, he took the girl into the woods, and the State Police tracked him down? Well, when they found him, he was babbling about demons. Said the forest was full of monsters and they were trying to kill him."

As I considered this, something occurred to me. "When they caught him, hadn't he been holding the girl at a campsite in a hollow?"

"Yeah, but I know what you're thinking, and you're wrong. It wasn't LeHorn's Hollow. Same forest, but a different place. Those woods are full of hollows, and if you ask me, every one of them is a bad spot. I said before, LeHorn's Hollow has got roots through that whole place. Maybe it infects the rest of the forest."

I thought about the hollow I'd been in today. How many others were there, I wondered, and did each of them have a satyr statue or a weird stone marker of some kind?

Merle grew silent, and I marveled again how fear could move my rustic, blue-collar neighbor to speak so eloquently.

I asked the next logical question. "Other than Patricia LeHorn, has anybody ever died in there?"

"Like I said, folks have disappeared. You mean have they ever found a body?"

I nodded.

Merle whispered, "I had a good friend, Frank Lehman, die in there a few years ago, actually. As for his body . . ."

He cleared his throat, spat onto the ground, and leaned back in his chair. I got the impression Merle was gathering his thoughts. He asked me for a cigarette and I gave him one. I hadn't seen Merle smoke since his last heart attack. He lit it up with the flair and familiarity of an ex-smoker who still misses the habit. Finally, he continued. His voice was rough, and thick with emotion.

"Frank and I went to high school together. Played football our junior and senior years. We were pretty good buds. Used to drink together down at the Maryland Line on Friday nights. A few years back, he went deer hunting with his sons, Mark and Glen, and their friends, Smitty and Luke. Frank got hosed down with Agent Orange over in Vietnam. It left him alone all those years, but then all of the sudden he got cancer. He was dying. Doctors couldn't do shit about it. So they went deer hunting. It was supposed to be their last, great trip together. Frank had a hunting cabin about a mile from the LeHorn place. They drove up there on a Friday night, and that was the last time anybody saw them alive."

He took a drag off the cigarette. "Damn, I miss these things. Fucking doctors . . ."

"You don't have to talk about this if you don't want to," I told him. "If it's too hard—"

"It's okay." He waved his hand, cutting me off. "They got to the cabin on Friday night. We know that because one of the boys, Mark, used his cell phone to call his wife and tell her they'd got there safely. That was the last anybody heard from them. By Saturday night, fire companies from six different towns were called to the cabin to fight a forest fire. Took out about thirty acres before they got it under control. They figure it started inside the cabin, but nobody is sure *how* it started.

Ronny Sneddon was there with the New Salem ladder crew. He told me it looked like a nuke had gone off. The cabin wasn't just burned. It was flattened. All the trees around it were nothing but ashes. No forensic evidence, and no bodies to identify, because the bodies were incinerated. There was just nothing left, not even their skeletons. A careless cigarette butt or a knocked over kerosene lantern wouldn't have caused a fire like that."

"So what did cause it?"

Merle shrugged. "Nobody knows. We'll probably never know. But it's just another bad thing to come out of that forest. And five more people that *didn't* come out."

A cloud passed over the sun, and the yard grew dark and chilly.

We sat in silence, while I thought about what I'd heard. Dale returned with a Styrofoam cooler filled with ice and beer, and we talked about less grim topics; the rising property taxes, why foot traffic was off for Merle's store, the Oriole's chances this year (we lived close enough to the border that we were allowed to root for Maryland's teams), the war in Iraq, and how all the good television shows were on cable.

Eventually, we heard the telltale crunch of car tires on our gravel driveways, as Claudine and Tara both came home from work, arriving within seconds of each other. (Even though Dale and Claudine were both retired, she volunteered every day at the library.) Tara gave me a look when she saw the empty beer cans on the table in front of me, but didn't say anything. They both joined us for a few minutes, but soon, the women pulled Dale and I away. Merle got up to go as well, and he looked wistful. I imagined he was wishing he still had a wife to drag him away from a bullshit session with the boys.

Tara and I went inside, and Big Steve crawled out from under my desk, stretched, and ran over to greet her. He smelled her shoes, investigating where she'd been for the day. She reached down to pet him and he wagged his tail and let her know how happy he was to see her. I was glad she was home as well.

"So what's for dinner?" Tara asked with a smile.

"Um, I guess time got away from me. Sorry. I didn't get the lawn finished either."

Her smile grew. "I noticed. Maybe you can get Merle and Dale to help you finish it tomorrow. If you guys can stay away from the beer long enough."

I gave her a brief hug. "How was your commute?"

"It sucked. How about yours?"

"It was a long walk from the coffee pot to the computer." I chuckled. "How are your feet?"

"Killing me," she sighed. "Have I ever mentioned how much I hate wearing nylons?"

"Once or twice."

"I'd like to get my hands around the neck of the guy who invented them." I grinned. "How do you know it was a guy?"

"Because a woman would never inflict this on her fellow females. Same goes for high heels." She bent over and rubbed her calf.

"Sit down," I suggested. "I'll massage them."

"You've got a deal."

We went into the living room and sat on the couch. Big Steve jumped up between us. Tara kicked her shoes off and then leaned back, putting her legs over Big Steve's back. I rubbed her feet while the dog served as a footstool.

Tara closed her eyes and sighed. "God, that feels good."

"Good," I replied, and felt the tension draining out of her. "How was your day?"

"Nothing but headaches. How was yours? Did you start the next book yet?"

"Not really," I admitted. "I tried like hell, but I just couldn't seem to get anything out. Writer's block, I guess."

Tara frowned. "You don't get writer's block."

"Well, like I told Leslie today, I guess I do now."

Her forehead creased. "So what did you and Steve do all day, then?"

I was speechless for a moment. The last thing I wanted to do was tell Tara about what I'd seen in the woods. She'd think I was losing my mind, or at the very least, get pissed off that I'd seen Shelly Carpenter naked.

"Research," I lied. "I went online and did research for the next book. And then I started to mow, until Merle interrupted me."

"Mmm-hmmm." She flexed her toes as I rubbed her heel. "And I bet he and Dale twisted your arm to goof off for the rest of the afternoon, too?"

"Yeah, now that you mention it. They held me at gunpoint. We may have to move."

She laughed, leaned forward, and gave me a kiss. "I love you, Mr. Senft."

"I love you, too, Mrs. Senft."

"Do you?" Her voice changed. She suddenly seemed sad.

"Of course I do," I said. "Why would you ask me that? What's wrong, honey?"

She shrugged, and began to stroke Big Steve's fur. "I started thinking about the baby again today. Our receptionist, Robin Harmic, is pregnant. She told us at lunch. I wanted to be happy for her, but I couldn't. It—it should be me, you know?"

I hugged her tight and kissed her forehead. "I know. And it will be, eventually."

"Will it?" she asked. "I don't know, Adam. Maybe there's something wrong with me. Maybe I can't have kids."

I spoke softly. "We've been through this, Tara. The doctors found nothing medically wrong with you. Chances are your body rejected the babies because there was something wrong with them. That doesn't mean that it will happen again."

"But what if it does? I can't go through this again. I just can't."

A lone tear slid down her face, and I held her tighter.

Big Steve shifted between us. His sad, brown eyes shifted from Tara to me and then back to Tara again. He knew something was wrong. Gently, he put his cold nose under Tara's hand and snuffled.

Tara patted him absentmindedly. "What if we keep miscarrying?"

"We won't," I promised, realizing how empty it sounded. "Next time, you'll see. A year from now, there'll be four of us. You, me, Big Steve, and the baby. Five of us, if we have twins."

She sniffed. "I'm just so scared. I know we haven't—haven't been intimate in a long while, and I'm sorry about that. I know it bothers you."

"No it doesn't." I was lying, of course. It did bother me, but I wasn't about to let Tara know that. The last thing she needed to hear right then was that her husband was sexually frustrated.

She wiped her nose on her blouse sleeve. "It's just that every time we try, I think about the miscarriage. I'm scared to try again."

"It's okay," I told her. "I understand. Remember what the grief counselor said? It's normal to feel that way."

"But not for this long, it isn't. I'm worried."

"About what?

"About all kinds of things. That you'll go elsewhere. Find another woman, or have an affair with one of your fans or another writer, maybe at one of these conventions, or when you're on tour again. I worry that you'll leave me, because I can't give you a baby and because we don't have sex anymore."

"Tara . . ." I was speechless.

"Maybe I'm just being silly, and I know that, but I'm scared."

I took her face in my hands. "Listen to me. I'm not going anywhere. I love you. I'd never cheat on you or leave you for another woman. You need to know that."

"I know. And I'm sorry. I'm tired of feeling bad. I want to move on, but I just can't seem to do it."

"It's okay," I repeated. "We'll get through this. Together. I promise."

We sat there and I held her for a long time, and whispered to her, and stroked her hair, and dried her tears, and softly reassured her. When she felt better, Tara went upstairs and changed clothes while I heated up some leftover meatloaf. We ate dinner, and then watched TV and played a video game. We didn't talk about the miscarriages or our sex life or anything else unsettling. We pretended that everything in our lives was normal.

Before bed, I took Big Steve outside. We'd missed his regular evening walk because I'd been drinking beer and listening to the neighbors tell me ghost stories.

A thin sliver of moon hung in the sky, and the stars seemed cold and distant. A screech owl called out from the top of the oak tree. Next door, the bass line from a Wu Tang Clan song thudded from Cory's apartment, along with the sound of screeching tires and gunshots as he played a video game. Cliff's lights were off upstairs and I wondered how he could sleep with all that going on underneath him.

Big Steve led me slowly towards the alley. When we reached it, he stopped and stared towards the woods. His tail was between his legs.

I reached down and scratched his head. "It's okay, buddy."

Big Steve didn't move. His body was rigid beneath my fingertips.

I followed his gaze, and stared at the forest. Despite the glow from the sodium lights in the Fire Hall's parking lot, the tree line was a wall of shadows. I looked at that impenetrable darkness and suddenly, I was very afraid.

Big Steve growled at something I couldn't see.

The events of that morning played back in my mind again. I'd tried to convince myself that what I'd seen were just Shelly and her boyfriend getting their freak on. But in my heart, I still didn't believe it.

Shivering, I turned back to the house. Our bedroom light was on upstairs, and it looked warm and inviting. Safe.

"Come on, bud. Let's go night-night."

He cast one last look at the forest, and then trotted along with me. He wagged his tail and sniffed the ground as if everything were normal again. We went inside. I turned off the light, and curled up next to Tara. Big Steve lay between us, facing the bedroom door, guarding it. He fell asleep, and I followed.

It was the last truly good night's sleep I remember having.

FIVE

On Tuesday morning, I tried very hard to pretend that nothing out of the ordinary had happened the day before. Some weird part of my brain convinced me that if I made believe everything was normal, it would be. Tara went to work, and I took Big Steve out for our morning walk, just like we always did. Shelly didn't jog down the alley, but I didn't let it trouble me. There could have been a million different reasons for her absence. Maybe she was sick, or she'd been early or was running late. I refused to think about what I'd seen any longer. Big deal. Shelly Carpenter was into kinky sex with guys in goat suits. So what? It wasn't any of my business.

A few years ago, our small town made *Forbes* magazine's list of 'The 200 Most Desirable Communities To Live In With Populations Under Ten Thousand'. At the time, I'd joked it was because we had a Wal-Mart, but there were plenty of other more tangible, realistic reasons. Our town offered instant access to Interstate 83, and a short, easy drive to York, Baltimore, Harrisburg, and Philadelphia, and it was only a little further to Washington D.C. or New York. Our property taxes stayed low, and housing was still affordable. We had good schools with teachers that still gave a damn, plenty of activities for adults and young people, the Lion's Club, Masonic Lodge, Knights of Columbus, the annual Volunteer Firemen's Carnival (which was held in the vacant lot across from our house), the antique district (which attracted tourist dollars), and a decent infrastructure. Churches abounded; Baptist, Lutheran, Brethren, Methodist, Catholic, Episcopalian, and a Jewish synagogue. Our residents loved the Lord in all of his denominations, and abhorred anything unholy (and in the opinion of some townspeople, their resident mystery writer fell into that category). As a result of these leftover Puritan attitudes, we were a dry town, meaning we had no bars, taverns, inns, or liquor stores within the borough limits. You couldn't buy a six-pack or a bottle of wine at the grocery store, and if you wanted those or a bottle of liquor, you went to York or Maryland. None of the establishments in town had liquor licenses, not even the restaurants. If you wanted to drink on Friday night, you had to drive down to the state line and pony up to the bar at the Maryland Line Bar and Grille. There was also no gambling (except for the state lottery tickets sold at the local convenience stores), no smoking in public places, no unleashed pets, and no skateboarding. Skateboarders were seen as just a notch above Satanists.

Maybe it was these attitudes and laws that contributed to our almost non-existent crime rate, (which was zero unless you counted Seth Ferguson and some of the other juvenile delinquents around town). Secretly, I thought the real reason we had so few serious troubles might be because the town was in heat. We may have paid attention to the rest of the Ten Commandments, but it often seemed like everybody in town coveted his neighbor's wife. At least once a week, when we got together in the backyard, Merle and Cliff would gossip about who was cheating on whom, which hubby had been spotted slow dancing down at the Maryland Line with somebody else's wife, who was getting divorced or separated, or climbing in and out of each other's bedroom window, who'd gotten whom knocked up, and what they planned to do about it. The townspeople liked the Lord, but they absolutely loved to fuck. Why should Shelly Carpenter be any different? She probably wasn't the only person in this town that liked to get peed on by men in goat suits.

I put it out of my mind, and focused instead on the weather. It was another beautiful day. I let the dog linger where he wanted, sniffing around our trees and bushes, and peeing on everything. I was in no rush to get back inside and start working. Instead, I soaked up the sun, closed my eyes, and listened to the bird's songs.

We crossed through the field and skirted around the park. Big Steve stopped before we got to the woods, and that was okay with me because I had no desire to re-enter them. An unseasonably warm breeze ruffled my hair, making the trees sway and bow, almost as if they were beckoning us toward them.

The dog lifted his leg and peed a few more drops, then turned around and started back towards the house.

"You done?"

He wagged his tail and began to pant, confirming that he was indeed finished, so I took him home. I got the impression Big Steve was pretending nothing had happened the day before, too.

I made a pot of coffee, pulled some hamburgers out of the freezer and left them sit out to thaw. I started a load of laundry, and then sat down at my desk. I went through the daily preparatory ritual, mouthing a prayer to the gods of writing that my muse would be there.

It was. Forcing myself to forget about the events in the woods had worked. My writer's block was gone, replaced with an overpowering urge to write. For an author, that's the best feeling in the world, and I took full advantage of it, sitting at the computer and pounding the keys until well past noon. I couldn't *not* write. I was so entranced with my tale of two brothers, one fighting for the North and the other for the South, that I didn't even get up to refill my coffee mug, which had grown cold. I paused only to light my cigarettes, and even that was done on automatic pilot.

Big Steve gnawed his daily bone, and then fell asleep at my feet. Occasionally, his paws would twitch or he'd growl softly, as he dreamed of chasing bunny rabbits.

At least, that's what I told myself he was dreaming about.

Around one that afternoon, I could no longer ignore the insistent urgings of my bladder. Happy with the progress I'd made, I saved my work, and took a piss. Then, satisfied that I'd written enough for the day, I put the laundry in the dryer, walked down for my daily nicotine fix from Leslie, and then mowed the rest of the lawn, basking in more of the same unseasonably warm weather. The lawnmower felt good beneath my hands. The motor roared, sounding nothing like a shepherd's pipe.

After finishing with the mowing, I brought Big Steve out and tied him to his chain. Then I raked the grass clippings into mounds and put them on my mulch pile. I'd use them as fertilizer in another month or so, after we'd planted our annual garden of tomatoes, cucumbers, sweet peas, parsley, and chives.

Big Steve started barking, and I turned to see what was bothering him. Out front, a young mother walked by pushing a baby stroller. She paused when she heard the dog, but as soon as she saw him cringing behind me, she visibly relaxed. The mother waved, and I waved back. She peered over the top of the stroller, smiled, and made baby talk to her child.

I was filled with a sudden, overpowering sense of anger. That could have been my wife and child. It *should* have been. I closed my eyes, picturing Tara pushing the same stroller, hearing her cooing to our child. Imagined the baby's laughter, the twinkle in its eyes, and the flush of its cheeks. I felt like screaming at the woman. How dare she walk her kid by my fucking house! Didn't she know what had happened here? Didn't she know we'd lost ours? It wasn't the first time I'd felt this unreasonable rage, but it had been a while, and the strength of the emotions surprised me. Immediately after the miscarriages, I'd experienced it all the time, anywhere there were children. At the mall, the county fair, down at the gas station, and the park—especially the park. Children playing on the swings and slides. Have you ever noticed that if you close your eyes and listen to a group of children's laughter, it sounds like they're actually screaming?

I'd thought those feelings had passed, but I'd been wrong.

The woman passed from sight. Big Steve settled down again and busied himself with digging a hole in the yard. Apparently, he'd heard there were good bones in China and was determined to find out for himself.

I checked the time. Three p.m. Tara would be home soon. I took Big Steve for his afternoon walk, and we stuck to the same shortened route we'd taken that morning. He wasn't his usual self. He seemed sedate.

When we got back, I pulled the grill out of the shed, cleaned it up, and made sure there was still propane left over from last summer. Then I tied Big Steve's leash around the oak tree and fired up the grill. The dog sniffed around the base of the tree, rooting through dead leaves, while I unwrapped the raw hamburgers.

I heard the purr of a motorcycle engine, and Cliff roared down the alley on his Harley. He pulled it into our garage, where he stored it, and then walked back outside and unsnapped his helmet.

I waved and Big Steve thumped his tail, but Cliff didn't notice us, for at that moment, a black and white State Police cruiser zipped down the alley. Its bubble lights flashed, but the siren was silent.

Cliff froze, one booted foot in his yard and the other in our driveway. I suppose he thought the cops were after him. He obviously hadn't been doing the alley's posted speed limit of twenty-five, and the cops had been cracking down on that lately, what with the playground nearby. But the police car cruised past him without slowing.

Cliff glanced towards Big Steve and me. His eyes were wide and he flashed us a lopsided grin.

"What'd you do now?" I hollered.

He shrugged. "Wasn't me, man. I don't know what the hell's going on."

One by one, I placed the hamburger patties on the grill. They sizzled and I breathed in the smoke, savoring the aroma. Meat cooking on the grill is the surest sign that winter is over, in my opinion, even more than the sighting of the first robin of spring. My mouth watered. Big Steve looked hopeful, his eyes darting from the burgers to me. I put the lid down and started towards the alley. Whining, the dog followed me to the edge of his leash.

"No," I told him. "You stay here and guard the burgers."

He gave me a mournful case of puppy dog eyes, and whined again, this time louder and longer. Relenting, I unclipped his leash from the tree trunk and took him along with me.

"You're incorrigible, you know that?"

He wagged his tail, confirming that he did indeed know that, and it didn't matter, because I loved him anyway. And he was right.

As we reached the alley, another police car, this one unmarked, sped by. Big Steve cowered and then shrank away to the end of his leash.

"It's okay, Stevie," Cliff said. "It's just the cops."

I nodded at the police cars. "What's going on?"

"Don't know." He flipped his long hair out of his face. "Thought maybe they were gonna give me a ticket at first."

"Me too."

A township police car flashed past us, tires humming, and Big Steve retreated a few more steps.

"State and township both," I observed. "Must be something serious, whatever it is."

Cliff pointed. "Looks like they're pulling into the Legerski's driveway. Wonder if Paul and Shannon are okay?"

Sure enough, all three cars were parked in the Legerski's driveway, six houses down. Paul's black truck was also there.

"He's home from work early," I said, indicating the truck. "He usually doesn't get back until around six."

"I don't think he went in today," Cliff told me. "His truck was parked in that same spot this morning when I went to work."

"Maybe he's sick," I suggested. "Or hurt."

"Then where's the ambulance?"

"Good point."

"Maybe that fucking Ferguson kid broke in or something," Cliff said.

Seth Ferguson was nothing but trouble. He lived across the street, thirteen going on thirty, and steadily working on a one-way ticket to the juvenile detention center in York. Leslie had caught him stealing gas from the pumps at the station a week before. Every neighborhood, no matter how Mayberry-like, has a Seth Ferguson. The type that shoots out windows with his bb gun, bullies other children, ties firecrackers to cat's tails, and soaps the windshields of cars.

We made small talk while we watched. Cliff wondered how my new book was coming along, and I asked him if he'd gotten lucky over the weekend. He had, with two different women he'd met at a bar in Baltimore's Fell's Point district. Spring fever had hit Cliff Swanson as well, it seemed. I secretly envied him.

A fourth patrol car raced down the alley. This one had its siren blaring, and it frightened Big Steve even worse. He pulled on his leash, cowering behind the shed. I took him inside the house, stopped to flip the burgers over, and then rejoined Cliff just as the ambulance finally arrived. Its siren was also on. I grew more concerned. This seemed like too much commotion for one of Seth Ferguson's pranks.

"Shit," Cliff breathed. "This is looking worse by the minute."

"Yeah," I agreed. "Something's up. Should we go down there?"

"Better not. Cops will just chase us off."

We both lit up cigarettes and watched the events unfold. I had a bad feeling in my stomach.

After hearing the sirens, Merle and Dale came outside to see what all the commotion was about, and joined us in front of my garage. As the four of us stood there talking amongst ourselves, I thought I heard something—that all-too-familiar piping from the day before. I froze, waiting to see if the others had noticed it, but none of them had. There were a few more brief notes, and then the music faded again. I chalked it up to my imagination—part of the background noise from the sirens—but then I noticed something strange.

I had another erection.

And I wasn't the only one.

Even as I tugged my t-shirt down over my pants to hide it, I noticed that Dale was staring at his own crotch, looking both very surprised and mildly uncomfortable. I followed his gaze, and saw that he had a bulge as well.

Merle noticed it, too. "What the hell, Dale? Am I that sexy?"

Dale's face turned bright red with embarrassment. "Not on your best day. I don't know what woke it up. First time in a while . . ."

"Did you pop some Viagra or something before you came outside?" Cliff joked, but I noticed that he was pulling his shirttail down over as well.

"N-no," Dale stammered. "It just . . . woke up."

Cliff chuckled. "One thing's for sure. Claudine will be happy tonight."

"I guess so," Dale said. "Hope it lasts till then."

Big Steve began licking himself. His own erection jutted like a pink candle.

Merle grinned, and scratched himself through his jeans. "Must be something in the air, 'cause I got one, too."

He squeezed it through the denim, and his grin grew wider. Then he shook his erect penis at Cliff, who backed away in disgust.

"Fuck you, Merle. Get the hell away from me with that thing."

"Come on, Cliff! Don't you want some action?"

"Not from you. You've got so many diseases, your dick probably looks like a cheese pizza with everything on it."

Merle playfully punched Cliff on the shoulder, and Cliff punched him back. The two of them started laughing, their erections forgotten. Dale still looked stunned, but he smiled along. I shook my head, wondering what in the world could have affected all five of us at the same time.

Before I could consider it any further, Tara pulled into the driveway. The guys all turned away from the car, trying to hide what was in their pants, but then the Legerski house caught their attention again.

"Hi honey," I hollered.

Big Steve ran around in an excited circle, jumping and panting, happy that his Mommy was finally home.

Tara got out of the car, balancing her briefcase, pocketbook, and travel mug, took one look at us and then followed our gaze to the activity in the Legerski's backyard.

"What's going on?" she asked.

I gave her a kiss on the cheek and took her briefcase from her. "We don't know. They showed up about five minutes ago."

Still watching the police, Tara bent down and scratched Big Steve behind the ears.

"Did you miss me, baby boy?" she asked.

He licked her face in response.

"Bet you it's a domestic dispute," Merle said. "Either he hit her or she hit him. Something like that. You guys watch and see."

I shook my head. "No way. Paul would never hit Shannon."

Merle snorted. "How well do you know him?"

"Well, not as good as I know you guys, but well enough. He reads my books. We like a lot of the same music. He's a nice guy. He wouldn't do something like that."

Merle turned his attention back to the police activity. "You might be surprised what happens behind closed doors. You can live with somebody for years, and suddenly, without warning, they'll fucking turn on you."

I wondered if Merle was talking about Paul and Shannon or his own ex-wife, Peggy, but I knew better than to ask. Then I realized something else. Without really thinking about it, I'd been holding Tara's briefcase in front of the bulge in my pants. But now my erection was gone. I cast a sidelong look at Dale's and noticed his had vanished too. I was relieved. Last thing I wanted was my wife standing out there while three of our male neighbors were sporting unexpected wood.

Tara looked at me quizzically. "Are you okay, Adam?"

"Yeah. I'm just worried about Paul and Shannon."

She sniffed the air. "What's burning?"

"Hmmm? What are you talking about? I don't think it's a fire."

"Yeah," Cliff said. "Ain't no fire trucks over there, Tara. So far, it's just the cops and that ambulance."

"Not that the fire trucks would have far to go," Dale commented, nodding towards the fire hall.

"No, I'm not talking about the Legerski's house." Tara pointed towards our grill. "Over there. Something is burning."

"Shit!" I'd forgotten about the hamburger patties. "That would be our dinner."

Tara rolled her eyes, and Cliff, Merle, and Dale all chuckled. I ran across the yard with Big Steve in tow, and pulled the blackened burgers off the grill. They were charred all the way through.

"Shit."

Tara hugged me from behind. "Looks like leftover meatloaf again, I guess?"

"I'm sorry, honey." I tossed the burned hamburgers onto the ground, and Big Steve greedily gulped them down, not minding that they crunched.

Tara stood on her tiptoes and kissed my forehead. "That's okay. At least you got the lawn mowed today."

I chuckled. "Yeah. And the laundry."

She looked genuinely pleased. "Good. I was running out of nylons."

"I started the book this morning, too."

Her smile grew wider. "Really? Adam, that's great!"

"Yep. Got about two thousand words written. I could have kept going, but there's no sense in burning out early. This weekend, I want to take a drive out to Gettysburg and do a little research."

Tara took the empty plate from me, along with her briefcase. "Let's celebrate. Maybe open a bottle of wine to go with our leftovers?"

I grinned. "Sure. Sounds good to me. What about dessert?"

She leaned close to me. I could smell her perfume, light after a long day's work, but still there.

"After dinner," she whispered in my ear, "we'll take a bubble bath. You can scrub me and I'll scrub you. And then we'll see about dessert."

I kissed the top of her head, breathing in her shampoo. "Promise?"

She sighed happily. "I promise."

"It's a date." I had another erection, but this time, I knew the reason why. Reluctantly, I pulled away and turned off the grill.

"Good. I'm going to go get changed, and then I'll heat up the leftovers."

"Okay," I said. "I'll be right in."

After Tara had gone inside, I rejoined the guys in the alley.

"Where's Merle?" I asked.

Cliff nodded towards the Legerski home. "He went down to talk to the cops—see if he can find out what's going on."

"He said he knows one of the township officers," Dale explained. "They drink at the same bar, apparently."

We watched and waited. Merle stood off to one side, talking with an officer. Two men dressed in suits and ties, that I assumed were detectives, were speaking to one of Paul's neighbors (I didn't know the old woman's name). Then the paramedics carried Paul out of the house on a stretcher, flanked by two state policemen. It was hard to tell from our distance, but Paul looked pretty out of it.

Dale shuffled his feet. "Well, that's not good."

"No," I agreed. "It isn't."

Cliff lit up another cigarette. "Wish Merle would get his fat ass back here and tell us what's going on."

We watched them load Paul into the ambulance. One of the cops got inside the vehicle with him, and then it pulled away. Gravel crunched under the tires. The lights and siren were both silent. After the ambulance had gone, the detectives went back into the house. Merle shook the police officer's hand and walked down the alley towards us.

"What's going on?" I asked him.

He panted, out of breath. "Shannon's gone missing."

Dale gasped. "What? When did this happen?"

Merle shrugged. "According to my buddy, Paul got home from work last night, and Shannon wasn't there. No note, no message on the answering machine, nothing like that. He figured that maybe she'd gone to visit her mom, or to the mall or the grocery store, so he went on about his business like normal. Ended up having a few beers and fell asleep in front of the TV. When he woke up this morning, she still wasn't home. Paul got scared then, or says he did. He called the cops, and they told him he had to wait twenty-four hours to file a missing persons claim."

Cliff grunted. "That's bullshit. Fucking cops."

"Well," Merle continued, "they didn't sit on their thumbs while the time frame passed. They checked with the Maryland state police, to see if her car had been involved in an accident or anything. And they checked with the hospitals on both sides of the border. Nothing. This afternoon, enough time had passed that they could treat it as a missing persons case. So they came over here and searched the house and talked with Paul."

"How could they search the house without a warrant?" Dale asked. "And why?"

Merle shrugged. "Do I look like an attorney to you? Maybe they swore one out before they came over. Or maybe they can legally search as long as Paul invited them in."

"Probable cause," Cliff muttered around his cigarette.

"How's Paul doing?" I asked. "Why are they taking him to the hospital?"

"Panic attack," Merle said. "He's a fucking mess. Looks like a zombie."

"So do they know anything yet?" Dale asked. "Any word on Shannon?"

Merle shook his head. "No, but my buddy told me the detectives suspect Paul may have had something to do with it. I imagine they'll want to ask him some more questions. And they're bringing in a forensic team right now, to go over the house."

I was stunned. "What, they think he's like Scott Peterson or something? That he killed Shannon and threw her body in Lake Codorus?"

"They don't know what to think at this point," Merle said. "But yeah, Paul's a suspect. For now, at least."

"That's ridiculous," I grumbled.

"They called him a suspect?" Dale asked.

Merle paused. "Not exactly. My buddy said he was a person of interest."

"Sounds like a suspect to me," Cliff said. "Ain't that what they call them now?"

"Well," Dale suggested, "maybe the investigation will turn up something else, instead."

"Let's hope so," I agreed. "Poor Paul."

Dale nodded. "And poor Shannon."

We talked it over for a few more minutes, and debated whether or not Paul was capable of killing his wife. Merle and Cliff seemed convinced that he'd done it. Dale and I weren't so sure. Then Cory and Claudine both got home from work around the same time and joined us in the back yard. Claudine informed us that word of the disappearance had already spread to the library, and that's why she was late. Cory was pissed off that he'd missed all the action, and immediately excited by the police presence in the neighborhood.

A news van from one of the local television stations arrived, and parked at the fire hall. A reporter and a cameraman piled out and began unloading equipment.

"Shit," Merle said. "There goes the neighborhood. In another hour, they'll all be camped out here."

"Like vultures," Cliff agreed.

"Hey!" Cory grew even more excited. "Maybe we can be on TV. That would rock, dude."

"Knock yourself out, kiddo," Merle told him. "I want nothing to do with them."

Cory reached into his pocket, pulled out his trusty hackysack, and started kicking it around, trying to attract the media's attention. He missed the ball with about every third kick, and Cliff mentioned that he wouldn't impress anybody that way.

Dale waved. "See you guys later."

He and Claudine went inside. Cliff and Merle snickered about his erection and how he'd better put it to use on Claudine while it lasted.

I excused myself and went inside as well. I had no desire to listen to their commentary on Cory's athletic skills and Dale's arousal, or stand in the backyard and watch the media circus. Paul's face would soon end up plastered across every newspaper and television station in the county, possibly in the country, if it was a slow news week and the national media got a hold of the story. Pundits would discuss it to death, and by next week, Paul and Shannon's names would be on everyone's lips. No matter what had really happened to Shannon, Paul would be tried and convicted in the court of public opinion before he even got his day in a real court.

There was a surprise waiting for me in the kitchen. Tara had heated up the remaining leftovers, and set the table with our best china, silverware, and tablecloth. She'd also lit red candles and the dining room smelled like rose petal potpourri. The radio played softly, and Whitney Houston promised that she'd always love me. Big Steve crawled under the table and lay down. His nose tested the air, hoping for some meatloaf.

I heard Tara bustling around upstairs. While I waited for her to come down, I turned on the television. Sure enough, there was a shot of Paul's house. A reporter was standing in the alley, reporting live on Shannon's disappearance. Behind him, Cliff and Cory mugged for the camera. Cory was flashing gangsta rap signs with his hands, and he looked like a white, idiotic version of Flavor Flav. I couldn't help but laugh. Then the local reporter told the viewers that Paul was considered a person of interest in his wife's disappearance.

"And so it begins," I said.

I turned the television off.

Cloth whispered behind me. I turned around. Tara stood in the doorway looking as beautiful as the day I married her. Fresh from the shower, she'd changed into a long, flowing nightgown, and red lace covered her every curve. Her long, dark hair spilled over her shoulders and breasts. Her feet were adorned with red high heels.

"What do you think?"

I opened my mouth to answer her, but nothing came out.

She smiled. "I'll take that as a compliment."

"Please do. You look beautiful."

Tara pulled out my chair and beckoned for me to sit down. Then she opened a bottle of wine and poured each of us a glass. Whitney Houston segued into Luther Vandross. Still thinking about Paul and Shannon, I half-heartedly smiled at Tara. She smiled back. The candle flames danced in her eyes.

She raised her glass. Her diamond earrings sparkled, reflecting in the wine. "Here's to you starting your next book."

"Cheers," I mumbled, and took a sip. It tasted bitter, more like vinegar than wine.

"You're quiet," she observed.

I nodded, and poked at the meatloaf with my fork. I didn't have much of an appetite.

Sighing, Tara sat her wine down and took my hand. "Adam, what's wrong?"

I filled her in on everything Merle had discovered; Shannon's disappearance and how the police were already looking at Paul as a prime suspect.

"God, that's terrible," she whispered. "I hope Shannon is okay. She's so nice."

"Yeah," I agreed. "They both are. I don't think Paul had anything to do with it. He couldn't have."

"I hope you're right."

We ate dinner, and I tried to get into a romantic mood and forget about everything else. Tara did the same. We talked about our first date, *Pulp Fiction* and coffee at Denny's, and of things we'd done since then, like our vacation trip to the Grand Canyon and the first roach-infested apartment we'd shared together, and our wedding day. We avoided mention of the miscarriages, and shied away from any events too close in time to those bad memories. Slowly, my appetite returned, and the wine kicked in. By the time our plates were clean, I felt much better. I was suddenly filled with love for my wife. If you've been married for a while, you've probably experienced the same thing. There are sudden moments where you feel that same electricity you felt when you first met. It's an overwhelming emotion, while it lasts.

Tara looked incredible, and I told her so again.

"I'm glad you like it." She thumbed the nightgown's thin material. "It doesn't really fit me anymore. I'm too big for it."

"Nonsense," I said. "You really do look beautiful."

She blushed. "Really? Tell me more, Mr. Senft."

I grinned. "You look good enough to eat."

She rolled her eyes. "Men."

"Hey, I meant it."

"If you insist." She drained her glass.

Smiling, Tara rose from the table, glided over, and sat in my lap. She put her arms around me, and our lips met. There was hunger in her kiss, a passion I hadn't felt since before the miscarriages. Our tongues met, dancing over each other. She tasted sweet, and I breathed in her scent, savoring it. My heart rate increased as her fingers ran through my hair. Her fingernails lovingly massaged my scalp, and she playfully nipped my nose with her teeth. Then she kissed me again. I brought my hands to her breasts and gently squeezed, running my thumbs across her nipples. They hardened at my touch, and my penis swelled in response.

Tara's lips left mine and she nuzzled against my neck, sighing.

"I should shower first," I said.

"Don't bother. You're fine. I like the way you smell."

I heard Big Steve's tail thumping under the table, and I fought to suppress my laughter.

Tara heard it too. She giggled. "Sounds like somebody's happy."

"He's not the only one." I kissed her chin and throat, and then teased her earlobe with my tongue. That was her secret spot, and it never failed to work magic.

Shivering, she leaned close, squeezed my hand, and whispered in my ear. "Let's go upstairs."

"I thought you'd never ask."

I scooped her into my arms and stood up. My back cracked like a gunshot and we both started laughing.

"Uh-oh," I said. "That didn't sound good."

"Put me down," she insisted. "I'm too heavy."

"No you're not." I crossed the living room and carried her towards the stairs. "It's just like when we got back from our honeymoon, and I carried you over the threshold."

"I've gained twenty pounds since then."

"And it looks good on you."

"No it doesn't. And besides, you're not as young as you were then. You'll be forty in a few years."

I kissed her cheek. "You really know how to romance a guy."

Big Steve got up to follow us, but I told him to stay. He lay back down, looking lonely and dejected.

With a little more effort than I cared to admit, I climbed the stairs with her in my arms. At twenty-five, or even thirty, I could have done this no problem. But Tara was right—I was almost forty, and I felt it. I was winded by the time we reached the bedroom, and my back was screaming.

Ignoring the pain, I lay Tara down on the bed and slid in next to her, still cradling her in my arms. We kissed again, long and lingering, as we slowly undressed each other. She was so warm. Our hands caressed each other's bodies, tracing familiar topography, stroking and touching in all of the right places, spots we knew blindfolded, our own version of Braille. She cooed and moaned, and I whispered words of love in her ear.

Grinning, I grabbed a bottle of long-unused massage lotion from the nightstand. Reading my intent, she rolled over onto her stomach. I rubbed the lotion into her back, massaging her shoulders and neck, and then working my way lower, to her tailbone, buttocks, and inner thighs. I took my time, enjoying the feel of her oiled skin as much as she enjoyed my attentions.

Finally, I gently rolled her over and brought my mouth to her breast, encircling her nipple with my lips, and flicking it with my tongue. Purring, she arched her back. I moved my hand lower, delved my fingers into her slick wetness, and it felt like returning home. It had been so long since I'd felt her there. Tara squirmed with pleasure as I gently massaged her clitoris. It pulsed beneath my thumb. She reached down and stroked me, and my penis felt ready to explode. Her fingers were electric.

"I want you," she breathed. "It's been so long, Adam."

"I want you to. I need you so much."

"Put on a condom. I don't want—"

I silenced her with a kiss, and then reluctantly pulled away. I reached over to the nightstand and pulled open the drawer. Tara wrapped her fingers around me and began to stroke me again. Groaning, I fumbled for the condoms. It had been so long since we'd used them, and they were buried beneath all the other assorted junk; a paperback, tissues, a bottle of aspirin, and a flashlight.

Her fingers continued stroking my shaft, keeping me hard, while I finally found a condom and tore the wrapper open with my teeth. I've often wondered why somebody can't design a condom that's easier to open. It kills the mood when you're biting and tearing at the wrapper, trying all the while to maintain an erection and keep your partner interested. I slid it down my length and then we embraced again. Tara leaned back on the pillows and arched her hips. I climbed between her widespread legs, looked at her glistening sex, and felt a wellspring of emotion and need erupt inside of me.

"Go slow," she whispered. "It's been a while."

I did, resisting the urge to plunge into her slick warmth all the way. I took my time, inch by excruciating inch. She flinched, and her body tensed.

"Are you okay?" I asked.

She nodded. "It's just a little tight. You're okay. Just keep going slow like that."

When I'd entered her completely, we lay still, kissing and caressing each other. I felt her inner walls begin to relax. Then, very slowly, Tara began to work her hips. I felt her stretching to accommodate me. After a moment, she relaxed.

"Better," she gasped. "Oh God, that's much better. You feel so good."

"So do you." I kissed her neck. "I missed this so much, Tara."

Slowly, I began to slide in and out of her, and she moved her hips in time with me. Soon, we found that familiar old rhythm that we both knew so well. We gasped each other's names, and our speed increased in time with our mutual needs. We moaned each other's name, tasted each other's sweat, and breathed in one another's scents. I sensed that she was close to orgasm, and even with the condom on, I knew I wouldn't be able to last very long either. Our movements took on greater urgency as we built towards a mutual climax.

Tara was dripping wet and I felt like a steel girder. Both of our bodies became tense as our orgasms approached.

Then, Tara grew stiff and silent.

I leaned down to lick her cheek. It was wet. At first I thought it was just perspiration, but as I kissed her eyes, I realized that she was crying.

I stopped in mid-stroke. “Tara, what’s wrong?”

“I’m sorry,” she sobbed. “I’m sorry. I just . . ."

She broke down, unable to finish. I pulled out, lay down beside her, and put my arms around her. I was confused—and in truth, a little disappointed as well. It had been so long since we’d made love, and something had gone terribly wrong. Now I felt rejected, and my balls were swollen and aching for release. It was painful, both physically and emotionally.

We lay there in the darkness and I held her, promising her that it was all right, even though I secretly didn’t understand what had happened. I wondered to myself if I’d done or said something wrong. Had I hurt her in some way? I wracked my brain, trying to figure it out, while Tara shook against me, her head buried in my chest.

“Do you want a tissue?” I asked.

She shook her head.

“How about a drink?”

“No.” She sniffled, and looked up from my chest. “No, I’m fine. Just stay here with me?”

“Of course.” I grabbed my cigarettes from the nightstand and shook one out of the pack. I lit it, inhaled, and settled back against the headboard. Tara lay across my chest. Her tears and mucous dried on my skin.

I stroked her hair. “Do you want to talk about it? I don’t understand . . ."

“I’m sorry,” she apologized again. “It felt so good, and all of a sudden, I just started thinking about the baby. I guess it reminded me.”

I nodded.

“I couldn’t help it. I started thinking about the miscarriage and the harder I tried to push it from my mind, the worse it got.”

"Why didn't you tell me to stop?" I asked.

"I didn't want to upset you. It's been so long since we made love. I didn't want you to be disappointed."

"I'm not," I lied.

She sniffled. "Are you sure?"

"Very much so. I totally understand." And I did, despite my own selfish need.

Tara sat up and wiped her eyes. She went to the bathroom while I lay there and smoked my cigarette down to the filter and tried to ignore the dull ache in my groin. While she was gone, I heard Big Steve's nails tapping on the stairs. He padded into the bedroom and jumped up on the bed with me. He stared into my eyes and then offered me his paw. I shook it.

"What are you looking at?" He curled up next to me, facing Tara's pillow.

The toilet flushed, and Tara came back to bed. She lay down next to me and took my hand.

"I tried, Adam. I really tried. You know that, don't you?"

"I know, honey. Let's not talk about it anymore tonight. Just get some sleep."

We snuggled close together, with Big Steve sandwiched between us, and I whispered my love and patience and understanding until she fell asleep. I lay there in the darkness for a very long time, listening to both Tara and the dog snoring, and thought about things. I was frustrated, and though I'd done a good job of hiding it from my wife, I couldn't hide it from myself. And I hated myself for feeling that way. It was selfish and insensitive—Neanderthal.

After a trip to the bathroom, I walked downstairs and went out into the backyard, hoping that the night air would tire me out. I turned off our motion-activated floodlight so that I wouldn't wake up the neighbors, lit a cigarette, and then stared up at the stars. Someone had once told me that the stars were God's eyes. I wondered if that was true, and then decided to find out. I stuck out my arm and extended my middle finger.

"Fuck you," I whispered. "This is all your fault. You've got a kid of your own. Why did you have to take ours? Oh, that's right— you let yours die on the cross."

The stars stared back at me, cold and silent and far away. I wasn't stricken down for my blasphemy, and hadn't expected to be. A grim sense of satisfaction settled over me. I snuffed out my cigarette on the sidewalk and continued stargazing.

My thoughts were interrupted by Cliff's voice. He stepped around the corner of his building, shirtless and barefoot, smoking a cigarette, his cell phone to his ear. Judging by the conversation, he was talking to one of his many girlfriends. He jumped when he saw me, and I waved. He feigned a heart attack, waved back, and then went back around the corner.

For a moment, I wondered what it would be like to have Cliff's life, being a bachelor in my early forties and having sex with different women every weekend. Then I gazed up at our bedroom window and felt guilty for thinking like that.

I went back inside, and fooled around on the computer. Eventually, I surfed my way to a free porn site. After looking at the pictures, I masturbated, careful not to make any noise. My orgasm was brief and unsatisfying, and when it was over, I felt guiltier than ever. I wiped myself with some tissues and buried the evidence at the bottom of the trashcan.

I started getting sleepy some time after midnight, so I went back upstairs and crawled into bed. Big Steve wiggled over next to me, sighed, and then went back to sleep. I closed my eyes. As I drifted off, floating in that comfortable zone between awake and sleep, I imagined I heard the sound of a shepherd's pipe on the breeze, outside on the street. It was faint and ghostly, and faded almost as suddenly as it had appeared.

I sat up and listened, but the music wasn't repeated. I glanced at the clock, pushed Big Steve's head off my pillow, and then lay back down. I figured I'd imagined it.

I closed my eyes again and went back to sleep, but it wasn't a peaceful slumber. My dreams were filled with eerie music and crackling flames. Naked female figures pranced around a bonfire deep inside the forest to the sound of beating drums. The satyr cavorted with them, playing a tune on his shepherd's pipe. In the dream, I could even smell the smoke from the fire. On the outskirts of the ring, a man had been nailed to a tree. His mouth was open, silently shrieking.

I woke up again, gasping and bathed in sweat, with the sounds of a shepherd's pipe floating through my head. Tara stirred beside me, but did not wake. Big Steve watched me intently, and I wondered if I'd woken him, or if he'd been having bad dreams too.

Sighing, he snuggled closer to me, and I breathed in his dog smell and hugged him tight, like a big old teddy bear. He licked my hand.

"It's going to be alright," I whispered in his ear. "Isn't it boy? Things will get better. They've got to."

We stayed like that for a long time.

Tara rolled over and moaned in her sleep. I kissed her forehead, slick with sweat, and her breathing grew shallow again. The worried creases in her face smoothed. She smiled, and then softly snored.

I fell asleep while thinking about the miscarriages, and how maybe it wasn't just our babies that had died. Maybe it was something more, a part of our relationship that could never be resurrected.

I dreamt no more that night.

And while the rest of the neighborhood slept, something prowled our streets with cloven feet.

SIX

Tara apologized again when she woke up the next morning. I reassured her that everything was okay and told her to stop being silly. There were dark circles under her eyes, and it didn't look like she'd slept well. Even though I'd turned in late, I'd gotten up a half an hour before she did. I surprised her with coffee and breakfast in bed, and despite the sadness still etched on her face, she smiled when I brought it to her, which made me feel better.

She sipped her coffee, an ice cube floating in it, just the way she liked. "You didn't have to do this, Adam."

"Sure I did. I had a good reason."

She chewed a strip of crisp bacon. "Oh really? What's that?"

"Because I love you. That's all the reason I need."

"I love you, too. And this was really sweet. Thank you."

After she'd finished breakfast and I'd cleared the plates away, Tara hopped in the shower. While she got ready for work, I lay back on the bed and turned on the television. Shannon's disappearance was all over the local morning news, and I saw Paul's house, the alley and playground, our houses, and even a shot of the forest, on every station. Shannon still hadn't turned up. Paul was in the hospital, and his condition was being guarded. They said he'd been treated for emotional stress, and that the police were waiting to speak some more with him.

Tara came out of the bathroom and began getting dressed. She pulled on a pair of nylons, and that drew my attention away from the television.

"Any news on Shannon?" she asked.

I clicked the television off. "Not yet. She's still missing, and Paul's in the hospital, being treated for stress. They're not saying much else."

"Do you think she's okay?"

I paused. "I don't know, hon. I hope so."

She responded, but the words were lost beneath the whine of her hair dryer. I closed my eyes while she brushed her hair. I'd awoken with a bad headache, and it wasn't going away, even after I'd swallowed two aspirin while making Tara's breakfast.

She turned the hair dryer off. "What's the matter?"

"Headache," I mumbled.

She walked over and gave me a quick kiss. "Are you sure you're not upset about last night?"

"Honey, I promise you that I'm not upset. It's okay. Really."

She sat down in front of the vanity table. "You'd tell me if you were, right?"

I nodded, and she leaned close to the mirror and began putting on her mascara.

"Maybe we can try again tonight," I suggested.

She looked up from the mirror, mascara brush in hand.

"Maybe," she said. "We'll see."

But I could tell from the tone of her voice that we probably wouldn't. Our troubled sex life was back to square one again. It was frustrating and depressing and I still didn't truly understand what had happened. I thought about how I'd jerked off the night before, and daydreamed about Cliff's bachelor life, and the guilt welled up inside me like a balloon. I lit a cigarette. It tasted like shit, but I smoked it anyway. My headache grew worse.

After she'd left for work, I took Big Steve outside for his morning walk. He stopped in the yard, sniffed the grass beneath our bedroom window, and then started barking. I looked around, but didn't see the source of his aggravation. The grass smelled strange; musky, but there was nothing amiss. I had to tug the leash hard to get him to move, and we walked to the alley.

Once again, there was no sign of Shelly Carpenter. I wondered if she was avoiding me, maybe out of embarrassment or anger. Perhaps she'd found a new jogging route. Maybe she couldn't face me, now that I'd seen what she was getting up to in the forest with her boyfriend, or she was freaked out that the local author who she often stopped and talked to was a peeping tom. But she certainly hadn't seemed to mind when I caught them. She'd seemed to enjoy it.

The weather was still nice, but it didn't feel like spring anymore. It felt—muted. Stale. The grass was brown. The lilac bush had no scent. The tree limbs slumped dejectedly, and their budding leaves seemed frozen in mid-sprout. There were no squirrels running around in the treetops. They were gone, along with the birds and the bees.

We had to thread our way through the media camp, and six different reporters asked if they could interview me. I declined. Big Steve peed on the power cables running to one of their vans. Law enforcement was present as well, both township and state. Big Steve pressed against my leg, trembling; so freaked out by the crowd that I had to cut his walk short.

When we got back to the house, I flipped through the newspaper while my second pot of coffee brewed. Paul and Shannon dominated the front page, relegating the President's trip to Saudi Arabia to the lower left hand corner. The rest of the news was child molesters, serial rapists, religious extremists, and corporate stock scandals; in other words, the same old shit.

Disgusted, I tossed the paper in the trash and started the day's writing. Some of the magic was gone, and I had to force the words to come. Big Steve assumed his usual position under my desk, and we stayed like that, uninterrupted, until around ten, when I heard a police siren race by on Main Street. I debated going to the window, but I knew if I got up, my concentration would be shattered and there'd be no more writing for the day. I resumed typing until eleven, when I was interrupted again, this time by a knock at the door.

Big Steve jumped to his feet and barked, pretending to be the vicious guard dog. I told him to be quiet and turned off the stereo, silencing Whitesnake's "In The Still of the Night" in mid-power chord. I went to the door and Big Steve nervously trotted along behind me.

A well-dressed Hispanic man, about my age or maybe a little older, stood on the front porch. His forehead was beaded with sweat and there were dark stains under his arms. I made him for a cop right away. He had a manila folder in one hand and a badge in the other. A black leather briefcase sat at his feet. I caught a glimpse of a shoulder holster strap beneath his suit coat.

"Hello, sir." He flashed the badge, tucked it into his suit, and stuck out his hand. "Sorry to bother you. I'm Detective Ramirez."

Caught off guard, I hesitated for a second. He smiled. I opened the screen door and shook his hand. It was slick with perspiration, but strong and firm. He smelled faintly of cheap cologne and cigarette smoke. Big Steve growled from the safety of my office, and the detective peered apprehensively over my shoulder.

"Don't worry," I told him. "Big Steve's a pussycat. If you get any closer to him, he'll run and hide."

"He's a big dog." The officer released my hand. "Nice to hear his bark is worse than his bite."

There was an uncomfortable moment of silence, and we stared at each other. I grinned, and felt idiotic doing it. The cop grinned back, and twitched his eyebrows up and down.

"Can I help you with something, Detective?" I finally asked.

"Sorry," he apologized again. "I've been knocking on doors all morning. We're investigating the disappearance of three of your neighbors. Shannon and Paul Legerski, and—"

I interrupted him. "Wait a minute. Paul's missing, too?"

The detective frowned. "Do you know Mr. Legerski, sir?"

"Yeah, I know them both. They live a few houses up the street."

"May I come in, sir? I'd like to ask you some questions."

My heart beat a little faster. There was no logical reason for it. Obviously, I'd done nothing wrong. I wasn't involved in Shannon's abduction, if that's what it was. But still, when an officer of the law says that they want to ask you some questions, it's human nature to be nervous.

"Sure." I held the screen door open. "Come on in."

He picked up the briefcase, cast another wary glance at Big Steve, and then stepped past me. The dog immediately ran into my office with his tail between his legs, and hid underneath the desk.

The detective laughed softly. "You weren't kidding. Cute dog, though."

"Thanks."

He glanced around the living room. "Nice place. I like the motif."

"My wife's doing. She's got a real flair for home decorating." I swept my hand toward the couch. "Please. Have a seat."

"Thank you." He sat down, loosened his tie, and pulled some photographs out of the manila envelope.

"Can I get you something to drink?" I offered.

He shook his head. "No thank you, Mr.—?"

"Senft. Adam Senft."

Detective Ramirez blinked. "Adam Senft, the mystery writer?"

I did my best to smile humbly. "That's me. You've read my books?"

"As a matter of fact, I just finished *Heart of the Matter* last weekend."

"No kidding? Small world."

"Yes it is. I knew you were local and lived here in York County, but I had no idea where."

"I don't like to be specific with my address," I explained. "I've known other authors who had trouble with intruders and overzealous fans. You know, disturbed people who wanted them to read their manuscript or accused them of psychically stealing their story ideas."

The detective grunted. "I can understand your need for privacy. The world is full of crazy people these days."

I laughed politely. "Well, Detective, I hope you enjoyed the book."

He shrugged. "I did, up until the ending. To be honest, I

thought maybe my book was missing a page or something. Couldn't believe you ended it like that."

"Yeah, I hear that a lot."

"I'll bet. You got your facts right, though. I liked that. A lot of writers seem to make it up as they go along, but you obviously did some research on armed robbery methods and police procedural responses to them. The book was a lot stronger for it."

"Thanks," I said, genuinely pleased. "Glad it rang true for you."

"Oh, believe me, it did. I used to work robberies myself."

"Why the switch?" I asked.

His face grew clouded. "Remember the bank robbery in Hanover about two years ago? The really *bad* one?"

I did remember, and told him so. It had been big news at the time, receiving nationwide coverage. A bank robbery turned into a hostage standoff. There were three robbers, one of whom, a young guy named O'Brien, had supposedly been dying of terminal cancer, and another that was wanted for a string of armed robberies on the West Coast. When it was over, several hostages were dead, including a young boy, a deliveryman, the bank manager, and one of the robbers. The boy was killed by crossfire when one of the suspects refused to drop his weapon and was gunned down by police commandoes. The other two robbers went to jail and died in prison about a year later. I recalled the tabloids had also been interested in the case. O'Brien, the robber who'd supposedly had cancer, insisted that the boy had healed him, and that another robber was possessed by demons.

"That was the weird one, right?" I asked. "In that jailhouse interview, the robber claimed he'd killed the Second Coming of Christ." The detective nodded. "That's the one."

"I remember watching that interview. He really seemed to believe it. And they said he wasn't crazy, right?"

"He was able to stand trial. In truth, I wish I had the strength of his convictions. Fantasy or not, he was convinced he was telling the truth."

"So you didn't believe him?"

"I'm short on belief, about a lot of things, Mr. Senft. I often wish I could believe. Maybe I just haven't been presented with the truth."

He grew quiet for a moment, his face clouding. I sensed a kindred spirit; someone else who was struggling with what he'd been raised to believe versus what the world continued to show him.

"Anyway," Detective Ramirez explained, "I was in charge of the response to that hostage standoff. I didn't do a very good job. People died because of decisions I made. I gave the order to storm the bank vault. It was a mistake. After it was all over, the brass made me take a sabbatical, and when I came back, I got reassigned to homicide. Not really a punishment. Homicide is the pinnacle of any cop's career. But I enjoyed working robberies, so they knew it was a demotion, far as I was concerned."

"Homicide? You think Shannon was murdered?"

His smile was tight-lipped. "This is an ongoing investigation. I'm afraid I can't say."

I anticipated more questions about my writing, the same ones I was always asked when somebody found out who I was and what I did for a living. Where I got my ideas and how come they hadn't made a movie out of one of my books and if I knew James Patterson, and if so, what was he like. But surprisingly, Detective Ramirez didn't ask any of them. Instead, he spread three photographs across the sofa cushions and got down to business.

"I take it you recognize two of these individuals?"

I nodded. "Sure. That's Paul and that's Shannon. I don't know who that third woman is, though."

He handed me the third photograph. "That's Antonietta Wallace. She lives a block away from here. Take a good look at it."

"Is she connected to Shannon's disappearance?"

"Again, I'm not at liberty to say, Mr. Senft. But I assume you haven't watched the news this morning?"

"Just the six o'clock round up. I've been working on a new novel all morning. Oh, and I read the paper. But I don't think there was anything about her."

"Mrs. Wallace is also missing, and since the details were already leaked to the press—although, apparently not in time for this morning's editions—I can tell you that it happened sometime last night, while she and her husband Walt were supposedly sleeping. The husband says that when he woke up this morning, she was gone."

My stomach sank. "Gone?"

He nodded, watching me carefully.

I studied her picture closely, and my dread increased. An older woman (probably in her mid-fifties but still strikingly beautiful) stared back at me. She was smiling. Her hair had streaks of white, rather than gray, and she wore wide-rimmed glasses, making her look like a librarian. Now that I had a closer view, she looked familiar. I'd seen Antonietta Wallace on the street, going into the antique shops and walking her dog, a miniature poodle. But I didn't actually know her, like I knew my neighbors.

I handed the photograph back to him. "Sorry to hear that. Is there a possibility she just went away on her own?"

He shook his head. "Doubtful. She left her purse behind, her car keys, driver's license, everything. Even her glasses, and according to family members, she couldn't see to drive without them."

Detective Ramirez put the photographs back in the envelope and took out a notepad. I sat down on the couch next to him and pulled out my cigarettes.

"You mind if I smoke?" I asked.

He grinned. "It's your house, Mr. Senft. Mind if I join you?"

I chuckled. "Feel free. Ashtray is to your right. And call me Adam."

We both lit up. I noticed he was smoking non-filtered. Hard core.

"So," I said as the nicotine rushed through my bloodstream, "if she's missing too, then that means that Paul is innocent, right?"

"Why is that, Mr. Senft?"

"Adam."

He nodded. "I'm sorry. Adam."

"Well," I explained, "it's got to be somebody else. I mean, two women missing in less than twenty-four hours? And Paul was in the hospital last night according to the news."

"Then you don't believe Mr. Legerski had anything to do with his wife's disappearance?"

"No, I don't. You've got to know Paul. He wouldn't do something like that. Earlier, you said he was missing. Have you talked to him at all?"

Detective Ramirez sighed. "Only an initial interview, while he was being treated. He was cooperative at the time. But Mr. Legerski checked himself out of the hospital late last night. We'd identified him as a person of interest, but no charges have been filed, so he was free to go. At this time, we're unsure of his present location."

"The news didn't say anything about that this morning, either."

"Nevertheless, it appears that he's gone." He tapped his cigarette in the ashtray. "Which brings me to my next question. Have you had any contact with Mr. Legerski in the last twelve hours? Or do you know anybody else who may have spoken with him? Your other neighbors, perhaps?"

"No, not at all."

"Do you know if the Legerskis were having any marital or financial problems?"

"I don't think so. Paul seemed pretty happy. He had a good job. Just bought a boat to take down to the Chesapeake Bay, so I don't think they were having trouble with money. But we never really talked about our incomes."

He wrote something down in his notepad. "What did you and Mr. Legerski talk about?"

I shrugged. "Music, mostly. Fishing. Sports. Stuff like that."

"Do you know if Mr. Legerski was having an affair, possibly?"

"No. I told you, he seemed very happy. He loved his wife."

But as Merle had pointed out, what did I really know about their relationship? Perhaps their sex life was unsatisfying, like Tara's and mine. Maybe Paul had been seeing someone else, and Shannon had found out about it. Immediately, I felt guilty for thinking like that, in regards to both my wife and our missing neighbors. I stood up and began to pace around the living room floor.

Detective Ramirez kept scribbling. "And you haven't seen or spoken with him today?"

"Nope. Maybe he went looking for Shannon?"

"Perhaps."

"Because I could see him doing that, you know? Especially if he thinks you guys are focusing on him and meanwhile his wife is still out there."

"Are you nervous?"

"Huh?"

"You're pacing. I thought you might be nervous."

"No," I said, more forcibly than I'd intended. "I'm just shocked, is all."

"Okay." He smiled again. "That's totally understandable."

I sat back down.

"And I need to ask, can you account for your whereabouts last night and this morning, Mr. Senft?"

"M-me?" I was startled. He'd gone back to calling me Mr. Senft again, rather than Adam. "Look, am I a suspect or something?"

Detective Ramirez smiled. "Not at all. We're asking this of all the neighbors. It just helps us get a handle on things. You might have seen something that can aid us in our investigation and not even realize it."

"Oh. You scared me for a second."

He looked up at me expectantly, but said nothing. His pen hovered over the notepad.

"I was here last night," I told him. "My wife, Tara, can vouch for that. We stayed home all evening. And my next door neighbor, Cliff Swanson, he saw me too."

He nodded. "Very good. And this morning?"

"Tara went to work. I was here."

"Where does your wife work?"

"Baltimore." I gave him the name of the company and told him what she did for a living. He paused in his writing.

"Huh."

"Something wrong?" I asked.

"Well, please don't take offense. I just assumed authors made a lot of money. Enough that their spouses didn't have to work."

"That's okay. Lots of folks think that way. I just wish it were true. For every bestseller you see in the front racks of the store, there's a bunch more of us on the shelves making the literary equivalent of minimum wage."

Big Steve paced in my office. His nails clicked on the hardwood floor.

Detective Ramirez resumed his questions. "And after she went to work? What did you do?"

"I took my dog for a walk, just like we do every morning."

He scribbled in his pad. "And where did you walk?"

I pointed to the back of the house. "Across the alley, and over into the field next to the park."

He frowned. "I didn't think they allowed pets in the park."

My cheeks flushed. "They don't. We just skirt around the edge of it. We used to walk in the woods down behind the park, but we don't go in there anymore."

"I see. And why is that?"

"It's—well, to tell the truth, Big Steve gets spooked by the forest. You know, with all the animals and stuff. He's afraid of the squirrels. Like I told you, his bark is worse than his bite."

"Mm-hmm. Did you see anybody during your walk?"

I thought of Shelly, whom we should have seen that morning, but hadn't.

"No."

Detective Ramirez stubbed his cigarette butt out in the ashtray.

"What time did you get back from your walk?"

"Around seven-thirty, maybe seven forty-five. We didn't stay out long, because of all the reporters."

He grimaced. "Can't blame you there."

"And then I wrote until just now, when you came by."

"Oh yeah?" He sounded genuinely interested. "New book?"

I nodded. "
What's it about?"

"I'm not sure yet. It deals with the Civil War. To be honest, I don't like to talk about the plots very much until I have them fleshed out."

"Trade secrets, huh?"

"Something like that."

His face fell, and I could see that he was disappointed.

Well, that's what you get for freaking me out, I thought.

He closed the notebook and slipped it back into the envelope. "Well, again, I'm very sorry for disturbing you."

"Don't sweat it. I'm happy to do whatever I can if it will help."

He stood up. "If you're serious about that, we're organizing civilian search teams later this afternoon, to help supplement our own people. The Fire Department is running the show, since it's still considered search and rescue at this point. But we'll be assisting, along with your local township police and other agencies. We're asking residents to meet at the firehouse at two o'clock if they'd like to volunteer to help search. Would you be interested?"

"Absolutely," I said. "I'd be happy to help."

"Well then, maybe I'll see you there."

"Sounds good."

We shook hands once more as I walked him to the door, and he told me again how much he'd liked *Heart of the Matter*. Then he reached into his pocket and handed me a business card with his contact information. He asked me to call him if I thought of anything else that might help with the investigation, no matter how trivial or seemingly unimportant. I promised that I would. Closing the door behind him, I watched through the curtains as he banged on Cliff and Cory's apartment doors. When he got no answer, he left business cards in each of their screen doors, and then moved on to Merle's house.

Big Steve crept out from under the desk and sniffed all around the carpet and the couch where the detective had been sitting. Satisfied, he looked at me and wagged his tail.

"You're so brave," I told him. "What a brave, brave boy

you are. What a vicious guard dog. He's lucky you didn't chew his leg off."

His tail wagged harder, and he offered me his paw. I shook it, noticing that his nails were getting long again and needed trimming. I scratched behind his ears, and Big Steve leaned into my hand and closed his eyes, shuddering with sheer bliss.

After I'd cut his toenails and played with him some more, I walked down to the gas station and bought two packs of cigarettes from Leslie. The disappearances were the talk of the town, and she'd heard every customer's theory that morning, everything from a serial killer to alien abduction. Leslie was convinced that Paul had killed Shannon, and was on the run, and that Antonietta Wallace's disappearance wasn't related. Leslie thought that maybe she'd just left her husband.

I told her I wasn't convinced that Paul had done it, and advised her to be careful. She shrugged it off and told me I'd written too many mysteries.

"You're beginning to sound like a character in one of your books, Adam."

Then she changed the subject, chattering with excitement about her big date that night.

"Well," I cautioned protectively, "don't do anything I wouldn't do."

She grinned. "What fun is that?"

"I'm serious. Be careful."

Leslie promised that she would.

Arriving back home, I decided to see if Detective Ramirez had paid a visit to Dale. He had, and while Dale and I discussed it in the backyard, Merle came out of his house, and joined us.

"What's up, Merle?" I greeted him.

"Not much," he answered. "That detective come by and visit you guys?"

Dale and I nodded.

"He stopped by my place, too," Merle told us. "Tried to sell him some antiques. Cheap bastard."

We laughed, and I imagined Merle pushing the hard sell on Detective Ramirez, probably for an ugly old lamp or an ancient Coke bottle.

"I see the scavengers are still here," Merle said, pointing at the media's encampment. "I was hoping they'd go chase another ambulance for a while."

"Slow news day," I said. "This is where all the action is."

"They'll probably want to get footage of the search," Dale said. "Either of you going to volunteer for that?"

"I am," I said.

"Me too," Merle agreed. "Got nothing better to do. Haven't had a single customer all day."

"How about you, Dale?" I asked.

"I told him I'd help. Not sure how much good I'll be. Can't go more than a few hundred yards without getting winded, it seems. But I'm willing to give it a shot. It's the right thing to do."

Merle watched the reporters. "Cliff and Cory are gonna be pissed about missing all the fun when they get home from work tonight."

A police car crawled down the alley, and had to turn on its siren to get the reporters out of the way.

"So, what do you guys think is going on?" I asked them. "I mean really going on, not what the cops and the reporters are feeding us."

"Paul's a serial killer," Merle said. "That's got to be it. Two women missing, and then he goes missing too?"

I groaned. "Oh, come on! Are you serious?"

He winked. "Serious as a heart attack."

"That doesn't mean he's a serial killer," I said. "We don't even know if he's involved."

Merle sat back and crossed his arms. "The detective sure as hell seemed to think he was."

I paused. "He told you that?"

"No." Merle shuffled his feet. "Not exactly. But you could read it in his actions. It's what they don't say that gives them away, you know? Paul did it. Watch and see. He's on the run, right now. Bet you he shows up on *America's Most Wanted* before the end of the month, if they don't catch him before then."

My cheeks flushed with anger. "That's bullshit."

"Why?"

"Just because he was married to Shannon doesn't mean he's involved. Yes, I agree it doesn't look good—him disappearing. But that still doesn't make him guilty."

"Sounds pretty reasonable to me," Merle said.

"If that's so, then why not Antonietta Wallace's husband? After all, she's missing too. Why don't you point the finger at him?"

Merle frowned. "Walt? There's no way he's involved in this mess. I know him. He wouldn't do something like that."

"And I know Paul. Neither would he."

Dale rubbed his forehead. "Both of you shut up. You're giving me a headache."

Merle turned to me, changing the subject. "So how's your girlfriend?"

"My girlfriend?"

"Yeah. Shelly Carpenter. Haven't seen her run by the past two days. Is she avoiding you or something?"

"She's not my girlfriend," I sighed. "And I haven't seen her either."

"Maybe she's missing," Dale suggested. "Like the other women."

Merle and I both stared at him.

"Think about it," Dale said. "Two women supposedly vanish from their homes two nights in a row. It's been two days since you've seen Shelly. Maybe she's gone, too. She could have been the first."

Merle punched his palm with his fist. "Son of a bitch! He's right. I never even though of that."

"No." I shook my head. "She's not."

"So you have seen her then." Merle asked.

"I saw her Monday morning," I admitted. "When I was walking Big Steve through the forest."

Dale pulled out a red handkerchief and blew his nose. "Sorry. These damn spring allergies."

"Shelly was in the woods?" Merle asked.

"Yeah. And—she wasn't alone. I saw her with . . ." I paused, unsure of how to continue.

Merle grew impatient. "With who?"

"Let's sit down," I suggested, pointing to the patio chairs. "Anybody else want a beer?"

"Damn," Merle snorted, "this must be one hell of a story."

"It's a little early to start drinking, isn't it?" Dale asked.

"I need a beer. Do you guys want one or not?"

Dale shook his head. "I'll pass."

"I'll take one," Merle said, "if you're gonna twist my arm."

I grabbed two beers from the fridge, hooked Big Steve up to his leash, and came back outside. Dale and Merle were seated at the table, watching the reporters and the cops mill about on the Legerski's lawn. After handing Merle a beer, I tied the dog to his outdoor leash and took a seat. Big Steve wagged his tail at Merle and Dale, and they tried to coax him over close enough to pet him. He'd get within inches of their outstretched fingers and then dart away.

"I was lost in thought," I said. "Wasn't really paying attention to where we were going. Next thing I knew, Big Steve and I had ended up pretty deep inside the woods. I'd certainly never been where we were before."

They listened attentively while I told them about the strange piping music, and the stone marker with the weird language—if it was a language—carved into it, and how the rock seemed to throb with a life of its own, and how the trees had seemed so sinister. I paused, taking a long swallow of beer before I got to the next part. Then I told them about that, too; Shelly and the guy in the satyr costume, the guy I'd thought was a statue at first.

I thought they'd laugh at me. Merle at the very least would probably have something sarcastic to say. But when I finished, neither one said anything. They just stared at me thoughtfully. Big Steve crawled under the table and sat between my legs. His panting was the only sound. Finally, I couldn't stand their silence any longer.

"Well," I said. "Let's hear it. Where are the jokes?"

Merle's face was serious. "Ain't a joking matter, Adam. Did you tell Ramirez about this when he stopped by?"

"No, I didn't see the connection at the time."

"And now?" Dale asked.

"Yeah," I admitted, "I guess I can see how it looks suspicious, in hindsight. But I still think she's probably just embarrassed and staying away from me."

Dale opened his mouth to say something, but then closed it again. "What?" I asked him.

"Adam, when you and Big Steve stumbled across Shelly and her . . . suitor . . ."

He paused, as if unsure of what he wanted to say next.

I motioned for him to continue. "Yeah?"

"How sure are you that it was just a man in a goat suit?"

I started to laugh, but Dale's expression was serious. I glanced at Merle, and his face mirrored Dale's.

"Well . . . it had to be," I stammered. "I mean, what else could it have been?"

"Yes," Dale whispered. "What else indeed?"

"Maybe we should make sure Shelly is all right," I suggested. "I mean, you guys might be right. With everything that's going on, it makes sense to check on her."

"Do you know where she lives?" Dale asked.

"Sure," I answered. "Big Steve and I have walked by there before. I've seen her out in the yard."

Merle stood up. "Like to, but I can't. I've got to finish up with some stuff inside the store if we're gonna help with the search this afternoon. You guys go ahead without me."

"I can't go either," Dale said. "Claudine's sister is dropping off some clothes that she doesn't want anymore, and I have to be here to let her in."

I reached down and scratched Big Steve between the ears. "Looks like it's just you and me then, buddy."

Big Steve licked my hand. I hooked him back up to his leash and stood to leave.

"Adam," Dale called, "be careful."

"It's just down the street," I said, taken aback.

"Yes, I know. And you're probably thinking I'm a crazy old man, but—"

Merle snickered. "I sure do."

"But be careful just the same," Dale finished. "I've got a weird feeling."

I studied him for a moment. His brow was creased, and he looked scared.

"What is it, Dale? You know something, don't you?"

He slowly got to his feet. "Actually, I don't. Not yet. But I'd like to see this stone marker for myself. Something about your description rings a bell."

Now it was Merle's turn to look surprised. "You're not thinking of going into the woods are you?"

Dale smiled. "That's where the search party's going, isn't it?"

Merle reached down and petted Big Steve. "They're going everywhere in town, I imagine. Except inside people homes."

I tried again to get Dale to talk about what was on his mind. "What's going on? Is the stone connected to all of this?"

He shrugged. "Like I said, I'm not sure. I want to check on something. But in the meantime, be careful."

"I will," I promised, wondering what Dale was onto. "Meet you guys over at the fire hall."

SEVEN

After Merle and Dale had gone back inside, Big Steve and I walked down the alley. The firemen had set up bright neon orange sawhorses to block it off at each end, so that the search party volunteers would have more room to assemble and not have to worry about vehicles driving through their ranks. They clustered around the sawhorses, apparently standing guard in case somebody decided to steal them. I nodded and exchanged hellos as we passed through the barricade. A reporter recognized me, asked if he could interview me, and I told him to fuck off. The look on his face brought a smile to mine. Big Steve wagged his tail. He thought it was funny, too.

We turned right, walked a few blocks up Forrest Avenue, and then turned left and went down another narrow alley. I saw a few people that I knew, and nodded politely, but didn't stop to chat. I was in no mood for small talk, especially since it would probably be centered on the disappearances. This was, after all, the biggest news to hit our town since former prom-queen Denise Riser's young husband got killed in Iraq the year before. They'd gotten married out of high school. The marriage lasted six months, which was five months longer than he lasted in the desert; killed by insurgents in an area that Iraqi legend claimed was the original site of the Garden of Eden.

Shelly Carpenter's house was on the left hand side of the alley, just across the railroad tracks, a small duplex with dirty aluminum siding and a black-shingled roof in desperate need of patching. A rusty chain link fence separated the duplex's yard straight down the middle, and both sides had more dirt and dead weeds than actual grass, along with empty hamburger wrappers and half-smoked cigarette butts that people had tossed from their car windows while passing by. Worse were the bare patches of dirt where nothing grew, littered with stones and broken glass. Despite the rundown appearance and her landlord's obvious lack of attention, Shelly's imprint on the place was still unmistakable. On her side of the narrow yard, a brightly painted lawn gnome frolicked with a ceramic fawn. A homemade welcome sign, woven out of wicker, hung slightly askew on the door. A similar welcome mat lay in front of the door, advising visitors to 'Wipe Paws Before Entering.' One of Shelly's first floor windows had a sticker advising firemen that, in case of an emergency, there was a cat inside the house. Her neighbor on the other side of the duplex had none of these personal touches.

Big Steve and I slowly approached Shelly's half. The shades were drawn, and three days worth of newspapers lay on the front stoop. Her mailbox overflowed with junk mail; credit card applications and offers for storm windows on a house she didn't own and coupon packets and magazine sweepstake entries. I looked away, feeling guilty for peeking at someone else's mail. A yellow slip of paper was stuck to her screen door, right beneath the welcome sign. I realized that it was a UPS missed delivery notice. So Shelly hadn't picked up the mail, the paper, or signed for a package in at least three days. None of these were good signs.

Her empty garbage cans sat on the curb. Trash pickup took place every Monday. This was Wednesday, and she still hadn't taken the cans back up onto the porch, a code violation, and one that the compliance officer loved to enforce with a nasty letter and a small fine. The cans sat abandoned; another bad sign. They stank the way long-used garbage cans do, but beneath that, there was another odor.

I opened the gate. The rusty hinges squeaked. I stepped onto the sidewalk, and the stench hit me full force; a strong, musky scent, like sardines or ammonia. I'd smelled the same thing in my yard earlier that morning, when Big Steve had acted peculiar, and before that, too—in the hollow, when the guy in the satyr suit had pissed all over himself and Shelly.

It smelled animal. I don't know of any other way to describe it.

I took another step and the leash yanked me backwards. Big Steve refused to budge. He sat down on his haunches and pulled at the leash. His collar slid up his neck, almost choking him, but he didn't seem to care.

"Come on, boy," I urged. "Let's go."

Instead, he lifted his muzzle, sniffed the air, and howled. The sound gave me chills, reminding me of our last trip to the woods. This was the same behavior he'd exhibited then. Suddenly, despite the bright sunlight and the fact that we were nowhere near the forest, I was afraid.

"Steve, what the hell is the matter with you? Stop it!"

He howled again. Then he gave the leash another tug. I began to worry that he might actually slip the collar and get loose.

As I tightened the collar around his neck, a screen door banged open behind me. Shelly's elderly next-door neighbor stood on her porch, scowling at us both. She wore a white apron with the words, *Praise Him* embroidered on the front, along with two hands clasped in prayer, but her own hands were not praying. One of them gripped the porch's handrail, and the other waved Big Steve and I away, as if we were mosquitoes.

"Shut that dog up," she commanded. "He's interrupting my soaps!"

Big Steve continued to howl. His nose worked overtime, quivering as he sniffed the breeze. Then he squatted and began pissing all over the sidewalk.

"Hey," the woman snapped. "He can't do that there! What's wrong with you? You think our yard is your dog's personal toilet?"

"I'm sorry," I apologized, embarrassed, and almost shouting to be heard over Big Steve's continued howls. "My name's Adam Senft, and I—"

"I know who you are." She squinted at me. "You're the one what wrote them mystery books."

"Yes, ma'm." I smiled. She'd obviously read me, was

probably a fan, so it should be a cinch to put her at ease. "I take it you like my books?"

"No, I don't go for that crap. Only thing I read is the Sunday paper, and books from the Christian Light Bookstore. And my Bible."

"Oh." I floundered, unsure where to go next. "I'm looking for Shelly. Is she home?"

"No, she ain't. Saw her Monday morning, and she ain't been back since."

"Are you sure?"

"'Course I'm sure. Not in the last few days. I know, because I can hear her at night through the walls, playing that god-awful rap music. She works the afternoon shift at the grocery store, so all morning long and all night long, it's that same crap, over and over again. 'Yo-yo-yo.' The bass is enough to make your ears bleed. Nobody listens to real music anymore. Just that nigger noise."

I cringed, the way I do any time I'm reminded that there are still small-minded racist assholes living in small town Pennsylvania—even ones with religious slogans embroidered on their aprons. Big Steve finally quieted down, but I could feel the tension in his body as he strained against the leash. He desperately wanted to leave.

"I'm sorry, Mrs.—" I paused, not knowing her name.

"Snyder. Hazel Snyder."

I gave her my best smile, the one I used on my editor and Tara when I wanted my way with either of them. "I'm sorry, Hazel."

"Mrs. Snyder."

Apparently, my best smile didn't work on her.

"Right. Mrs. Snyder. It's pretty important that I speak with Shelly. Do you know where she's gone or how I can reach her?"

"No," she snarled. "I don't know. I done told you already, she ain't been home since Monday morning. No telling where she went. Probably got scared and left town; what with these other two women missing and all. Wouldn't surprise me one bit."

"Maybe she has a cell phone?"

The old woman sniffed. "If she does, I don't know about it. Those things will give you brain cancer."

I bent to scratch the dog, trying to reassure him. He scrambled away from me, refusing to come near the yard.

"You need anything else?" Shelly's neighbor asked.

"No," I said. "Thank you, Mrs. Snyder. I'm sorry to have troubled you."

Rather than replying, she just sneered at me and then went back inside. The screen door banged shut behind her. I heard her turn the television up loud—*Days of Our Lives*, by the sound of it.

I turned back to Big Steve. He was cowering on the sidewalk, and a puddle of urine spread out around him. He flipped the tip of his tail, which was still between his legs, and gave me a look.

That didn't go so well, did it, master?

"Well, it's all your fault. What got into you, howling like that? We're nowhere near the hollow."

He did his best to make his big, brown eyes look mournful and apologetic. Then he lowered his head and glanced back the way we'd come, signaling that he wanted to go home.

I gave Shelly's house one last look, debating whether or not I should try knocking on the door. Her neighbor had said she wasn't home, true, and it looked like the mail was piling up, but I wondered if I should make certain, just in case. Maybe she was sick, or injured. A vision of Shelly lying on the kitchen floor with a broken back came to mind. I shuddered. Or what if Dale and Merle were right, and she was missing?

Big Steve pulled with all his might, trying to lead me away. As I turned, something on the ground caught my eye.

There, right next to the cracked cement sidewalk, pressed into the soil of the grassless yard, was a single hoof print; cloven, twotoed, about seven inches long and five inches wide. The impression was deep, which meant that whatever had made it was heavy, probably over two hundred pounds. The track looked fresh, maybe from within the last day or two. I'd gone deer hunting with my father every November from the time I was fourteen until he passed away four years ago of prostate cancer, and as a result, I was a pretty good tracker. He'd taught me everything he knew, and that had been a lot. It would have been easy for someone less skilled to mistake the hoof print for a deer or a goat's, except that deer didn't get that big. Neither did goats.

Unless they were satyrs . . .

Big Steve howled, even louder this time. He lifted his leg and pissed on the fence, and when Mrs. Snyder charged outside to holler at us again, I almost screamed.

EIGHT

I thought about it on our way home. It didn't make sense. If the satyr had been a statue, then it couldn't have been stalking Shelly outside her apartment. So they must have returned together after I'd seen them in the woods.

By the time we got back to the house, the volunteers had all assembled in the rear of the fire hall's parking lot. It was an impressive turnout, one hundred or so people, mostly men, but women and teenagers as well, an assortment of law enforcement officers from both local and State precincts, medical crews, a few State Police canine units, six different fire departments (ours and five from neighboring towns), television and newspaper reporters, and a few National Guardsmen. Seth Ferguson and his buddies had even turned out, and they sullenly eyed the proceedings with mixed looks of derision and appreciation. I wondered why they weren't at school, and guessed they were playing hooky. Scanning the crowd, I caught sight of Dale and Merle amidst the throng, and waved. They waved back.

Big Steve did not like the crowd at all, and I had to pick him up and carry him because he refused to budge. I lugged across the alley, grunting with the effort, and put him inside the house. I gave him a bone to chew on, and then came back out to join my neighbors.

Doug Fulton, our Fire Chief, a paunchy, balding guy in his mid-forties, had climbed on top of a huge ladder truck and was addressing the crowd with a bullhorn. As I weaved my way through the crowd to Merle and Dale, I caught sight of Detective Ramirez, standing next to the ladder truck. Even though I'd only seen him an hour or so before, he now looked tired and beaten, and I wondered how much sleep he'd gotten since being assigned to the case. His feet must have hurt from walking around town and knocking on doors all morning.

"Was she home?" Merle asked me, raising his voice to compete with the chief's echoing bullhorn.

I shook my head, but before I could respond, several people in the crowd gave us dirty looks and made shushing sounds, urging us to be quiet and pay attention.

"Sorry," Merle apologized. His stubbly cheeks turned red from embarrassment.

"We'll coordinate from here," Chief Fulton said. "And let me stress again how much we appreciate your help and support, as do the Legerski and Wallace families."

He nodded towards a silver-haired man standing next to Detective Ramirez. The man looked exhausted. His face was haggard, and there were dark circles under his bloodshot eyes. His clothes were rumpled and dirty.

"That's Walt Wallace," Merle whispered to me, quieter than before. "Antonietta's husband."

"We're pressed for time this afternoon," Chief Fulton continued. "Every minute counts, so I'll make this quick. We've broken the search into a grid pattern, based on a topographical map of the area. We'll be searching everywhere—the town and the adjoining fields and woodlands, even the golf course. Each of you will be assigned to a search crew, and you'll be responsible for searching one particular grid. None of you are authorized to enter a residence, so please keep that in mind. Be respectful of people's properties. Most importantly, stick to your assigned grid. Don't go off by yourselves, wanting to play detective and search elsewhere. That's not the objective here. Obviously, we all hope to find Mrs. Wallace and Mrs. Legerski, or even Mr. Legerski. Hopefully alive."

A murmur of assent ran through the crowd.

"If you don't know them, or don't know what they look like, there are pictures posted on that cork board over there. Please study them before you leave, and familiarize yourself with their faces. Also study the signs around you as you search. Are there turkey buzzards circling an area, or maybe an unlocked barn that should be secured? Anything out of the ordinary like that—investigate it. In addition to searching for these three individuals, we're looking for their personal belongings, clothing, identification, jewelry, or anything that may have belonged to one of them. Possibly even hair, a fingernail—things like that. Each search team will have a radio. If you find anything like this, don't touch it. You could damage the crime scene. Immediately notify us back here at the command center via the radio. The same rule applies if you find a body."

The word 'body' seemed to hang in the air. Walt Wallace hung his head and began to cry. Everybody stared at him. Another man took him by the arm and slowly led him away.

"Poor guy," Merle said. "This must be tough on him."

"What about Paul?" I asked, reminding him that there were two distraught husbands involved.

Merle swept his hand in a circle. "You see him here? His wife's missing and where is he?"

"Not here," I admitted.

"So what does that tell you?"

"Quiet, you two," Dale whispered. "I want to hear what he's saying."

"Okay," the Chief called. "Let's start setting up the search teams. I'll take you in groups of ten. Line up front here, so we can assign you to an area."

The crowd moved forward, forming a loose line, and the television cameras followed, filming it all. Hushed whispers gave way to babbling conversation. Soon, everybody was talking at once, discussing Paul and Shannon and Antonietta, and offering theories as to what had happened. But I also caught snatches of other conversations—gardening and fishing and the Baltimore Orioles and NASCAR racing and who got hurt at the foundry last week. Some people laughed, and others joked and teased one another.

They're excited, I realized. *Sure, they're here to help, but this is exciting to them. This is something different. Something fun. They don't even realize how morbid that is. After all, it's not every day they get to search the neighborhood for missing persons. They're hamming it up for the cameras, hoping to see themselves on the six o'clock news tonight.*

I was filled with a sudden deep and unexpected loathing for my fellow man. I mentioned it to Dale and Merle in a hushed whisper, not wanting anyone around us to hear me. Merle just shrugged it off. Dale suggested that maybe this was their way of dealing with the fear and uncertainty the disappearances had put on our town.

Eventually, we reached the head of the line, and found out we'd been assigned a section of the woods beyond the park. Upon hearing this, my newfound disgust with our fellow citizens turned into apprehension. My stomach twisted into knots. Dale, Merle and I exchanged glances, but none of us said anything. If the Chief noticed our misgivings, he didn't comment.

There were seven other volunteers assigned to our search team; Seth Ferguson, three other civilian volunteers whom I didn't know (and who didn't introduce themselves by name), two search and rescue trained volunteer firemen named Bill and Ned, a canine officer who introduced himself as Trooper Harrison, and his dog, Honcho. Honcho was a huge, hulking German shepherd that would have easily towered over Big Steve. He seemed friendly enough. Honcho sat quietly by Trooper Harrison's side, unmoving, but watching everything with attentive interest. I thought about petting him, but decided against it. His formidable size was intimidating. Plus, had I come home smelling like another dog, Big Steve would never forgive me.

After introductions were made among our team, we departed, crossing over the playground and heading straight for the woods. The officer and his dog took the lead, and Seth Ferguson shuffled along behind him, hands stuffed into the pockets of his low-slung jeans, which nearly fell off his hips. Bill and Ned brought up the rear, talking amongst themselves, as did the other three volunteers. Bill carried the radio for our group, and the cop had one of his own. Merle, Dale and myself kept to the middle. They didn't say much. Merle was already out of breath, and I got the feeling Dale was saving his. I shook a cigarette out of my pack and was about to light it when Seth stopped me.

"Yo, can I bum one of those, Mr. Senft?"

"Don't think you're old enough yet."

"Shit." Seth sneered, and it made the acne on his cheeks and nose really stand out. "I smoke all the time, dude. My Mom lets me."

Merle frowned. "Yeah, you and your buddies have been smoking out back behind my tool shed. Does your Mom know about that?"

Seth shrugged, but wouldn't meet his eye.

"I didn't think so. Bet you guys didn't think I knew about it either, did you? And you ain't been smoking cigarettes out there either. You've been smoking weed. I found a roach."

Seth snorted in derision. "A roach? Man, what are you like an old hippie or something? Nobody calls them roaches anymore, dude."

But despite his bravado, he snuck a wary glance at the cop to see if he'd overheard us. The trooper hadn't.

"Shouldn't you be in school?" Dale asked him.

"Shouldn't you be in the old folks home?" Seth shot back.

Dale's face grew red. "Why you—"

Trooper Harrison cleared his throat. "Nobody is smoking this afternoon, I'm afraid. Not as long as we're out here. The smoke can throw off Honcho if he catches a scent. I'll have to ask you all to please refrain."

He turned away and led the search dog towards the forest. I glared at Seth and put my lighter away. He glared back. Merle mouthed something crude, and Dale chuckled behind us. Bill radioed back to the Fire Hall and let them know we'd arrived at our grid and were commencing the search.

As we neared the tree line, Honcho slowed his pace. Trooper Harrison gave a short verbal command and directed him with the leash, and Honcho stuck to his side—but the dog's eyes looked frightened and wild, as if he'd caught scent of something he didn't like. His behavior reminded me of Big Steve's. He let out a short, low whine, and then stopped walking altogether.

Trooper Harrison snapped the leash impatiently. "Honcho. Come." His voice was stern and authoritative, and Honcho obeyed him, but moved with obvious reluctance.

"Maybe he wants a cigarette," Dale joked.

Trooper Harrison didn't laugh. He turned to face us. "Okay, spread yourselves at least thirty feet apart. Stay within sight of each other, but keep enough distance between yourselves so that you don't cover each other's ground. Go slow, and remain alert. I'll let Honcho off his leash, so he can track. If he smells something, he'll start barking and take off like greased lightning. Don't let it startle you, and try to keep up."

He bent over and unclipped Honcho's leash. Then he lightly slapped the dog's hind end.

"Honcho. Go."

The dog stepped into the tree line, sniffed the ground, and then backed out of the woods completely. He lifted his muzzle into the air, howled, then turned tail and ran away.

"What's it mean if he does that?" Seth asked.

Trooper Harrison's face turned red with anger and embarrassment. "Honcho! Come!"

Bill peered into the forest. "Looks alright to me. Wonder what spooked him?"

"Shit," muttered his buddy Ned, "these woods spook me, too. I won't let my kids play here. You ever hear the stories?"

"Local ghost stories," one of the other civilians said. "If you believe them, I've got a bridge in Brooklyn I'll sell you."

"Oh yeah?" Ned shrugged. "Let's see you spend the night out there, buddy."

The other man turned away and studied his shoes.

I watched Trooper Harrison chase after Honcho and thought about Big Steve's similar reaction back at Shelly's house. He'd been scared of something, possibly a scent. And he'd done this on Monday morning too, when we first discovered the hollow. Before that, Big Steve had never minded the woods. Ever since Monday, he'd seemed terrified of them.

Now this police dog was acting in the same manner.

And I didn't feel that good about the woods either. Nor,

apparently, did Merle or Dale or our volunteer firemen.

Trooper Harrison stopped running and cupped his hands together. "Honcho! Get back here right now! Stop!"

Honcho reached the edge of the playground, then turned around and faced us. He stood there panting, but refused to return. When Trooper Harrison started towards him, he darted off again back to the parking lot.

"Goddamn it!" The cop sighed, exasperated. "I'm sorry, folks. I don't know what's got into him. He's never done anything like this before. You'll have to start without me. Meanwhile, I'll see if I can get another canine unit over here."

He trudged off after the dog and radioed for another officer and dog team. We heard the Chief respond that none were available.

We all looked at each other. Nobody moved.

"Well," Dale finally said. "I guess we should get started."

Bill nodded. "Yeah, time's-a-wasting."

The volunteer firemen stepped into the forest, spacing themselves about thirty feet apart. We followed along behind them. The sinewy tree limbs closed over our heads, and the gloom surrounded us. My heart beat faster. Leaves rustled overhead. I told myself it was just a squirrel.

"Yo, Mr. Senft?" Seth tapped me on the shoulder. "The dog is gone, and so is five-oh. Can I get that cigarette now?"

I thought about it for a second. "You know what, Seth? I can't believe I'm saying this, but that's not a bad idea."

I pulled out the pack and tried not to let him see that my hands were shaking. I gave him one, and cautioned him not to tell his Mom, even though I knew she wouldn't care. Stacy Ferguson worked nights at the Foxy Lady strip club in downtown York, and pretty much let her son get away with murder.

"So seriously," I said in a confident tone, "why aren't you in school today?"

He made a face. "Fuck school. People are missing and shit. This is my hood too, dog. Know what I'm saying?"

"Not really," Dale muttered, "because you talk like a two-bit drug dealer from Baltimore."

Seth's ears turned red, and he stalked away.

I chuckled at Dale's comment, but secretly, I was impressed that our local delinquent cared enough about the neighborhood to skip school and help with the search.

We slowly went deeper into the woods, picking our way through the undergrowth. The smell of rotting flora hung thick, yet once again I could see no source for it. The forest was quiet, and had that same oppressive atmosphere I'd felt before. There was no wildlife moving about. No birds or squirrels or rabbits. Even the insects were quiet. The silence was infectious. None of us spoke as we searched. We remained spaced apart but proceeded at the same pace. Dead leaves crunched under our feet.

Despite the chill in the air, I was soon hot, sweaty, and tired. I stumbled along, trying to focus. A thorny vine pricked the back of my hand and drew blood. I brought it to my mouth and accidentally dropped my half-finished cigarette. I bent down to pick it up, and froze.

"Jesus . . ."

There, in a muddy spot between the leaves, was another cloven-hoofed footprint. Next to it was a huge, stinking pile of feces. Black flies crawled sluggishly over it. I recoiled in disgust.

The others noticed that I'd stopped and came over to see what I'd found. They gathered around me in a circle and stared at the pile of manure. The flies buzzed away, angry at the disturbance.

Bill studied the ground intently. "Don't tell me you stopped for a pile of dog shit?"

I glanced at Merle and Dale, and then at the rest of the group. Their expressions were confused and irritated.

"The footprint," I explained, immediately realizing how idiotic it sounded. "It's strange, isn't it?"

Ned smacked his forehead. "It's a frigging deer print, Mr. Senft. How does that help us? They're all over these woods."

"I don't think so," Dale commented, his voice low. "It's much too big for a white-tailed deer, which is all we have in Pennsylvania. That print is human-sized."

"So it's a big fucking deer then," Bill snapped. "We don't have time for this."

I picked up a stick and prodded the droppings. The turds were also bigger than a deer's. I caught a faint whiff of that same musky stench I'd smelled at Shelly's house.

Seth laughed. "Mr. Senft-dude, what are you doing? You're playing with fucking dog-doody, yo! Wait till I tell everyone."

Merle towered over him. "Get bent, you little prick."

"Enough!" Bill shouted. "We don't have time for this shit."

All of us were quiet for a few seconds, and then we all began to snicker at the same time. Bill, not understanding his own unintentional pun, took a moment longer, and then he got the joke and smiled.

"Ha ha," he said. "Very funny. 'Time for this shit.' Can we keep searching now, please?"

The tension between our group dissipated, and we spread out again. Dale, Merle, and I cast one more lingering glance at the foot print, and then we moved on.

"We'll talk about it later," Dale whispered before heading back to his section of woodland.

The thorn prick on my hand began to itch. As I walked down the trail, I saw two more scattered hoofprints, and a half impression that could have been made by a shoeless human foot, but I kept it to myself. I would only be met with derision, and I was tired and sweaty and in no mood to argue. But I made a mental note of the tracks locations, so that Dale, Merle and I could find them again if we needed to.

We ventured deeper into the woods, and the gloom increased. It was mid-afternoon outside the forest's perimeter, but beneath those sinister trees, we walked in eternal dusk. The farther we went, the darker it got.

"Shit," Merle muttered. "It's cold in here. I can see my breath."

Seth wrapped his arms around himself and shivered. I wondered if he was cold or scared or both.

As we continued on our way, I got the distinct impression

that the trail had changed in some subtle way. I didn't know this part of the forest well, having been this far inside only once, but something was off. Where I thought I remembered a curve, the path was straight. Yellow moss covered the forest floor in places where it hadn't three days ago. It seemed like there were more trees and vines clustered together than there had been before, and I had the uncanny impression that they were watching us, and didn't approve of the intrusion.

The others must have felt it too, because we began to walk closer together, narrowing the distance between us from thirty feet to ten, and then to five. Soon, we found ourselves grouped together in the middle of the path.

"This is no good," Bill complained. "The undergrowth is too thick. Those damn thorn vines are everywhere. Can't see shit, let alone walk through it."

"I think I stepped in poison ivy," Seth moaned. "This sucks."

For once, I think we all agreed with him.

"So what do we do now?" Dale asked, turning to Bill and Ned. "We can't go on. Not without sickles to clear away this brush."

Bill toyed with his radio. "I guess we go back to the command center and check in with Chief Hanson. They'll have to bring the National Guard or the forest rangers in here to deal with this. Antonietta Wallace's body could be lying right here at our feet and we wouldn't even know it."

I shuddered at the thought.

"How about this," Ned suggested. "As we head back out, each of us will take a different section than the one we had coming in. We might as well double check each other since we're going back the same way."

"Works for me," Bill said.

We all nodded in agreement, except for Seth, who looked tired and moody. Despite my strong dislike for the kid, I found myself pitying him, and decided to cheer him up.

"Hey man," I said. "You want another smoke?"

He eyed me warily. "You serious?"

"Sure."

"Hell yeah! Hook me up, dog." His face brightened, and for one second, he didn't look like the town bully, but a regular teenage kid. I handed him a cigarette, and one of the other civilian volunteers asked me if he could bum one as well. As we lit up, Seth's attention focused on something further in the woods.

"What's that?" He pointed behind us.

We turned and I recognized it immediately. It was the white stone marker, still jutting out from between the deadfall. But something was different. It took me a second, but then I realized what it was.

The trees had moved.

When I'd been there with Big Steve, the path had been bordered on both sides by a dense wall of black and gray trees. The foliage had formed a tunnel, which led directly into the hollow. Now, there was no wall and no tunnel. Even the hollow seemed to be missing. Stranger still, the narrow path now veered away from the stone marker, turning sharply west. It was as if the trees were leading us in a different direction.

"Listen," I said, and held my finger to my lips.

"What?" Bill asked. "I don't hear anything."

I cocked my ear and after a moment, I heard the quiet murmur of a trickling stream. There had been a creek inside the hollow, as well. Which meant one of three things. Either somebody had moved the stone marker, or this was a different one, or . . .

Well, I refused to entertain the idea of the third option. The landscape couldn't have changed itself like this in three days time. That would be impossible. Supernatural even.

Just like the satyr . . .

"The fuck is that thing?" Seth asked again. "Looks like a tombstone."

"Let's have a look," Ned agreed. "Probably nothing, but it won't hurt to check, just to be sure."

We stepped off the path and approached the stone. Above us, the tree limbs swayed back and forth.

There was no wind.

"What did you hear, Mr. Senft?" Bill asked me.

"Water," I said, trying to sound like everything was normal. "Thought maybe there was a creek or something nearby."

We reached the vine-covered deadfall and gathered around the marker. Dale knelt beside it and squinted. Hesitantly, he reached out and brushed it with his fingertips. He jerked them away as if he'd been shocked.

"What's wrong?" Merle asked.

"Nothing," Dale said. "Just static electricity."

He was lying and I knew it. He'd felt that same weird throbbing sensation that I'd experienced when touching the stone.

I looked over the deadfall, expecting to see the hollow. But instead, all I saw was more trees. The hollow was gone, as if it had never existed. The stream was still there, but there was no lush grass, and no satyr—statue or otherwise.

Bill nudged me. "Looks like you were right about the creek. You got good ears."

I saw Merle looking around too, and when he caught my eye, he frowned.

I pulled him away from the others and whispered in his ear. "The hollow was here on Monday. I swear to God."

"Well it ain't here now, Adam," he whispered back. "You sure you didn't imagine the whole thing?"

"No. I'm not crazy, Merle. It was here. Right over there—beyond the stone. I told you about the marker, and there it is, right? Well, the hollow was there, too."

"So what happened to it?"

I glanced around and made sure the others weren't listening. "I think the trees moved."

"What?"

"You said it yourself Monday afternoon. You said there's stories about the trees moving in here."

"At LeHorn's Hollow, but we're far from there."

"You also said that maybe LeHorn's Hollow infects the rest of this place. Now, if you'll accept folklore that the trees move down near LeHorn's, why is it so hard for you to believe they moved here, trying to hide the hollow I saw

Monday morning?"

He muttered something, but I couldn't hear him.

"What?" I asked.

Merle grabbed my arm. "Because I'm scared to believe. Alright?"

"I am too, Merle. I am too. But we need to talk about this shit."

He nodded reluctantly. "Okay. We'll talk about it later."

The rest of the search team was still studying the stone, and hadn't noticed our private exchange.

"So what is that thing?" Seth asked a third time.

"I think you were right, kid," Ned told him. "It looks like an old grave."

Seth scrambled away from it.

Bill scratched his chin. "Do you think one of the missing could be buried here?"

"No," Ned replied. "Look at the ground. It hasn't been recently disturbed. And check out the writing. That's old."

Dale let his index finger hover just over the carved letters, tracing them in the air.

DEVOMLABYRINTHI
NLEHORNPOSSVIT
PROPTERNVPTIAS
QUASVIDITSVBVMRA

"Anybody know what it says?" Bill asked.

"I've seen this before," Dale whispered. "But I can't remember where."

"I think it's Latin," one of the civilian searchers said. "Or some weird version of it, anyway."

"Pig Latin," Ned joked, but nobody laughed. They kept staring at the stone.

Merle stirred. "It's getting darker. We should get back. I don't know about you guys, but I don't want to be in these woods after dark. They give me the fucking creeps."

"No arguments here," Bill agreed. "Looks like this is just another dead end anyway."

We turned back to the path, and I swear it had moved again while our backs were turned. As we'd approached, the trail had led to the west, away from the stone marker. Now it ran straight up to where we stood, and pointed back the way we'd come. It seemed wider, too, as if the trees had drawn back to give us more room to walk side-by-side, rather than single file, allowing for a quicker exit.

We took advantage of it.

I didn't voice my fears, and if any of the others noticed the shifting path, they didn't comment on it. But I noticed that as we started back up the trail, they each moved a little faster, and they all kept looking upward, as if expecting a tree limb to come crashing down on top of us at any moment.

"Those trees give me the creeps," Seth said.

"Me too," Bill agreed. "The township ought to let the pulp wood company over in Spring Grove come in here with some chainsaws and clear them out."

A branch creaked above us.

We walked faster. Bill and Ned took the lead. Bill tried radioing ahead, but he couldn't get any reception beneath the foliage. The three civilians were in the middle. Seth followed them, and Merle, Dale and myself brought up the rear.

As we left, we all heard something behind us, coming from deep inside the forest. It sounded far away—and yet all too close.

Everybody stopped and spun around.

"The fuck is that?" Bill hissed. His eyes were wide.

"Sounds like a flute," Seth whispered. "Maybe Jethro Tull is in the woods."

"Shut up," Merle warned him. He'd balled his hands up into fists, and his knuckles were white. His lips were pulled into a tight grimace, and I realized he was just as uneasy as me.

The shepherd's pipe continued to play; a high, lilting melody. It was definitely getting closer.

Like clockwork, my penis began to stiffen. I noticed that the others were affected by the music too. Each of them had a bulge in his pants.

The leaves rustled over our heads. As I watched, the tree limbs shook. I opened my mouth to speak, and found that I couldn't. The music filled my ears and my cock grew harder. The others seemed frozen too. They stood there, listening and aroused.

Ned finally stirred, and tugged on Bill's arm. Bill jumped.

"It's got nothing to do with what we're looking for," Ned said. His voice had taken on a pleading tone. "Let's just leave, okay? Let's get the hell out of here."

Blinking, Bill shook his head, as if awakening from a dream. He glanced down at the bulge in his pants.

"Yeah, man. I think that's a good idea."

We left, and the music faded, along with our erections.

We were quiet for the trip back, each person lost in their thoughts, or maybe too shocked to speak. When we finally stepped out from under the trees and back into the sunlight again, everyone's spirits seemed to soar. Suddenly, they were all laughing and joking as if none of it had happened. And maybe it hadn't. Maybe it had just been my overactive writer's imagination.

But I knew that wasn't true, and when I saw Dale and Merle's expressions, I knew they didn't believe it either.

Bill and Ned thanked us for our help, and then walked away to give their report. Seth gave me a curt nod and said, "Thanks for the smokes, dog," and then slunk away. The other three members of our team also left.

Dale, Merle and I walked across the playground and headed home.

Merle sighed. "So. . . no luck finding them."

"No," I agreed.

"I'll tell you guys one thing," Merle said. "I've had enough of the fucking woods to last me all summer. Don't think I'll go camping this year."

I laughed, but Dale remained quiet and pensive.

"What's wrong?" I asked him.

"Let's meet in the backyard at seven o'clock tonight," Dale said. "Everybody okay with that?"

"For what?" Merle asked. "You gonna tell us stories

about the time you went to Tijuana as a young man and saw a donkey show?"

"I think you know why," Dale told him. "We've got things to discuss."

Merle didn't reply.

"Why not talk about it now?" I asked. "I mean, you're talking about the woods, right? You think that what I saw is connected to what happened to Shannon and Antonietta?"

"I do, but I want to check on something first," he said. "When you told us about the stone, it sparked something in my head. I meant to do it earlier today, before the search began, but I got sidetracked. But seeing the marker for myself, I think I remember now why it seems so familiar. Just let me make sure and then we'll talk. Before we go to the cops, we need to have all the facts."

"Seven o'clock," I repeated. "I'll be there."

"Merle?" Dale demanded.

"You gonna bring the beer?"

Dale smiled. "But of course. Only the best for you."

"Then I'll be there. Ain't got nothing better to do, and besides, I promised Adam inside the woods that we'd talk later. I'll see if I can't round up Cliff and Cory, too."

"Merle," I prodded, "do you still think Paul had something to do with this?"

He stopped walking, and stared at me long and hard before answering.

"No, Adam. I don't. And that scares the fucking piss out of me. Scares me even worse than those woods do."

We went our separate ways, and I wondered what Dale was onto. When I walked inside the house, Big Steve was missing in action. I hollered for him, but there was no answer. Usually when I came home, he'd be under my desk thumping his tail, or prancing at the top of the stairs, his nails clicking on the wooden floor.

I walked upstairs and into the bedroom. Big Steve was sprawled on his back in the middle of the bed. He was sound asleep, but his paws twitched, and he whined and growled softly, in the grips of a nightmare.

I sat down on the mattress beside him and gently called his name. He kept whining. I reached out and shook him. His eyes snapped open and his jaws almost clamped shut on my hand. His low growl changed into a vicious bark. I yanked my hand away and jumped up.

"Whoa! Take it easy buddy. It's me. You were having a bad dream."

Still growling, Big Steve glanced around the room. Then he recognized his surroundings and calmed down. He flipped the tip of his tail, and gave me his best apologetic look.

Sorry, master. Didn't mean to almost take your fingers off.

"You're okay," I assured him. "Must have been a bad one, huh?"

He wagged his tail harder, in confirmation, and then stretched out his paws and yawned.

"I wish you could talk," I told him. "I'd love to know what you were dreaming about."

But deep down inside, I already knew. Knew too damn well. And knowing that what haunted my dog's nightmares was the same thing haunting my own made me afraid all over again. So I patted his head and whispered soothing words and rubbed his belly in little circular motions the way he liked.

It occurred to me that Big Steve was braver in his nightmares than he was when confronted by the real thing.

We sat there together in the bedroom for a long time and waited for Tara to come home.

And even though I didn't believe in Him anymore, I thanked God when she did.

NINE

Before we ate dinner, Tara and I sat and chatted for a while. I rubbed her feet and asked about her day and told her all about mine, leaving out my suspicions regarding Shelly, what may have happened to Shannon and Mrs. Wallace, and the emotions we'd felt inside the woods earlier that day. It was funny. Tara was my wife and I trusted her implicitly, but for some reason, I couldn't voice my suspicions to her. Maybe it was because she was my personal and emotional barometer, and I was afraid of what her reaction would be. What if she flat out didn't believe me, or worse yet, questioned my sanity? A husband never wants his wife to doubt him or the strength of his convictions, because as soon as that happens, a little part of us dies inside. And Tara and I had suffered through enough death.

I popped a frozen pizza into the oven, and when it was done, we sat down in our matching recliners and ate pizza and drank water in front of the television, while Big Steve stretched out on the couch and watched the pizza slices hopefully. He wasn't exactly begging, but he wasn't making it a secret that he'd love to have some either. I tossed a piece of crust onto the floor and he leaped from the couch and snapped it up in one bite. Tara hollered at us both, me for putting it on the floor and him for eating people food.

When a commercial for car insurance came on, I flipped to the local news. Sure enough, they were showing footage from the afternoon's search and interviews with some of the volunteers. I caught a glimpse of Merle, Dale, and myself. Just a quick flash, and then we were gone. Luckily, I was just another face in the crowd, and the station didn't identify me as 'Adam Senft, Local Author.' I had a love-hate relationship with our local media, who always seemed to misquote me.

"Hey look, I'm on TV."

Tara smiled around her slice of pizza. It was a false smile.

There was still nothing new to report. Paul, Shannon, and Mrs. Wallace were all still missing, the search had turned up nothing despite the massive amount of manpower, and the police refused to discuss the details of the case. Detective Ramirez was quoted as saying that they had some promising leads, but despite the press peppering him with questions, he wouldn't comment further since the investigation was still ongoing. He advised the public to remain cautious and alert. The number for a toll free tip line scrolled across the bottom of the screen. The smiling anchorwoman reminded viewers that the Wallace family, the Lion's and Rotary Club, and several other organizations were offering a cash reward for information. Then they followed the report with a public interest piece on 'Ten Tips To Protect Yourself From Being Abducted'.

Groaning, I began flipping through the channels, bypassing more news and commercials, two game shows, C-Span, and an old *Highway to Heaven* rerun. I finally settled on an episode of *Seinfeld* that I liked.

"Is this okay with you?" I asked Tara.

She shrugged, and then nodded. Her plate still had half-eaten slices of pizza on it, and Big Steve was parked in front of her, patiently waiting for some.

"I can change the channel if you want me to," I offered. "We've seen this one a million times. They get lost in the parking garage, and then Jerry and George wind up in jail for pissing in public."

"That's nice," she said, not looking up from the program. Her tone was flat, disinterested. She sat the plate on the floor and Big Steve proceeded to do his best impression of a pig, complete with grunting noises as he wolfed it down. I started to point out that she'd just finished hollering at me for feeding him table scraps not minutes before, but then thought better of it.

Instead, I asked, "You okay, honey?"

She sighed, and rubbed her temples. "I'm just still a little depressed. And tired. I'm really, *really* tired. I didn't sleep well last night. Tossed and turned a lot, and had weird dreams all night long."

"What about?" I took a sip of water from my bottle.

"I don't remember all of it. There was somebody outside. It may have been you, but I'm not sure. He had more hair than you, so maybe not. In the dream, I woke up and went to the window and he was standing right underneath it, right there in the backyard. I wasn't scared. I can't recall his face, though. It's blurry. That's all I remember. Oh, and there was a flute or something."

The bottom fell out of my stomach.

I choked on my water. It was Tara's turn to be concerned. "You okay?"

"Wrong pipe," I gasped. "A—a flute? You dreamed about a hairy man, and a flute?"

Tara nodded. "Yeah. Isn't that weird? I'll have to get out my dream dictionary and see what that means. It must symbolize something. Anyway, when I woke up, I didn't feel rested. You know what I mean?"

I didn't respond. She'd dreamed about somebody standing outside our window. A hairy man, she'd called him. And she'd heard a flute. I'd heard music too, right before drifting off to sleep, notes from a shepherd's pipe. At the time, I'd chalked it up to the weird dream of my own that I'd been having, the one with naked women dancing around a bonfire inside the forest, while the satyr played his shepherd's pipe. Was it possible that my wife and I had had the same dream?

"I thought maybe we'd try again tonight," Tara said. "You know, after what happened last night. That we'd make love and it would be okay this time. Better. But I'm just so tired. I don't think I'm up for it after all."

"No biggie."

"I'm sorry."

"It's okay." I gave her my best smile. "I'm getting together with the neighbors tonight anyway. We're supposed to meet in Dale's back yard at seven."

Despite her fatigue, she looked curious. "What about?"

"Merle's having trouble with Peggy again," I lied. "She wants more alimony. He's really depressed about it, so we're going to drink a few beers, cheer him up."

"Don't drive anywhere if you're drinking," she warned. "I'll probably just go to sleep early, if that's okay?"

"Sure. I think that's a good idea. You need your rest. I won't be outside long, and when I come in, we'll both get a good night's sleep. And no bad dreams."

"No bad dreams," she repeated.

My smile faltered at the corners.

Yawning, Tara stood up and gave me a goodnight kiss. Then she went upstairs. Big Steve trotted along behind her. I heard her shut the bathroom door, followed by the sound of running water. Within five minutes, she'd be wearing her pajamas and crawling into bed, and would probably be sound asleep within another ten.

I put our plates in the dishwasher and then headed outside. The sun was just starting to set, and the sky was on fire with red and orange hues. A cool breeze chased leaves across the grass. Some teenagers in a Mazda roared down Main Street, the bass in their car stereo turned up loud enough to rattle the windows of the house they passed. Out back, the media encampment was still present, but there were less of them now than there had been before. Most of the reporters had moved off in search of the next big story.

Thinking about Tara's dream, I stopped underneath our bedroom window. Our motion detector light clicked on as I walked by it, and the beam illuminated that section of the yard like it was daylight. The musky smell was gone. I bent down and looked at the grass beneath the window, remembering how earlier in the day, Big Steve had barked at this particular spot.

Now I saw why.

There were two cloven footprints in the grass. Whatever had made them had stood directly beneath our second floor bedroom window. Stood there and gazed upward while we slept. Tara hadn't been dreaming. Neither had I.

Panicking, I whirled in a frantic circle, cursing over and over again and trying to keep from screaming. I didn't want Tara to hear me, didn't want her to come outside and see this.

Next door, Dale had just stepped out onto his patio. He held a thick stack of papers in his hands. When he saw my agitated state, he rushed over.

"Adam?"

"Fuck fuck fuck fuck fuck!"

Dale grabbed my shoulder and stopped me in my tracks. "Adam, calm down. What's wrong?"

Rather than responding, I just pointed at the ground. Dale bent down and examined the grass. I heard a sharp intake of breath and then he slowly backed away.

"It's real," I said, trying to catch my breath, and keep my voice calm and in control. It was a struggle. Instead, I wanted to run and scream and pull my hair out.

Dale closed his eyes, and took a deep breath.

"The damned thing is real," I repeated. "It wasn't a guy in a suit, Dale. The satyr is real and it was right outside our fucking house! We need to call that detective. Ramirez. We've got to tell him right away."

Dale slowly shook his head. His eyes were still closed.

"What do you mean, no?" My voice rose in pitch, and I was very close to shouting. "You saw the hoofprint. That *thing* was right here, man, playing its pipe and stalking my wife. That's who's taking the women!"

Dale's eyes snapped open. He held up a finger and silenced me.

"Get a grip on yourself. We need to talk about this—this and other things. Yes, something weird is happening in our neighborhood. But we can't go off half-cocked. If you called 911 and told Detective Ramirez that you think a satyr is abducting women from their homes for unknown purposes, they'd not only put you in the hospital for observation, but you'd rise to the top of their list of suspects as well. We all would."

I fumbled for my cigarettes. "You're right. Sorry."

"Don't apologize."

We grew quiet, and the click of my lighter sounded very loud in the silence.

I inhaled. My hands were shaking.

"Dale, I'm fucking scared, man."

"I'm scared, too," he admitted. "And for what it's worth, I think you're right. Claudine had a dream last night. Said she heard music outside our window."

"Tara did, too. Did you check under your window for tracks?"

"No," Dale said. "Wouldn't do any good. It's all cement sidewalk there."

"Oh." I resisted the urge to go check his yard anyway.

He patted the stack of papers in his hand. "But I did check something else."

"What's all that?"

"Research. You'd be amazed what one can find out just by using a simple search engine."

"Like what?"

He held up his hand. "Let's wait till the others get here. Then we'll talk all about it. No sense covering the same ground twice."

We each took a seat in one of his green plastic patio chairs. Dale reached into an ice chest full of beer, and he offered me one. I accepted gratefully, and drained the can in four long gulps. My heart rate began to slow down to a normal pace again, and the alcohol took the edge off my fear. But it didn't dissipate completely. I still felt sick to my stomach every time I glanced over at the hoof print.

"Remember when we built this patio?" Dale asked.

Despite my fears, I smiled. "Yeah. Me, you, Merle, and Cliff— spent a whole weekend on it. Why?"

"No reason. Just trying to get your mind off things while we wait."

"Thanks." I smiled, took another sip of beer, and tried my best to ignore the hoof print.

We didn't have to wait long. Soon enough, Merle, Cliff, and Cory joined us, pulling up chairs around Dale's patio table. Each took a beer from the chest and settled in. Cliff and Cory made small talk and played hackeysack, but Merle was silent and dour.

The sun disappeared beneath the horizon, and the dusk to dawn lights in the Fire Hall's parking lot automatically clicked on, bathing the playground, vacant field, and the parking lot itself in a sickly, yellow glow that extended all the way to the forest. I noticed that the light did not penetrate the thick shadows beyond the tree line. The treetops swayed in the still, cool air.

I shivered.

Dale cleared his throat, signaling that he was ready to begin. Cory stuffed the hackeysack back in his pocket. Cliff and I lit cigarettes.

"So," Dale began, "some strange things have happened over the last three days."

"Boy, I'll say." Cory chugged his first beer and reached for a second one. "People have been horny as shit at work. It's like a fucking soap opera in there."

Merle started on a second beer as well. "That's not what we're talking about, dip shit."

Cory blanched. "Oh, you mean like what happened with Paul and Shannon and that other lady? Yeah, that's strange, too."

"How'd the search go today?" Cliff asked. "Any news?"

Merle, Dale, and I looked at one another. Merle drained his beer in one long swallow.

"Before we get to that," I said, "maybe we'd better fill you guys in on everything else that's happened."

"I think that's a good idea," Dale agreed. "Let's get all the facts out on the table before we draw any conclusions. Okay with you, Merle?"

Merle shrugged, and then grabbed a third beer from the ice chest.

"Slow down, big guy," Cory laughed. "Just because they're free doesn't mean you have to drink them all in ten minutes. Save some for the rest of us."

Merle didn't respond. I watched him as he gulped the third

beer, and got the impression that he was trying very hard to get drunk—and failing miserably.

Cliff looked puzzled. "What the hell are you guys talking about? You know something about what happened to the Legerskis and the Wallace woman, or not?"

Merle stared at the ground. Dale motioned for me to go ahead.

So I did. I told Cliff and Cory about what had happened that Monday morning; the weather had been unseasonably warm and I remembered thinking it was the first day of spring—the rutting season. I recounted meeting Shelly Carpenter in the alley, and her flirting and my getting turned on, and how uncharacteristic it had been for each of us. I talked about how I'd first heard the phantom strains of the shepherd's pipe while still in the alley, just after Shelly had jogged away. Big Steve heard it too, and he'd growled, instantly disliking it. And when we heard the pipe, both of us got erections.

I continued with our walk into the forest, telling them how Big Steve and I got sidetracked and ended up in a section of the woods that we'd never seen before, a part of the forest where the trees seemed sinister.

Cory and Cliff both scoffed.

"They moved?" Cory asked. "You mean like they were smart?"

I looked over at Merle for confirmation.

"That's what they say," he muttered. "Don't know if I ever truly believed it until this afternoon, though. Now I do."

"Why," Cliff asked. "What happened today that changed your mind? You drank too many beers?"

"Don't you worry," Merle said. "We'll get to that part in a minute."

I was discouraged by Cory and Cliff's reaction. "Maybe this isn't such a good idea."

"Go ahead," Dale encouraged me. "You're doing fine."

"The trees formed a little tunnel over the path with their leaves," I continued, and went on to tell them about hearing the pipe a second time, along with Shelly moaning, and how the music affected both mine and the dog's libidos again. I described the white stone marker, and the nonsensical words carved on it, and how it throbbed when I ran my fingers across it.

"I can verify that," Dale interrupted. "I touched it myself today, and it was like grabbing an electric fence. But without the shock."

"I saw it too," Merle said. "Didn't touch it, but you could almost feel it humming inside you. Like one of those frequencies that only a dog can hear."

"That don't make sense," Cory said.

Merle sat up. "Adam's the writer, not me. That's the only way I know to describe it."

I drank my beer. Despite the evening's chill, the coldness warmed me as it slid down my throat.

Dale filled Cory and Cliff in on the search party, and how the police dog's behavior had been similar to Big Steve's. Then he motioned for me to continue where he'd left off.

I took another long swallow of beer before going on. I wanted to think it over and choose the right words for the next part, because it still sounded fantastical to me, and I'd been there. I could only imagine how it would sound to Cliff and Cory. They were already skeptical. Cory was on his fourth beer by then, and working on a hangover. He'd slumped down low in the chair, and his head bobbed back and forth. The kid was a lightweight—but so was I at that age. For a second, I wished I could go back to that.

I picked up the story, describing how I'd seen Shelly on her knees in the hollow, performing fellatio on a satyr statue. I had to pause in the narrative while Dale explained to Cory what a satyr was. Then, when I had his attention again, I recalled every little detail; from the bird shit on the statue's shoulder to the tattoo on Shelly's back, even the size of the satyr's dick. Cliff shifted in his seat when I talked about the statue coming to life, but he didn't interrupt. I continued with how the creature had spoken to me, asking me to 'celebrate the season and bear witness while it sowed its seed'. And how I'd convinced myself it was just a guy in a costume, which sounded silliest of all to my own ears, now that I knew the truth.

Cliff frowned. "So you thought it was a dude in a suit, but now you think it's real. You believe there's a half-man, half-goat sticking it to Shelly Carpenter out in the woods?"

"Yeah," I admitted. "I do. I know it sounds crazy, Cliff, but it's true. Ask Merle and Dale."

"Well?" Cliff lit another cigarette and looked at them. "You guys believe this shit?"

Dale nodded. "I do indeed. As impossible as it sounds."

"You too?" Cliff asked Merle.

Merle drained his beer and opened another one. "Yeah, Cliff. I do. There's more to it than what Adam's told you guys." Cory belched, then grinned. "Like what?"

Dale stood up. "Well, for starters, do you guys remember on Tuesday when we were watching the police arrive at Paul and Shannon's house?"

We all nodded, even Cory, who had been on his way home from work at that point.

"You weren't there yet, Cory," Dale continued, "but while the rest of us were standing there, I thought I heard something. It sounded sort of like a flute. I didn't mention it at the time, but all of us—well, we got erections."

Cory snickered.

"It's not funny," Dale snapped, surprising all of us with the outburst.

Cory's laughter abruptly fizzled.

"I haven't had a hard on in over five years, not even with Viagra. A few years ago, I was diagnosed with prostate cancer. I survived, but the treatment left me impotent."

Cory's face clouded. "I'm sorry, Dale. Don't take offense."

He shrugged. "It happens. Just hope that it doesn't happen to you when you're my age. It's no picnic."

"How come you never told us about the cancer?" I asked.

"I didn't know you and Tara well enough then. You'd just moved in. Cliff and Cory weren't living here yet either. And besides, there are some things that you just want to keep private, you know?"

I nodded, silently thinking about the miscarriages. Despite the fact that they were my friends, I'd never told any of them about those. We told Tara's family, and some of my fellow authors, but I'd never told them.

"What about me?" Merle grumbled. "Thought I was your friend."

Dale smiled sadly. "You are, and it's because you're my friend that I didn't tell you about it. Peggy was already cheating on you by then, and I didn't want to burden you with anything else."

"Wouldn't have been a burden."

Cory slumped further down in his seat. "Wish I was back in college. Things seemed simpler then."

Cliff clapped his back. "Yeah, but you flunked out."

Dale reached over the table and shook Merle's hand.

"Still wish you would've told me," Merle said. "Ex-wives are a dime a dozen. Friends are something else."

"Well, I'm sorry. The point is that I can't get an erection. It's medically impossible. But I got one today, in the woods, and I got one yesterday evening. We all did. And both times we heard the pipes."

"I'll give you that," Cliff agreed. "And now that you've mentioned it, I thought I heard something, too. Could have been a pipe. But what does all that have to do with anything?"

"Allow me to explain." Dale filled them in on Wednesday's events; my trip over to Shelly's house and the rest of what we'd all experienced in the woods. Then he sat back down and patted his stack of papers.

"When we got back this afternoon," Dale continued, "I hopped online and did some research. First thing I looked up was satyrs. Did you know they have no females? Only males. They lived in woodlands and forests in Greek and Roman mythology. The Romans called them fauns, rather than satyrs, but it's the same thing. Satyrs served a god named Bacchus, pouring his wine and playing their flutes for him. They were also very fond of females, since they had none of their own. They preferred human women, but would mate with wild animals, livestock, or even pets, if they had to."

His expression was one of pride and satisfaction. I got the impression that Dale was enjoying the role of our own small town Van Helsing.

Cliff toyed with his lighter. “So they liked to drink and get laid. Sound like decent enough guys.”

Dale smiled. “Yes, I guess you could say they were the original party animals.”

That made us all groan, except for Cory, who was too drunk to understand the joke. We had to repeat it to him, and then he laughed a little too loud and long. While his attention was focused on Dale, I slid his half-finished fifth beer over to my side of the table. He’d had enough, and I was flagging him.

“Have any of you ever heard of Pan?” Dale asked.

I had, but the others hadn’t.

“He was the Greek god of the woods,” Dale explained. “As well as the god of green fields and the guardian spirit of the shepherds.”

Cory giggled. “Sounds like he was a busy dude.”

“He was. Pan was also a satyr. So even though they served gods like Bacchus, the satyrs themselves were worshipped, too. Some think their animal attributes and wild sex drive reflect the way satyrs embody the ‘uninhibited forces of nature’ or some such. People worshipped them in conjunction with the Spring Equinox, and farmers asked them to bless the planting season. They were also called upon during fertility rituals and livestock breeding.”

I saw where he was going. “All of this started on Monday, the first day of spring.”

“And satyrs like to fuck,” Merle said.

Dale pointed at him. “Exactly. They like to fuck. Adam saw Shelly having sex with one during the Spring Equinox. She hasn’t been seen or heard from since. And now there are more women missing.”

“Okay,” Cliff said, tapping ashes into an empty beer can. “Are you guys saying a statue of a goat man came to life and is running around town raping women? Even if Shelly Carpenter was kinky enough to get it on with a satyr, you can’t tell me Shannon Legerski or Antonietta Wallace would do the same thing. That’s *bestiality*, man.”

“Not necessarily,” Dale said. “I think it has something to

do with the shepherd's pipe."

"I've been thinking that too," I admitted. "But I'm not sure how or why."

"Well . . ." Dale shuffled through the papers until he found what he was looking for. "According to legend, Pan invented the shepherd's pipe. One day, he came across a beautiful woman named Syrinx."

Cliff broke into an impromptu chorus of Rush's "Temples of Syrinx." He stopped when he realized Dale was glaring at him. I suppressed a giggle.

"Sorry," Cliff apologized.

Dale continued. "Pan tried to rape Syrinx, but she escaped. Pan chased after her until they came to a river, at which point Syrinx turned into a reed."

"A reed?" Cory squinted. His eyes were watery and his lids drooped. "You mean like camouflage or something?"

Dale waved him away. "Yes, just like the ones that lined the bank of the river. Pan grabbed a handful of reeds, hoping to capture Syrinx, but he couldn't find her. So he sat down beside the river and started tying them together."

"Thus inventing the shepherd's pipe?" I guessed.

"Bingo." Dale winked at me. "Also known as the Pipes of Pan. The pipes were supposed to be magic, giving Pan control over people's minds, especially females. He even defeated Apollo, the god of music, with his shepherd's pipe. Pan's music swayed the mind of King Midas, who was judging the contest."

Merle pushed his beer aside and sat up straight. "So the satyr's pipe can take over people's minds?"

Dale nodded. "At the very least, it affects people's emotions. Pan used it to seduce females. Stands to reason that it would work on males, too. It worked on King Midas. And what happened each time one of us heard the pipe?"

"We got hard ons," Cliff said. "So the satyr wanted to fuck us too?"

"Not necessarily," Dale said. "Maybe our arousal keeps us docile while he rapes our women. Or could be it was just some kind of side effect. Adam said that Shelly looked like she was in a trance, and that he was starting to feel it too. And Cory, you said earlier that your coworkers were horny. What did you mean?"

Cory glanced around for his beer. "They're all hot-to-trot, man. Seems like over the last few days, more people are fucking each other. Wayne Taylor banged Stephanie Ennis in the warehouse, and Connie Miller gave Joey Potter a blowjob out behind the dumpsters—and Connie strictly likes other chicks."

"It's effecting the whole town," Merle said. "Just like my damn wife."

His face clouded, and I suddenly pitied him. For Merle, this whole situation was just another reminder of his Peggy's infidelity, and was probably stirring up emotions that he'd tried to lock away.

"We don't know that for sure," Dale cautioned. "But it's a good bet."

"So how does the stone marker fit into this?" I asked.

Dale ruffled through his papers and slid several sheets across the table.

"Earlier, I said it looked familiar? Well, I saw it on the History Channel. Wasn't until I'd started my research that I remembered."

"What are these?" I asked, picking up the sheets of paper.

"Photos," he said. "Taken inside a museum in Caermaen."

"Where?"

"It's a town in Wales."

"Never heard of it," Cory said. "Is that near Iceland?"

"No, dip shit," Cliff corrected him. "Wales is part of England. See what happens when you flunk out of college?"

"Fuck you, Cliff."

"Will you two idiots shut up?" Merle growled. "Wales is a separate country."

Cory pouted. "Where's my beer?"

I tuned them out and studied the photographs. They'd been printed out from a website and the black and white images were grainy and dark. The pictures were mostly Roman artifacts, according to the text beneath each one—

coins, jewelry, sculptures, weapons, coffins, and even a chunk of ancient pavement. I flipped through them, and one sheet near the bottom of the stack caught my eye. It showed a small, square pillar, carved out of white stone.

Dale whispered, "That was discovered in Wales by an archeologist named Machen. He found it in some woods alongside an old Roman road. According to the website, some of the letters had been defaced, but Machen was able to restore them when the stone was moved to the museum. Next page has a close up."

Cliff, Cory, and Merle leaned closer, reading over my shoulder. I passed the papers I'd already looked at over to them, and then studied the next one. Sure enough, it was a close up shot of the block-lettered inscription carved into the Roman pillar.

DEVOMNODENTI
FLAVIVSSENILISPOSSVIT
PROPTERNVPTIAS
QUASVIDITSVBVMRA

I handed the photograph to Merle. "It looks kinda like the one we found, but some of the letters are different. What does it mean?"

Consulting his notes, Dale translated. "To the great god Nodens, Flavius Senilis has erected this pillar on account of the marriage which he saw beneath the shade."

"Who was Nodens?" Merle asked, staring at the paper.

"According to several websites," Dale said, "Nodens was the god of something called the Great Labyrinth."

Cliff sipped his beer. "Is that like Hell or something?"

Dale shook his head. "It's not Hell. Or Heaven. Some ancient cultures believed that the Great Labyrinth existed alongside those places, along with something called the Void and the Great Deep. Nodens lived in the center of the Labyrinth."

"Man," Cory mumbled. "I ain't drunk enough to understand any of this. Where'd you guys put my beer?"

Dale ignored him. "Nodens isn't even his real name. That's what the Romans called him, because to say his real name out loud was to invite certain death and destruction. Most cultures just called him 'He Who Shall Not Be Named.' He pops up, in different guises, across Roman, Greek, Byzantine, and Sumerian legend. Always in connection to this Labyrinth place—where satyrs are also said to originally come from."

Merle scratched his head. "So Nodens is a satyr, too? You said they were gods of the woods? If that's so, then what are these satyrs doing hanging out in a maze?"

Dale shook his head. "I'm not sure. And I don't think Nodens is actually a satyr, either. It sounds like he could take any form he wanted. Smoke. Fire. A child. A satyr. Anything. But according to at least one Sumerian myth, all of the old gods originally came from this Labyrinth."

I sensed that we were getting off on a theological track, and turned the conversation back to the inscription. "This carving is similar to the one we found, but I still don't understand how this helps us right now."

"I thought you might say that," Dale said, smiling. "So I drew this."

He held up a sheet of paper. On it, he'd transcribed the inscription we'd seen on the stone marker in the forest.

"Look at it again," he told us, "using the inscription on the museum's pillar as a guide."

We studied the paper closely. The last two lines were exactly the same, but the first two were different.

I pointed. "This first line. It starts with 'Devom', just like the one from the museum. And ends with 'Labyrinthi.'"

"Is that Latin for 'Labyrinth'?" Merle asked.

"You'd think so," Dale said. "But it's not. The person who carved our stone didn't know Latin, but faked it anyway. Like if Cliff tried to pick up a girl in Spanish, and only knew 'Que pasa,' but tried to speak it beyond that."

Grinning, Cliff leaned back in his chair and exhaled smoke. "Chinga tu madre, motherfucker. I've banged plenty of Spanish chicks."

"Then you've done your part to bridge the cultural divide."

Dale flashed him the finger. "I'm guessing that whoever carved our stone meant 'Labyrinth', but didn't know Latin, so they fudged it. A farmer or logger, maybe—somebody with a high school education."

I took a swig of Cory's beer. "Any guesses as to who that person was?"

"Look at the second line," Dale said. "You tell me. I want to make sure that I'm not jumping to conclusions here."

I traced the second line with my finger.

NLEHORNPOSSVIT

"I don't see anything but gibberish," Merle admitted.

"Me either," Cliff said.

Cory belched.

I stared at the letters, running them around in my head. And then it dawned on me.

"N LEHORN. Nelson LeHorn. He made the stone marker we found?"

Dale nodded. "I think so."

"Jesus Christ . . ." Merle's jaw went slack.

Dale's voice was low. "To the great god of the Labyrinth, Nelson LeHorn has erected this pillar on account of the marriage which he saw beneath the shade."

"What marriage," Cory asked, "and seriously, where did you guys put my beer?"

None of us answered him. We stared at the inscription, not speaking. A hush seemed to have fallen over the neighborhood. There was no traffic on Main Street and the houses around us were silent, no televisions blaring or children playing or parents hollering. A cloud passed over the moon, and the backyard grew darker.

The bug light on Dale's garage crackled loudly, and I jumped in my seat.

"Okay," Merle said. "The old man made it. But why?"

"Because he was fucking crazy," Cliff sneered. "LeHorn killed his wife, man. He was a frigging witch."

Cory leaned forward in his seat and reached for the ice

chest. Dale closed the cooler's lid before Cory could get a beer.

"I think he summoned the satyr," Dale continued. "Nelson LeHorn worked black powwow, but first and foremost, he was a farmer. Maybe he brought it here, asked it to bless the planting season or help him breed his livestock or something."

"Then how did it end up a statue?" I asked. "And if it was out there in the woods all this time, why hasn't anybody ever seen it before this?"

"Maybe the forest has been protecting it," Merle guessed. "Until Shelly came along. All of this started on the first day of spring, right? Maybe the time was right for it to wake up again."

I thought it over. As I said earlier, our town had always had a secret reputation for being randy in the spring. Maybe the satyr struggled to break free from his stone prison every year. Maybe he called to the townspeople when we were feeling horny. Maybe he'd even been calling to Becky and I back in 1987, when we'd gone parking.

I shivered. "That still doesn't explain how it ended up a statue in the first place."

Dale sighed. "There's a lot we still have to figure out. But we know enough. The question is what do we do with it? Should we tell Detective Ramirez?"

"Hell yes," I said, and reached in my pocket for my cell phone. "Let's get him over here right now."

"So he can arrest us all?" Merle cracked his knuckles. "Shit, Adam—this morning, I still thought Paul was behind this. Now I know the truth, and I still realize how fucking crazy it all sounds. What makes you think Ramirez will believe us?"

"He's got to," I insisted. "He's a cop. It's his job to protect people. To track down any lead, no matter how bizarre. And besides, if we all stick together, he'll have to take us more seriously."

Cory hiccupped. "I say we call the cops. Tell this Ramirez dude what time it is."

Dale rubbed his forehead, looking aggravated with Cory. "Your vote is duly noted."

"No offense guys," Cliff snuffed out his cigarette and stood up. "But I don't believe any of this shit. And if the cop asks me, that's exactly what I'm going to tell him."

"How can you say that?" I asked. "You've seen the proof. The fucking hoof print is right over there beneath my window. Take a look."

"Doesn't prove a thing." Cliff shrugged. "For all we know, it could have been a deer, wandered in from the woods. Do I believe you saw something? Sure. But it wasn't some half-man, half-goat. That's fairy tale shit, Adam. The same fairy tales that Dale's been reading to us tonight."

"What about the stone?" Merle reminded him. "It's just like the one in the museum. How do you explain that?"

"I can't explain it because I haven't seen it," Cliff said. "Let's go look right now. You guys show me the one you found. Then maybe I'll change my mind."

He glanced from Merle to Dale to me. All three of us turned away.

"I'm not going back into those woods," I muttered. "Not tonight."

Merle shook his head. "Me neither."

Cliff looked at Dale, expectantly. "How about you? Want to show me this stone?"

Dale stared at his feet. "Not now, not after dark. Tomorrow, when it's light . . ."

Swaying, Cory stumbled to his feet. "Shit, I'll go with you, Cliff. Just give me a beer for the road."

"You've had enough, kiddo," Merle said, gently forcing him to sit back down.

Cory sagged back into the seat, pouting. "You guys treat me like I'm in fucking high school."

I stood, and squeezed Cliff's shoulder. "Listen, man. We're friends, right? Not just neighbors, but friends?"

"Sure we are." He reached up and squeezed my hand. "You know that, brother."

"I'm worried about Tara," I told him. "Dale's worried about Claudine. Can't you try to believe this, just for us?"

Cliff was silent for a moment. He walked over to my yard,

stared down at the impression in the grass, and then turned back towards us.

"I'm sorry, but I just don't see it. Looks like a regular old deer print to me, and that's all. You guys are scared. I understand that. Shit, the whole fucking town's scared. Somebody is running around kidnapping women. But that somebody ain't the goat man, and if you tell that to the cops, they'll lock you up in the cell they've got reserved for Paul Legerski. They'll treat you the same way they treat these guys that look for Bigfoot and flying saucers. You'll be laughingstocks, and every disc jockey and late night talk show host in the country will be making fun of you by this time tomorrow night."

He paused, lit another cigarette, and then continued.

"Are we friends? Hell yes, Adam. You guys are some of the best friends I have. And I don't want to see any of that shit happen to you. But I ain't gonna bullshit you either, just because it's what you want to hear. You want me to tell you I believe in satyrs and musical flutes and that a crazy old farmer summoned up a demon from hell—I'll tell you that, man. I'll stand here and say it out loud. But that don't mean I believe it, and I sure as hell ain't gonna repeat it to no cop."

"Okay," I said, defeated. My shoulders slumped. "I understand."

Dale nodded. "We all do."

After that, Cliff said good night and went inside, taking Cory along with him. Cory leaned against his shoulder, babbling drunkenly about satyrs and serial killers and how none of us ever took him seriously. Cliff helped him into his apartment and then went upstairs to his own.

"Well," Dale sighed. "That didn't go as well as I'd hoped."

Merle sat back down at the table. "I hate to say it, but Cliff's right. I mean, what have we got, really, other than a rock with some weird writing on it, out in the middle of the woods. Some pictures of a similar stone in a museum across the ocean, and hoof prints in the yard. That's it."

"What about Big Steve's reaction, and the police dog's?" I began peeling the label off my beer. "Or how we all got erections when we heard the flute?"

"The dogs got scared and we got erections. It still doesn't prove anything. Ramirez will think we're a pack of idiots. Even if he does decide to humor us, all he'll have are more questions."

"For which we don't have any answers," Dale said. "You're right."

"What about LeHorn's family? I asked. "You guys know how to contact them? Maybe they could fill in the blanks for us."

Merle shook his head. "His son is doing time upstate. We could see him in prison, but since we're not cops, we'd have to write him first, have him put us on his visitor's list. That could take months."

"Claudia moved to Idaho after her mom was killed," Dale said. "I don't know her married name."

"Neither do I," I admitted. "And her little sister, Gina, is teaching school somewhere in New York. I have no idea where, though."

"I could look her up on the internet," Dale suggested. "See if we can find a phone number or an address."

"No." Frustrated, I lit a cigarette, the last one in the pack. "It'll take too long. While we're trying to track them down, how many more women will go missing? And even if we do find them, how do we know they'll talk? The girls have tried to get as far away from this town as they can. It's pretty obvious they don't want anything to do with their old man."

Dale frowned. "Can't say that I blame them."

Frowning, Merle slapped at a gnat. "So how about this? First thing tomorrow morning, we get some hunting rifles and go into those woods and track that satyr son of a bitch down ourselves. Mount him on the fucking wall."

"No," I said. "We don't know where he is, for one. Those woods are huge, and a lot of it is private property. We can't just go traipsing through it. And remember, the trees tried to hide the hollow from us. They could be doing the same thing with the satyr."

"Yeah," Dale agreed. "And while a 30.06 might bring

down a satyr, it's not going to do much against an oak tree."

"You really think that could happen?" I asked. "I mean; we know they move. But could they actually attack us?"

"I don't want to find out," Dale said. "Unless I'm armed with a chainsaw, and even then, I'd prefer not to learn the hard way."

"Guess you're right," Merle admitted. "Shit, we don't even know if a deer rifle would hurt this thing. It was a statue before Shelly brought it to life."

I took a long drag off my cigarette, watching the tip glow in the darkness. "If LeHorn really did summon this satyr from elsewhere, then conventional weapons might not work on it. But we don't know for sure. Just another question to which we need the answer."

"So again," Merle asked, "how do we find out?"

I exhaled, watching the smoke curl between us. "We go to LeHorn's Hollow. First thing tomorrow morning, we drive out there to the house and look around."

Merle's eyebrow twitched. "For what?"

"Answers." I shrugged. "I don't know—books, notes, LeHorn's copy of *The Long Lost Friend*. Anything that helps us to understand what it is we're dealing with."

"The LeHorn place is a crime scene," Dale reminded me. "Surely the police confiscated everything during the murder investigation."

"Nelson LeHorn threw his wife out of their attic window. If the cops took stuff, it would be related to the murder itself. They wouldn't bother with crap about satyrs. They'd think it was just nonsense."

The night sky grew darker, and the wind picked up.

"It's going to rain," Dale said.

Merle rocked backward in his chair and appraised the sky. "You really think it's that simple, Adam? That we'll find a book called *The Care and Feeding of Satyrs*?"

I dropped my cigarette butt into an empty beer bottle. "You believe in magic, Merle?"

He blinked. "You mean like powwow? Sure. I told you, my Grandma did it."

"So did my great-grandmother. How about ghosts? You believe in them?"

"Well . . ." He paused. "Yeah, I do. Sometimes I think my place might be haunted. Supposedly, a guy died there during the Civil War."

The leaves rustled overhead, and for a second, I wondered if the trees in our yard could move like the ones in the woods. A single cold raindrop splattered on my head. I ignored it.

"So you believe in the supernatural?" I continued. "You believe that LeHorn's Hollow is haunted, and that whatever forces are at work in there have spread out into the rest of the forest?"

Merle looked up at the sky again. "Where are you going with this, Adam?"

"If you believe all that, then you've got to believe that there are supernatural answers to our supernatural questions. Answers we can only find in LeHorn's Hollow. I don't know what form those answers will take. But it's sure as hell better than running off into the woods like we're going squirrel hunting. I'd rather be armed with something more than a gun if we're going after this thing."

More rain fell, still sporadic, but hinting of the downpour to come.

"Like a spell or something?" Dale asked, wiping his glasses.

I shrugged. "Something like that. It's worth a shot, isn't it?"

They both nodded reluctantly.

"Okay." Merle stood up. "I don't feel like getting wet. What time do you want to head over there?"

I got up as well, and grabbed one of the handles on the ice chest. Beer bottles clanked inside, and the ice sloshed around.

"Soon as we wake up. That okay with you guys?"

"Yeah," Dale said, lifting his corner of the cooler. "I'll make a pot of coffee."

"Screw that." Merle grinned, returning to his old, jovial self. "Your ass is making breakfast. I take my eggs over easy."

Dale smiled. "Want me to bring it to you in bed?"

A blast of thunder ripped the sky open above us, and the rain began to fall in earnest. Within seconds, we were soaked.

"Shit!" Merle trotted across the yard, waving over his shoulder. "See you in the morning."

I helped Dale get the ice chest into the house. "Sleep well, man."

"I don't think so, Adam. In fact, I don't intend to sleep at all tonight."

I paused, ignoring the rain. "You think the satyr will come for Claudine again?"

He nodded, wiping off his glasses again with his shirttail. "I think it might."

I wondered if he was right, or if it was his own fears speaking, brought about by his impotence. He had to worry that Claudine would go elsewhere. Now he had reason to.

"Stay awake," he said. "Alert. If either of us hears anything, we'll call each other immediately. Deal?"

"You got it. Be careful, man."

I shook his wet hand and then ran back across my yard though the rain. I slammed the door behind me and stood there, dripping on the carpet. The house was quiet. I grabbed some paper towels from the rack in the kitchen and dried my hair and face. The rain beat against the windows and drummed over the roof. Lightning flashed outside, and for a second, the kitchen turned blue. It was the first big thunderstorm of the season. It was possible we'd lose power before it was over. Tomorrow morning, the streets would be full of downed tree limbs, and the gutters and storm drains would be choked with leaves.

I wondered what else the storm might bring.

Grabbing some candles from the kitchen junk drawer, I made my way upstairs. Tara was sound asleep, and Big Steve lay at the foot of the bed, facing the bedroom door. He looked up as I entered the room. His ears were plastered against the sides of his head, and he was shivering; his eyes wide and frightened.

I tiptoed over to him and kissed the top of his head.

"It's okay, buddy," I whispered softly, so as not to wake Tara. "It's only thunder."

He pressed his cold nose against my cheek and then licked my face.

I changed out of my wet clothes and put on some pajamas, and then brushed my teeth. When I came back into the bedroom, Big Steve had crawled underneath the covers. Only his nose was sticking out. He was still quivering, and the blankets moved over him.

I slid into bed, lifted the sheets, and patted him on the head just as another blast of thunder shook the house. Big Steve whimpered, trembling harder. Tara mumbled in her sleep, and rolled over to face us. Her breathing was shallow. I tried reassuring the dog with one hand and stroking her hair with the other. I don't know if it helped them, but it made me feel better.

Big Steve crawled out from under the covers and cautiously edged between Tara and me. She still didn't wake up. I reached for a smoke, and then remembered that I was out of cigarettes. Instead, I lay there in the darkness, petting my dog and listening to the rain tap-dance across our shingles.

Eventually, the thunder and lightning died down, and then, the storm was over as quickly as it had begun. Big Steve rose, turned in a circle, and lay back down, his head pointing back towards the bedroom door again. I noticed that he was still shaking.

And then it occurred to me that maybe it wasn't the thunder he'd been afraid of after all. Maybe it was something else. Something in the darkness, standing beneath our bedroom window, with cloven hooves and horns and a king-sized dick.

I sat up and listened for the now-familiar shepherd's pipe, but there was only the soft, throaty sound of Tara's breathing. I lay back down and reminded myself to not fall asleep. I'd promised Dale. He was counting on me. So were Tara and Claudine, for that matter. I couldn't fall asleep.

I decided to get up and make some coffee. Maybe do some writing. That was the last thing I remembered thinking.

When I woke up again, all hell had quite literally broken loose.

TEN

Big Steve woke me with an alarmed series of barks. Startled, I propped myself up on one elbow and glanced around the bedroom in confusion. The dog stood on all fours at the edge of the mattress, facing the window. I reached for him, cursing myself for falling asleep. The fur on his neck stood up, and his white teeth glowed in the darkness.

I rubbed sleep from my eyes. "What—"

Outside, lightning ripped the sky, and rain hammered against the windows. The storm had returned in all its fury while we slept. Immediately, I felt for Tara, to reassure her that it was okay.

The bed was empty.

My heart fluttered. The fear was electric. My wife was missing. Before I could act, thunder boomed, followed by another sound, almost lost beneath the noise of the storm and the dog's barking— the faint melody of a shepherd's pipe. Despite my panic, I instantly had an erection. The arousal was a terrible feeling.

I ripped the covers off the bed.

"Tara? Where are you?"

The lightning flashed again, bathing the bedroom in an eerie blue half-light. Tara was not in the room. Outside, the music continued. Then, I heard a floorboard creak in the hallway. I looked up in time to see my wife's shadow disappearing down the stairs.

"Tara!"

Encouraged by my shout, Big Steve leaped off the bed and sprang for the door. Growls continued rumbling from deep inside his chest, and his nails scrabbled on the hardwood floor.

He darted down the stairwell.

I ran after them both, pausing only to grab the baseball bat I kept underneath the bed. Tara didn't approve of guns and wouldn't let me keep one in the house. Before the miscarriages, she'd asked me to get rid of the ones I owned, not wanting our child to stumble across them some day. I'd agreed at the time, and hadn't brought the subject up since the miscarriages because it was just another reminder of what we'd lost. Now, running across the bedroom clad only in a pair of pajama bottoms and wielding the bat like a sword, I wished I had.

The floor was cold under my bare feet. I reached the top of the stairs and shouted again. Tara was at the bottom, standing at the door with one hand on the knob. Big Steve was behind her, the hem of Tara's nightgown clenched firmly between his teeth. His legs were locked and spread apart, and he tugged with all of his might. Tara didn't budge.

"Tara, stop!"

I took the stairs two at a time, almost losing my balance. I clung to the rail with one hand, struggling not to fall. Big Steve kept trying to pull Tara away from the door. She ignored us both. Without a word, she wrenched the door open just as I reached the bottom.

Dropping the baseball bat, I spun her around. Big Steve released her nightgown, sniffed the air gusting through the screen door, and stepped back, whining. The rain hissed on the street outside.

"Tara, what are you doing?" I shook her.

She stared at me as if I wasn't even in the room. I guided her towards the couch and sat her down. Immediately, Tara stood back up and walked towards the open door. Big Steve glanced nervously from the door to us.

I forced her back down on the couch just as the melody came again. My erection poked out of my pajamas, but I had no time to think about that. Quickly, I ran to the door and peered outside. Main Street was rain-slicked and deserted. Nothing moved, except for the water trickling down the storm drain. Leaves and a few scattered tree limbs littered the sidewalks.

It was darker than normal, and the streetlights were out. The music continued playing, and I realized it was coming from our backyard.

When I turned around, Tara was standing behind me, trying to get through the door. I shoved her backward, harder this time, and slammed the door behind us. The dead bolt clicked into place, and I fastened the chain with one trembling hand.

"Tara, can you hear me?"

"Yes." Her voice was sleepy and toneless.

"I need you to stay inside, honey. Can you do that?"

"No." She shook her head slowly. "He needs me."

My stomach leaped. "Who, Tara? Who needs you?"

"Hylinus."

"Who's Hylinus?"

"My love."

"Why does he need you?"

She grabbed my hand and thrust it beneath her nightgown. The crotch of her panties was soaked, her clitoris swollen beneath the fabric. I yanked my fingers away, shocked.

Tara smiled. "See what he does to me? You can't do that. I've got to go be with him."

"Stay," I told her, and Big Steve sat down instead, thinking the command was meant for him.

I forced Tara towards the chair again. She struggled—slapping, clawing, and pulling my hair. My cheeks stung, and one of her fingernails scratched a furrow across my chest. I wiped the blood off and stared at her, dismayed. My first urge was to strike back, but I repressed it, swallowing my anger.

The piping continued, and Big Steve howled.

"What the hell is wrong with you, Tara?"

She giggled. "I need it. I need it bad. Hylinus."

"Fuck this."

Grabbing the baseball bat, I stalked to the back door. My palms were slick with sweat, and the bat slipped in my grasp. I clung tighter. Big Steve slunk along behind me, but when I ripped the back door open, he shrank away. I stepped outside. The rain pelted my bare skin. Blood dribbled down my chest. I rounded the corner of the house and skidded to a halt.

The satyr stood between my yard and Dale's, playing his shepherd's pipe. His eyes were closed, and he swayed slightly, in time with the music. Claudine walked towards him, her arms outstretched as if to embrace a lover. Her dreamy face was ecstatic. She licked her lips. Her thin t-shirt and panties, soaked from the rain, clung to her body like a second skin. Her breasts sagged but her nipples were hard beneath the wet material.

"Hylinus," Claudine shrieked with joy. "I'm here!"

There was a blur of movement in the corner of my eye. I turned just as Tara dashed past me. I grabbed for her, but my wet fingers slipped off her arm. She and Claudine reached the satyr and knelt at his feet. His massive erection was only inches from their faces, and despite the overall weirdness of it all, I was filled with sudden, overpowering jealousy when I saw the look in Tara's eyes as she admired the creature's engorged member.

"Tara?" My voice cracked.

The satyr opened his eyes and beamed down at them both. Seconds later, my jealousy turned to rage as Tara reached out and began to stroke its cock. Claudine joined her, rubbing vigorously. Rainwater streamed down their exposed flesh and dripped from the tip of the creature's penis. Something else dripped from it as well; a clear, dime-sized droplet of pre-cum.

"Leave my wife alone, you fuck!"

Hefting the bat, I stepped forward. The satyr's eyes flicked towards me.

"Come no closer," the beast warned. Its voice was like gravel.

"Tara," I shouted, ignoring the monster. "Get away from him!"

Her lips closed over the head of its penis, while Claudine's tongue lathed the shaft. Both of them cradled his plum-sized testicles with one hand and caressed the thick, wet fur on his thighs with the others.

Dale's screen door banged open, and he rushed outside, his bathrobe flapping behind him, a Marlin 30-30 rifle clutched in his shaking hands. He wasn't wearing his glasses, and he blinked twice at the scene unfolding in the yard. When he realized what our wives were doing, his jaw dropped.

"Son of a bitch," he gasped. "Claudine . . ."

Dale slammed the rifle butt into the hollow of his shoulder and squinted, trying to sight through the falling rain without the aid of his glasses.

"Get the fuck away from my wife!" I inched closer; holding the baseball bat over my head, ready to swing.

Tara turned back to me, the tip of the creature's shaft still in her mouth. Her left cheek bulged like a chipmunk's. She pulled her mouth off of it and smiled. More of the satyr's pre-cum dribbled from her lips.

"I want to have his babies, Adam. The ones you give me are no good. You're tainted. Weak. That's why our babies died. Hylinus can give me strong ones."

She turned her attentions back to the satyr. Her head bobbed up and down.

I made a strangled, choking sound. Tears spilled from my eyes and ran down my already wet face. "You bitch . . ."

Claudine stripped off her panties, turned around and crouched on all fours, presenting her ass and swollen sex to the monster. Her fingers clenched the wet grass.

"Me too," she groaned. "I want to feel you inside me, Hylinus. My man can't get it up."

Dale clicked off the safety. "Adam, step away from them."

The satyr's ears twitched, and it jumped backward. Its huge penis plopped out of Tara's mouth with a wet, smacking sound. Regret shone in her eyes as she pouted.

"This is the second time you have interrupted my pleasure," Hylinus said, fixing me with a baleful stare. "I remember your scent from the hollow. I must procreate, and your wife wishes to do the same. It is the season. Time for my kind to live again and walk the woods of the earth."

He turned to Dale, his laughter swallowed by a blast of thunder.

"And you," Hylinus continued. "You are old and weak. You cannot give her what she so obviously desires. Neither of you can. Why not let me share the fruit of my loins?"

My fingers tightened around the bat. Claudine waited patiently for the thing to mount her, while Tara continued her ministrations. Dale just stood there, mumbling the Lord's Prayer under his breath. His bathrobe rippled in the breeze. Rain lashed at his face and dripped off the barrel of the Marlin.

"Dale," I shouted. "What are you waiting for? Just shoot the fucker."

"I can't! The girls are in the way."

Lightning flashed overhead as Hylinus thrust his hips forward.

"Aim high," I hollered. "Shoot it!"

The satyr pointed at me with one taloned finger. "I'll be back for you, son of Adam."

I wondered how it knew my name, and then I realized it meant another, much older Adam—the original version.

Scooping up his shepherd's pipe, Hylinus dropped to all fours and fled towards the alley. His speed startled me. Dale squeezed the trigger and the rifle bucked against his shoulder. Smoke curled from the barrel. My ears rang. The shot missed, slamming into my shed instead. The creature disappeared into the darkness.

"Did I hit it?" Dale peered through the rain.

"No." My shoulders slumped in defeat. "It's gone."

Tara and Claudine stumbled to their feet and started to chase after Hylinus. I rushed forward and gabbed Tara from behind, wrapping my arms around her waist and lifting her off the ground. She struggled with me. Her breath was sharp and musky.

Dick breath, I realized, shuddering. *She smells like that thing . . .*

Her lips were glazed with the satyr's fluids. I turned away.

"They're still under its spell," Dale said. "What do we do?"

"Hylinus," Claudine cried. "Come back!"

Dale dropped the Marlin and restrained her. Then, both women suddenly went limp in our arms.

"Adam?" Tara blinked as if awakening from a dream. "Wwhat's going on?"

"It's okay, honey." I hugged her to me, crushing her against my chest.

"Why am I outside?" she whispered. "What happened?"

I could still smell the stink of the creature on her, with each gasping breath. I closed my eyes and held her tight. Claudine clung to Dale, sobbing in confusion.

The gunshot had woken our neighbors. Lights clicked on in the houses around us. Within minutes, Merle, Cliff, and Cory were in the backyard. Merle, dressed in ratty sweatpants and a too-small tshirt, clutched a Colt .45 pistol and a flashlight. Cliff, shirtless, but still wearing his jeans, had a golf club. Cory carried nothing and wore nothing, except for his boxer shorts. His eyes were bloodshot, and he still appeared drunk. All three of them looked confused. They stared at our half-dressed wives, and then quickly looked away in embarrassment.

"Who's shooting?" Merle asked. "What the hell's going on?"

"It was here," I told them. "That thing. The satyr. It came for Tara and Claudine."

Tara mumbled, "What thing?"

"They okay?" Merle's voice was shocked.

I shrugged. "I hope."

Cliff glanced around. "So where is it now?"

"It got away," Dale said, one arm wrapped around Claudine, supporting her weight. "I shot at it, but missed. Couldn't see. It ran off towards the park."

Cliff fished his cigarettes out of his jeans pocket, tried lightning one in the rain, and then gave up.

"Come on, guys," he grumbled. "Stop with the bullshit. Enough is enough."

I resisted the urge to drop Tara, rush across the yard, and hit him.

Merle shined the flashlight beam across the yard, revealing dozens of muddy hoof prints, heading in the direction of the alley.

"They're telling the truth," he said. "How else do you explain those?"

Cliff's eyes widened. The unlit cigarette tumbled from his mouth.

"Still think it's a fucking deer?" Merle asked him.

Tara slumped in my arms. I looked down and saw that she'd fallen asleep. I shook her gently, trying to wake her up.

"Tara?"

There was no response. I glanced over at Claudine and noticed that she'd done the same.

"Let's get them inside," Dale said. "Merle—you guys check around. Make sure it's not out there somewhere, hiding. Take my Marlin."

Grinning, Cory picked up the rifle. A second later, Cliff snatched it from his grasp.

"Hey," Cory protested. "What do I get to use?"

"This." Cliff handed him the golf club.

"Gee, thanks."

"Try not to hurt yourself with it," Merle said.

While they searched the yards, Dale and I took our wives back inside. I stripped Tara out of her wet clothes and put on dry ones. She didn't wake up, remaining limp as a rag doll. Her breathing was shallow. Big Steve pranced around, concerned, then jumped onto the bed and lay down beside her.

"Stay," I told him. "Guard Mommy."

He wagged his tail in confirmation. This was a job he could handle.

I bent over to kiss her, but in my mind I saw Tara's mouth on the satyr's cock. I caught another whiff of her breath and noticed the crusted glaze on her lips. I kissed her forehead instead. I hated myself for feeling that way towards my wife. I loved her. It hadn't been her fault. And yet, I felt disgusted and angry. My stomach was in knots. I took a deep breath and tried to clear my head.

Sliding into a raincoat and shoes, I then returned outside. The rain had slowed to a light drizzle, the storm's intensity vanishing with Hylinus. Dale stepped out of his house, breathing hard and rubbing his shoulder where the rifle had kicked against it.

"You okay?" I asked.

"I'm too old for this shit," he gasped, trying to catch his breath. "And Claudine. She was . . ."

He couldn't finish. All that came out of his mouth was a highpitched gobbling sound. Dale's face was wet, and not just from the rain.

I put my hand on his shoulder, and he winced. A tear slid from the corner of his eye.

"I know," I told him. "Tara was doing it, too. Best not to think about this right now."

"How can I not? They were *enjoying* it, Adam!"

"No," I said. "They were under its spell. That's all. They didn't know what they were doing. Tara would never willingly do something like that. Neither would Claudine."

Even as I said it, I realized that I wasn't just trying to convince him. I was also trying to convince myself, because the alternative was unthinkable.

"The things it said," Dale whispered. "How did it know?"

I shook my head. Tara's voice mocked me.

I want to have his babies, Adam. The ones you give me are no good. You're tainted. Weak. That's why our babies died.

I clenched my teeth. "I'm going to kill that fucking thing."

"How did this happen?" Dale asked. "Did you fall asleep?"

I hung my head in shame. "Yeah. I didn't mean to."

"I was in my den," he said. "Doing some more research on the computer. I didn't even know Claudine had left the house until I heard you shouting for Tara."

Shadowy figures rustled towards us in the darkness. Dale and I both jumped, but it was only Merle, Cliff, and Cory, returning from their search.

"Find anything?" I asked.

"Nothing," Merle reported. "The tracks lead to the alley and then stop. There's a car parked over near the playground, so we didn't go any farther."

"Whose car?" Dale asked.

Merle shrugged. "I don't know. Probably just some kids making out or something. The interior light was on, but the windows were fogged up."

Dale turned to me. "Think they heard anything, or saw it?"

"Maybe," I said. "Did any of you guys call 911?"

Cliff stepped underneath my gutters and lit a cigarette. "I

didn't. Was too busy throwing my jeans on."

"Me neither," Merle said. "I heard the gunshot and came running."

"I was asleep," Cory mumbled. "Didn't know what the fuck was going on."

I took a drag off of Cliff's cigarette. "Could any of the other neighbors have called?"

"Stacy Ferguson works nights at the strip club," Dale said. "And since she's not home, I doubt Seth is home either. Probably out getting into trouble. Mrs. Jefferson's ninety. Doubt she heard anything. And the Legerski's . . ."

He trailed off. Obviously, Paul and Shannon hadn't called the police.

"So what do we do now?" Merle asked.

Cliff sneezed. "How about we get out of this fucking rain?"

I started towards my door and Dale glanced at his house.

"I'm not leaving Claudine alone," he said. "Not now. And we can't go to sleep, either. You hear me, Adam? No sleep."

"I'm sorry," I apologized. "I didn't mean to."

He smiled. It looked faked. "It's okay. I'm not blaming you. But we can't let it happen again."

"Believe me," I said. "Last thing I can do now is sleep."

"Should we move Claudine and Tara into the same house?" Merle suggested. "That way, we can all stick together. Keep an eye on things."

"No," I said. "Let them rest. They've been through enough tonight. I don't think we should wake them if we don't have to."

Dale nodded. "I agree."

"I'll go with Dale, then," Merle offered. "Cliff and Cory can stay with you and Tara."

"Me," Cliff said. "Cory still needs to sleep it off."

Cory nodded drunkenly. "Word."

"You okay on my couch?" I asked Cliff. "I want to stay upstairs with Tara. But I'll make us some coffee and you're welcome to watch movies or something."

"Illiterate fucker can read one of your books," Merle said,

and we all laughed, a little. It felt wrong, however, and the laughter dried up, followed by an awkward silence.

"Are we still going to LeHorn's tomorrow morning?" I asked.

They all nodded, even Cliff.

We bid each other good night and went inside. While the coffee brewed, I grabbed a towel for Cliff to dry off with and stowed the baseball bat back under the bed. Tara hadn't moved. She snored softly, and the sheets rose and fell in time with her breathing. Big Steve lay pressed up against her. His eyes shone in the darkness. I patted him on the head and he licked my hand. Then I went downstairs.

Cliff had helped himself to a cup of coffee. He stood at the living room window, and peered out the blinds, watching the rain.

I lit one of his cigarettes, inhaled, and coughed. The nicotine rushed through me, and I felt better.

"I appreciate this, man."

He stepped back from the window and sat on the couch. "No sweat, brother. Sorry about scoffing earlier. Anybody tries to get at Tara, they'll have to go through me."

"So you believe now?"

Cliff propped his feet up on my coffee table. "I believe that there's some weird shit going on, and I believe something scared the piss out of you guys tonight. I still don't know if it's a goat man. I need proof. More than those tracks."

"You come with us tomorrow," I said, "and we'll find the proof."

Neither Big Steve nor myself slept for the rest of the night. We lay there in the darkness and watched over Tara. Cliff stayed downstairs on the couch, drinking coffee and watching television. Snatches of old movies and infomercials drifted up the stairs. He came upstairs to piss once, and Big Steve timidly wagged his tail as Cliff passed by the closed bedroom door, but that was it for activity.

I rolled over to pet the dog. He looked at me with those big, brown eyes and sighed. His normally soft fur was coarse, and as my hand passed over his flank, I felt ribs instead of fat.

I realized that while I'd been focused on Tara and myself, the weirdness and stress were affecting him as well.

"You're a good dog," I whispered. "You know that?"

He thumped his tail against the mattress, indicating that he did.

I scratched behind his ears the way he liked, and Big Steve leaned into it, tilting his head against my hand. When I was done, he straightened and shook his head, jowls and ears flapping. Tara and I called it his helicopter impression.

Despite the commotion, Tara didn't stir.

Her words kept running through my head. I tried to block them out, tried to forget the hurt they'd caused, but it was no use. I knew that she'd been under some kind of spell from the satyr's pipe. That's why she'd done the things in the yard. I gritted my teeth, remembering the look on her face as she'd knelt in front of Hylinus and begun giving him a blowjob. She'd never had that look on her face when she did the same to me. I was sure of it. But as painful as the images were, the words were worse. That taunting laughter as she'd spoken them, telling me it was my fault we'd miscarried, saying I was weak and the satyr—her lover—was strong. That hurt in ways the sex itself never would. It cut deep, and I knew the scars might never completely heal.

Just like the scars left behind by the miscarriages themselves.

I reached for her in the darkness, but pulled my hand away at the last moment. I wanted to hold her while she slept, but I was afraid to touch her. Afraid of *her*. Until then, I'd no idea she could hurt me this way.

Around four in the morning, the rain stopped. Eventually, dawn arrived, but things seemed no brighter.

The dog snuggled up between us. I wrapped my arms around him and soundlessly cried into his flank. Gummy fluid leaked from the corners of his eyes.

Big Steve cried, too.

ELEVEN

The birds greeted the dawn outside our bedroom window. A garbage truck rolled down the street, its sputtering engine and the clang of the sanitary workers throwing trashcans around both loud enough to wake the dead. Daylight filtered through the blinds, bathing our pillows and the bedspread. Despite all of this, Tara slept on. Big Steve remained sprawled out between us, all four feet planted firmly in my back, his claws poking my skin. He opened one eye and glared at me when I moved.

I got up, stretched, and rubbed my tired eyes. They felt like they'd been sandpapered. Big Steve stretched, and jumped off the bed, following me. The mattress springs creaked, but Tara didn't stir. I turned off her alarm clock so that it wouldn't buzz when it was time for her to go to work.

Big Steve and I went downstairs. Cliff lay on the couch, aimlessly flipping through the television channels. He waved a greeting and I yawned.

"I've been thinking," he said. "One thing's for sure. You can get a good book out of all that's happened so far."

I thought about that. All fiction writers are semi-autobiographical when it comes to their work, and all fiction contains an ounce of truth. If a writer tells you that's not so, they are lying. Characters share the same traits as those around us—and often ourself. Situations mirror things we've gone through in real life. The names may have been changed, but it's there. Sometimes, this is a conscious decision. Other times, we aren't even aware we were doing that until the work is finished. But it is always there, the truth. This is called writing what you know.

I considered everything that had happened; the odd weather, Shelly and the satyr, the disappearances, what had happened in the yard last night. Or even before that; the miscarriages, and the sadness that had fallen over our home. Cliff was right. It would have all made a hell of a book.

But there was no way I could write it. Therein lay madness. In truth, I wondered if I'd ever write again at all.

"I made more coffee," Cliff said. "Figured we'll need it."

"You're a gentleman and a scholar."

Cliff grunted, his eyes not leaving the television. "A scholar's somebody who's smart. And a gentleman is a guy who can count all the hairs on a girl's pussy without getting a hard on. I'm neither."

I started to laugh, but then I remembered the sound the satyr's penis had made as it fell out of my wife's mouth. Grimacing, I walked into the kitchen and poured myself a cup of coffee.

Big Steve went to the door, sniffed around, and then looked back at me.

"Hang on," I told him, sipping coffee. It tasted good, and the effect on my exhausted body and mind was even better.

"Good coffee," I called.

Cliff muttered his thanks.

I sat the mug down, put Big Steve's leash around his neck, and took him outside to pee. The satyr's tracks were still in the yard. Big Steve smelled them, growled, and then began to bark.

"Hush," I commanded.

Ignoring me, he growled louder.

"I know. It was here. Just like at Shelly's house. But quiet down. You'll wake up Mommy."

Snorting, Big Steve lifted his back leg and pissed all over the tracks, covering them with his scent. Then he followed the hoof prints through the yard, his nose to the ground. Every few feet, he'd stop and pee some more.

"Well," I said. "At least you're getting braver about it."

We stopped when we reached the alley. The media circus was back, as were the cop cars. They were gathered around a car in the Fire Hall's parking lot, a red Mazda with its interior light still on. The driver's side door hung open, and there was blood splattered on the inside of the windshield—enough that I could see it even from my vantage point. A crow shrieked above us. I hurried Big Steve back to the house and went inside.

In the living room, Cliff had settled on an old episode of *The Herculoids*, and he looked up from the television as we walked in.

"Dude," he yawned. "I'm fucking tired, man."

I didn't reply.

"What's wrong?" Cliff asked.

"What kind of car did you guys see in the parking lot last night?"

"You mean when we were searching? A red Mazda, I think."

I poured dog food into Big Steve's dish. "Turn on the news."

Cliff flipped to the local news channel while Big Steve devoured his food in five huge gulps. After pouring myself a mug of coffee, I carried the coffee pot into the living room, refreshed Cliff's mug, and turned back toward the kitchen to get mine.

Cliff said, "Shit."

Pausing, I turned. The screen showed the parking lot out back, and the same red Mazda with an open driver's door and a cracked, bloody windshield. Cliff thumbed the volume on the remote, and the announcer's voice filled the room.

"Not too loud," I cautioned. "You'll wake up Tara."

He ignored me, his attention fixed on the news report. A pretty, blonde reporter stood in the alley, right at the edge of our backyards, smiling for the camera even as she reported something ghastly.

"—apparently the victim of a homicide. Police say Michael Gitleson, of York, was killed sometime between one and three this morning. Missing is Gitleson's companion, twenty-three year old Leslie Vandercamp, of Shrewsbury. The two were on a date."

Cliff bolted upright. I almost dropped the coffee pot.

"Dude," Cliff stared at me, his mouth agape. "Did she just say Leslie? Our Leslie, from the gas station?"

I nodded, unable to speak.

The newscaster continued. "Sources close to the case say they had just come from a movie at Regal Cinemas. Gitleson and Vandercamp were parked here in the lot behind the volunteer Fire Hall, next to a neighborhood playground. This is the same area where Shannon Legerski and Antonietta Wallace have disappeared in subsequent days. Yesterday, York City detective Carlos Ramirez named Shannon Legerski's husband, Paul, as a suspect in both women's disappearances. There's no word on whether this morning's horrific discovery is related or not, but some of the neighbors we've talked to are assuming it's connected."

They played a pre-taped interview with old Mrs. Jefferson from down the street. It must have been filmed earlier. Then the blonde reporter came back on screen.

"Gitleson's body was discovered this morning by an elderly couple walking their dog. Vandercamp's whereabouts are still unknown and police spokespersons have refused further comment. They also refused to confirm reports that the victim's head was missing."

"Holy mother of fuck." Cliff slipped on his boots. "You said this thing—whatever it was—ran towards the alley last night."

"Which would have put Leslie and her date directly in its path," I said. "Hylinus couldn't take Tara and Claudine, so he took Leslie instead."

"Who?" Cliff looked confused.

"The satyr," I explained. "Tara and Claudine called him Hylinus."

I sank onto the recliner, still holding the pot. Hot coffee sloshed inside it. Big Steve trotted out from the kitchen and lay down at my feet. He looked troubled.

A smiling anchorman sitting in the studio replaced the pretty blonde reporter. "Jennifer, is there any word on whether or not these cases are related to the additional disappearance of a fourth young woman, Shelly Carpenter?"

I stopped breathing.

The blonde reporter, Jennifer, came back on screen. "No word at this time, Ron. Apparently, police weren't informed that Carpenter was missing until early this morning. We have no further details at this time."

While she was talking, the camera panned over the bloody Mazda. Cliff and I stared at the screen, and I tried to catch a glimpse of Ramirez amongst the assembled throng of crime scene investigators. I didn't see him.

"They know about Shelly," I said. "That means the cops will come here next."

Cliff sipped his coffee. "Why's that?"

"Because I stopped by her house yesterday, to check on her. I talked to Shelly's neighbor, and she knew who I was. Ramirez is sure to have talked to her already. Hell, she's probably the one who reported Shelly missing. They'll know I was there, and they'll want to know why."

"You were worried about her," Cliff pointed out. "That ain't no crime."

I nodded. "Yeah, but not reporting what I knew might be."

Cliff lit a cigarette. "Shit, man. It ain't like you could tell them what you saw in the woods. You said so yourself."

I stood up. Cliff and Big Steve both followed me into the kitchen. I put the coffee pot back on its burner and took a sip from my mug. It had already grown cold. "

What the fuck are we gonna do, Cliff?"

As if in answer, there was a knock at the back door. Cliff and I stared at one another, our eyes wide.

"Answer it," he whispered, nodding towards the door.

"You answer it," I said. "It might be Ramirez."

He shook his head. "It's your house, man."

The knocking continued, loud and insistent, the kind that indicated the visitor was very anxious to have the door opened.

Swallowing hard, I turned the knob.

Merle stood in the open doorway, looking excited. His thin hair was askew, and his eyes were bloodshot from fatigue. "

You guys hear the news?" he asked.

"We're watching it now. Have you or Dale been out back yet?"

"No. Dale thinks we should hit the LeHorn place before we go to the cops. Or before they come to us."

"You heard about Shelly too, I take it?"

"Yeah. They know, so Dale figures it's just a matter of time before Ramirez shows up. He said to tell you to get ready. Him and Claudine will be over in a bit."

"How is she?" I asked. I was surprised to hear that she was coming over, let alone awake.

Merle's face darkened. "She doesn't remember any of it. Woke up complaining about a bad taste in her mouth, and an even worse headache. That's about it."

"So why are they coming over?"

"Dale thinks the women should stay home today. Claudine is too sick to go to work, anyway. If Tara refuses, Dale said we should tell her that we're worried about their safety, now that there are four women missing and at least one murder. He said we can leave somebody here with them while the rest of us go to the house."

It made sense to me. "Cliff and I will be ready."

"Okay." He turned away. "I'm gonna go get dressed. Need some coffee."

Cliff left for his apartment as well, to grab a shower and change clothes.

"Wake up Cory too, on your way back?"

"Will do." He waved over his shoulder, and departed.

After he was gone, I went upstairs. Tara was still sleeping. I crawled into bed beside her and wrapped my arm around her waist. I breathed in her scent. My lips nuzzled her ear. Slowly, she stirred.

"Morning, sleepy-head," I said. "How do you feel?"

She opened her eyes, glared at the alarm clock, and then shut her eyes again.

"Like shit," Tara groaned. "Headache. Nausea. Feel like I'm hung over. And I'm going to be late."

"No work today," I said, keeping my voice steady. "Leslie's vanished, just like Shannon."

She stiffened. "Oh no . . . Leslie from the gas station?"

"Yeah. And there's more."

Tara rolled over and stared at me, blinking the sleep from her eyes. Her forehead wrinkled in concern. "What?"

"Leslie's date is dead. Somebody murdered him. Right out back. They were parked next to the playground."

"Oh my God . . ."

"Dale and I want you and Claudine to stay home today, just to be safe. Okay?"

She groaned again. "Believe me, the way I feel, I'm not going to argue. Feel like shit. Going to call in sick, anyway."

"I'll get you some aspirin," I offered. "Coffee, too."

"Mmm." Tara smiled. "I love you."

"I love you too," I said. And I did.

Then the image of her sucking the satyr's cock came rushing back again.

You're tainted, she'd said. *Weak. That's why our babies died.*

I got up and left the room before Tara could see the expression on my face. I suppressed the urge to scream, to rant, to hit her, curse her, and curse Hylinus, Nelson LeHorn, God, and anyone else involved in this fiasco. I wanted to break something, felt like smashing my fist against the wall. But that wouldn't help.

What would help us were answers. Answers from the LeHorn place, with any luck.

In the kitchen, I poured Tara a cup of coffee, with an ice cube to cool it down, just the way she liked it. I tried to push the memories from my mind, but all I could see was my wife's lips wrapped around that—*thing*. I closed my eyes, and saw my dead baby's eyes, still staring back at me from the toilet.

It's your fault, Daddy. Your fault we died. You were supposed to keep us safe, but you didn't. You couldn't protect us, and you can't protect Mommy either.

I collapsed to my knees and wept silently, conscious enough not to let Tara hear me. Big Steve walked over and pressed his cold nose against my cheek. I hugged him tight, afraid to let go. He was my anchor. My sanity. All I had left.

"Seems like all we've done the last twenty-four hours is cry," I told him. "I'm sorry, buddy."

He nuzzled me again, letting me know it was okay. I hung on tight.

A half hour later, we gathered together in my living room. Claudine and Tara looked like hell; dark circles under their eyes, hair mussed, skin pale. They sat together on the couch, clutching steaming mugs of coffee and squinting against the sunlight. Both were convinced they'd picked up the same bug, the suggestion made easy by the fact that there was indeed a flu bug going around town. They put up no argument when we suggested they stay together for the day, especially after we filled them in on Leslie and Shelly's disappearances. Cliff, Merle, Dale, Cory and myself didn't look much better. Hung over, Cory moved at a snail's pace. The rest of us were tired and irritable from stress and lack of sleep.

While the girls talked, we stepped into the kitchen to go over the plan. Someone had to stay behind to safeguard Tara and Claudine, and we decided it should be Cory. He protested, but we explained how important his role was, how we were entrusting him with the safety of the women we loved, and how he'd better not fuck it up. Cory got very solemn after that, and promised us he'd do his best. In truth, I wasn't too worried. Hylinus didn't seem to be active during the day, and this way, Cory wouldn't annoy the rest of us once we were inside LeHorn's house.

We stepped back into the living room. Despite their symptoms, Tara and Claudine wanted to know what was going on and where we were going. I opened my mouth, unsure of what to say, but Dale cut me off.

"Search party," he lied, apparently having already rehearsed our excuse. "They're going to go back over some of the ground we missed yesterday. They didn't want a lot of people this time, so you probably won't see it on the news. Something about too many searchers tramping over possible clues. They asked for a few volunteers, and since Merle, Adam, and myself are home all day, we agreed to help."

"Yeah," Cliff said, "and I needed a day off work, anyway.

Can't let these guys have all the fun."

"Cory's going to stay here with you until we get back," I said.

Tara frowned, looking suspicious. "Why?"

"Just to be on the safe side," I told her. "Nobody really knows what's going on. It will make us feel better about leaving you here."

"Besides," Dale added, "if you're both sick, Cory can take care of you."

"How?" Claudine asked.

Dale shrugged. "Make you some chicken soup or something."

Both women glanced dubiously at Cory, who was seated in front of my media shelf, thumbing through our video games.

I cringed. "Please?"

Tara nodded. "Okay. If you insist."

Cory glanced back at us, clearly oblivious to the conversation.

"Dude!" His eyes sparkled. "You've got the new *Grand Theft Auto*. Care if I play it?"

"Knock yourself out," I said.

"Sweet."

"But remember what Dale and I told you."

Cory's face grew somber again. "I will."

Claudine sipped coffee. "And just what did you guys tell him?"

Dale kissed her forehead. "That he had to wait on the two of you hand and foot and obey your every whim. He is your slave and you two are his masters."

The girls laughed, then both of them stopped suddenly and winced, rubbing their heads.

"Oh," Tara groaned. "Hurts to laugh."

Merle and Cliff filed out while Dale and I kissed our wives goodbye.

"Be careful," Tara whispered.

I hugged her tight. "It's just a search party."

She pulled away and looked me in the eyes.

"No, it's not." She kept her voice low, so that Dale and

Claudine wouldn't hear her. "I know you, Adam Senft, and I know when you're bullshitting me. Like now."

I started to deny it, but she interrupted.

"Whatever's going on, I trust you. Just promise me you'll be careful, and that you'll tell me about it later?"

I squeezed her hand. "I promise."

She squeezed back. "Then go."

"If you need us," Dale told them, "just call Adam's or Cliff's cell phone."

Cory and Big Steve followed Dale and I to the back door. Cory's demeanor had changed. He looked nervous and scared.

"Guys, what if that detective shows up? What do I tell him?"

"Don't answer the door," Dale told him.

"But what if Claudine or Tara answer it instead? If they let him in and he starts asking questions . . ."

"Then tell him the truth," I said. "Tell him we went to the woods."

"And if he asks about Shelly?" Cory grabbed my shirt. "Am I supposed to tell him about the goat-man?"

"Hopefully, by then, we'll have the proof, and we'll tell him everything."

"Yeah," Cory said, "but if I tell him, he'll think I've been drinking and shit."

"Cory," Dale sighed. "He'll probably think you've been drinking anyway. Just be careful, and watch over the girls."

I bent down and patted Big Steve's head. "And you watch over them all. Don't let Cory give you any shit."

He wagged his tail slightly, but the worried expression lingered in his eyes. He whined mournfully. I was suddenly overcome with emotion. While Dale and Cory watched, I knelt down and hugged my dog.

"I love you, buddy," I whispered into his neck.

Big Steve licked my face. I didn't want to let him go. Didn't want to let go of my rock. As if sensing that, he slipped out of my arms and stepped backward. His eyes never left me.

They said, *Go. . .*

Dale and I stepped out onto the sidewalk, and Cory shut

the door behind us. The last thing I saw was Big Steve's head, tilted, his eyes still watching me.

"Okay, ladies," Cory called from inside, "who's up for some video games?"

The grass was still wet from the previous night's rain, and the muddy satyr tracks remained. They seemed to put things into perspective—made what we were doing more real.

Merle pulled his Chevy Suburban behind my car, and we all piled in, Merle and Cliff up front, Dale and I in the back. Merle turned the stereo on, and Ray Charles sang a cover of Hank Williams Sr.'s "Your Cheating Heart." The song summoned up the image of Tara and Hylinus, and I fought to keep from puking.

We drove in silence.

TWELVE

After stopping off for more coffee and cigarettes, we went through Shrewsbury and Seven Valleys, passing into farm country, and then spent twenty-five minutes driving along one narrow back road after another. The weather was perfect and we rolled with the windows down.

"Nice day," Cliff said. "Feels like summer."

We nodded in agreement, but said nothing.

I tried to get my head around the fact that we were going to the deserted home of a black powwow magician, where we'd search for answers regarding a horny satyr who'd come to life in our neighborhood. It seemed so bizarre. All around us were signs of normalcy; kids climbing into a school bus, a man mowing his lawn, a cop giving a ticket to a motorist, construction workers standing alongside the road, doing nothing but watching the cars pass by. We didn't seem to fit into that equation.

"I brought guns," Merle said from up front, as if to accentuate my thoughts. "In the cargo space behind you guys. Couple of deer rifles."

Dale adjusted his window. "For what?"

"Just in case."

"We won't need them," I said. "It's just an abandoned farmhouse. The satyr isn't hanging out there."

Merle stared straight ahead and kept his eyes on the road.

"Anybody care if I smoke?" Cliff asked.

They didn't, and he lit a cigarette. I joined him. The rush of nicotine woke me up, and calmed me down. My cell phone rang— my publisher wanting to know if they could set up an interview with a newspaper. I told them to call back later. They asked if they'd interrupted my writing. I lied and told them yes.

Eventually, we turned off onto the dirt road leading to LeHorn's Hollow.

"This is the right way, isn't it?" Merle asked. "Been a while since I was out here."

"Yeah." I remembered my own last trip down this road, on my date with Becky back in high school. Things hadn't changed much since then.

The trees cast long, sinister shadows across the road. A vast expanse of barren cornfields stretched off to the left of the road, the rolling hills not worked since Nelson LeHorn's disappearance twenty years earlier. They reminded me of NASA's pictures from the surface of Mars. Nothing grew there now. The red clay-dirt was strewn with rocks and unturned clods of earth. To the right lay miles and miles of woodlands, untouched by the explosive development that had marred other parts of the state, with the exception of the portion Gladstone Pulp Wood Company logged for their paper mill.

"Spooky back here," Merle mumbled. "Pretty dark, even in the daylight."

On the radio, Willie Nelson's "Dandelion Wine" was drowned out by a sudden burst of static. Merle pressed the seek function, looking for another station. Snatches of disembodied voices cut through the white noise; an infomercial for hair replacement medicine, the driving beat of a hip-hop song, a preacher or a conservative talk show host, it was hard to tell which. His voice swelled, seeming to boom from the speakers.

"In Ecclesiastes nine, verse three, King Solomon tells us that 'there is an evil among all things that are done under the sun'. . ."

Cliff groaned. "It's way too fucking early and I've had way too little sleep to listen to this shit."

"Sorry," Merle apologized. "Reception sucks back in these woods. You guys might have trouble with your cell phones, too."

"I didn't bring mine," Cliff said. "Was I supposed to?"

On the radio, the pastor's disembodied voice faded in and out.

"Wouldn't have hurt," Dale answered. "I told the girls you had it on you."

Cliff shrugged. "We still got Adam's."

I glanced at mine. Sure enough, Merle had been right about the backwoods reception. I barely had one bar.

"Won't do us a lot of good back here," I told them. "Must not be any towers around. Why didn't you bring yours anyway, Cliff?"

"Didn't want work calling me all day."

"But you told them you were sick."

"Yeah, but they'll still call. Place would shut down without me."

"*And chapter eleven,*" the sermon continued, *"says 'for thou knowest not what evil shall be upon the earth, and if the tree falls toward the south, there it shall be.' And evil is upon the earth, brothers and sisters. It walks the earth with cloven feet and a burning lust . . ."*

"Give me a break." Cliff reached out and clicked the stereo off.

"Hey." Dale leaned forward. "What was he saying about cloven feet?"

"Who cares," Cliff said, turning around to look at us. "It's just more superstitious bullshit."

"You don't believe in God?" I asked.

His lip curled up in a sneer. "Hell, no. Why? Do you?"

I thought about Tara and the satyr, rutting in the backyard; about Tara's miscarriages; our baby floating in the toilet, and the sound the commode made when I flushed it.

"I don't know anymore," I admitted. "I used to believe in God. Believed in powwow magic, too, somewhat, but not the paranormal. I wanted to believe more, but I never saw a ghost or a flying saucer. Needed to see proof. But I always believed in God. These days, I'm not so sure. I think my beliefs may have gotten reversed. I've seen proof of monsters, but I haven't seen proof of God."

"Well I believe," Merle said. "When Peggy left, I had nothing. No one. So one Sunday morning, I come stumbling home drunk, turned on the television, and watched this preacher. Got up, still drunk, and drove to that Episcopalian church on the edge of town, right down near the Maryland border."

"And you found God?" Cliff asked, his voice thick with derision.

"I found peace," Merle said. "If you want to say that God is peace, then yeah, I found God."

I considered the look on Merle's face when somebody mentioned his ex-wife, and the way he still talked about her every day, and secretly wondered just how much peace he'd actually found. But I didn't say it. Instead, I turned to Dale.

"What about you? Do you believe in God?"

Dale stared out the window, watching the trees rush past. "I did," he whispered. "Until last night. After Claudine and that—that thing." He choked back an angry sob. "If God exists, then He let that happen. Like you said, we've seen the monster. Where was God while that was happening?"

Cliff muttered something under his breath.

"What's that?" Dale asked, leaning forward.

"He was inside Adam's house. Big Steve."

I frowned. "What does that have to do with God?"

Cliff grinned. "God is dog spelled backwards."

He laughed at his joke, but Dale and I just shook our heads.

Merle kept driving. We passed by the burned-out skeleton of a cabin. Charred timbers jutted skyward, and the ground beneath them was ash. The destruction extended out into the outlying forest, carving a large swath through its center. The greenery had just started to creep back into the empty space, a fresh crop of new undergrowth sprouting from the scorched earth. Miraculously, an outhouse, untouched by the flames, sat nearby.

Merle glanced at the wreckage and then looked away. His expression was grim.

"Adam, you remember when I told you about my buddy Frank?"

I nodded.

"That was his place we just passed."

"The guy who's hunting cabin caught on fire?" Cliff asked.

Merle nodded, his knuckles tightening around the steering wheel.

"It's remarkable how the forest is already growing back," Dale said. "Almost as if it's reclaiming the spot."

We rounded a curve in the road, and suddenly, LeHorn's Hollow lay spread out before us. The farmhouse, barn, and other buildings stood weather-beaten and empty, providing a haven for rats, groundhogs, and other scavengers. More unplowed fields and oldgrowth forest surrounded the place. In the center of the forest, at the bottom of a steep depression formed by four sloping hills, sat the hollow itself. The trees sprouting from its center seemed taller than the others, up to the point where they joined the rest of the forest.

"Just think," I said. "Those woods reach all the way back to our place."

Merle chuckled. "Want to walk home and see if you beat us back?"

"I don't think so."

He parked a few yards away from the farmhouse and turned the Suburban off. We grew quiet.

Bright yellow police tape fluttered in the wind, ends still tied to various parts of the farmhouse. A few *POSTED—NO HUNTING, FISHING, OR TRESPASSING* signs hung from the tree-trunks at the outer rim of the woods.

Cliff whistled, staring at the buildings. "Damn, this place is falling apart."

"Did somebody finally buy the land?" Dale asked, pointing at the signs.

"No," Merle said. "Those were leftover from when LeHorn was still living here. I'd guess you could hunt there now, if you really wanted to."

Cliff nodded. "Your friend did, right?"

"Yeah," Merle grunted. "And look what happened to him."

Stretching, I cracked my neck. "So, we gonna sit here all day or are we going in?"

I opened my door, and reluctantly, the others followed. We got out of the Suburban and studied the house. Red, faded paint peeled from the walls, revealing gray, insect-eaten timber beneath. Several of the windows were cracked or broken, unboarded against the elements, and a bird's nest sprouted from the top of the chimney. Shingles were missing from the roof. One of the front porch steps had sunken, and the others looked rickety. Wasps had built a home above the screen door. The barn was in even worse shape. One entire section of roof had collapsed, and the doors hung off their hinges, creaking back and forth in the breeze.

I checked my cell phone. It flashed a message telling me there was no service.

Despite the fact that we were outdoors, it was quiet. No insects or birds. No distant traffic. No airplanes passing overhead. It felt like we were a million miles from civilization, deep in the middle of nowhere.

Merle opened the trunk and pulled aside an old, grease-covered blanket. Beneath it were two hunting rifles—a Mossberg .22 and a Remington 30-06. Boxes of ammunition lay beside them, along with a pair of binoculars and a heavy-duty flashlight.

I took the flashlight. Merle and Cliff each selected a rifle. Cliff lit a cigarette and sighed.

"Let's do this," he said. "Lead the way."

Even with the sun overhead, the area between the house and the barn was covered in shadows, and I shivered as we crossed it. In the distance, the trees of the hollow loomed over it all, watching us. I had the uncanny impression that the entire place was holding its breath.

We walked across the yard, if you could call it that. Years of neglect had transformed it into a tangled, overgrown mass of brown weeds. As we neared the house, something crunched under my feet. I knelt down, brushed the weeds aside, and picked up a fragment of glass.

"Came from up there." Cliff pointed.

I looked up at the third floor attic window, still broken from the day of the murder, twenty years ago. Someone had nailed a piece of plywood over the opening, but that was all. It reminded me of a mouth. Jagged shards of glass stuck out of the rotting frame like teeth. A loose strand of police tape hung from one corner, flapping like a tongue.

"This is where she died," I said. "Patricia LeHorn. Right here. On this spot."

The weeds swayed silently in the breeze.

"Come on," Dale urged. "Nothing here now but broken glass."

We stopped at the sunken porch steps.

"Who's first?" I asked, trying to smile and failing miserably.

"You are," Merle said, nudging me with his elbow. "This was your idea."

"And you've got the flashlight," Dale pointed out.

"Yeah, but like Cliff said, you guys have the firepower. Maybe one of you should go first."

"Can't shoot what we can't see," Merle explained. "Flashlight's gotta go first."

I swallowed hard. "Want to trade?"

"Not on your life."

I put my foot on the first step, experimenting with it. The wood groaned, but supported my weight. I reached out and grabbed the handrail, then ascended. There was a sharp pain in my hand. I jerked it away. A gray splinter jutted from my palm, drawing a small drop of blood.

"It fucking bit me."

The stairs groaned again, as if the wood had tasted my blood and was now hungry for more.

I reached the top, and the others followed.

"Watch out for that wasp's nest," Dale cautioned. "Don't stir them up. I'm allergic."

"It's empty. Leftover from last year." I pushed the fluttering police tape out of the way, pulled open the screen door and rattled the doorknob. It was locked. I turned back to them. "What now?"

Cliff sighed. "You mean we drove all the way out here and you guys don't even have a plan for getting inside? Why not just break in?"

"We're already guilty of withholding information from

the police," I told him. "We don't need to add breaking and entering."

Cliff shrugged. "Who's gonna know? We're in the middle of nowhere, man."

"The back door?" Dale suggested. "It's probably locked, too," I said.

Merle pointed to the side of the house. "Saw some storm doors over there. Maybe we can get in through the cellar."

"Fuck that," Cliff said.

"I thought you didn't believe in any of this?" Merle said.

"I don't, but that doesn't mean I'm gonna go traipsing around through some old basement, either."

"You scared?"

"No, I ain't scared. I just got a thing about spiders. And basements have spiders."

I grinned. "You're afraid of spiders? You? Cliff Swanson, ladies man and all around bad boy?"

"Fuck off, Adam." He flicked his cigarette butt into the grass, and then stomped on it with his boot heel. "Let's go try the storm doors. Probably locked anyway."

They weren't. The hinges were rusty, and we had to tug hard to get them open, but we did, revealing a wooden staircase descending into darkness. The air smelled like mildew. I thought I heard something skittering in the shadows, but I couldn't see anything.

Brushing a long abandoned spider web out of the way, I clicked on the flashlight and started down. Dust floated in the beam of light. Dale grabbed my shoulder. His Adam's apple bobbed in his throat and his eyes were frightened.

"Adam, we don't have to do this. We haven't slept. We could go see Ramirez right now, and tell him what we know."

I shrugged him off. "No. We do have to do this, if not for us, then for our wives. You saw what we're up against, Dale. I know I did—but I still don't understand it. We need to find out. Arm ourselves."

He closed his eyes and nodded.

I slowly descended into the darkness, and when I got to the bottom, I looked back up at them. They looked like three bluecollar angels, their faces silhouetted in the sunlight. "You guys coming?"

Reluctantly, they followed. Merle started humming "The Eensy, Weensy Spider" and Cliff punched him in the arm.

We let our eyes adjust to the darkness. Despite the warm spring day, it felt like winter in the basement. Our breath hung in the air. The cold crept into our bones, rising from the cracked and pitted concrete.

Another staircase led up to the first floor. Judging by our position, I guessed that the kitchen was directly over our heads.

I trailed the flashlight beam around the cellar. The walls were made of cracked cinderblocks. Moisture seeped in through the fissures. Black-green mold grew in the crevices like slimy tendrils, glistening in the flashlight's beam. The air was thick with rot and decay, and we all breathed through our mouths. The cellar was filled with debris, and in the shadows, everything took on sinister shapes. Rust covered the furnace and hot water heater. Moldering cardboard boxes, stuffed to overflowing with old newspapers and magazines, sat stacked up against one wall. Empty wooden crates occupied another corner. All around us were the castoffs of another family's life. A ten-speed bike, the spokes entwined with cobwebs; rusty tools; threadbare furniture; forgotten toys; an unused coalburning fireplace; oak storage chests, their contents hidden beneath the layers of dust on the lids; rags; old brooms and mops. A worktable stacked with rusted paint cans, plastic and metal jugs of turpentine and gasoline, and bottles of spray-paint. A potato bin contained blackened, stinking lumps that must have once been potatoes but now looked like shrunken heads. One wall was lined with steel shelving, and the shelves were filled with self-canned goods— peaches, apples, squash, green beans, peas, corn, and beets. A faded, delicate scrawl labeled each jar, identifying the contents— the handwriting of a dead woman, thrown to her death from an attic window at the hands of her husband.

"It's chilly down here," Merle whispered.

"Yeah," I rubbed my arms. "It is."

"Should we be breathing in that mold?" Cliff asked.

"Probably not," Dale answered. "But I wouldn't worry.

We won't be here long enough for it to have any effect."

"You hope."

I cocked an ear, listening for mice or rats. I saw evidence of their existence; nests made from newspaper and mildewed scraps of clothing, and scattered rodent droppings on the eaves and floor; but nothing alive. The cellar was silent, and somehow, that was the chilliest part of all.

Cliff lit a cigarette, his lighter flaring. The darkness seemed to gather around the flame, as if trying to extinguish it.

"Why are we whispering?" His voice echoed off the walls. "Ain't nobody here." Above us, the floorboards creaked.

We froze. Dale reached out and grabbed my arm. I held my breath. My heart thundered in my chest, trying to leap into my throat.

"Somebody's upstairs." Merle's voice was so quiet we had to strain to hear him. Despite that, his terror came through loud and clear.

"Can't be," I whispered. "There weren't any cars out front."

"They could have walked."

"From where?" Dale hissed. "There's nothing around for miles."

He was breathing heavy, and I wondered if his heart was okay. Last thing we needed in the midst of all this was for Dale to have a heart attack here in the cellar of an abandoned farmhouse.

"The house is old," I reasoned. "It's just the wood settling."

The floorboards creaked again, once, twice, three times. The sound was spaced apart—like footsteps. Then they fell silent once more. The darkness seemed to grow more powerful, pressing against us like a solid entity. I resisted the urge to lash out at the gloom. The noise was not repeated.

The flashlight beam reflected off Merle's face, bathed in sweat.

"What if Dale's right?" he asked. "If there's nobody here except us, maybe it's Patricia LeHorn."

"A ghost?" I whispered.

"Let's go," Merle insisted. "Just get out of here and go home."

I opened my mouth to reply, but Cliff snatched the flashlight from my hands. Then he grabbed the 30-06 from Merle and worked the bolt, putting a round in the chamber.

"Fuck it." His voice echoed across the cellar. "We came for answers and we're gonna get them. If somebody's up there, then they can answer this shit for us. Ghost or not."

He stalked towards the stairs, picking his way through the debris. "Cliff," Merle stage-whispered. "Get back here!"

"Hello," Cliff shouted. "Anybody home? Yoo-hoo? Mrs. LeHorn? Goat-man?"

Silence.

"Come out, come out wherever you are, or I'll huff and I'll puff and I'll blow your house down!"

"Goddamn it, Cliff," I raised my voice. "Stop it."

He looked back at us, flashed a grin, and then started up the stairs. They creaked under his boots, but the floorboards above us were still.

"We're coming up," he continued yelling, purposely stomping his feet to punctuate each step. "Put away your eyes of newt and frog toes. We're just here to talk about the goat-man!"

Sighing, Dale hefted the Mossberg. "Come on. If there is somebody in this house, they know we're here now. All we can do is damage control."

We started up the stairs—Dale in the lead, me in the middle, and a now weaponless Merle bringing up the rear. When we reached the top, Cliff handed the flashlight to Dale, who handed it back to me. Then, still grinning, Cliff slammed the Remington's butt against the doorknob. The door shuddered in its frame. He rammed it again and the wood splintered.

Dale grabbed his arm. "Cliff, what the hell is wrong with you?"

Cliff laughed.

He's scared, I realized. *He stayed awake all night. He's exhausted and just as scared as the rest of us, and this is how he's coping. He believes more than he's let on.*

Cliff brought the rifle down several more times, and the door finally burst open. Cliff tumbled through.

"Hey, goat-man! Come on out."

We leaped after him. I'd been right; the room above us was the kitchen. Like the cellar, it was dark and deserted. No residents, no squatters, not even a mouse. Nothing to account for the footsteps we'd heard. Cracked linoleum floor. Wallpaper peeling away to reveal cracked, dingy plaster. Appliances—refrigerator, oven, and sink—all dead and covered with dust and splotches of black mildew. Wooden cupboards, several with the doors hanging open, empty except for cobwebs and dustballs. No people, and no ghosts—at least, none that we could see.

We could feel them, however. Feel something. None of the other guys mentioned it, but I could see it in their actions, read it in the expressions on their faces as they looked around. The air felt oppressive. Heavy. It seemed *wrong*. Like it had in the cellar, but stronger now. Closer to the surface. I got the impression that the house was watching us, determining whether or not we were a threat. The shadows seemed to swell.

Craving sunlight, I approached one of the kitchen windows that wasn't boarded up and parted the blinds. The windowsills were piled high with dead insects, almost an inch deep in some places; flies, bees, ladybugs—and others, their shells too desiccated to determine their type. For a moment, I wondered what had killed them. Fear? Did bugs know fear? Had they fluttered helplessly against the windowpanes while that same oppressive darkness closed in on them? Had the darkness *squeezed* them before completely enveloping their bodies?

Merle nudged me. "Anybody outside?"

I shook my head, and let the blinds fall.

Cliff's temporary madness had drained away. He stood in the center of the kitchen, staring about sheepishly. He clutched the rifle, and when Merle tried to retrieve it again, he backed away, shaking his head.

"We shouldn't be here," he said. "You guys feel it too, don't you?"

"I thought you were the skeptic?" Dale muttered.

"Just because I don't believe in the goat-man doesn't

mean I ain't spooked. This place feels wrong."

There were two exits from the kitchen. One led to the dining room. From where I stood, I could see the corner of the table and several chairs. What lay beyond the second exit was concealed behind a dirty curtain hanging over the doorway. Cliff and Merle crept into the dining room, alert and ready to jump should the mysterious floorwalker decide to reveal itself. Dale quietly opened a few cabinets and peered inside. I poked my head through the cur

tained doorway, looking into a laundry room. The washer and dryer were covered in dust, and there were mouse tracks trailing through it, along with small nuggets of rodent feces and more dead insects. At the rear of the laundry room was a door leading out onto the porch. Taped above it was a yellowed scrap of paper that said:

I.
N. I. R.
I.
SANCTUS SPIRITUS
I.
N. I. R.
I.

"What's that?" I asked.

Dale shrugged. "Some kind of powwow charm, I guess. Maybe to protect the house?"

I stepped back into the kitchen. Merle and Cliff had ventured into the living room, and I heard them shushing each other. There was a soft thud, and then Merle cursed under his breath. Cliff apologized for bumping into whatever it was he'd brushed up against.

Dale stared at a photograph on the wall. I joined him. Looking back at us was the LeHorn family in happier times. Judging by their clothes, I guess the portrait had been taken in the early Eighties. Nelson LeHorn looked like your typical, old-fashioned Pennsylvania farmer. He was standing; tall and thin, yet his frame and the set of his shoulders hinted at powerful strength. He was not smiling; his expression was dour and serious. A long, black beard framed his narrow, pointed face, curling down to his chest, and his close-cropped hair was slicked back against his scalp. His eyes were like two dots of India ink. His wife, Patricia, stood next to him, smiling and beatific. Yet her smile seemed sad, and her eyes looked haunted. She was heavy-set, her hair bland, and she wore no make-up, yet despite this, she had a natural beauty that caught the eye, the type of beauty a woman like that retained well into her sixties and seventies—had she not been murdered. Seated in front of them were the kids; Matty, Claudine, and Gina. The girls both had the 'big hair' style so popular during that era, and Matty looked like a young Tom Cruise, circa *Risky Business*. Obviously, he'd taken after his mother, rather than his old man.

I stared at Nelson LeHorn. His frozen, black eyes seemed to stare back at me.

The floorboards creaked behind us, and Dale and I both jumped.

"Family portrait," Cliff observed, looking over our shoulders. Merle stood beside him. "You guys scared us," I whispered. "Didn't hear you coming."

Merle sighed, fixated on the photograph. "It's a damn shame. Guy had a beautiful wife and three beautiful kids. The kind of family some of us would give our left nut for. And he killed them. Killed any chance at happiness they'd ever have."

Merle looked away from the portrait, and I saw him wipe away a single tear. I knew he was thinking about his Peggy, and I started thinking about the miscarriages. I quickly changed the subject, before we grew too maudlin.

"Did you guys find anything?" I spoke a little louder. "Any signs that someone has been here?"

"Nothing," Cliff said. "There's an inch of dust on everything. No one's been here. The whole place is going to shit. Who knows how long it's been exposed to the elements."

"What about the upper floors?" Dale asked.

Cliff shrugged. "We didn't go up, but the stairs are dusty, too. There'd be footprints on them if somebody were here.

I'm thinking Adam was right. It was just the house settling on its foundation."

"Okay," I said, breathing a sigh of relief. "Let's search it, top to bottom."

Cliff pulled out his cigarettes and offered one to me, which I accepted.

"I still don't know what the hell we're looking for," he said.

"You will." I borrowed his lighter and lit up. "You'll know it when you see it."

"What?"

"Anything that will help us to understand what the hell we're up against. Books, papers, something like that."

Cliff took his lighter back. "I still think the cops would have cleaned that shit out."

"Not necessarily," Dale said. "Think about it. Nelson pushes Patricia from the third story attic window. The kids confirm that's what happened. Nelson flees before they can charge him. They'd be looking for evidence of affairs, insurance policies; stuff like that. Even if they came across something about satyrs, they'd discard it as fantasy."

"Maybe," Cliff said, but he didn't seem convinced.

Animals and the elements had eroded the living room's interior, turning it into a disaster area. Strips of wallpaper peeled away, revealing more yellow, mildewed plaster. The carpet was a layer of filth, and the hardwood floor beneath it was warped. Rats had chewed holes in the sofa and baseboards. The family had left a lot of personal belongings behind; china, books, photo albums, record albums and cassette tapes. All of it was worse for the wear. Even if some brave soul had actually wanted to loot the LeHorn place, there wasn't much left that was worth anything.

After spending an hour searching the downstairs, we moved up to the second floor. Conditions were slightly better there; most of the windows were sealed, but there were still signs of infestation; old mouse droppings and chewed papers. My flashlight beam trailed over a pile of dead cockroaches.

A cursory check of the bathroom turned up nothing, so we moved on to the bedrooms, starting with Matty's.

"Have you guys noticed the rats?" Dale asked, rifling through dresser drawers.

"The nests," Cliff said. "Haven't seen one yet, though."

"No," Dale agreed. "You haven't. Neither have I. How about you two?"

Merle and I shook our heads, and Dale continued.

"We've seen evidence of mice and rats, but we haven't actually encountered any. And the bugs. Plenty of dead ones, but we haven't seen a live one yet. Not a moth or a cockroach, or even a fly. Plenty of spider webs, too, but no spiders."

"That's a good thing," Cliff muttered, sitting down on the bed. He looked tired.

I knew how he felt. The caffeine from the morning's coffee had worn off, and the cigarettes weren't helping. I stifled a yawn.

"No spiders are always a good thing," Cliff repeated.

"Is it?" Dale's eyebrows twitched. "I wonder . . ."

Merle opened the closet door and peeked inside. "What are you getting at, Dale?"

"There's nothing living here. This place should be crawling with vermin, but it's not. It's just full of dead things."

As he was talking, I bent down and shined the flashlight under the bed. The space beneath was full of dust balls.

I stood back up and wiped my hands on my pants. "Damn."

"You give up?" Cliff asked, checking his watch. "It's noon already. Can we go home now?"

"No," I told him. "We haven't checked the attic yet."

Sighing, he heaved himself off the bed. "Well, let's get it over with."

The attic was accessible from the master bedroom, via a narrow, winding staircase. It was blacker up there than anywhere else in the house, including the basement. Whoever had nailed the plywood over the attic's broken window had done an uneven job. Daylight filtered through a few small cracks around the edges, but that just made it seem darker. The flashlight beam weakened, unable to fully penetrate the gloom, and I wondered how much longer the batteries would last.

"Jesus," Merle gasped when we reached the top.

The attic held even more clutter than the cellar. Boxes and chests were piled high on top of each other. Some had their contents scrawled on the side in black magic marker. Others were blank. We waded through the junk, opening boxes and looking for anything that would give us insight into Hylinus. Cliff used his cigarette lighter to give us more light, until the tip grew hot and burned his fingers.

"This is fucking pointless." He sucked his index finger. "We'll never find anything in this mess."

"Adam," Dale said. "Shine that light over here a second."

He studied an old-fashioned, wooden steam trunk, buried beneath a stack of boxes. Frowning, he ran his fingers over the lettering on the side, stirring up dust particles.

Cliff sneezed. "Frigging dust."

"What is it?" I asked Dale.

"This lettering," he said. "It looks similar to the lettering on the stone."

Merle knelt beside him. "LeHorn's?"

Dale nodded. "I think so."

Cliff and I gathered around them. Cliff's eyes were watering from the dust. We looked at the trunk. The letters did seem familiar, crafted by the same hand. But the message, whatever it meant, was different. It said:

Ito, alo Massa Dandi Bando, III. Amen J. R. N. R. J.

Beneath that, in the same erratic handwriting, was some kind of prayer, followed by more gibberish:

Mary, God's Mother, traversed the land,
Holding three worms close in her hand;
One was white, the other was black, the third was red.

SATOR
AREPO
TENET
OPERA
ROTAS

"What the fuck is this?" Cliff asked, rubbing dust from his eyes.

"A charm," Dale said. "That prayer, at least, is classic powwow."

Cliff wasn't convinced. "How do you know?"

"Because I've seen it before," Dale told him. "When I was a kid. If I remember correctly, it's supposed to be a spell against worms, termites, and the like."

"He's right," Merle said. "It sounds like the stuff my Grandma used to recite."

"So what's the rest?" Cliff asked.

Dale stroked his chin. "I'd guess a protection of some sort. Safeguards. Protecting the trunk, or whatever's inside it."

"Sator." Merle pointed at the word. "You think that's supposed to be 'Satyr'?"

"Maybe," Dale said. "I don't know."

I trained the light on the trunk's hasp. "It's not locked. Open it."

Merle sat his rifle aside, and then he and Cliff moved the boxes off the chest. Dale unfastened the hasps and raised the lid, sending another cloud of dust and the faint scent of mothballs wafting into the air.

The trunk was full of books. We huddled around and began examining them. On the top was a small, thin hardcover, its binding made of brown leather and the title embellished with gold lettering; *The Long Lost Friend, A Collection of Mysterious & Invaluable Arts & Remedies* by John George Hohman.

I whistled, my fatigue and disquiet forgotten. "Guys, I think we've found what we were looking for."

Dale picked the book up, blew the dust from its cover, and turned to first page. He squinted at the tiny lettering.

"Nineteen Sixteen; older than I am. This thing would probably fetch a pretty penny on eBay. And it's even signed by the man himself."

He held it up. Nelson LeHorn's signature was scribbled in the upper margin. The handwriting was the same. I realized now that it was also the same handwriting on the charm we'd seen above the back door in the laundry room.

"LeHorn's spell book," Merle said. "So all we gotta do is find a charm against the satyr."

"Let me see the flashlight," Dale said.

I handed it to him, and he sat down cross-legged, and began thumbing through the book. While he was perusing it, I rifled through the other books. Some of them looked very old, others were cheap modern paperbacks; a King James version of the *Holy Bible*, *The Golden Bough* by Sir James G. Frazer, *De la Demonomanie des sorciers* by Jean Bodin and *De Praestigiis* by Johan Weyer (neither of these were in English), Aleister Crowley's *Magick In Theory and Practice*, a paperback biography of John Dee (missing its cover), several slim paperback volumes by Charles Fort, and *The Encyclopedia of Witchcraft and Demonology* by Russell Hope Robbins. At the very bottom were *Der Lang Verbogene Freund*— which looked to be *The Long Lost Friend* translated into German; *The Sixth and Seventh Books of Moses* (which was in English and purported to be based on magic and cures that Moses learned while living in the house of Pharaoh), another German translation of the same (*Sechstes Und Siebentes Buch Mosis*); a three-volume set by Albertus Magnus called *Egyptian Secrets*; something called the *Daemonolateria*; and an old ledger, the kind farmers used to record their crops and accounting in. Paging through some the books, I saw what appeared to be mystical incantations, prayers, and magic symbols.

I was confused. "Some of these are in Latin and German. Now, it's conceivable that he knew German, but if LeHorn didn't read or speak Latin, then what was he doing with them?"

"Maybe he was a collector," Cliff said.

"Or maybe they had power on their own," Merle whispered. "I wouldn't fuck with them, if I were you, Adam."

Shrugging, I picked up the hardcover of *The Golden Bough* and flipped through it. It smelled musty, and the edges of the pages were yellow with age, but otherwise it was in good shape. I came across an underlined segment dealing with 'Ancient Deities of Vegetation As Animals'. It was hard to read (Dale still had the flashlight), but sure enough, the passage concerned Satyrs and other goat and horse-like creatures. I scanned a few paragraphs. It didn't tell us anything new, and I put the book back down.

Dale had better luck. "Listen to this. You know the writing on the outside of the steam trunk? We were right about the second part. *The Long Lost Friend* describes it as a remedy for worms and insects. The first part, that begins with 'Ito,' is supposed to protect houses and property against theft."

"And what about the 'Sator' bit?" Merle asked. "What's that?"

Dale turned the page. "Didn't have anything to do with satyrs, apparently. Says here it's a charm to extinguish fire without water. I'm guessing that LeHorn wanted to protect these books. So he put them in the trunk and covered it with charms."

I picked up the ledger. It was a hardcover, with lined, white sheets of paper, and a sewn-binding; just like you'd find in a stationery store. I opened it near the back. The pages were filled with cramped handwriting—a man's. I squinted at the dates, and realized it wasn't just a ledger after all.

My heart beat faster.

"Or maybe he wanted to protect this."

"What is it?" Dale asked. "What did you find?"

I grabbed the flashlight from him and shined it on the book, letting them see.

"Nelson LeHorn's journal."

The attic grew even darker. Outside, the wind picked up, whistling through the cracks in the house. Inside, we slid closer to each other without really thinking about it. Something rustled behind the walls, and I told myself it was just a mouse.

Turning to the last few pages, I began to read out loud.

THIRTEEN

March 01, 1985

Changed the spark plugs in the tractor today and now my hands and fingers hurt. Arthritis, I reckon. I'm no spring chicken anymore. Spring. Spring chicken. Spring Fever. Got spring on my mind. It ain't till later this month, and even then, I've seen snow in April and even May some years, but it feels like spring today.

It may feel like spring outside, but inside this house, it's still winter. My wife and children think me a fool. They don't love me no more, and I feel cold. They say they do. They still mouth the words; give me a peck on the cheek. But it's in their stares. When they look at me, sometimes it feels like a blizzard. Maybe it's cause we've grown away from God, or grown away from each other. I don't know. All I know is it makes me feel like crying.

Will make me a remedy for the arthritis later. Need a quart of unslacked lime, two quarts of water, a pint of flaxseed oil, and a little lard. Mix it all up and apply it and I'll be right as rain again.

Wish I could remedy our family just as easy.

March 03, 1985

Arthritis feels much better. Was cutting brush today, down near the hollow, and saw something mighty strange. There was an old elm tree with a knot about halfway up the trunk, right about level with my head. The knot looked like a face. Nature's art, I reckon. Reminded me of the one they call the Green Man, who there are pictures of in some of my other books. It stared at me and I stared back. Felt like it was seeing inside of me.

The face in the tree looked sad.

Patricia and the kids were grumpy tonight. Went outside to smoke my pipe, but in truth, I really just wanted to be away from them all. Don't like the way they make me feel. I feel like the tree.

I wonder if it cries too, when nobody's looking?

March 04, 1985

Saw a groundhog out in the field today. Reckon he was a little late for Groundhog Day. Had his summer coat already, which ain't normal. That don't usually show up until May. The creek down in the hollow is running slow, almost a trickle, but it ain't dammed up anywhere. The air feels funny. And that face in the tree is gone; or else I had the wrong tree when I went back to look today. It up and vanished. Sometimes I wish I could do that, but I've got my responsibilities.

March 06, 1985

Went to the feed mill over in Seven Valleys today, to pick up some grain. It was near lunchtime, and the workers were all piling out the door to go eat. Suddenly, somebody yells 'Mad dog', and I see a huge Doberman tearing straight toward us with froth coming out of its mouth. It's growling and racing at us, and there was nowhere to run because the men were still blocking the door. So I stepped between them and the dog, and said the words from the book, 'Dog, hold thy nose to the ground, God has made me and thee, hound.' Then I made three crosses at it and stared it in the eye. The dog quit frothing and sat down on his rear end and wagged his tail. Old Man Wellman, who knew what I was about and knows the way of powwow, wanted to take him home for his grandkids, but Paul Melniczek, who owns the mill, called Animal Control and they took the dog away. I reckon they'll put it to sleep, which is a shame. Poor thing. Would have liked to see it come to a better end. Dogs are close to God.

March 07, 1985

Matty got in trouble again at school. Caught him smoking out back behind the woodshop, and he gave the teacher a hard time and talked back when they took him to the principal's office. They gave him ten days of in-school detention. I told the principal they ought to just tan his hide. She said they can't do that no more on account of the lawyers. Don't know what to do with that boy. Ain't got a lick of sense. All he does, when I don't have him working around the farm, is sit up in his room and play Atari and listen to that music. The Devil's in it, I can tell. Songs with names like "Number of the Beast" and "Shout At the Devil." Heavy metal, they call it. Some of the singers look like women. Wear more makeup than a woman, too. I ought to make him throw them out. Patricia says I'm too hard on the boy, but I'm starting to think I ain't been hard enough. She coddles him. Coddles them all.

You know what she wants to get? Cable television! Imagine, paying for TV when you can get it for free right out of the air. She says the kid's friends all have it, and we should to. I put my foot down and said no. We can't afford a new combine or a roof for the chicken house. How are we to pay for television?

That stuff is a fad, anyway. In ten years, nobody will still have cable. It will be like those pet rocks and eight-track players. I remember when the kids all wanted eight-track players and I told them we couldn't afford it. Now they never even bring it up, because nobody listens to those eight-track tapes anymore.

Nothing good on TV no how.

March 08, 1985

Luke Jones come by the house today. Said his cattle keep getting out and he can't afford to put up a new fence, on account of he owes back taxes to the government. He says it's all Reagan's fault, but I'm of a mind he'd owe no matter who was in office. I told him to pull out three bunches of their hair, one from between the horns, one from the middle of their back, and one near the tail, and mix the hair in with their feed. The Book says that will make them return to the same place.

March 10, 1985
Got me a German copy of the Book at an estate auction over in Lancaster today. Picked up a skid of bricks too, for less than five dollars. I'll use them to shore up the retaining wall. The German translation cost a bit more, but was still a steal. Looking through it now, as I write this. I reckon it pretty much matches up to my English copy. Can't read it, but it's nice to have. It's important that things like this not get lost through time. Besides, I can't read Latin neither, but those other books written in it have come in handy. Been able to use the drawings and sigils out of them and such.

It was very hot today, hotter than normal for this time of year. Means it's going to be a dry season. There's a drought coming this summer. Squirrels and groundhogs have their summer coats already (I saw another one today) and the spiders are making their webs low to the ground. The creek in the hollow is almost dried up. These are bad signs. A bad season's coming.

March 11, 1985
Had a fight with the wife tonight. That woman tests me. Says I don't fancy her no more because we don't make love. She never used to talk like that. It's these damn talk shows she watches, like that Phil Donahue, and those magazines she reads. Anyway, Patricia said she'd go get it somewhere else if I didn't give it to her. I told her go ahead, long as it meant I could get some sleep.

She won't though, and I'm glad for that. I love her, but I'm just too tired.

Still warm outside. Spring has come early. No denying it now. Gnats are out already, swarming around in little clouds. Another bad sign.

March 13, 1985
The warm spell continues unbroken. I've seen the signs, all of them bad. Drought coming this summer for sure, unless I do something to head it off. First day of spring is next week. Perfect time to work some powwow. Only thing is; I can't

use the Book. Will have to turn to one of the other books, the Daemonolateria, to do it right. I don't like fooling with that one, but there's no other way. The Long Lost Friend don't provide for this.

The Daemonolateria is in Latin. Wish I could read it. There's a fella out in Hanover named Saul O'Connor that can help me translate the parts I need. He's aided me before, when it suited his purpose. Hell, he's the one who gave me the Daemonolateria in the first place, on account of you're supposed to make one for yourself, and I didn't know how, and he needed money. He's a bad one, but I've got no choice but to seek his help again. If the crops fail this summer, we'll be ruined. I don't know how to do anything else and I'd hate to see this land get sold to the developers. The girls want to go to college. Can't let this harvest fail.

Patricia's been sleeping on the couch the last few nights. She ain't happy and I don't know how to make her happy anymore. Yesterday, I brought her some flowers that I picked down in the hollow, first flowers of spring, blue and yellow. Real pretty, just like her. I give them to her while she was doing dishes. She just grunted and then put them in a vase. I think she forgot about them already. Tried making love to her last night, before she went down to the couch. She didn't make a sound, barely moved. I don't think she enjoyed it.

I'll win her over again, just as soon as I take care of this planting season.

Need to study and meditate until the equinox. Will have to fast too, as according to what O'Connor said was written.

Don't have much of an appetite these days, no how.

March 17, 1985

Hungry and weak. Made myself some tea from the inner bark of a birch tree, and that's remedied the weakness in my limbs some. Would do more, but I can't. Have to observe the fast. Can't put nothing else into my body, or it could ruin the powwow. Still, I don't feel good. Been having headaches all the time, and been grumping at Patricia and the kids, too.

They know some of what's going on, but not all. The kids

don't take an interest in powwow and Patricia's forgotten a lot of it from when she was younger. My daddy done it and her mother did too. That's how we met. Our families worked it together on occasion. Patricia used to practice. She was a novice, but she still believed. But now she says I ought to stop it. She don't believe no more. Don't observe the rituals. Don't practice. Don't do much of anything anymore. Hasn't told me she loves me in a long time, and sometimes a man likes to hear that. Doesn't laugh anymore, unless it's to laugh at me. I feel alone, even in my own house with my own family. That ain't how a man's supposed to feel in his home.

If only they knew I was doing this for them. For all of us. The old ways are the best ways, and in another generation, I wonder who will do it when I'm gone? Maybe I'm the last one in these parts. I've heard tell of an old fella down south, a Korean War vet. Folks call him Silver John. Walks the Appalachians with a silver-stringed guitar and works some really strong powwow. Hear tell he's got a real nice singing voice, too. But he's getting up there in age, and I don't think he's ever made it this far north. Sticks below the Mason-Dixon. And there was an old Amish fella, but he passed on five years ago. And there was that kid, Levi Stolzfus, and his Daddy, but the boy run off on account of what happened to that girl, and his Daddy... Well, now, here in Central Pennsylvania, it's just O'Connor and me.

O'Connor is a bad one, no mistake. Wish that I could read Latin; I wouldn't give him the time of day. But I can't, so I'm stuck with him. Ain't nobody else in these parts that can fool with the Daemonolateria, except for old Rehmeyer, and he's been dead nigh on fifty years. My Daddy spoke highly of him. But he got himself murdered by that Blymire fella. Killed Rehmeyer for his copy of the Book, but it burned up with him.

That will never happen to me. When I pass on to the Lord's house, I'd like to be surrounded by Patricia and the kids. Even if they don't love me no more. I'd still like their faces to be the last things I'd see. Maybe then, I'd see some love.

O'Connor's schooling me. Been learning my lines and

what to draw on the ground, and what to bring. I aim to call up a minion of Nodens, who O'Connor says is the father of Pan. That ain't the way I read it in other books, but O'Connor says a lot of the history books are wrong. Nodens is one of the Thirteen, those who weren't angels or demons, but something else—something that exists outside of Heaven and Hell, in another place that connects those realms to this world. It's called the Labyrinth. O'Connor says that Nodens' minions can bless the planting and make sure we have a good crop this summer, drought or not. O'Connor also says we have to be careful, or else we could bring forth one of the others, one of the Thirteen themselves, rather than a minion, and that would be bad for all. I dare say it would. Don't want to mess with them.

O'Connor says you ain't supposed to say Nodens' name out loud, but he didn't say nothing about writing it, so I reckon I'm okay.

The Farmer's Almanac says that March 20, at 11:10am is when spring starts. I'll cast the spell then, and everything will be okay, long as I keep my wits about me.

March 19, 1985
Tomorrow is the day. I can hardly sleep. Feel excited, like I haven't in a long time. Things will be okay. Patricia come upstairs and slept beside me tonight. After she fell asleep, I lay there and held her, listened to her breathing and smelled her hair, and I was happy.

I still love her. Now more than ever. Just wish she felt the same. Maybe she will after I've saved the day.

March 21, 1985
O'Connor lied. He tricked me. At least, I think he did. Something went wrong. The words didn't work. I couldn't send it back. And now I've done a terrible thing. I've brought something bad into this world. It's out there now, on the loose. In the hollow.

Patricia and the girls are out there with it. And what I saw . . . what they were doing.

No, can't write about it. Not yet.

Something's gotten inside the trees. They're different now. Dark. They're moving by themselves and I hear them whispering to each other on the wind. Except that there's no breeze.

There are faces in the trees. Lots of faces. And these faces don't look sad. They look angry.

March 22?

I don't know. Can't remember what day this is. Maybe it's only been a few hours or maybe it's been days. I don't know. I'm drunk. Haven't let a drop of liquor pass my lips in almost thirty years, but I'm drunk now. Or trying to be, anyway. Not having much luck, because I'm still awake. Feel light-headed. Woozy. But it's not enough. I need to feel numb. Dead. Need to not think. And when I close my eyes, I don't want to see.

O'Connor's dead. I don't know where to start, so I reckon that I might as well start with that. Saw it on the news this morning. They found him in his backyard, all burned up and lying next to a burn barrel. There was still some trash on fire inside of it. Sounds to me like he was working some powwow.

In his house, they found a dead dog□and a boy. Both of them had been carved up. Butchered. Sliced open like a pair of fish; symbols cut into their flesh. Guts missing. O'Connor had been using them in rituals. Cops don't know that, but I do. I do now. And I know what kind, too. He was trying to go somewhere else. Trying to open a door to a place no door should lead to. Damn fool!

All three, O'Connor, the boy, and the dog; were covered with some kind of weird fungus. Don't know what that's all about. Neither does the law. Coroner's report hasn't come out yet. News didn't say they'd found his books, so I reckon O'Connor must have squirreled them away somewhere, like I do. If they find them, they should burn them. Some things just shouldn't be.

He always said he wanted to find doorways to other worlds, and go through them. Now, I reckon he has. I wonder what he saw in the flames inside that burn barrel? Did he see the world he expected to see on the other side?

I found a doorway to another world, too, right down yonder in the hollow. I didn't go through it. But something else come through, into our world. Something that walks around on hoofed feet and plays the pipes of Pan.

It didn't come alone, either. Other things come through with it, and they've gotten inside the trees. I'm thinking they could be Elilum, which I've read about in my books. They are kin to Legion, I think, and led by a demon named Ab, who's another one of the Thirteen. They possess plants. But I don't know for sure if that's what they are, and I can't do anything about them without knowing their name. Names are power. If you know something's name, then you can bind it or banish it. Naming gives you control. But if you don't know its name, or if you take a guess and wind up calling it by the wrong name, then you can make things worse.

The hollow ain't safe no more. And if it spreads to the rest of the woods, then there's no help for anyone.

I don't know the names of what's gotten into the trees, but I know the name of the other thing. Hylinus. I looked the name up in my books, but couldn't find it. Ain't no mention of him. But that must be his name, because that's what Patricia called it, while she was . . .

I need another drink.

Patricia.

We went down to the hollow that morning just after the kids caught the bus for school. Matty was sleeping over at a friend's house for a few nights (the Pastor's kid—I thought that might straighten him out a bit.) The girls would be back in time for dinner. That gave us plenty of time for what needed to be done. In truth, I'd reckoned to have it finished before noon. 11:10 was the appointed time, when everything had to align.

Even though we'd been alright the night before, and I thought maybe things were changing again, Patricia groused the whole way to the hollow, making fun of me, making fun of the old ways. I reminded her that her own folks believed in these ways, and that she'd believed too, once. She said something mean and we didn't talk after that. But she come along just the same. On the way, I noticed the spring was all dried up now, too.

We got to the clearing. I was weak and tired, and hadn't had any food, on account of the fasting for preparation. Patricia hadn't fasted but I didn't need her for the actual ritual, so I figured it would be okay. I just needed her help setting things up.

I put our things down in the middle of the clearing. A magician's tools; what was needed for this particular powwow. A coffee can filled with salt and powdered limestone; three strands of goat hair bound together with a single human hair (my own); two new candles, made of beeswax from our own hives and mixed in the moonlight with the menstrual blood of a virgin (I nipped one of Gina's tampons from the garbage pail in the bathroom); a bone, found by accident while walking through the forest (because, according to O'Connor, the book said if I was purposely looking for it, the bone wouldn't be no good. My eyes had to settle on it by accident); a willow branch, one that had been pointing to the sunrise and was cut in one swoop after winter's thaw; pine shavings and sage sprigs to burn; a small copper urn to burn them in; and olive oil.

We raked the leaves clear. Then we poured the lime and salt on the ground, copying the sigils O'Connor told me to use. I used the willow branch to draw them into the soil. O'Connor was specific about that. Nothing else would do. It took a couple hours, getting everything just so, dotting our i's and crossing our t's. Then we were ready.

I placed a drop of oil on my forehead, and another on Patricia's. I told her to stay out of the circle. I made sure I was clear of it, too. Then I lit the sage and pine shavings and waited for the smoke to build. When it had, I picked up the bone and began chanting the words, just as O'Connor had told me they were pronounced. My tongue had a fit trying to say them. Twisted itself into knots almost.

The hollow grew dark, but when I looked up, there weren't no clouds over the sun. The powwow was working. I lit the candle and put it at one end of the circle. Then, while saying the rest of the words, I had Patricia throw the goat hair into the urn. It stank as it burned. But then, I smelled something else. The inside of a barn. A horse, sweating after a run, or a sidewalk after a thunderstorm. How your bedroom smells after you've been with your wife.

It smelled animal.

I kept up with the words, talking faster and louder. Waved the bone around. The smoke got thicker. Didn't seem like such a little fire could make so much smoke, but that's the way of it. There was no wind, but the smoke drifted towards the circle, and seemed to swirl around in the middle of it, like a cloud.

The hollow got real still. Even Patricia was quiet. She watched. Licked her lips. She looked excited and I reckoned that maybe she was remembering how good this could be, when it was working right. Maybe things would be okay after all.

The darkness went away, and at the same time, the smoke seemed to spread out like tentacles or snakes maybe, and it was sucked up into the trees. Where it had been, there in the center of the circle, stood a wood spirit. I'd seen pictures of them before, and The Golden Bough talks about them a bit. Some folks call them Satyrs. That's what we'd caught. A satyr. It looked at me like it wanted to kill me. No doubt it would have, if it could have gotten out of the circle. Then it noticed Patricia, and its face softened. I happened to look between its legs, because there weren't no real way to ignore what was there. I dare say Patricia had an effect on it. The satyr stepped towards her, and then shrank back with a growl when it hit the boundary.

"You can't pass the circle," I told it.

The satyr's voice was deep, and sounded like a goat's. "I was asleep. I was—elsewhere. Who calls?"

"I do." I tried to keep the fear out of my voice. "And you are bound, as you can see."

It snorted. Looked down at the circle. "By whose name do you bind me?"

O'Connor hadn't covered this with me, so I switched to what I knew from the Book.

"Our Lord and Savior, Jesus Christ," I said. "By his blood

do I bind thee, and by Matthew, Mark, Luke, and John; and by my name, Nelson Amos LeHorn."

"Why am I summoned?"

"Hard times is coming for my farm. I command you to bless this planting season, and make it fruitful and bountiful."

"Only this, and nothing more?"

I nodded. "Only that, and then I'll release you back from where you came. You can go back to sleep."

"Very well."

The satyr raised his hand to his lips, and it was then that I noticed he had a pipe. He started to play, and the music was beautiful. I reckoned this was how he worked his blessing. Played a song and the drought wouldn't happen. I stood there, kind of swaying to the music. Something started happening down below in my pants, something better suited for the bedroom. Embarrassed, I looked over at Patricia and saw she was feeling it, too. She took a step forward and licked her lips.

The satyr stopped his playing. "Come."

He motioned to her. She took another step. I started to shout, but it was too late. Her right foot broke the circle. Smudged the salt and lime. There was a flash of bright light as the barrier went down. The satyr moved fast as lightning. He grabbed Patricia, bent her over, tore off her clothes, and . . .

Need another drink. Bottle is getting low. Be empty soon. That's okay. Got some cough syrup around here somewhere. I can drink that.

She enjoyed it. It took her right there, in the circle. No foreplay. Just like the horses and cows do, out in the field. He slid into her with a grunt and she slammed her hips back to meet him. They rutted in the middle of the hollow, right there in the dirt, in the middle of the summoning circle, and Patricia smiled at me while they did it. Blood was running down her thighs, but she didn't seem to mind. I thought I might be sick, but I wasn't.

It looked at me. "Will you join us? Will you celebrate the season?"

I dare say I wouldn't. I tried then to send it back, using the words from the Daemonolateria, just like O'Connor had told me to do, but it was no good. Nothing happened. O'Connor give me the wrong words. The satyr must have realized what I was about because it laughed. Then, it lay my wife down on the ground and stepped towards me. Stepped out of the circle. Dropped the pipe and reached for me. Its breath stank like a pigsty. Claws tore into my skin, right above my heart, and drew blood. The wound burned.

I stepped back and hit it with the sign of the cross. Said, "Dullx, ix, ux. Yea, you can't come over Pontio; Pontio is above Pilato." The Book says that's to prevent wicked or malicious persons from doing you an injury, and it's always worked for me before. But it didn't this time, maybe because that thing weren't no person. The spell had no effect. The satyr kept coming, and I kept walking backward, staying out of reach.

Tree limbs rustled above me, and at the time, I didn't think nothing of it, but now I know. They were waking up.

Patricia lay there on the ground, her legs spread out and her womanhood showing. I'd loved that place. Watched my children be born from it. Now, I almost didn't recognize it. She looked ruined, and the satisfied expression on her face turned my stomach. Wanted to scream, but instead, I kept trying. Using what I'd memorized from the Book, I tried to bind it, charm it, turn it, and slow it. I used every prayer, spell, and benediction I could think of, but nothing worked. The satyr kept coming at me. I hollered at Patricia to run, but she just laughed at me. Said she'd found someone who could finally satisfy her. That hurt in ways I never imagined. The whole time she said it, she was playing with herself. Both hands. Her fingers were wet and red.

When I reached the edge of the hollow, I'd gotten a good lead on the satyr. It hung back, then turned and loped off to my wife. Reckon it figured on getting me later. It had other things on its mind, and Patricia seemed willing enough. I thought about going after it, but that was foolish. It pained me to leave her, but there was no help for it. I run back to the house instead.

First thing I did was stop the bleeding. I'd lost a good bit. Felt woozy. Took four different charms from the Book before

I could get the blood flow stopped. Even then, my skin still burned. Went to the medicine cabinet and poured peroxide over the wound. Watched the bubbles and tried not to pass out. Felt a little better after that, so then I charmed the house against evil spirits and all manner of witchcraft. Took a white piece of paper, as the Book says to do, and wrote:

I.
N. I. R.
I.
SANCTUS SPIRITUS
I.
N. I. R.
I.

That's the only Latin I know; what's in the Book, and what O'Connor give me. Wish I knew more. Said the benediction over the paper, "All this be guarded, here in time, and there in eternity. Amen." Then I taped the paper up over the front door and made another one for the back door. That way, the satyr couldn't get in the house. All I had to do was get Patricia back inside. It was pretty plain that she was under its spell. Get her back here to the house, where that thing couldn't tread, I could undo that charm.

It got into my head that silver might hurt it. Silver's good for hurting things of that kin. But I didn't have no silver bullets and no time to make them, either. Had a silver knife that I used in some powwows, and I tucked that down into my belt. Then I went back to the hollow.

The trees kept me out. They'd grown closer together, while I was gone, and they made a wall around the hollow with their trunks. Each time I tried to get between them, they'd groan, and their limbs would grasp at me, or fall off, aimed at my head. I tried several charms from the Book, but they weren't no good. Whatever was inside those trees was because of the Daemonolateria, and spells from the Book were useless against them. I needed their names, and their banishing rituals.

I had both, but they were in Latin.

I hollered for Patricia, but she didn't answer me. All afternoon, I edged my way around that hollow, and the trees kept me out. Sometimes, I'd hear my wife inside, laughing with that thing, and making other sounds that I don't want to write about. Sounds she ain't never made with me in all our years of marriage. She cried out its name over and over again. Hylinus. That's what she called it.

Listening to them, I got angrier and angrier. Tried to shove my way through the tree line, but the branches tore at me, raking my skin. I stabbed one with the knife. The blade sank into the trunk and the whole tree started shaking something fierce. I reckon it didn't like the silver too much. There was a sound like the wind was screaming and then the tree was still. The rest of them started grabbing at me worse. I tugged on the knife hilt but it was stuck fast. I tore away from the branches and went stumbling back out again.

I was beside myself. Judging by the sun, the girls would be home from school soon. I didn't know what to do next. Thought about calling the police, thought about calling my neighbors, thought about burning the whole damn woods down. Eventually, I reckoned on my chainsaw. That would even things up a bit. Silver seemed to have done good on them that was inside the trees, and I wished I had silver teeth on the chain. But still, the chainsaw would even the odds.

While I . . .

Can't write about it yet. I'm tuckered out. Tired. Been awake a long time and my fingers are starting to hurt from holding this pen. Later. I'll write about it later.

Later

Passed out for a bit. Liquor must have done its work after all. My head hurts. Somebody is screaming upstairs. Not sure who. Matty will probably be home soon. Phone's been ringing but I ain't answered it.

While I walked back to the farm and went to the woodshed, the school bus must have dropped Claudia and Gina off at the end of the lane. Never heard it, but I reckon that's what happened. The girls come home, and didn't find us in the house.

If they hollered for us, I never heard them. The woodshed sits back a ways; down between the corn crib and the outhouse that we don't use no more, but still, I should have heard them. So maybe they didn't holler. I got no way of knowing what happened next. What went through their minds, while I was out in the woodshed, sharpening the teeth and oiling up the chain, and making sure the saw had gas? Did they decide to go for a walk, or maybe went to look for their Ma? I don't know.

I fired up the chainsaw, made sure it run good enough, and then shut it off again. Stepped outside the woodshed and that's when I heard the music. It affected me down below again, and I was ashamed. It was the satyr, playing on his pipe. I ran for the hollow. The chainsaw slowed me down some. When I was younger, it wouldn't have been no problem, but now, I was out of breath and sore and scared for my wife.

I crested the hill and down there, near the tree line, was the satyr. It was dancing around and piping away, and my daughters were following after it. They were . . . I feel sick. They were taking their clothes off. Just dropping them on the ground. I shouted but they paid me no mind. The satyr slipped between the trees, back into the hollow. So did Claudia and Gina. I run after them, and fired up the chainsaw. Drowned out that damned music.

My girls. I remember when each of them was born, Claudia right here at home and Gina at York Memorial. They were both so darned pretty, just like their mother. Claudia curled her little fist around my finger and I almost cried. And Gina, she smiled at me. Nurse said it was gas, but I know. A father knows.

The tree branches closed in front of me and I laid into them. Swung the saw upward. Tore through them. The trees, they screamed. I was grinning. Said me a charm from the book and kept swinging the saw. Chain bit wood. Wood hit the ground. Trees got out of my way. But then, there was a sharp pain in my leg. I looked down and a limb had punched through my calf. Just a twig, but it had speared me, sticking clean through the flesh. Reached down with one hand and snapped the twig off, and I'm a fool for that very reason. Because when I did, a branch whipped out and yanked that chainsaw away from me. Then it brought it around and tried to cut my head off. I ducked, screamed, and backed away. My hand brushed up against the bark of another tree, and it bit me. I turned and saw a face, just as clear as day, and my fingers were in its mouth. Bit them down to the bone, and if I hadn't yanked them free, it would have bit them clean off. The branches grabbed at me, trying to hold me in place as the chainsaw swung towards me again. I managed to shake them, and jumped back out of the hollow.

I stood there, panting. The trees rustled, but I was out of their range. They couldn't move. Couldn't leave the hollow, at least not yet. The claw marks on my shoulder were bleeding again, and that weren't a good sign. The charm should have took hold and healed it, but it hadn't. The Book had failed me. The Lord had failed me. And I had failed my family because of it.

Weren't no help coming from God, so I reckoned I'd have to turn to another.

And I did. Stumbled home, bleeding and crying and cursing God. Snot bubbled out of my nose and the gnats crowded my face, trying to get at it. Bandaged up my wounds as best I could, and then turned to my books. First one I pulled out was The Long Lost Friend, and I threw it across the room. Opened the Daemonolateria, and tried to make sense of things. Tried to understand what the spells were for by looking at the pictures and diagrams. Looked at other books, too. Anything what had to do with satyrs or wood spirits or things of nature. And as the sun went down, I got me a plan.

First thing I did was load every bag of lime I had onto the wagon. It was hot, heavy work, and I did it like I was twenty years younger. Then I hitched the tractor up to it, and made sure the tractor had gas. Wouldn't do to run out halfway through this. Gathered all the other things I thought I'd need, the ingredients to make it work, as best I could tell from the pictures. Then I wrote in this journal and studied, studied harder than I ever have in my life. Prayed to the Lord, asked His forgiveness for the things I'd said, explained that I was hurt and scared for my wife and daughters, asked Him for His strength and guidance. But the Lord was silent. Didn't feel His presence the way I could sometimes, assuring me when things got tough, like in the old Footprints poem. He was not dwelling in my house or in my heart. Can't say much as I blame Him, on account of who I was going to call upon to save my family.

When things were ready, I climbed onboard the tractor, turned on the headlights, and drove down to the hollow. It was dark outside, couple hours after nightfall, but the hollow was darker than the rest. The headlights didn't seem to cut through it, like the darkness was swallowing them up.

Deep inside the forest, I heard the pipes, and Patricia and the girls. Tried to ignore them, but I couldn't. Started shaking. They were in there with that thing, and I knew what they were doing. My wife. My daughters. My two little girls. My babies.

When I'd got myself under control, I climbed down off the tractor and grabbed the first bag of lime. Cut the top open with my pocketknife and then started spreading it in a line around the hollow. Made sure I stayed out of reach of the tree limbs. They grabbed at me the whole time, but I was too smart for them. The treetops rustled and whispered, swaying back and forth. The sounds kept coming from the center of the woods. Animal sounds, but they were made by my family.

Took most of the night but I made a circle around the entire hollow. Did the symbols and everything, just like I'd seen in the book. I said the words by what they call phonetically. Don't know if I got them right or not, but since I don't read Latin, I'll just have to hope. If I done right, then the things what are inside the trees can't spread to the rest of the forest.

But that was just the first part. While looking at the books, I'd come across a spell that I thought was supposed to petrify wood. At least, that's how it looked. I cursed O'Connor for up and getting himself killed, and wished I knew for sure, but I didn't. Once the circle was finished, I stood on the outside and said the words as best I could, hoping I was sounding them out right. Then I stepped back and held my breath. Like someone had flipped a switch, the sounds stopped. The trees didn't turn into wood, but they stopped moving. The pipes fell silent, and there were no more moans or sighs. Everything got real quiet.

I reckoned it had worked good enough.

And then the screaming started. Patricia first, then the girls, and it all sort of blended together. I stood outside the circle and hollered for them, and after a minute, they answered me. They come out of the hollow, stepping over the circle without paying it no mind. I wasn't worried about them breaking it. The first part of the spell I'd worked was only supposed to affect the things from another plane.

Patricia and the girls looked like they'd stepped off a battlefield; like those fellas that come back from Vietnam. Shellshocked, they call it. They were naked, and all scratched up. There were twigs and leaves in their hair and stuck to their backs and behinds. The satyr had done the same thing to the girls that he'd done to Patricia. I took one look at the blood on their legs and couldn't look no more. Threw up next to the tractor and it burned my throat. Didn't think I'd ever stop shaking.

They couldn't remember any of what happened. Had amnesia or something. Patricia accused me, thought it was part of the powwow we'd worked that morning. She got the girls pretty worked up with her talk. I got them all calmed down as best I could and then loaded them into the wagon and drove them all home. It took about five minutes. All three of them were asleep before we got back. They slept till this morning.

But not me. When the sun come back up, I went back to the hollow. Said my prayers and drew a sigil on my forehead, but I didn't need them. Whatever was in that forest was dead. The trees was just trees again, and when I stepped in between them, they didn't attack me.

In the center of the hollow, I found Hylinus. He'd been turned to stone, so I reckon the second part of the spell worked after all. I knocked on him with my fist (the one I'd bandaged after the tree tried to bite it off) and it hurt. He was solid. Petrified. Even down there between his legs. Hard stone.

There was one last thing to do, and I did it. Found a picture in one of my history books. It's all in Latin, but the caption translated it. It was a marker, a totem to Nodens, one of the Thirteen, who I'd called upon to help me end this. The marker had been discovered by a scientist fella named Machen. I didn't understand it all, but making a totem of my own was something I reckoned I should do, just to make double sure. The caption give me enough information to know where my name went and where Nodens' name was supposed to be. I remembered that O'Connor had said we weren't supposed to say Nodens' name out loud. I'd written it earlier in this here journal, and maybe that's when the badness started. So rather than carving his name, I used the Labyrinth instead. He's the god of it, so I reckoned it would work. Figured as long as I copied the rest just like in the book, I'd be okay. I carved it into one of my stone property markers and then I put it in the center of the hollow, right next to the satyr. Here are the words I engraved on it.

DEVOMLABYRINTHI
NLEHORNPOSSVIT
PROPTERNVPTIAS
QUASVIDITSVBVMRA

After I'd put up the totem, I stepped back and looked at my handiwork. I was sweating something fierce but things soon cooled off. The wind picked up and thunder come rolling in over the hills. Sure enough, it started to rain. I was bone tired and I couldn't even feel the drops on my skin.

When I come back home, Patricia and the girls had woken up. They were scared, and whatever poison that thing put into them had gotten into their heads. Patricia locked the three of them up in the attic. She was afraid I'd try to hurt them. Said I'd done something terrible to them down in those woods. When I tried to get in, she threatened to kill me. I thought maybe it was some leftover influence from the satyr. Maybe Hylinus was still alive inside that stone. Reckoned I should do something about that.

I took a sledgehammer down to the hollow. Reckoned if

I smashed him to bits maybe his hold over them would be broken. Walked through the rain. Thunder and lightning was crashing all over the place, but I paid it no mind. Didn't even notice the rain had washed the circle away until it was too late. The lime and salt were just blurry smudges, spread out all over the ground.

The satyr was gone. Escaped, even as a statue. My marker was gone, too. And the trees inside the hollow were different trees. The whole hollow had moved. Shifted. Escaped. Gone somewhere else. I don't know where. Maybe from wherever they first come from, or maybe just to another part of the forest. They hid from me.

They're screaming upstairs again. Gonna go up and try to talk to them. I love my wife. I love my family. I just want things to be normal again. I want us to be a happy family. Everything I done, I did for them. If I can make them see that, then maybe we can get through this.

I want them to love me the way they used to.

Will write more later. Put this back in the chest with the other books, so that it stays safe.

Going up to the attic now. Try to make things right.

It's funny. I been up in that attic a million times, but those stairs have never seemed steeper than they do right now.

Lord, I'm tired.

FOURTEEN

I closed the journal. Nelson LeHorn's final words seemed to hang in the air, echoing in the darkness. My throat felt raw, and I wished I'd brought some water with me. The guys were quiet, each of them mulling over what we'd learned.

What had happened next, I wondered. What had ultimately led to Patricia LeHorn's fatal plunge from the attic window—the same attic we were sitting in now, twenty years later? The official account was Nelson had pushed her out the window. His owndaughters had testified to that. But I was beginning to question it. According to the diary, he'd loved Patricia. I almost felt sorry for him. Poor, rustic farmer, uneasy with the effect that encroaching modern life was having on his family; unable to stop its advance; at odds with the culture of the Reagan years, the era of yuppies and greed and heavy metal and video games, the beginning of the postmodern techno-sex revolution. He'd loved his wife, would have done anything to make her happy—to save their marriage. It didn't seem possible that he could have written those words, and then murdered her immediately after. So what really occurred in this attic? And more importantly, what happened to LeHorn after Patricia's death? Gone before the cops arrived, and never seen again. Somewhere, in the State Police barracks in Harrisburg, or maybe hanging in the corner of a post office somewhere, was a wanted poster with Nelson LeHorn's picture on it, a picture from twenty years ago. He'd disappeared; fallen off the face of the planet. I wondered if he was even still *on* the planet. His journal had spoken of doorways to other places, other worlds. Had he gone through one of those portals, never to return, and leaving us to clean up his mess?

While I'd been reading, it had grown dark outside. No light came through the cracks in the plywood around the attic window, and I wondered just how long we'd been up there. Merle sat silently, his head in his hands. Dale looked thoughtful. Cliff smoked and said nothing. None of them seemed to notice the change in lighting.

"So," Dale whispered. "Now we know."

"Yeah," I agreed. "We do indeed."

Merle shifted the rifle on his lap. "I remember Saul O'Connor. It was all over the papers when they discovered that kid in his house. Think I might still have a copy of *The Evening Sun* with that headline."

"Yeah, I remember that, too." Cliff sucked his cigarette down to the filter and sighed. "So it really is true. All of it. The goat man ain't a guy in a suit."

"You're a believer now?" Merle asked.

Cliff shrugged. "That was pretty convincing, dude. He wrote that shit twenty years ago, but a lot of it matches up with what you guys have been saying. The pipes. The stone. Hylinus—it's the same. . .thing. It got his wife and daughters just like it has Shelly, Leslie, Shannon, and the Wallace woman. Can't believe I'm saying it, but I'm sold on the idea."

Merle clapped him on the shoulder. "Glad to have you aboard."

"Well," Dale said, "now that we're all on the same page, what do we do? I hate to say it, but despite everything in that journal, we still don't have the proof we need to convince Ramirez we're not crazy."

"No," I agreed, "but at least we really know what we're up against. We're not guessing anymore. LeHorn managed to trap the trees in the hollow and turn Hylinus into stone. But then the rain came and washed away his magic circle before he could come up with a more permanent solution, and the trees got loose. Somehow, they moved the actual hollow into the forest; marker and everything."

"But the hollow is still outside," Cliff said. "We saw it when we drove in. How can it be in two places at the same time?"

"Different trees," Merle suggested. "LeHorn said a lot in there about things moving from one world to the next. What if these things replaced themselves with other trees?"

"You mean they teleported to another part of the woods? Exchanged places with regular trees?"

"Why not?" Merle stood up and brushed off the seat of his pants. "It's no more unrealistic than any of this other stuff."

Cliff shrugged. "You got a point."

I continued. "So all this time, they hid inside the forest, safe from prying eyes. Occasionally, they killed somebody. That would account for some of the people who have disappeared over the years. But for the most part, they stayed in hiding. Maybe they move around during hunting season, when the woods are full, so they won't be discovered. Until Shelly came along and woke the satyr up by—well, we already know how she woke it up."

Cliff nodded. "The blow job."

"But why Shelly?" Dale asked. "And why now? It just doesn't make any sense."

"I don't know," I admitted. "Maybe the time was right. Maybe the stars were aligned and all that. Could be the spell wore off after two decades. I heard the pipes before Hylinus came back to life. Maybe he sent out a psychic summons or something like that."

I thought about my own encounter in high school, when Becky Schrum and I had heard something in the woods. I had a good idea now what it was, and how incredibly lucky we'd been. Then something else occurred to me, something terrible. What if it had been our own teenage lust that had actually awoken him? What if it was me that had set this whole thing in motion, back then?

Merle shook his head. "Seems like for every answer we get, there are still more questions."

Dale stood up, wincing as his knee joints popped. He looked tired and pale. I was worried about him. Worried about us all.

"Fuck the questions," Cliff said. "We know enough. All we have to do is repeat the spell, turn the fucker back into a statue, and then smash him into tiny little satyr bits with a sledgehammer."

"Easy enough," Merle whispered.

Cliff nodded. "So what are we waiting for?"

"Do you know Latin?" Dale asked. "Because the spell is in Latin. And besides, the journal doesn't tell us which spell LeHorn actually used. There must be hundreds of them in this Daemonowhatever. It's a thick book. We could study it for the next week and still not be sure of the proper incantation. And we know what happens if you mix them up."

I got to my feet. "Silver. LeHorn's silver knife blade worked against the trees, and he seemed to think it would work against the satyr as well. I say we try that."

"Where you gonna get silver?" Cliff asked.

"Tara's got silver earrings and stuff. We can use those."

Dale nodded. "So does Claudine."

Cliff laughed. "You're gonna stab it with your wife's jewelry?"

"No," I said. "But we could drop the silver jewelry down the barrel of a gun and shoot it."

Dale shook his head. "Wouldn't work. When the bullet goes off with the jewelry in front of it, it's going to hit the silver and screw up the trajectory. You've got dissimilar metals coming into contact under high force. Not a wise combination, especially if we're facing down Hylinus."

Merle clapped his hands together in excitement. "I've got it!"

"What?" Cliff smirked. "Herpes or the crabs?"

"A shotgun," Merle said, ignoring him. "We cut open the top of shotgun shell, pull out the pellets and keep the wadding, then replace the pellets with the jewelry, seal it back up with duct tape, and load the shell into the gun. I've got a double-barreled 12-guage at home that will do the trick."

"I've got a shotgun, too," Dale said.

"Duct tape?" I was doubtful. "Wouldn't that fuck it up?"

Merle grinned. "Duct tape is a miracle of modern science. It can do anything. Seriously. Friend of mine cut his leg open with a chainsaw one time. Almost down to the bone. He bandaged it up with duct tape until he got to the hospital. And I once took off a wart with duct tape."

I winked at him. "Merle Laughman, High Priest of the Cult of Duct Tape. Let us pray."

"Hey," he said, smiling. "I'm a big believer in the stuff."

"Kind of like your own personal powwow?"

Merle paused, considering. "Yeah, I guess it is sort of like that."

"Actually," Dale said, "That's not a bad comparison. None of us knows the first thing about casting spells, but maybe we can use magic of our own against this thing. What is powwow—or any kind of magic? It's just a belief structure. Folk remedies and folk tales. Things that people once believed would heal them and protect them. Maybe we can incorporate some of our own beliefs—like Merle's duct tape. Might make for good magic."

I shrugged. "Anything's possible. What else do we have?"

"My wedding ring," Dale said. "I love Claudine, and I've never once taken this ring off my finger since the day we were married. Not even to go swimming. I was in an accident about twenty years ago, and the paramedics were going to cut it off my hand, and I wouldn't let them. I believe in what this ring represents. Hylinus went after Claudine. This gold band is my power against that happening again. It's my talisman."

I saw where he was going, and came up with some powwow of my own. "Big Steve. LeHorn said in his journal that dogs were close to God. I've always thought the same thing. Big Steve has been my rock through this entire thing, and he's just as involved as the rest of us. Maybe more. He's been in it since the beginning. I'm drawing power from my dog."

Dale and Merle nodded, looking pleased with my choice.

"And if we're using Tara and Claudine's silver jewelry," I added, "That has to be good for something, right? They've been affected by this, too."

We looked expectantly at Cliff.

He scowled. "What?"

"Come on, dude," I urged. "Merle's got a roll of magic

duct tape, Dale's got his wedding ring, and I've got the dog. You need a talisman of your own before we go up against this thing."

"This is stupid. You guys know that, right?"

"Yesterday," I reminded him, "you thought the satyr was stupid, too."

He stood up, shook a cigarette from the pack, and put it in his mouth. He clicked the lighter and once again, the darkness seemed to surround the flame. He touched it to the cigarette, inhaled, and put the lighter back in his pocket.

"These." Cliff pulled the cigarette from his mouth and held it up, the tip glowing in the darkness. "These are my magic. I always figured smokes would be the death of me. I mean, I know they're gonna give me cancer, but I don't quit. Never even really tried. They're going to kill me someday."

Dale looked puzzled. "Cigarettes are your personal powwow?"

"Yep. If the cigarettes are gonna kill me, then that means the satyr can't. So I'm safe."

I began to feel hopeful. For the first time since this whole thing had become a reality, I felt confidence—confidence in myself, in my marriage, in my friends. Nothing else mattered now. We would beat this thing.

Then the flashlight batteries died, plunging us into total darkness.

Cliff said, "Oh shit."

I shook the flashlight and banged it against my hip, but the beam did not return. As if in response, the rustling sounds in the walls suddenly increased. Something banged downstairs. The house shook slightly.

Merle gasped. "What was that?"

"Just the wind," Dale said, keeping his voice calm and steady. He stood rock still. "Knocked something over downstairs. That's all."

"And that rustling noise?" Merle whispered. "That the wind, too?"

"Just mice. Nothing to be afraid of. Still, Cliff, maybe you could get out your lighter again?"

Cliff flicked it on and the rustling sound stopped.

"Scared it off," Dale whispered.

"Okay, can we get the hell out of here now?" Merle's eyes darted around the attic nervously.

"Yeah," I said, trying to hide my own apprehension. "Let's go satyr hunting."

"Wait a minute," Dale said. "What about the trees? We haven't discussed how to deal with them."

"We do it on the way home," Cliff whined. "This lighter is getting hot, man. I'm burning my damn fingers."

"I've got stuff in my woodshop that will take care of the trees," Merle said. "Right now, I agree with Cliff."

We fumbled down the darkened stairs, back into the bedroom. Merle and Cliff carried the rifles, and I carried LeHorn's journal, his English copy of *The Long Lost Friend*, and his tattered *Daemonolateria*.

The shadows were just as solid on the second floor. There was no hint of daylight outside. "How long were we up there?" I asked.

"Maybe an hour?" Merle guessed. "Don't worry, we'll be home before dark."

"It's already dark," I pointed out. "It's only around noon, but I don't see any daylight between those cracks in the boards."

Dale crossed the floor. There was a small knothole in the plywood covering the bedroom window, and he peered through it. Gasping, he pulled away.

"What's wrong?" I asked. "Take a look." He sounded terrified.

I put my eye to the hole and peeked outside. It was pitch black, and it took a moment for my eyes to adjust. When they did, I saw tree branches.

Behind me, Dale whispered, "There were no trees in the yard when we got here."

He was right. The yard had been devoid of plant life, save for scraggly weeds and overgrown grass. Now there was a forest out there. Giant, old growth oaks and maples and elms and pines clustered together, encircling the house, pressing against its sides, close enough that I could smell the pine trees' sap and needles. There was another stench as well; rotting vegetation. I'd smelled it when Big Steve and I first encountered Hylinus, and here it was again.

As if sensing my presence, the branches of a dogwood leaned towards the window and scratched the side of the house. They scraped along the wood, searching for a way inside. The sound was unnerving, like fingernails on a chalkboard.

I looked at the others. "We're trapped."

Cliff dropped the lighter and sucked on his burned fingers. "What are you talking about?"

"The trees. They've surrounded the house."

"Oh shit," Merle said. "They know what we're up to! They know we're trying to stop it."

Cliff gingerly picked up the hot lighter. "How? How can they know?"

"Because they're magic, stupid!" Merle punched the wall in frustration. "They're possessed by fucking demons. You heard what LeHorn said."

The clawing sounds increased, and then the screeching was replaced with a thump. Then another. And then a third, louder than the rest. The plaster cracked. Above us, the light fixture rattled.

"They're beating at the walls," Dale said. "Trying to get inside."

Another thud reverberated through the foundation. The floorboards shook beneath our feet. Wood splintered and glass shattered as the branches slammed into the walls. The cracks spiraled through the plaster in a spider web formation, and pieces of masonry crumbled away. A picture frame fell from the wall. The bed's headboard rattled, sending knick-knacks crashing to the floor.

"Downstairs," I shouted. "Hurry!"

It was hard to hear each other beneath the racket. We ran down the stairs. The tremors rocked the house, and we clutched the railing just to keep our balance. There was a torturous screech above us as the roof was peeled back from the frame. More glass shattered, and I heard the squeal of nails being pulled from wood. I guessed that they'd succeeded in pulling the plywood away from one of the windows.

The first floor was no safer. We stumbled through the darkness, choking on swirling clouds of dust, stirred up by the assault. The light fixtures swung back and forth like pendulums, shelves collapsed, and the house's frame groaned on its supports. We stared in horror as an entire section of the living room wall cracked, then exploded in a shower of plaster and wood fragments. Massive tree limbs thrust their way through the gaping hole, their tendril-like branches seizing everything in reach. One of them grabbed a porcelain figurine and squeezed until it shattered. Another speared the sofa cushion, burrowing into the stuffing. A third hooked the carpet we were standing on and tried yanking us toward it. A thin vine grasped at Dale's arm, and he shrank away.

We ran into the kitchen. Panicking, Merle reached for the old rotary phone hanging on the wall. He put the receiver to his ear, a hopeful expression flashing across his face. Then it died.

"There's no dial tone."

"Well of course there's no dial tone," Cliff yelled. "The fucking place has been abandoned for the last twenty years, you dipshit!"

"Don't call me a dipshit you son of a bitch!"

"Dipshit."

Merle's face turned red. "So help me God, you say it one more time and I'll knock you on your ass, biker boy."

Cliff opened his mouth, but I cut him off.

"Both of you knock it the fuck off! This isn't helping."

In the living room, the trees smashed the front door off its hinges. It crashed to the floor, sending up another cloud of dust. The wind howled through the opening, whistling into the kitchen. Over the sink, a window that hadn't been boarded up exploded, showering us all with shards of glass. An oak branch, thick as an elephant's trunk, thrust its way through. One of its branches snaked towards Dale, slithering across the kitchen counter. Dale grabbed it in his hands and tried to break it, but the branch twisted, pulling away. Dale cried out.

An ugly red welt marked his palms.

"The cellar," he shouted. "I saw rags and turpentine down there when we came in. We can make torches!"

Cliff and Dale darted for the cellar door. Merle stood transfixed, watching the bigger tree limb move closer. More branches and vines crawled through the open window and began pressing against the sides. Tiny cracks and fissures spread through the wall.

Merle gaped. "That charm over the door ain't working."

"Move it!" I shoved him towards the door. "They're gonna tear the wall down."

Merle looked at me as if seeing me for the first time. He blinked twice, and then slowly turned away. His double chins quivered. When he spoke, I had to strain to hear him. His voice echoed of hopelessness and defeat.

"We're screwed, aren't we?"

"Think about Tara and Claudine," I told him. "And all the other women this thing has preyed on. Leslie, Antonietta, Shelly, and Shannon. Should we let this Hylinus fucker keep raping our women? Hell, think about Paul and that guy Leslie went out with— Michael Gitleson. You want it to keep happening?"

That seemed to galvanize him. He hurried for the stairs.

In the cellar, dust and dirt rained down upon us as the house shook. Cliff wrapped his shirt around his fingers and held up the lighter so we could see. We snapped the broom and mop handles in half, then found some relatively dry rags at the bottom of the pile, untouched by mildew. We wrapped them around the sticks and then doused them with twenty-year old turpentine.

"Is that stuff still flammable?" I asked Dale. I had to shout so that he could hear me over the destruction.

He held out his torch and Cliff touched the flame to it, setting the cloth ablaze.

"I think so," Dale hollered. "Let's move. These won't last us long."

Outside, we heard the trees striking something metal.

"Adam," Dale said, "you carry the turpentine. Splash it on

every one of those things that crosses our path. We'll do the rest."

"What about the rifles?" Merle glanced over to the workbench, where we'd left them. "We can't carry the torches and the rifles at the same time."

"The hell with the rifles," Dale insisted. "They aren't going to do us any good against these things anyway. We'll come back and get them after we're done with the satyr."

Cliff lit his own torch. "No way, man. I ain't coming back to this house again. Not in a million years."

Silently, I agreed with him. It was a bad place, built on bad ground. The atmosphere was spoiled. Poisoned. The best thing the county could do was to bulldoze it over.

I grabbed the can of turpentine, then, as an afterthought, took the plastic gas can too. I shook it, making sure there was still liquid inside, and then I unscrewed the cap and stuck a rag in the opening.

"Molotov cocktail," I explained. "Saw it on an old episode of *The A-Team*."

"Good idea," Dale said. "Now lets move, before this whole place comes crashing down and buries us in here."

I tucked LeHorn's books into my waistband and nodded.

We crept back up the stairs. Scraps of flaming cloth fell from our torches, drifting to the floor.

"What if we catch the house on fire?" Merle asked.

I clenched my teeth. "Let it burn."

A quick glance into the kitchen and we hurried back down the basement steps. The trees had bashed down both the front and rear doors, as well as breaking through the windows and the walls. A forest was blooming inside the house, as smaller saplings slowly worked their way inside. The bigger trees kept up their assault, circling the home with their towering forms.

"Can't get out that way," Dale gasped.

We glanced around the cellar. It occurred to me that we were underground, just like in a grave. The trees began battering the cellar door.

"Too bad LeHorn didn't leave some chainsaws down here," Cliff mumbled.

"Now what?" Merle asked. "Our torches are getting low and that door ain't gonna hold."

Dale nodded towards the storm doors. "We go out the way we came in."

"You sure about that?" I asked.

"No." Dale shook his head. "I've never been more scared in my life. I can barely think straight."

Merle stood at the bottom of the stairs. "Just don't have a heart attack once I push these storm doors open. We ain't dragging your ass back to the Suburban."

"Try to keep up with me, fat ass."

"Old fart."

They grinned at each other, and then Merle's expression hardened.

"Let's do it."

Bellowing, Merle charged up the stairs and slammed against the doors with his shoulder, pushing them upward. He heaved, grunted, and then the storm doors flew open. Immediately, a giant oak tree swung towards us, clubbing at Merle with its limbs. It reminded me of a spider, the way it crawled on its roots. But despite its ferocity, the tree's girth slowed it down, and Merle was faster. He struck at it with the torch, and something inside the tree screamed.

"It works," Merle shouted. "It fucking works!"

He struck it again in a different spot. The flames caught hold, flickering across the bark. The tree drew back. Something shadowy swirled inside the smoke billowing off the burning wood.

Dale shoved me forward. "Come on!"

I dashed up the stairs. Merle waved his torch back and forth, holding several trees at bay. Cliff and Dale came up behind me, distracting my attention for a second. When I looked back, a limb snaked across the ground towards Merle. Before I could warn him, it curled around his leg like a tentacle and jerked him off his feet. There was a meaty smack as he hit the ground, and the air rushed out of his lungs. His torch rolled away from him, setting the weeds on fire. The tree yanked Merle towards it. Two giant limbs loomed above him, ready to impale him. Merle screamed as roots slithered over his body.

Snatching up his torch, I lit the rag on the gas can and tossed it at the tree. The effect was like a miniature can of napalm. The flames engulfed the trunk, and the frenzied tree released Merle's leg and thrashed across the yard. Another shadowy form poured out of it and shot into the sky.

"It was gonna drink me," he squealed. "Those roots . . ."

He clambered to his feet, panting for breath. Without a word, I handed him the torch and then splashed turpentine in each direction, flinging it on every branch within reach. Cliff and Dale thrust their torches forward, and dozens of small fires erupted. The air grew thick with the smell of burning leaves.

Angered, the trees closed ranks, coming at us from three sides. The ground shook with their advance.

Dale shouted, "Get to the Suburban!"

Except that the vehicle wasn't there anymore. We screeched to a halt. The trees had bludgeoned it almost beyond recognition. The roof was flattened down to the dashboard, the hood creased and buckled, the windows broken. All four tires were flat, and one of them had been wrenched from its rim. Oil, gasoline, and antifreeze pooled beneath the wreckage.

I poured the remaining turpentine in a C-shape behind us, making a magic circle of my own. Cliff touched his torch to the liquid and it erupted into flame, cutting us off from the marching plants.

"Jesus." Merle stared at his Chevy in disbelief. "I've still got three years of payments left on this thing."

"Head for the road," Dale said. "Nothing else we can do now except run."

"What about you?" I asked, alarmed.

"I'll be right behind you. Now get going."

We didn't argue. Cliff, Merle, and I fled down the dirt road, stopping at the crest of the hill. When we glanced back, Dale tossed his torch beneath the wrecked Suburban and ran after us. There was a whooshing sound, and then the vehicle was a ball of orange flame. The fire quickly spread, merging with the one I had started, and jumping from tree to tree. A tall pine went up like a Roman candle, while a sturdy oak smoked and sparked. The fire lapped at them hungrily. The trees screamed in unison.

We continued down the road, to the bottom of the hill. Out of the tree's menacing shadows, daylight returned. The sun hung high in the afternoon sky. Behind us, the flames roared. We kept running, until it was clear that we were out of reach. Then we stopped to catch our breath in front of the burned-out remains of Merle's friend's hunting cabin; a grim reminder of fires past.

"My fucking Chevy," Merle groaned. "They wrecked it."

Cliff lit a cigarette with his still-flickering torch. "You got insurance, right?"

Merle nodded.

"Well, just tell them you ran into a tree."

Merle stared at him. Cliff snickered, and tossed his torch to the side of the road.

Slowly, a broad smile spread across Merle's face. "You're an idiot, Cliff. You know that?"

"Yeah." Cliff grinned. "But you love me anyway. Sorry I called you a dipshit, man."

"Don't sweat it."

Dale and I were silent. I was thinking about Tara and I'm sure he was thinking about Claudine.

"Try your cell phone," he suggested.

I patted my pockets, and came up empty. My stomach lurched. I double-checked; my key ring, loose change, a wadded up tissue, and LeHorn's books (in my waistband)—but no cell phone.

"I must have dropped it back at the house."

The words hung in the air; felt like an epitaph.

Dale tossed his fluttering torch aside, then stomped on it until it was out.

"We've got a long walk ahead of us," he said. "Might as well get moving."

Exhausted, we shuffled down the road. My feet hurt, and my throat was dry and scratchy. As we walked, I watched the sun drift steadily towards the western horizon. My heart sank with it. I prayed we'd be in time, and knew we wouldn't. On foot, we'd never make it home before dark. Nightfall would bring the sound of pipes.

And only Cory and Big Steve—a stoned college drop out who worked at Wal-Mart and a cowardly dog that ran from squirrels—stood between Hylinus and our wives.

FIFTEEN

For the next two hours, we walked along the lonely dirt roads, winding past fields and woods, making our way back out to the main road. We'd cringe each time we passed a section of forest where the trees loomed over the road, expecting an attack that never came. Each time the branches swayed with the breeze, we fled beyond their reach. We saw no one, and not a single car passed us. We couldn't call for help. Houses were scarce. We stopped at two different farms, looking for assistance. There was nobody home at the first, and a nervous looking housewife greeted us at the second. She refused to open the door, obviously wary of four strangers.

"My husband's not home," she yelled. "You'll have to come back later!"

"Listen," Dale pleaded. "We've been in an accident. If you won't let us in, could you at least make a phone call for us?"

"Phones are out. Been out all morning. Happens a lot around here. Weird things with the phones and electricity. Messes up our TV reception, too."

Thick, black smoke rose from the direction of LeHorn's Hollow. The fire was obviously spreading. Despite that, no fire trucks arrived. I realized just how totally cut off from civilization we were, walking in a remote area where even a forest fire didn't attract attention.

"What if they find Adam's cell phone inside LeHorn's house,"

Merle asked, suddenly sounding frightened. "Or my rifles? They'll know it was us."

"Who's going to find them?" Dale rubbed his knee, wincing in pain. "It doesn't look like anybody is responding yet. With luck, by the time they know about the fire, there will be nothing left of Adam's cell phone and your guns."

Merle stopped walking. "What about LeHorn's steamer trunk? The charms kept it protected from fire, right?"

"So?"

"Our fingerprints are on it. Adam's got some of the books. They could trace it all back to us."

Dale shrugged. "Doubtful they'll take fingerprints off that old trunk. Even if it didn't burn, chances are they won't find it beneath the ashes—or if they do, they won't think twice. Why would they? You're being paranoid."

"Maybe," Merle said, sounding unconvinced. Then he hurried to catch up with us.

The dirt road seemed endless. With every mile, Dale's age and Merle's weight caught up with them, slowing their pace, but every time Cliff suggested they stop and rest, both men refused, insisting that we keep going. To be honest, Cliff and myself, though both younger and more physically fit, weren't in much better shape than they were. The events of the last twenty-four hours had taken their toll on us as well.

We stumbled on. I found an empty plastic bag lying in some weeds. I put the books inside it and continued down the road.

Once we'd reached the main road, traffic picked up and we had to walk single file along the side. Cliff and I stuck out our thumbs, begging for a ride. Several cars sped past, choking us with exhaust fumes and spraying us with gravel and dust. One guy in a pickup truck honked his horn as he swerved around us, either saying "Sorry I can't give you a lift," or "Get out of the road you idiots." A few cars slowed down as they drew alongside us, and each time my spirits lifted, sure that we'd found a Samaritan. But then they'd speed up again. I didn't blame them. The four of us must have looked pretty rough.

"Doesn't anybody pick up hitchhikers anymore?" Cliff complained. "It's not like we're serial killers or something."

"It's the hollow," Dale said, breathing hard. "Its aura is following us—like a cloud. Can't you feel it?"

"All I feel," Merle gasped, "is tired."

The sky grew darker and the sun began its descent, slipping lower towards the horizon. Now Cliff and I gestured at passing traffic, clasping our hands together like we were praying, and shouting out pleas. Still nobody stopped.

Please, I prayed for real. *Please, please, please make somebody stop. I'm sorry I doubted you. I'm sorry for all the shit I said after the miscarriages. Just let somebody stop and pick us up.*

The sun sank lower, its lower half gone for the night. Blue twilight deepened. The warm temperatures vanished with the daylight.

"We're not going to make it," I said.

The words caught in my throat, choking me. What was it Leslie had said to me when we were discussing Shannon and Antoinetta's disappearance? *You're beginning to sound like one of the characters in your books, Adam.* She'd been right. If this were a novel, my heroes would have arrived just in the nick of time, and saved the day. But real life didn't work like that. Real life had no happy endings. Despite our best efforts, despite my love for Tara and my determination to protect her, and after everything we'd been through at the LeHorn house—fate conspired against us. We were still nine or ten miles from home, and night was almost upon us. By the time we got there, it would already be too late. I fought back tears. I had the urge to just lie down in the middle of the road and let the next car run over me.

"We're almost to Seven Valleys," Cliff said. "I've got a buddy that lives there. Carl, a dude I work with. Maybe he can let us use his phone or give us a ride."

The sun disappeared, and night descended. The blue-gray sky was littered with cold pinpricks of starlight. Each one felt like an accusatory eye. The moon seemed huge. I beat myself up over losing the cell, and kept hoping that we'd find a payphone, but there were no stores or garages or even factories this far back in the country. We were on our own and running late. Too late.

I closed my eyes and whispered, "I'm sorry, Tara."

Merle squeezed my shoulder. "Cory's a good kid. Sure,

he's scatterbrained, but we all were at that age. He won't fuck up."

Behind us, Cliff snorted. "Who are you kidding? Cory would fuck up a wet dream."

Merle spun around. "I don't think that's what Dale and Adam want to hear right now, Cliff."

A car rounded the curve, spearing us with its headlights. I stuck my thumb up until it passed us; then watched the taillights fade.

"What do you guys think happened to Paul?" Cliff asked. "You think he knew about any of this?"

"I imagine Hylinus or the trees killed him," Dale said.

"So then where's his body? We didn't find it."

Dale shrugged. "Out there in the woods somewhere. Yes, we didn't find it, but that doesn't mean it's not out there somewhere. Remember, the hollow has the power to move—to camouflage itself. It could have hidden Paul's body, hid the evidence, so that nobody would interfere with the satyr's plans."

"But why would Hylinus go after Paul anyway?" Merle asked.

"I don't think he did," Dale said. "More likely Paul went out into the woods to look for Shannon on his own."

Stopping, I bent over to tie my shoe. "You know what else is bothering me? If the hollow could teleport, then why did it let us find the marker when we were with the search party?"

"Maybe its power weakens the farther away it is from the original spot," Dale suggested. "Or maybe it was too busy hiding Hylinus. Maybe it can't do both at once. If he was in a separate location at the time, maybe it focused on him."

"How do you know that?"

"I don't. I'm just guessing. This is magic we're talking about, Adam. I'm a retired engineer. I don't know the first thing about the supernatural."

Standing back up, I pulled LeHorn's books out of the bag. "We do now."

Dale frowned. "I wouldn't fool with those if I were you. Better that we stick to the plan. Create magic of our own."

"At this point, I'll use anything I can."

Tired and depressed, our conversation turned sporadic. We focused on putting one aching foot in front of the other. Blisters had formed on my toes and my heels felt like balls of flame. My calves cramped, and my mouth was parched. As bad as I felt, Dale and Merle looked like they were in even worse shape. Merle's tongue stuck out of his mouth, and rivulets of perspiration ran down his red face. He stank—smoke and sour sweat. We all did.

I paged through the books as we walked, squinting in the twilight, and it occurred to me that I'd yet to read them in broad daylight. My only other exposure to their contents had been under the flashlight's beam. Now I studied them under the sun's last dying embers. *The Long Lost Friend* was more of what I'd expected; folk remedies and cures, some of them intriguing and others—odd; glyphs, wards and sigils to protect against everything from evil spirits to slander; recipes and remedies to cure fevers, heal sore mouths, relieve toothaches, and catch fish. The *Daemonolateria* was different. There was no publisher or author listed, and the font and layout changed from page to page—giving the impression that it had been compiled from various other books. I couldn't read it, but some of the illustrations filled me with dread. They weren't cartoonish *Tales From the Crypt*-style monsters, but hideously detailed renderings of depravity, torture, and what I guessed were demons. Some of the caricatures had names next to them; Ob and Meeble, Leviathan and Behemoth, Kandara and Shtar, something called Kat, which looked like anything but its namesake, and Purturabo, who appeared almost human. Shuddering, I closed the book. Maybe Dale was right, I thought. It might be better to not use them.

About twenty minutes later, we heard a siren in the distance, drawing closer. Soon, a fire engine raced past us, its tires humming on the asphalt. A ladder truck quickly followed. Both of the emergency vehicles had SEVEN VALLEYS VOLUNTEER FIRE DEPARTMENT painted on their sides. We paused, watching them rocket by.

"Wonder if they're going to LeHorn's?" Cliff asked.

"Should we flag them down and ask?" I suggested.

Merle frowned. “And tell them we started the fire? I don’t think so. Let’s keep moving.”

The taillights and sirens faded into the darkness. Far away, over the hills, we heard another siren, probably from the fire hall in either New Salem or Jefferson or Spring Grove (it was hard to tell in the dark.)

“If they are going to the hollow,” Dale said, “then I hope they’re too late.”

We reached Seven Valleys around eight o’clock. Immediately, we headed for Cliff’s friend’s house. That took us another fifteen minutes. His friend, Carl, lived on the other side of town in a ramshackle trailer. It squatted on a small lot, sandwiched between two other trailers, and looked like it had been new back in the Sixties. A gray-primer colored Trans-Am and a rusty mini-van sat in the driveway. The Trans-Am needed a new state inspection sticker and registration, and the mini-van needed its engine block lifted up and a whole new van shoved beneath it. The side panels and tailpipe were rusted out, and a large crack ran across the passenger’s side of the windshield. The yard was full of trash; junked cars, bald tires, broken children’s toys, a chipped ceramic deer; empty beer cans (Old Milwaukee, the discriminating Pennsylvanian redneck’s beer of choice), and other debris. The only thing missing was a big Confederate flag hanging from the porch. Inside the trailer, somebody had the television turned up as loud as it would go. They were watching wrestling.

I stepped in a pile of cat shit and it did nothing to improve my mood. I wiped my heel off in the grass.

“Nice place,” Merle cracked.

“Beggars can’t be choosers,” Cliff said. “Unless you’d rather keep walking?”

“No, this will be fine.”

I grabbed Cliff’s arm. “No small talk, okay? Dale and I need to call home right away.”

“Adam . . ." Cliff looked offended. "Trust me."

He knocked on the screen door. There was no answer. Cliff knocked again, louder and more insistent. The television’s volume faded.

"Who is it?"

"Cliff Swanson, from work!"

"Who?" Cliff frowned. "It's Fuckstick!"

There was a brief pause, and then heavy footsteps plodded across the floor. The trailer creaked and groaned on its supports. Merle, Dale and I glanced at each other, then at Cliff.

Merle grinned. "Fuckstick?"

Cliff scowled. "Don't ask."

The four of us were good friends, as close as neighbors could be, but it amazed me sometimes how little we knew of each other's lives outside the neighborhood. The others were oblivious to the publishing business, we had no clue where Merle bought all of his antiques, had no idea Dale had suffered from prostate cancer a few years ago, and now, apparently, Cliff had a nickname we knew nothing about.

The trailer door swung open, revealing a prodigious beer gut, clad in a white, pizza-stained, wife-beater shirt. I couldn't see anything else from where I stood—just the gut.

"Fuckstick," the man greeted Cliff. "The hell are you doing here?"

"Hey Carl." Cliff grinned, then glanced back at us. "We had an accident, man. We were hoping we could use your phone?"

"Shit. You okay?"

Cliff nodded. "We're fine. But my buddies really need to call their wives. They'll be worried about us—we've been gone a long time. I called off work today."

Carl leaned out the door and eyed us. The man was a walking stereotype, and none of it good—ruddy complexion; two-days worth of whiskers; a bulbous, red-veined nose. He clutched a can of beer in one meaty hand and waved at us with the other. The way he was weaving in the doorframe, I suspected this wasn't his first beer of the night.

"Meetcha," he grunted.

We nodded back.

"There but for the grace of God go I," Merle whispered.

Carl held the door open. "Come on in."

"Thanks, man." Cliff beckoned us when we hesitated, and

then followed his friend. Merle, Dale, and I glanced at each other and then did the same.

The trailer's interior was even worse than the yard. Mounds of garbage lay everywhere, and there were skinny pathways running between them. The air stank, and the surfaces of the furniture and walls looked greasy.

"You took off today?" Carl asked Cliff. "So did I. Decided to get drunk instead."

He heaved his bulk into a stained recliner, and Cliff took a seat on the soiled couch. Cliff introduced the three of us and then asked about the phone. Carl pointed it out, and I threaded my way through the debris. I dialed my house. Dale stood beside me, looking as anxious as I felt. Carl turned the television back up, and I put a finger in my ear so that I could hear.

The phone rang—and kept ringing. Three times. Four. My heartbeat increased. I smiled at Dale, trying to reassure him. On the sixth ring, the answering machine picked up. I heard my own voice, telling me that Adam and Tara weren't home right now, and that if you wanted to, you could leave a message. The beep that followed had never seemed longer.

"Tara, it's me. Pick up."

She didn't. Instead, I heard the subtle hiss of white noise that always lingers at the other end of an empty phone line.

"Tara? Baby, if you're there, I need you to pick up now. It's important."

Dale drew closer, practically standing on my feet. I was aware that Cliff and Merle were both watching as well.

"Tara?"

Silence.

"Claudine? Cory?"

Nothing.

"Goddamn it, somebody pick up the—"

The machine beeped again, cutting me off in mid-sentence, followed by a dial tone. I put the phone back on its cradle.

Dale and I looked at each other. We didn't have to say anything. Our eyes said it all. Something had gone wrong. We felt it in our guts.

Nearby, the fire siren began to wail.

"Neighbor's a volunteer fireman," Carl told Cliff. "Said earlier there's a big forest fire out towards the old LeHorn place."

Cliff kept his expression neutral. "Really?"

Carl belched, then nodded. He crumpled the beer can and looked at us. "Any of you guys want a beer? Help yourself."

"No thanks," Dale said. "To be honest, we need to get going."

He shrugged. "Suit yourselves. Any luck getting hold of your old ladies?"

"No," I replied. "They're not home."

Cliff stood up. "Carl, any way you could give us a ride home?"

"Shit," he slurred. "I been drinking since nine o'clock this morning. I ain't in no shape to drive."

My spirits sank even lower. I was nearly frantic now, and it took everything I had not to start screaming. Something was terribly wrong. I felt it with every inch of my being. We had to get home—*NOW*.

"Why don't you let us borrow your van?" Cliff suggested.

Carl eyed us suspiciously. "I dunno. I mean, you're okay, Fuckstick, but I don't know these other guys. What if something happens to it? The Trans-Am ain't inspected."

Cliff pointed at me. "Adam is a famous writer. Real responsible kind of guy. He wouldn't let anything happen to your ride, brother."

"That true?" Carl asked, sitting up straight. "You a writer?"

I nodded.

"What kind of books you write?"

"Mysteries." I glanced at the door, anxious to leave. Despite my fatigue, I felt like running home.

"I don't read," Carl said. "But that's pretty cool. Beats the hell out of going to work every day."

"Look," Cliff said, steering the conversation back to more pressing matters. "If it makes you feel better, I'll promise not to let anybody drive it but me. And I'll bring it back as soon as we're done. Cool?"

"Pick me up another case of beer?"

"Sure."

Carl tossed the keys to Cliff. "Old Milwaukee pounders. Cold ones, too, not any of that warm shit."

"You got it," Cliff said, already heading for the door. "Thanks, Carl! I owe you one."

"You owe me a case," Carl shouted after us. "Nice meeting you guys."

We piled into the van, Cliff and Merle up front, Dale and I in the back. The vehicle's interior matched that of the trailer, and we tried not to sit in anything too offensive.

Cliff flicked on the headlights and turned the key.

Nothing happened.

He turned it again.

The headlights dimmed and the van refused to start.

"Fuck!" Cliff opened the door. "Merle, pop the hood."

"What's wrong with it?" Merle asked. "Why won't it start?"

"If I knew that, I wouldn't have you popping the hood."

I leaned forward and rested my forehead against the back of the driver's seat. It felt oily, and I pulled away. Merle popped the hood and Cliff vanished beneath it.

"He'll fix it," Dale said. I couldn't tell if he was trying to convince me, or just reassuring himself.

"How?" I opened my door. "He doesn't have any tools."

I walked around to the front of the van. Cliff was under the hood, scowling at the engine.

"Any luck?" I asked.

"Could be the starter," he said. "Or the battery, or the alternator. Or it could be that it's just a piece of fucking shit. I don't know, man."

"Can you fix it?"

He slammed the hood. "No."

I clenched my fists. "This just keeps getting worse. It's like we're cursed now."

"No offense, Adam, but I think you're letting what happened back at LeHorn's get to you."

"Of course I am. I want to get home to Tara, man! The

sun's gone down. You know what that means? Ever since we escaped the hollow, it's been one roadblock after another. I can't fucking take it!"

"Calm down . . ."

"Don't tell me to calm down. Just fix the fucking van!"

Cliff wiped his hands on his jeans. "Look, I'll go convince Carl to let us use the Trans-Am. Hopefully, we won't get pulled over because of the tags and inspection sticker. It's dark. If we pass a cop, maybe he won't notice."

He rounded the corner and went back into the trailer. Inside the van, Merle and Dale looked at me warily. They'd seen the exchange.

I opened the door and grabbed *The Long Lost Friend* out of the bag.

"What are you doing?" Dale asked. "You okay?"

"Never better. You said we had to make our own magic, right? Well, I'm going to heal the van."

"What?" His tone was incredulous.

"Look," I snapped. "I don't know a lot about this stuff, but I know it's real. We were attacked by carnivorous fucking trees, man. It doesn't get more real than that. But maybe it's like voodoo. Maybe it doesn't work if you don't believe in it. So get out here and help me. I need your belief. Our wives need it, too. Something's wrong at home. I feel it, and I know you do too. Help me."

Solemnly, without another word, they slid out of the van.

"What the hell," Merle said, shrugging his shoulders. "Beats sitting here."

I flipped through the book, looking for something that might suit our needs, but since it had been written in a time before automobiles, our pickings were slim. Then two caught my eye: 'To Prevent Witches and Evil Spirits From Bewitching Cattle and Horses', and, 'To Unfasten Cattle and Horses Which Have Been Bound'.

"Let's try this one," I said, picking the second. "It's to unbind horses, and horses were their cars."

"You're reaching," Merle muttered.

Dale shook his head. "It's worth a shot. What do we do?"

"The book doesn't say. It just gives me a spell I'm supposed to recite."

"Lets put our hands on the hood and bow our heads," Dale suggested. "Like a benediction."

Merle looked skeptical. "You serious?"

Dale nodded. "Adam's right. Do it, at least for Claudine and Tara. Okay?"

"Okay."

Both men bowed their heads and rested their palms flat on the van's hood, like faith healers preparing to cast out automatic transmission demons.

Clearing my throat, I recited the passage. "Trotter Head, I forbid thee my horse and cow stable. I—"

"Trotter Head?" Merle whispered. "Who the hell's Trotter Head?"

"Shush," Dale hissed. "He's reading it the way it's written. Doesn't matter who Trotter Head is."

"I'm just saying; it's a weird name."

"Thou mayest not breathe upon me or upon my horse," I continued. "Breathe upon some other house, some other horse, some other stable, until thou has ascended every hill, until thou has counted every fence post, and until thou has crossed every water. Ut nemo in sense tenat, descendere nemo. At precedenti spectator mantica tergo. In the name of God the Father, the Son, and the Holy Ghost."

Merle and Dale said, "Amen."

We stared at each other. I suddenly felt very foolish. Nearby, a dog barked.

"What now?" Merle asked.

"Try it," Dale said.

Merle slid behind the steering wheel and turned the key. Nothing happened.

"Well," Dale said, "it was worth a try."

"We did it wrong," I said. "We're supposed to make our own magic, right? So we need to add our own ingredients to it."

"Adam." He reached for me, squeezing my shoulder. "Enough. We tried and we failed. I'm just as worried about

Claudine as you are about Tara, but this isn't helping. Let's wait for Cliff and then we'll take the Trans-Am."

"Again," I insisted. "Please? Just one more try?"

Sighing, he closed his eyes, bowed his head, and put his hands back on the hood.

I paused, summoning up the writer within me.

"Please," I whispered. "I command thee to start. Our loved ones are alone and in terrible danger. They need help, and we cry out now to be with them. Stand not in our way, nor prevent us. Start, fired by our determination and our love. Start, so that we may keep them safe. Start, and carry us safely and quickly. I ask this in the name of Tara and Claudine and all those who have been harmed by Hylinus's evil."

I returned to the book and repeated the last portion of the spell. "Ut nemo in sense tenat, descendere nemo. At precedenti spectator mantica tergo. In the name of God the Father, the Son, and the Holy Ghost. And in the name of love. Amen."

"Amen," Dale repeated, opening his eyes. He nodded to Merle. "Try it again."

Merle turned the key. The engine choked, sputtered and then roared to life. Blue smoke belched from the tailpipe. The headlights came back on. Behind the wheel, Merle jumped. Dale's jaw went slack.

I grinned. "Our own magic."

Cliff came back out of the trailer. "Carl says we can—"

He paused, staring at the van.

"How the hell did you get it started?"

Dale clapped him on the back. "Powwow."

"What?"

"Let's get going."

"But . . ."

Dale nodded towards the van. "Please, Cliff? With every second that we waste, Tara and Claudine are in more danger. Not to mention Adam's dog and Cory."

Merle slid over into the passenger seat and Cliff took the wheel. Dale and I jumped into the back.

"Take us home, Fuckstick." Merle grinned.

Cliff punched him in the arm.

Hope stirred inside of me for the first time since leaving the hollow. It wasn't just dumb luck or some coincidence that the van had started. It was magic—the power of our beliefs. It actually worked. Before this, I'd always looked at powwow as nothing more than superstition. But now, I understood the appeal it must have had for people like Nelson LeHorn. It was an incredibly powerful and liberating feeling.

"Our own magic," I repeated. "It really did work."

"Indeed it did," Dale agreed. "Now, let's just hope it works on Hylinus."

My buoyed spirits sank again as we rushed home.

SIXTEEN

As we sped down the narrow alley behind our homes, fire trucks rocketed towards us, pouring out of the Fire Hall. Cliff slammed on the brakes, and we skidded to a halt, waiting for the engines to pass.

"Bet they're responding to the fire," Merle said. "Jesus, I hope that house burned down. I don't want to spend my golden years in jail for arson."

"Why not?" Cliff teased. "You'd be popular with all the big cons."

"Not as popular as your Mom, Fuckstick."

"Stop calling me that. I put up with that stupid nickname at work. I don't need to hear it from you guys."

More emergency vehicles squeezed by, their sirens blaring. Their formidable size took up most of the alley, and there was no way for the van to get past them. We were literally yards away from our homes, and still, bad luck seemed to intervene.

"Come on," Cliff shouted at the passing firemen. "Get out of the way!"

I flung my door open and hit the pavement running. Dale was right behind me, trying hard to keep up. The firemen gave us odd looks as we zipped by. Dale tripped in front of the ambulance, and the driver hit the brakes, blowing the horn. Barely pausing,

I gasped, "You okay?"

He nodded, clambering back to his feet.

Merle and Cliff hollered at us to wait, but we kept going, dashing past Merle's house, then Cliff and Cory's apartment, and finally into my yard. The lights were out in the house, but Tara's car was still in the driveway. A quick glance at

Dale's house confirmed that Claudine's car was, too. Cory's apartment was dark as well, and the shades were drawn.

My back door was open. The screen door swayed in the breeze. We'd shut it that morning, heard Cory lock it behind us. Dale and I glanced at each other. I put my finger to my lips. We burst through the open door, into my office.

"Tara!"

"Claudine," Dale shouted. "Where are you?"

I whistled for Big Steve, clapping my hands together, listening for the thump as he jumped off the bed and the telltale click of his nails on the stairs.

The television was on in the living room, tuned to CNN, and Larry King's grating, lizard-like voice was the only thing to welcome us. The clock ticked in the kitchen. It seemed louder than normal. Something stank.

"Look," Dale whispered, pointing at the floor.

The carpet was filthy, covered with muddy cloven hoof prints—and a fresh pile of feces, still steaming. It didn't look human; too large for that.

Satyr shit, I thought. *The son of a bitch marked his territory.*

"Oh God . . ."

Panic took over. I ran through the house, screaming for Tara and Big Steve, for Claudine and Cory, for anybody that would answer. I didn't notice the blood pooling on the living room carpet until I slipped in it.

The blood belonged to Cory. He lay face up, sprawled on the floor between the television and the sofa. His sightless eyes were glassy and dry. I remember wondering why he didn't blink—his eyes were drying out. Despite his wounds, his face seemed alive.

He'd been gored to death. Long, ugly slashes crisscrossed his chest and abdomen, revealing his insides. Ropy, purple and white lengths of intestine looped from an extremely deep gash in his belly. His forehead and the left side of his face were crushed. Cloven hoof prints were stamped into his flesh. One of his feet was wedged beneath the coffee table. The other leg was bent at the knee and curled up under his body. His limp arms extended straight out from his sides. One hand clutched my baseball bat, the tip matted with blood and fur. Apparently, Cory had gotten in at least one good swing before dying. A vase had been knocked over, and the pieces were scattered across the floor. Movies and video games had been knocked off the shelves.

Cory. The kid. Our neighbor and our friend. We all picked on him, but we loved him just the same. He'd been young. Had his whole life ahead of him. Worked at Wal-Mart, liked James Bond movies, and couldn't hold his alcohol or play hackeysack worth a damn. Wanted a girlfriend but seemed to have bad luck with women. He'd liked to draw cartoons and play video games. And now he was dead, ripped open and spilling out all over my floor.

From behind me, Dale asked, "Is he?"

Without turning to face him, I nodded.

"Any sign of the others? The dog?"

"No."

My shoes stuck to the carpet as I backed away from the body, leaving bloody footprints. In the kitchen, Dale vomited into the garbage can. I felt my own gorge rise, and bit my lip to fight it off.

"Dale?"

He wiped his mouth with the back of his hand. "W-what?"

"Check your house. Cory hit the satyr at least once. It's obvious he went down fighting. Maybe the girls escaped while he was defending them. Maybe they're hiding over there."

He nodded, then leaned forward and retched again.

I ran up the stairs. A quick glance in the bathroom, bedroom, and spare room showed them all deserted. I paused in the spare room. We'd intended it to be our baby's room one day. The walls still had the Eeyore border that I'd put up before the second miscarriage.

"Tara. . ." Choking back tears, I could barely speak her name.

Something thumped in the bedroom.

"Hello?"

Thump.

"Tara? Honey, is that you?"

Thump. Thump.

"Big Steve?"

Thumpthumpthumpthump.

I raced into the room. Big Steve crawled out from underneath the bed where he'd been hiding. His tail wagged furiously. Sobbing, I collapsed to my knees and wrapped my arms around him, hugging him tight.

"Oh buddy, I thought you were . . ."

He cowered against me, body trembling beneath his thick fur. I petted him and he licked my face with his rough tongue, and despite my fears and sorrow, I laughed.

"Where's Mommy? Where is she, boy?"

He whined at the mention of Tara. His soft, brown eyes had never looked more terrified than they did at that moment.

The door banged downstairs, followed by the sound of footsteps.

Cliff shouted, "Adam? Dale? Where you guys at?"

"Come on, buddy." I snapped my fingers and Big Steve trotted along behind me, his courage returning now that Daddy was home.

Merle and Cliff stood staring down at Cory's body. Cliff's eyes were full of tears.

"He . . ." Cliff worked his mouth, but the words would not come.

"The girls?" Merle asked hopefully.

I shook my head. "They're not here. Dale went next door to check."

Enraged, Cliff kicked the recliner. Frightened by his sudden outburst, Big Steve scrambled back up the stairs.

"Cory didn't deserve this shit," Cliff yelled. "He was a good kid!"

"No," I agreed sadly, "he didn't."

"I'll go get my shotgun," Merle said. "You calling Detective Ramirez?"

"Fuck Ramirez," I spat. "We've wasted enough time today. Let's kill this son of a bitch."

Merle cast one last glance at Cory, then left. Cliff sank into the recliner, resting his head in his hands. Big Steve crept back down the stairs and sniffed his boots. Cliff reached out to pet him and Big Steve licked his hand.

"You okay?" I asked.

"No." He looked up at me with red-rimmed eyes. "You?"

"No." I pried the bat from Cory's fingers. "I'm most definitely not okay."

I studied the fur and blood on the bat's tip.

"Cory nailed him, huh?"

I nodded.

"Good. Hope he split the fucker's head open."

I pulled the tuft of fur off the bat. It was sticky, but soft.

"What are you doing?" Cliff asked.

I stuffed the fur in my pocket. "Making up my own pow-wow."

Dale returned with his shotgun, and reported what we already suspected; there was no sign of Tara or Claudine at his house, and no indication that they'd been there at all during the day.

He looked around the living room. "Where's Merle?"

"Went to get his shotgun, too" Cliff said.

"Good," Dale replied. "I brought Claudine's silver jewelry along."

Remembering our plan for the silver, I excused myself and went back upstairs to the bedroom. Big Steve trailed along behind me, hopping up onto the bed. Tara's musical jewelry box (it had belonged to her Grandmother) sat on her dressing table. I opened it and was greeted by the faint strains of "When You Wish Upon A Star", Tara's favorite childhood song. Our wedding picture was taped to the inside of the lid. We looked young and happy, free from the sorrows and perils that I now knew had been lying in wait for us, ready to eradicate those smiles forever. The music box lied. We'd wished upon a star the evening we were married, standing on a hotel balcony and looking up at the night sky. We'd wished to be happy forever, to have a family and a wonderful marriage, free of sorrow and tears, but despite what the song promised, our dreams hadn't come true.

I rifled through the jewelry box and grabbed every silver

ring, necklace, brooch, pin, and earring I could find. I also came across a silver dollar that her father had given her. I grabbed that, too. When Big Steve and I got back downstairs, Merle had returned, carrying a shotgun and a chainsaw.

"Let's not waste any more time," I said. "Cory's blood hasn't congealed yet. I'm not a medical examiner, but I'm guessing this happened within the last hour. We may still have a chance."

Dale's face was drawn and pale. "Don't worry. The girls are still alive. Hylinus wouldn't hurt them. He wants them for . . .you know."

"Okay," Merle gasped, out of breath from running. "Dale's got a gun, and I've got a gun. Those should handle the satyr. But in case we didn't get all the trees, which one of you wants to carry the chainsaw?"

"Give it to Cliff," I answered, picking up the baseball bat. "I'll use this."

"Ain't gonna do you much good against that thing," Cliff said. "At least, it didn't for Cory."

"He drew blood," I pointed out. "That's enough."

A plan was beginning to formulate in my head, but I wasn't sure of the specifics yet, and didn't want to voice it until I was. When the others weren't looking, I dipped the baseball bat in Cory's blood; letting his fluids mingle with the satyr's. Big Steve watched me, his head tilted in curiosity.

"Come on," I said, snapping my fingers so he would follow.

"You're bringing the dog along?" Cliff asked.

"Sure," I said. "I'm drawing power from him, remember? He's part of my personal powwow."

I clipped Big Steve to his leash, and the five of us went outside. Immediately, his nose went to the ground, investigating. He growled, and then pointed at the woods with his paw and snout.

"Can he track Tara?" Dale asked.

"I think so." I tugged the leash. "Come on, bud."

Reluctantly, he followed. The five of us went to Merle's woodshop. While we watched, Merle cut open the tops of the shotgun shells and dumped the pellets onto the floor. Then, he replaced them with the silver, putting the jewelry on top of the wadding.

"Here," I said, reaching into my pocket and pulling out the clump of fur. "Put this in, too."

Merle eyes it dubiously. "What is it?"

"Some of Hylinus's hair."

"How is that going to help?"

"It's part of him. I don't know how else to explain it, but adding it to the mix feels right."

Grimacing, he took it from me, and divided the strands between the shells, dropping it on top of the jewelry.

Dale twirled his gold wedding band, his own magic item. "Hylinus took a dump on Adam's floor. We should add some of that, too."

"No," Merle said emphatically. "Hair is one thing. I'm not touching satyr shit."

Big Steve lay down in the corner and whimpered.

"It's okay," I assured him. "We're going soon. We'll find Mommy."

Finished dividing the fur amongst the shells, Merle looked up from the workbench. "Now for the magic duct tape. Want to say some words over it?"

On the corner of the workbench was an empty coffee can, stuffed full of grease pens, hobby-knives, and magic markers. I plucked a black permanent marker from the assortment.

"I've got a better idea. Cliff, run out to the van and bring me LeHorn's books."

Surprisingly, he didn't argue or ask questions. He returned a minute later and handed me the bag. While I flipped through *The Long Lost Friend*, Merle carefully sealed the shotgun shells back up with duct tape. Then, using the marker and the spell book, I drew a sigil on each strip of tape; three stars in an upside-down triangular pattern, with three crosses directly beneath them, also in the shape of a triangle. Then, I held my right hand out over the shells and read from the book.

"Ut nemo in sense tentat, descendere nemo. At precedenti spectaur mantica tergo. Hecate. Hecate. Hecate. Papa, R. tarn,

Tetregammaten Angen. Jesus Nazarenus, Rex Judeorum."

"What spell was that?" Cliff asked.

"Two of them," I said. "A benediction against evil and a charm for guns and other arms. Figured it wouldn't hurt to double up."

Dale fidgeted impatiently. "Are we ready?"

"One more thing," I said.

"Adam—"

"Dale, my wife is out there, too. Just one more second, please?"

Pulling a pair of safety goggles over my eyes, I switched on Merle's grinding wheel and sharpened the edges of Tara's silver dollar. Then I hammered one end into the tip of the baseball bat, letting the other end stick out like a razor.

I took off the goggles and appraised my weapon.

"Now I'm ready."

Cliff grinned. "Fucking barbarian, man."

I left the books on Merle's workbench, grabbed Big Steve's leash and the baseball bat, and followed them outside. Merle and Dale loaded their shotguns. Cliff made sure the chainsaw started, and then left it running. He sat it down, lit a cigarette, and then picked it up again, revving the engine.

The full moon hung in the sky like an engorged, unblinking eye. It reminded me of Cory's unseeing stare. I closed my own eyes and when I opened them again, the moon was still watching. It looked heavy, as if it could fall to the ground any moment.

It was directly over the forest.

And it was blood red.

Like gunslingers, the five of us walked side by side—Merle on the left, then Dale, then Cliff, and then me and the dog, armed with our weapons and our totems; Cliff's cigarettes, Merle's duct tape, Dale's wedding ring, and my dog. Big Steve seemed to draw courage from our resolve. Not even the sputtering chainsaw disturbed him. He walked tall and proud, his back rigid, his white teeth bared, flashing in the darkness.

We crossed the alley. The woods loomed just beyond the

parking lot and playground. In the distance, on the other side of the forest, the horizon glowed orange from the forest fire. Even though we were dozens of miles away, we could smell the smoke, carried on the breeze.

"Look." Merle sniffed the air. "We did that."

Dale grunted. "It's a good start."

We continued on across the parking lot, heading towards the playground. The spot where they'd discovered Michael Gitleson's wrecked vehicle after his and Leslie's fateful date, along with an adjoining section of the playground, were roped off with fluttering yellow police tape.

Big Steve looked at the forest and barked once, echoing into the night.

We're coming for you, goat-boy—me and my master and our friends. Coming to bite your hairy ass.

His enthusiasm was infectious. I gave the bat an experimental swing, jabbing at the darkness. Merle and Dale jacked their shotguns, chambering shells. Cliff raised the chainsaw and thumbed the throttle. Its roar filled the air.

"I'm a lumberjack, baby," he sang, "and I'm gonna cut you down to size."

He thrust and parried with the chainsaw as if it were a sword, then let the motor idle down again.

We laughed.

And that was when Detective Ramirez stopped us.

SEVENTEEN

The black and white sat in the shadows beneath a telephone pole, out of reach of the soft glow of the parking lot's sodium lights. We didn't see it until we heard the car door slam. All five of us jumped at the sound. The chainsaw sputtered, then died, and the night seemed suddenly quiet.

"Good evening, gentlemen." Detective Ramirez stepped towards us. "You guys are up late."

A uniformed officer with brown hair slid out of the passenger's side, and another with red hair walked around to the front of the patrol car. Both stood stiffly, hands resting on their holsters.

"D-detective Ramirez," I stammered. "What are you doing here?"

He smiled thinly. "I could ask you the same thing, Mr. Senft. We're on stakeout. Watching the neighborhood, seeing if the perp returns to the scene of the crime. I'll spare you the details. Surveillance is always boring."

He eyed our weapons, and continued.

"But something tells me that you guys are having much more excitement tonight."

Merle tried to grin but succeeded only in looking ill. "You know how it is, Detective. Quiet night in a small town and all that."

Cliff attempted a laugh that immediately died on the wind.

Ramirez's smile vanished. "Indeed. Maybe you should lower your weapons."

Slowly, Merle and Dale lay the shotguns on the ground, and stepped away from them. I did the same with the bat. The sharpened silver dollar glinted in the moonlight.

The redheaded officer inched closer, nodding at Cliff. “Want to put that thing down?”

Cliff sat the chainsaw down and backed away.

“So,” Detective Ramirez said, his smile returning. “Which one of you wants to go first?”

I stepped forward, and the dark-haired cop pulled his gun.

“Keep away from the bat,” he shouted. “Down on the ground!”

I froze, my testicles crawling up inside me. Suddenly, I felt very cold. Next to me, Big Steve cringed. Glass crunched under my feet, and I wondered if it was from Michael Gitelson’s shattered windshield.

Ramirez held up his hand. “Easy, Sam. This is Adam Senft, the famous mystery writer. He wasn’t going for the bat. We’re you, Mr. Senft?”

I shook my head, too afraid to speak. Big Steve relaxed.

“Officers Sam Young and Al Uylik,” Ramirez continued, “Meet Merle Laughman, Dale Haubner, and Cliff Swanson. And the furry guy is Big Steve. His bark is much worse than his bite.”

Big Steve’s tail wagged at the mention of his name.

Ramirez’s smile faded again. “So which was it?”

I inched farther away from the bat. “Sorry, Detective?”

“Which was it? Were you guys going squirrel hunting or cutting firewood? It must be one of those explanations, right?”

“You wouldn’t believe us if we told you.”

“Well, you’d better tell me something. The four of you are running around out here in the middle of the night, armed with shotguns, a chainsaw, and a modified baseball bat. We call that suspicious behavior.”

“Neighborhood watch,” Dale lied. “With all that’s happened, we’ve got a right to protect our homes.”

“Not like this you don’t. The law frowns on vigilante justice, Mr. Haubner. And besides, if you were watching for prowlers, you gentlemen wouldn’t have been laughing and singing and revving that chainsaw as loud as it would go.”

“Our wives are missing . . ."

I hadn’t meant to say it. I’d opened my mouth to verify

Dale's explanation, and instead, the truth had tumbled out.

"We got home about twenty minutes ago," I continued. "Dale's wife and my wife are gone. It looks like somebody broke into my home. And our friend is dead." Ramirez's face was expressionless. "Murdered?"

"Yes."

"Did you call 911?"

"No."

"Why not? Your wives have been abducted and your friend was murdered. Wouldn't you call for help?"

"I. . .I guess we were too freaked out. We were looking for Tara and Claudine."

"And I take it this deceased friend would be Cory Peters?"

I nodded, swallowing hard.

"Where's the body?"

"In my living room."

"Did any of you touch anything inside the home, or disturb his body?"

We shook our heads in unison.

Ramirez turned to Officer Young. "Call it in."

"Can we leave?" Dale asked.

"No." Ramirez shook his head. "You guys just hang tight till our backup arrives. Then we'll go have a look, and I'll have some questions for you."

My stomach sank. Dale made a small, whimpering noise in the back of his throat. Our bad luck seemed to have returned—in spades. We glanced at one another. Merle was sweating bullets and Cliff's cigarette was down to the butt. The filter was burning, but he didn't seem to notice.

I stepped forward. Ramirez and Uylik both eyed me warily. Inside the patrol car, Officer Young was talking into the radio.

"Detective Ramirez," I said, holding out my palms. "Please, just listen to me for a second."

"Mr. Senft, I would advise you to not say anything else for the moment. I'll be taking statements from each of you as soon as Officer Young is finished."

"But our wives are out there, right now." Dale's voice trembled with emotion. "We've got to find them."

"That's right," I said. "We have reason to believe that Antonietta Wallace, Shannon, Leslie, and Shelly Carpenter are still alive, and our wives are with them."

"Where are they? Do you know who took them?"

Dale started to respond, but then looked at me. "You tell him."

My mouth had suddenly gone dry. I licked my lips.

"Look." Annoyance crept into the detective's voice. "One of you better start explaining now, or I'm going to read you your rights and you can explain it in detail at the Loganville barracks."

I took a deep breath. "Do you know the name, Nelson LeHorn?"

Ramirez shook his head. "No. Should I?"

"He was a local farmer, and a powwow magician. He disappeared in the Eighties, after his wife was murdered."

"I remember that," Uylik said. "Happened when I was in college. Never caught the guy."

"I moved here from Baltimore," Ramirez said. "Probably why I haven't heard of him. Do you suspect he's involved in these disappearances?"

I shrugged. "In a way, yes. But it's more complicated than that, and we don't have time to go into it right now. My point is, we know who's behind this, and we think he's in the woods right now, with our wives and possibly the other missing women."

"So who is he?" Ramirez pulled out his notepad and a pen.

"His name is Hylinus."

Ramirez wrote it down. "Last name?"

"We don't know. Look, if you can just come with us, we can lead you to him. Please? Our wives—"

"I understand," he interrupted, "but you need to understand my position as well. You just informed me that your friend has been murdered—inside your home. And I see the four of you walking through the neighborhood, heavily armed. And you're being vague with your answers. What am I supposed to think?"

Dale spoke up. "It's not that easy to explain, Detective.

Hylinus is not your average suspect."

"I'm listening."

"Remember when you interviewed me the other day?" I asked. "We were talking about the O'Brien robbery in Hanover, and some of the weird, paranormal stuff involved with it?"

Ramirez nodded.

"Well, this is sort of like that. There's not enough time to explain it all to you, but there's some supernatural stuff occurring. If you come with us, we can show you."

Ramirez chuckled. "I'm not Fox Mulder, Mr. Senft. I think we'll stay right here until the others arrive."

Officer Young got back out of the car and walked around to us. "Units are on their way."

"ETA?" Ramirez asked him.

Young shrugged. "Ten minutes. Maybe fifteen. Traffic's a mess because of the forest fire."

"Fifteen minutes?" Dale exploded. "God damn it, we've been more than patient. We did nothing wrong. Our wives are out there right now, in jeopardy. You've got to listen to us!"

Ramirez held up his hands. "Calm down, Mr. Haubner."

"I will *not* calm down! You're treating us like suspects, and we've done nothing wrong."

Big Steve shrank against me, frightened by Dale's outburst. I reached down to reassure him, and Officer Young's eyes darted to my hands. I held them back up again.

The wind shifted, and the smell of wood smoke grew stronger. There was something else on the wind, too.

The sound of a shepherd's pipe.

Immediately, my penis stiffened. Judging by the way Merle, Dale, and Cliff fidgeted; theirs were doing the same. The three police officers looked uncomfortable. Young readjusted his holster and belt, and Ramirez held his notepad in front of his crotch. Uylik shuffled his feet.

"Oh shit." Cliff's cigarette butt dropped from his mouth.

"What the hell is that?" Officer Young asked, glancing around. "Sounds like a flute."

"It's Hylinus," Merle said. "We tried to tell you."

Ramirez's face turned red. He was clearly embarrassed by

his body's reaction.

"This suspect plays the flute?" he asked.

I changed tactics. "You've got erections right now, don't you guys?"

"Fuck off," Officer Young snapped. "I don't—"

"You've got one because of the music. We all do. That's part of it. That's how he lures them. It's like he hypnotizes them or some thing."

Ramirez didn't respond. His complexion grew scarlet.

"Look," I tried again. "Remember when we were talking about the bank robbery in Hanover? You said that you found O'Brien's story hard to believe. You said that you wanted to believe him, but that you just haven't been presented with the truth. Right?"

Ramirez toyed with his moustache. "What's your point, Mr. Senft?"

"If you want the truth, then let us show you. Right now. You can't seriously believe we're involved with this."

He glanced down at the bulge in his pants.

Dale tried another angle. "Have you discovered hoof prints at the crime scenes?"

Ramirez was visibly startled. "This Hylinus—would he have some way of leaving hoof imprints in steel?"

We stared at him, too shocked to reply.

"Gitleson's vehicle was damaged in such a way. One of our technicians said it was like somebody had clubbed it with a goat's foot. Can you gentlemen explain that?"

"No," I said. "But we can show you."

"Can you also show me what would have left behind traces of animal fur that, so far, our lab technicians haven't been able to identify?"

"Yes, we can."

"Please?" Dale begged. "Before it's too late."

Ramirez seemed to consider our request. Then he said, "Give me your keys, Mr. Senft."

"What?"

"Your house keys. Give them to me."

I grew nervous again, but did as he asked.

Sighing, Ramirez handed them to Young. "Secure the crime scene. It's that house over there, with the white vinyl siding."

Young refused. "Sir, that's totally—"

"I know it is," Ramirez interrupted. "And I don't give a damn. Last time I went by the book, a lot of innocent people got killed. These men's wives are missing. I'll be damned if I'm going to let that happen again."

"But sir, you can't possibly—"

"I can and I do. Come on, Sam. You can see as well as I can that these men aren't killers. It's called playing a hunch. Go ahead and make fun. Tell me I sound like a television cop. You know as well as I do that there's all kinds of weirdness associated with this case. Has been since day one. If they can explain it, I want to know about it. Now go secure the scene and wait for backup. When they get here, send some of them along after us."

"What about me, sir?" Uylik asked.

"You're coming along," Ramirez said.

Dale flashed me a thumbs up.

Ramirez turned to us. "Where are we going, exactly?"

I pointed towards the forest. "There."

Uylik scowled. "You realize there's a forest fire several miles away. The way this wind is picking up, it could spread."

"That's where my wife is," I said. "So that's where I'm going. And I'm going now. If you're going to arrest me, then arrest me. If not, then get the fuck out of my way."

Taking a chance, I stooped down and seized the baseball bat. Nobody stopped me. I walked towards the park, and Big Steve trotted along at my side, nose to the ground. I prayed that he was tracking his mother and not a rabbit or squirrel. When we reached the grass, I turned around. The others were watching us.

"Well, Detective? You coming?"

Cursing softly, Ramirez followed. Dale, Merle and Cliff hesitantly retrieved their weapons.

"No," Uylik said. "Leave the chainsaw here."

"We'll need it," Cliff replied.

"For what? The detective's got a Glock .40 and I have a

9mm and your friends are armed with shotguns."

"It's not for Hylinus," Cliff said. "It's for the trees."

Ramirez and Uylik stared at him in disbelief.

"Let me make something very clear," Ramirez said. "See that patrol car? It's got a dashboard mounted recording device. The entire time we've been standing here, it's captured your images and our conversation. Now, perhaps you were thinking, 'Oh, we've fooled the cops. Now we can get away with something.' Maybe you think I one hundred percent believe your story—what little bit of it you've shared with me. I don't, but I also don't believe that you're involved in any foul play. Other than that, I don't know what to believe at this point."

"We can help you with your belief," I said. "All we've got to do is show you."

"Well, that may or may not be. Just don't get any ideas inside those woods."

"Don't worry," Dale said. "It's Hylinus we want."

We walked through the playground, weaving our way around the swings and monkey bars. Big Steve stopped long enough to lift his leg and pee on the slide. Then he returned to tracking.

"I still don't think this is a good idea," Officer Young called out.

Big Steve led the way, with Dale and I right behind him. Merle and Cliff walked behind us, Ramirez and Uylik brought up the rear, probably so they could get the jump on us if we proved to be the killers after all.

We stood at the forest's edge. Thin wisps of smoke floated between the trees like strands of gossamer. The wind increased, and above us, the leaves hissed.

"Just the breeze," Dale said. "Just the breeze making them hiss."

"Of course it is," Ramirez answered. "What else would it be?"

"Hopefully, Detective, you won't find out."

Pushing aside the branches, we stepped through the tree line and into the forest. Beneath the green canopy, the moon was eclipsed, and darkness surrounded us like a shroud.

EIGHTEEN

The muted strains of the shepherd's pipe floated through the forest, borne on the smoke. The music was no longer mesmerizing or haunting, but celebratory, full of life and frivolity. It still affected our libidos, but it hinted at something else, too, some indefinable base emotion, suppressed by years of evolution and civilized behavior, hibernating deep inside our gray matter.

Vines and roots snagged our feet, and briars and thorns drew blood, yet the undergrowth itself remained stationary. It wasn't possessed, like the trees at the hollow's core, but it was still a hindrance. The footpath would have been easier—and quicker—to take, but it had disappeared, swallowed up by the forest.

Just like our loved ones had been.

Though the fire was still miles from our location, the smoke soon grew thick enough to sting my eyes. I licked my parched lips. My mouth tasted like burned charcoal.

Big Steve dutifully led us onward. I had no doubt in my mind now that he was following Tara's scent, because the direction he took us was the same general direction the music was coming from. I wondered if the forest itself would let us find her. I wondered what I'd find if we did.

The dog halted about a half mile into the woods, lifted his muzzle, and howled. My pulse beat faster, and I looked around for Tara, squinting into the darkness. Then I smelled it, the stench strong enough to blot out the smoke.

Paul Legerski lay sprawled in front of us. Had we gone a few more feet, we would have stepped on him. His head was missing, but I knew it was Paul. The body wore the same

Winger t-shirt that Paul had worn, the same shirt I'd picked on him about countless times. Despite the absence of light, I was close enough to make out the garish details. He'd been gored, just like Cory. The skin on his arms was gray; and waxy, like fake fruit. The stump of his neck was filled with leaves and twigs. Insects crawled on his extremities, and I had no doubt they were burrowing through the rest of him as well.

I inched closer, but Detective Ramirez pulled me back.

"Don't. This is a crime scene."

He flipped open his cell phone and tried to make a call. While we waited, Cliff and I lit cigarettes. The lighter's flame showed us more details as to the state of Paul's corpse. He'd clearly been here for several days. I was secretly glad when Cliff put the lighter away. Ramirez tried dialing again. His expression grew more frustrated.

"No signal." He snapped the phone shut and slipped it back into his pocket. "There's a cell phone tower right here in town. I don't understand it."

Uylik frowned. "My radio's not working either."

Dale shifted restlessly. "What now, Detective?"

"I know you gentlemen are anxious, but I'll have to secure this crime scene. We can leave Officer Uylik here while we go on, but I'll need to make some quick notes, document the scene and my observations. I'll try to be quick. Meanwhile, please stay back, and keep the dog back, too. If you finish your cigarettes, don't discard the butts anywhere in the vicinity."

"Where's his head?" Cliff asked, stunned.

Ignoring the question, Ramirez held his tie over his nose to block the smell and knelt beside the body. He pulled out a small penlight and began his examination, pausing to make observations in his notebook. Uylik hovered over him, watching.

The rest of us huddled close together. The wind whistled, rustling the leaves above us. The temperature had dropped, and our breath clouded the air. The pipe's sporadic tune continued mocking us; first faint, then loud, and then drifting away again.

Big Steve pranced uneasily.

"Poor little guy." Merle scratched the dog's head. "He's worried about his Mommy."

Cliff and I nodded. Dale gave no indication that he'd heard. Instead, he stared off into the darkness, scowling. I assumed he was thinking about Claudine.

"Don't worry," I said, as the music swelled again. "We'll find them."

He looked nervous. "We came through this spot with the search party. I remember that white boulder over there."

"Hard to tell in the dark," I replied. "But I'll take your word for it."

"I'm sure of it," he insisted. "We passed that rock, and that fallen log to our right. I remember thinking how pretty it was, all covered with moss."

Merle stopped scratching Big Steve. "Yeah, I remember it, too. I thought about bouncing Seth Ferguson's head off that boulder."

Above us, the branches creaked, rocked by the wind.

Cliff exhaled a plume of smoke. "So what? How's that help us now?"

"We were here in broad daylight," Dale explained, "with a search party that included two members of the fire department trained in search and rescue operations. Why didn't we find Paul's body then? Seems like we would have stumbled across it."

Big Steve growled at the darkness.

"One of the other volunteers could have missed it," I suggested. "We were kind of spread out."

"Why no turkey buzzards flying overhead?" Dale shivered, pulling his jacket tight around him. "Every time there's something dead in the field or the woods, you see them circling. But we didn't. Why not?"

"Maybe the body was hidden," Merle said.

"Hidden by what," Dale asked, "and if it was, then why show it to us now?"

Ramirez must have mistaken our hushed chatter for impatience. "Almost finished, gentlemen."

The leaves rustled again. A pinecone plummeted to the

ground, almost hitting Merle on the head. Big Steve growled again.

"It's the hollow," Dale whispered. "The trees are delaying us. It's kept Paul's body hidden all this time, but now it wanted to slow us down."

The leaves continued rustling. All around us, tree limbs groaned, reaching forward. The forest came alive.

Big Steve exploded, barking at the moving foliage.

"Oh shit." Cliff dropped his cigarette and reached for the chainsaw.

"They set a trap," Merle shouted. "They set a fucking trap!"

Ramirez and Uylik whirled around, their weapons drawn.

"What's happening?" Ramirez yelled.

A maple tree lurched towards us.

I glanced up—and screamed.

"Cliff—"

I tried to finish my warning, but it was too late. Even as Cliff's fingers brushed against the chainsaw, a massive oak limb, thick as a railroad tie, punched through his back and straight through his chest, impaling him. Ribs splintered like twigs, and there was an awful, wet sound. Cliff tried to scream, but could only gurgle as dark blood erupted from his mouth and nose. He reached for me, his eyes wide and frightened. I tried to grab his hand, but Big Steve pulled me away, jerking his leash. The dog was terrified, trying to flee. But even in the midst of the chaos, I noticed he wasn't running for home. He was determined to go deeper into the forest.

Tara! The realization flashed through my mind. *Something's happening to her. He can sense it.*

The oak tree straightened its trunk, lifting Cliff high into the air. He dangled above our heads. His blood fell like rain. I blinked the droplets out of my eyes, and tried hard to ignore the warm, salty taste as it splattered into my gaping mouth.

Detective Ramirez shouted something in Spanish.

Have we helped you with your belief now, Detective? I thought.

Two more long limbs from the maple shot forward

and grasped Dale's arms, pinning them to his sides. As he struggled, a branch whipped forward and seized the chainsaw. Merle made a grab for it, but more branches lashed across his hands and face, whipping him away from it. The maple tree flung the chainsaw into the darkness, far beyond our reach.

Uylik shrieked. A monstrous willow towered over him, pinning his body to the ground with its roots. Those same roots had punctured his legs, chest, and arms, and were draining him dry. His body deflated, the skin sagging and wrinkling like a prune. His eyes fell back in his head.

Detective Ramirez squeezed off three shots. The bullets slammed into the willow, gouging the wood, but had little effect. My ears rang. Ramirez hollered at me but I couldn't understand what he said. The ringing also drowned out the shepherd's pipe— and Cliff's final, gurgling scream, as another massive tree limb smashed his head open like a rotten pumpkin. His body went limp, still dangling in mid-air, an oak tree sprouting from his chest.

To the left, Dale struggled with the maple tree. His arms were pinned tight against his body, and the tree limbs wrapped around him like a snake, slowly squeezing him to death. He struggled to breathe, and his face turned purple. His shotgun lay at his feet, fully loaded and completely useless.

Merle's weapon boomed from my right, as he and Ramirez opened fire on the oak tree that had murdered Cliff. Once again, the tree shrugged off the detective's bullets. But Merle's silver-loaded shotgun shells had a much different effect. I don't know if it was the spell we'd said over them, or the silver itself, or a combination of the two, but as the jewelry hit the bark, the wood split open, belching smoke and sap. The tree's scream was deafening. The crack in the wood widened, and more smoke poured through, thick and black—and alive. It moved with purpose, fleeing from its organic shell and soaring into the night sky. Then its screams faded.

Shouting, Ramirez and Merle turned their attentions to the willow. They didn't notice the maple attacking Dale, and couldn't hear me above the gunfire. Dragging Big Steve with me, I swung the baseball bat at the maple. The sharpened silver dollar sank into the trunk, embedding itself in the wood. The tree shuddered, then split apart. Again, writhing tendrils of black smoke erupted from the wound. Enraged, the shadowy form flew away. The coiling tree branches went limp, and Dale gasped for breath.

"You okay?" Coughing, Dale nodded.

Merle, Big Steve and I stood back to back, forming a half circle while warily watching the rest of the forest for signs of movement. Ramirez, mopping blood from his forehead with his handkerchief, ran over to Uylik's side.

"Officer down," he moaned. "Oh shit, officer down!"

We didn't know how to respond, so we said nothing.

"I think that's it," Merle panted after a moment. "The rest aren't moving."

I peered into the darkness. "Are you sure?"

"Yeah." Merle dropped the shotgun and bent over, hyperventilating. "Jesus . . ."

I glanced over at Cliff, and then threw up all over my shoes. Big Steve scampered out of the way.

"What the fuck is going on?" Ramirez's eyes were wide, scared. "What was this?"

Ignoring him, I retched again. I hadn't eaten since breakfast, but my body didn't care. Big Steve kept his distance.

Dale called out, struggling to free himself from the branches. "Hey guys, a little help?"

Merle grabbed the clinging flora and ripped it aside, and Dale collapsed to the ground. Merle helped him up. The two leaned against each other, resting.

Cliff's mangled form still hung suspended from the tree, a human scarecrow. His bowels had loosened in death, dripping down the legs of his pants. My breath caught in my throat and I turned away, closing my eyes. I didn't want to see him like this. I wanted to remember Cliff riding around on his Harley, cigarette dangling from his mouth, always ready with a wisecrack—not as the leaking bag of meat dangling over our heads.

Dale and Merle shuffled over. Dale hugged me. Merle looked up at our friend and sighed.

"Oh Cliff . . ."

Ramirez lashed out, kicking a pile of leaves. "What the fuck was this? I've got a man down—a cop!"

Merle's face darkened. "Fuck you, Ramirez. In case you haven't noticed, we lost a friend, too."

"But what happened? The trees . . ."

I stepped toward him. "I'm sorry. To be honest, we weren't sure if this would happen again. We thought maybe we'd taken care of them earlier."

"Taken care of what?"

"The trees act as guardians," Dale explained. "They protect Hylinus."

"What in God's name are we up against?"

"Hell," I said simply. "You wanted help with your beliefs. Well, this is it. The devil is out there, complete with horns and cloven feet. Hear those pipes? He's calling us to the dance."

Ramirez stared at me, unable to speak.

Dale bent over and picked something up off the ground beneath Cliff's body—his lighter and cigarettes. Dale shook four out of the pack and handed one to each of us.

Ramirez shook his head. "No thank you. I don't smoke."

"Then I suggest you start," Dale advised him. "This is serious white magic here. Not smoking could be hazardous to your health."

Merle took the lighter from Dale and lit his. "Didn't help Cliff much."

We stood in a circle and smoked our friend's cigarettes. Ramirez refused to light his. Instead, Ramirez tucked it in his shirt pocket. While we said goodbye to Cliff, he closed Uylik's eyes.

"He had a wife and three kids," the detective murmured. "One of his kids had multiple sclerosis. How are we going to explain this to them?"

We didn't answer. Merle pulled more shotgun shells from his pockets and reloaded. Dale retrieved his weapon.

I took another drag off my cigarette. The smell of wood smoke grew stronger. The woods seemed brighter, too. I searched for the source of illumination, and noticed an orange glow coming from between the trees to our left, perhaps a football field's length away.

"Is it me," I said, "or is that fire getting closer?"

The music grew louder and clearer, mixing with the sound of drumming. Then came voices and laughter. Women's voices.

Barking, Big Steve sprang forward, almost jerking the leash out of my hands. I had time to grab the baseball bat before he dragged me forward. I had no choice but to follow, lest he wrench free of the leash and take off on his own. Dropping their smokes, Merle and Dale scrambled for their weapons and ran after us.

"Wait," Ramirez called. "We can't just leave them!"

Ignoring him, we ran on, letting Big Steve guide us. He made a beeline for the orange glow. We darted between trees and stumbled over roots and stones. The underbrush tore our skin, but we pushed on, oblivious. I resisted the urge to call out for Tara, and noticed that the dog had grown silent too.

Panting for breath, he halted next to a wild tangle of raspberry bushes. The others caught up with us.

"You can't just run off like that," Ramirez warned.

"Quiet," I whispered. "Listen. We're close."

Slowly, we peeked over the thicket. Our eyes widened as one.

The glow wasn't cast by the inferno sweeping through the forest, but by a huge bonfire, built in the middle of a clearing. Hylinus danced around it in a circle, playing his shepherd's pipe. Tara, Claudine, Antonietta, Leslie, and Shannon danced with him. The firelight reflected off their naked, sweating bodies. Shelly sat on a nearby stump, playing the drums.

Dale reached out and squeezed my arm.

The drums were human heads. Now we knew what Hylinus had done with the rest of Paul Legerski. I recognized the other head, too. Had seen it on the news that morning, when they'd shown a picture of him, a picture in which he'd still been alive and smiling. It was Leslie's date, Michael Gitleson. Their lips were blue; their eyes open.

Ramirez's stare grew wider and wider.

"Well, Detective," I whispered. "Do you believe now?"

"Holy shit . . ."

I knew how he felt.

And then, before we could move, Big Steve finally found his courage. Tara pranced by again, writhing in time to the music. Big Steve watched her pass. Then he slipped his collar and leaped from the undergrowth, landing in the midst of the circle, interrupting the orgy. The women screamed and scattered. Big Steve barked. The music stopped.

I clutched the dog's empty leash in my hand.

Roaring, Hylinus charged.

Snarling, Big Steve sprang to meet him.

NINETEEN

Everything happened so fast; chaos erupting around the bonfire, screaming and howling and cries of pain and anger, gunshots and more screams.

Big Steve and Hylinus slammed into one another with an audible smack. The satyr had his head lowered in an effort to disembowel Big Steve, but the dog was quicker, twisting out of his path in mid-air and landing behind him. His jaws snapped shut on the satyr's tail. Growling, Big Steve planted his feet, shaking his head viciously, intent on pulling the tail out by the roots. Enraged, Hylinus tried to turn around and strike him, but Big Steve moved in a circle with him, staying out of reach of those wicked claws, the tail gripped firmly between his clenched teeth. I thought about all the times the two of us had played tug-of-war and knew Hylinus wasn't getting free.

We crashed through the vines and into the clearing. Merle raised his shotgun, aiming it at Hylinus, but I pushed the barrel away.

"No, you'll hit Big Steve!"

Apparently, Detective Ramirez had no qualms about my dog. Before I could stop him, he raised the forty-caliber and fired three shots into the satyr's chest, the groupings close enough to be covered with the bottom of a soda can. The bullets parted fur and flesh and exploded out the back, spraying the leaves and trees with satyr blood, but Hylinus merely grunted and continued struggling with Big Steve. Cursing, Ramirez readjusted his aim.

"It's just like the trees, Detective," Merle hollered. "You got to use silver."

"Where the hell is that backup?" Ramirez fumbled for his cell phone and tried to place a call. When he still couldn't get a signal, he pointed the Glock into the air and fired in an attempt to let them know our location.

Wailing with fear, Shelly dropped Paul and Michael's heads, and joined the other women on the far side of the bonfire. The severed head rolled through the leaves, coming to rest against a fallen log.

"Release me," Hylinus roared. "Release me now, lowly cur!"

Growling in defiance, Big Steve tugged harder, dragging the satyr towards us and away from Tara and the others. The bullet wounds in Hylinus's chest had already healed, and all that remained were three singed patches of fur.

Dale circled the bonfire, running after Claudine. She seemed to recognize him for an instant. Confusion flashed in her eyes. He swept her up into his arms and pulled her close. I was torn between my dog and my wife. I needed to get Tara to safety, away from the satyr's influence, but I couldn't just leave Big Steve behind, struggling with the creature.

Merle must have seen the indecision in my expression. "Go help Tara. I've got this."

He stalked towards Hylinus, intent on shooting him at point blank range, but before he could reach him, the satyr raised the shepherd's pipe to his lips and played a new tune, one that didn't invite erections or inspire lust; a darker, sinister-sounding song. The notes hung heavy in the air.

Instantly, the women changed. Their expressions and demeanor transformed with the music. Gone was the fear and uncertainty, replaced with horrifying looks of hatred and loathing. The firelight cast writhing shadows on their naked bodies. As one, they attacked. Claudine pushed away from Dale, clawing at his face. Her nails sank deep into his cheek, raking the flesh. Dale yelled in surprise and pain. Antonietta Wallace joined her, beating Dale's back with both fists. Leslie and Shannon dashed towards Merle, shrieking obscenities, and Shelly went after Ramirez. Tara came for me, and in the firelight, I barely recognized her as the woman I'd married.

Her lips pulled back in a hideous snarl, and something flashed in her eyes that I'd never seen before. Murder. She intended to kill me with her bare hands.

The music continued. Big Steve wrenched his head to the right, ripping the tail out by the roots. Bellowing in agony, Hylinus tumbled backward into the dirt, still clutching his pipe. Big Steve dropped the bloody stump and leapt for his throat. His teeth flashed in the darkness, and sounds rumbled from his chest that I'd never heard him make before.

Both my wife and my dog, the two people closer to me than anybody on Earth, were different now. Big Steve's animal instincts had taken over. Tara's had, too.

The satyr kicked out with both feet, catching Big Steve in midleap. Yelping, the dog flew through the air, crashing into a tree. He landed in a pile of dead leaves and lay still. Before I could run to him, Hylinus brought the pipe back to his mouth and resumed playing. Tara fell upon me again, kicking and scratching. She knocked the bat from my grasp, and her hands closed around my throat and squeezed.

From the corner of my eye, I saw Ramirez point the pistol at Shelly and order her to halt. Then Tara swung me around, blocking my vision. A gunshot rang out. I heard Big Steve making the helicopter noise with his ears as he shook his head, so I knew he was alive at least, and able to move. Relief coursed through me, even as the blood pounded in my temples, and my lungs screamed for air. I was dying, but that was okay because my dog was still alive.

“T-ta . . ." I tried to speak her name, but couldn't.

“I should have done this a long time ago,” she spat. “Your are fucking worthless, Adam. I want babies and Hylinus can give them to me. Unlike you, he's a real man, with a real dick.”

My vision blurred. Tara's foul breath was hot on my face; her spittle ran down my cheek, mingling with my tears.

“He's so much bigger than you. *And I love it!*”

With all my remaining strength, I brought my knee up hard, kicking her in the groin. Tara's breath whooshed out of her lungs, and her grip loosened around my throat. I gasped for air and then swung my fist, striking her in the breast. She crumpled to the ground, gasping in pain. My lungs felt like they were on fire. Coughing, I glanced around.

Dale had gone down under Claudine and Antonietta's continued assault. Merle and Ramirez both had their hands full as well. Shelly had backed the detective up to the bonfire. He warned her again to step back, told her to lie down on the ground with her hands behind her back, but she ignored him, flinging taunts and curses. Ramirez pointed his weapon at her, but his aim wavered, and I could tell he didn't want to shoot her. Merle, however, had no qualms. Shannon Legerski aimed a kick at his stomach and Merle sidestepped, and then swung the stock of the shotgun, striking her in the chin. Shannon collapsed, screaming through a broken jaw. From behind, Leslie grabbed a fistful of Merle's hair and gave it a savage yank.

"That wasn't nice, old man," Leslie cackled. "All those times you were checking me out at the gas station, staring at my ass— let's see that dick now, so I can tear it off!"

Hylinus continued to play. The bonfire's flames grew higher, and the woods filled with smoke as the raging forest fire drew closer.

Tara didn't move. Stumbling forward, I reached for her. "
Honey, are you—"

Shrieking, she flung a handful of dirt into my face, blinding me. Her first punch caught me square in the groin. My testicles shriveled as cold pain coursed through me. I didn't even feel the second punch. I fell. Dale screamed from somewhere to my left.

Blinking the dirt out of my eyes, I tried to roll over, but Tara leaped on top of me, straddling my chest. Her vagina gaped like an open wound, raw and bleeding. The satyr's sperm dripped from it like poison. I tried to scream, but Tara's fist smashed into my mouth. My lips shredded against my teeth. Blow after blow rained down upon my face. Another gunshot rang out, but I barely heard it over the ringing sound in my ears. Frothing at the mouth, Tara ranted incoherently.

"Killyoukillyoukillyoukillyoumotherfuckingkill. . ."

Something dark and hairy jumped between us, brushing

against my face. I thought it was Hylinus, but when I sat up, Tara was on her back. Big Steve held her down with his front paws. Whining, he licked her face.

"Adam!"

I turned. Ramirez stumbled toward me, reloading the Glock. Behind him, Shelly Carpenter lay still, dead. He'd shot her after all. There were two wounds; one in her leg, and a second in her head.

Tara struggled beneath Big Steve. "Get off me, you god damned dog!"

He responded with a worried bark, and then licked her face some more.

"Ramirez." I pointed towards Dale, all but invisible beneath Claudine and Antonietta's thrashing bodies. "Help Da—"

A wailing, high-pitched scream cut me off. It seemed to have no end, reminding me of a fire siren—a breathless, warbling screech that went on and on and on until it seemed that the vocal cords of whoever was making its vocal chords would rupture.

It belonged to Merle.

He was on his back against a log. Somehow, they'd managed to get his pants off. Shannon clubbed him repeatedly on the head with the shotgun, while Leslie sat between his spread legs. One of her hands clutched his manhood, stretching it out. The other hand sawed back and forth at the base of his penis with a sharp rock. Blood poured from the wound. Merle's arms and legs jittered spasmodically. He tried to sit up, but Shannon struck him again with the stock. He sank back, still shrieking. Leslie continued hacking through his dick with the rock.

"Drop your weapons," Ramirez warned.

A crazy part of me wondered if he meant the shotgun or the rock. I started to laugh, but it turned into a scream.

Ramirez snapped the Glock up and squeezed off a shot. The back of Shannon's head exploded. Still holding the shotgun, she toppled over onto Merle. The exit wound was the size of a fist. At the same instant, Leslie leaned back and with a triumphant cry, held Merle's severed penis over her head like a prize. A second later, Ramirez shot her, too.

Hylinus stopped playing. Roaring in furious indignation, he ran towards his fallen harem.

"Help Dale," I shouted at Ramirez.

Springing to my feet, I seized the baseball bat and charged Hylinus. Big Steve jumped off Tara and dashed along behind me. I swung the bat, but the satyr was faster. He ducked beneath the blow and punched me in my already battered face. One of my back teeth crunched beneath his massive fist. I flew backward, landing next to Leslie. Blood trickled from her mouth and nose, and her chest was as pink as her hair. Her eyes were open. She blinked.

". . .Adam?"

With the music halted, her senses had returned.

"Don't move," I said, sitting up. "Just lay still, Leslie. You're hurt."

"I . . ." Her lips stopped moving.

Big Steve sprang into the air, knocking Hylinus to the ground. The two of them wrestled with one another, rolling through the leaves, growling and clawing and biting. Big Steve's teeth ripped into the satyr's side, tearing through fur and flesh.

"Adam," Merle moaned. "My fucking dick's g-gone. . ."

"Ssshhh." I patted his hand. "Just lay still, man. Help is coming. It's gonna be okay."

"Okay? M-my fucking d-dick's gone!"

"You'll be—"

"Where's Cliff?"

I choked back tears. "He's okay. He's just waiting for you to get better. Now you just rest, okay?"

He grabbed my hand. "T-tell Peggy. . .that I. . ."

"Yeah? I'm listening, Merle. Tell me."

"T-tell Peggy . . ."

He died with his ex-wife's name on his lips.

Then Big Steve yelped, louder than I'd ever heard him before.

I turned away from Merle—and screamed.

Big Steve thrashed in the satyr's grip. Hylinus held him aloft, dangling him from his back legs. One clawed hand gripped Big Steve's hind paws, and the other still clutched the shepherd's pipe. The satyr's horns were buried in Big Steve's underbelly. Blood stained both their fur. The dog struggled helplessly as Hylinus ripped into him, goring him further. Big Steve howled, and then Hylinus pulled his head away from the dog's torn abdomen and threw him to the ground.

Something spilled out of Big Steve's insides, and I snapped. "You motherfucker!"

Hylinus grinned. "Now it is your turn, son of Adam. At the hands of your wife, I believe."

Grabbing Merle's shotgun, I stumbling to my feet and pointed the weapon at him.

"Oh, what fools you mortals be," Hylinus laughed. "Your weapon cannot harm one such as I."

He raised the shepherd's pipe to his lips and began to play.

"It's silver, you son of a bitch."

Hylinus stopped playing. His eyes grew wide.

I squeezed the trigger.

The blast hit the satyr in the chest, knocking him to the ground. Blood poured from the wound, hissing like bacon grease in a frying pan. His fur burned. Hylinus screamed in a language that I didn't understand. It sounded like something from one of Nelson LeHorn's books.

Looming over him, I jacked another shell into the chamber.

He pointed at me with one clawed finger. "Know this, son of Adam. I have tasted the nectar of your wife's loins. She has presented herself to me and we have rutted beneath the moon. Forever, when she orgasms, my name will be on her lips. This is my curse upon thee."

I pressed the smoking shotgun barrel between his legs, right against his penis.

"No!" His eyes grew wider still. Terrified.

"Yes."

I pulled the trigger again, obliterating that monstrous phallus. His terrible, agonized cries filled the night, music to my ears. I squeezed the trigger a third time, unloading into the bite wound Big Steve had delivered. Blood bubbled as the silver hissed, burrowing deeper into his flesh.

I spat in his face. "That is silver from those who you defiled, delivered with duct tape owned by Merle, and emptied into a wound caused by my dog, Big Steve. Our magic is stronger than yours."

I glanced around the clearing. Tara knelt over Big Steve, gently stroking his fur. Claudine sobbed, rocking back and forth on the balls of her feet. Antonietta shivered, looking about in bewilderment. Dale and Ramirez moved to my side.

"What is that thing?" Ramirez asked.

Ignoring his question, I held out my palm. "Hand me that cigarette that Cliff gave you earlier."

Hylinus twitched, moaning in shock and pain.

Dale slid his gold wedding band off his finger, knelt over, and thrust it into the gunshot wound in the creature's chest. "This is a band of gold, a perfect circle, and a symbol of my wife's and my undying love. You cannot break the circle. You cannot break us. This is our magic."

Hylinus screamed; his thrashing increased.

Ramirez handed me Cliff's last cigarette. I lit it and bent over, my face inches away from the satyr's.

"This is smoke from Cliff's magic cancer sticks. As I breathe his last breath into you, may it be yours as well. By our names do I slay thee; Adam Senft and Dale Haubner and Merle Laughman and Clifford Swanson and Cory Peters, and by the names of our wives, Claudine Haubner and Tara Senft, and all the other women you've fouled; Shelly Carpenter and Shannon Legerski and Antonietta Wallace and Leslie Vandercamp; and in the names of those men whom you slaughtered, Michael Gitleson and Paul Legerski and Officer Al Uylik; and for Nelson and Patricia LeHorn and their children; and for anyone else that you've harmed through the ages . . . die now and never return!"

I inhaled. The tip of the cigarette glowed. Then, leaning closer, I placed my lips to the satyr's and exhaled smoke into his lungs. His spine arched, and he threw his head back, choking. Then, spasms wracked his body. I stood back, hurrying Dale and Ramirez away from him.

I'm not sure what I expected to happen. He didn't burst into flames or explode or vanish in a flash of light. It was anti-climactic, really. Hylinus flopped on the ground like a fish out of water, and finally, lay still. His chest rose one final time, and then did not rise again.

"You okay?" I asked Dale.

He nodded. "Got the shit beat out of me, but I think you look worse."

"Claudine?"

"She'll be. . .well, she's unharmed, physically at least."

I pointed at Hylinus. "Throw him on the bonfire. Fire purifies, right? So that's good magic. Make sure you throw his pipe on there, too."

Dale and Ramirez grabbed the satyr's arms and legs and dragged him towards the fire, grunting with the effort.

I knelt beside Tara. Her hands were red with Big Steve's blood. Tears streamed down her face.

"I—I don't understand what's happening," she cried. "Adam, what's going on?"

"It'll be okay," I lied.

Something wet brushed against my knuckles. I looked down and Big Steve nuzzled me again with his nose. His big, brown eyes were filled with pain, but also mirrored love and affection. He licked my hand—

—and then he died.

I hung my head and wailed. Sobbing, Tara leaned against me. We held each other, crouched there in the dirt and leaves, and cried. So many were lost, Leslie and Cory and Cliff and Merle; some of the best friends and neighbors I've ever had—but the toughest loss of all was Big Steve. He'd been a part of us, a part of Tara and me— a part of the family. It felt like losing another child. The pain was a raw, open wound, and I wept in a way I hadn't done since the miscarriages.

"Adam." Dale squeezed my shoulder. "The forest fire is getting closer. We've got to go. Now."

I helped Tara to her feet.

"Big Steve," I said to Dale. "We can't just leave him

like this. And what about Merle and Leslie and Shannon's bodies?"

Tears spilled from his eyes. "We can't carry them. There's nothing else we can do."

Antonietta Wallace shrieked, tripping over Paul and Michael's severed heads. Detective Ramirez ran to her.

"This isn't right," I insisted. "They deserve better."

"Yes," Dale agreed, "they do. But we can't give it to them, Adam. Look at us. We've both had the shit beat out of us. I can barely stand, let alone carry Merle. Neither can you. We don't have time to bury them."

The bonfire roared, the satyr's corpse now engulfed in flames. His skeleton blackened as the flames licked at it. The shepherd's pipe had melted. In the distance, the forest fire's orange glow drew closer, crackling and popping. The sound reminded me of the ocean. The smoke grew thick as fog.

Tara coughed. "Please, Adam. I want to go home."

"Okay," I whispered. "Let's go home."

Slowly, I led her away. The firelight lit our path, parting the darkness. The trees stood frozen, unable to flee the advancing destruction—unmoving, as normal trees are supposed to be. Dale and Claudine limped after us. Detective Ramirez and Antonietta Wallace brought up the rear. I found Big Steve's leash and collar lying amongst the vines, and I picked it up. His tags jingled.

"What has happened to us?" Antonietta rasped, choking on the drifting smoke.

"You wouldn't believe it if we told you," Ramirez said. "In truth, I didn't believe it either."

"And now, Detective?" Dale asked. "Now do you believe?"

"Oh yes, Mr. Haubner. I'm a believer. I'm just not sure what it is I now believe in."

"Hell," Dale said. "We've seen proof of hell."

When I glanced back for one last look, the clearing was an inferno.

TWENTY

That was six months ago. The Forest Fire of Spring 2006, as it came to be called, destroyed over five hundred acres of woodlands, including LeHorn's Hollow and the adjoining farmhouse and out buildings. Nothing was left. Investigators suspected arson, but were never able to determine the exact cause. In the end, it was speculated that a careless cigarette or an untended campfire had sparked the conflagration. It made national headlines, and for a week, we had even more reporters than before hanging around. It overshadowed the original story—the disappearances.

Eventually, the media and the authorities pulled out that reliable old chestnut; the satanic cult, and got the public to believe it. Dale, Ramirez and I knew the truth, of course, but we kept silent. Ramirez believed, but he knew that others wouldn't. I don't know who the spin-doctor was, but by month's end, the rumor was that Shelly Carpenter and the Legerski's were leading a coven, which practiced black magic somewhere in the woods and worshipped Nelson LeHorn.

It didn't hold up in the light of day; there were too many unanswered questions and too many loose ends. But the authorities were never able to answer them. The fire had destroyed much of the evidence, aside from Cory's body, Michael Gitleson's car and his headless corpse, and a few hoof prints outside Shelly's and the Legerski house, along with that tuft of fur they'd recovered from Gitleson's car. Tara, Claudine, and Antonietta Wallace had no memory of their abductions, or anything that happened after that, up until the time we'd rescued them. Paul and Michael's deaths were investigated, as were Cory's, Cliff's, and Merle's. I suppose it was just easier for the authorities to take those bits of information that didn't match up with the cult theory and sweep them under the rug. It's not like television. Other crimes were being committed and there were other cases to solve. This one had been neatly wrapped up, complete with a bow. It did them no good to examine the wrapping paper for holes and tears. The national media didn't even report on it after the first week. There were other things going on; natural disasters and terrorist attacks and wars and corporate scandals.

For the most part, we managed to keep our total involvement out of the paper. Tara was never mentioned by name, and the only thing the news really reported was that Cory's body had been found murdered inside my home—or, as they put it, *BODY FOUND MURDERED INSIDE HOME OF LOCAL AUTHOR*. That caused all kinds of questions and speculation, but like I said, after a few weeks, the questions stopped and people looked elsewhere at the other stories happening in the world.

Ramirez retired—at least, publicly. I'd heard he was forced out for bungling the investigation, just like he'd fumbled the bank robbery and hostage standoff in Hanover. I felt sorry for him, but I never revealed the truth to his superiors. If Ramirez was happy to keep his mouth shut, then so was I. Last I heard, he was working for a private security firm somewhere down south. I hope that he found what he was looking for.

Antonietta Wallace and her husband moved to Florida a few weeks ago. Leslie's kid went to live with her parents. They live up north, near Allentown. I don't walk down to the gas station anymore, and buy my cigarettes at Wal-Mart. Paul and Shannon Legerski's house sold to a nice young couple from Maryland. They're expecting a baby. I met them once, and have avoided them since.

Merle's house is up for estate auction. He left everything to Peggy, his ex-wife. Dale and I saw her in the weeks that followed, as she went through Merle's belongings. We told her how much he'd loved her, that his last thoughts had been of her, and she cried. She asked us how he actually died, and we lied to her. The auction is next month. They'll sell everything; the antiques, the house, even the wood shop out back. The only thing missing is LeHorn's books. I'd left them in the wood shop when we went to confront Hylinus, and I rescued them the same night.

New tenants moved into Cliff and Cory's apartments; a young couple downstairs and an elderly woman in Cliff's. Dale and I refuse to talk to them, other than nodding hello, or exchanging pleasantries. That's the way it is these days. You really don't know your neighbors, other than minor small talk. Sometimes it's better that way.

Our neighborhood has changed. It's no longer home.

I haven't written since that night. I tried to, eventually. Went through the daily ritual, my own personal writer's powwow. But the words would not come. There was something missing—a key ingredient, the essence of my muse.

Big Steve.

His collar and leash still hang on the door. I can't bring myself to take them down.

I don't take walks anymore, and I've put on weight.

At night, I lay in the darkness next to Tara and there's an empty space in our bed that wasn't there before. I wake up in the morning, expecting to feel his cold nose, listening for his snores or the helicopter sound he made when he shook his ears, but instead, there are only the quiet sounds of my own muffled sobs.

I cry a lot more these days. Seems like I cry all the time.

Big Steve's absence isn't the only space between Tara and I. We have grown distant, two strangers sharing a house. I'm worried about her, worried about us. I don't think she loves me anymore and the thought scares me to death, because she's all I have left. I remember how she used to be, before all this happened. She's different now. Cold. Unemotional. We don't hold hands. We don't talk. We don't make love. At first, I figured it was because she'd been raped. Figured we'd get through it together, just like we get through everything else. But it wasn't because of that. It was because. . .

She's pregnant.

We found out a month and a half after the incident. Her

period was late. We chalked it up to the emotional and physical trauma she'd been through. But then she took a test and a trip to the doctor confirmed the results. We haven't made love since the spring, and we supposed that it happened the last time we did, right before Hylinus abducted her. Yes, we'd been careful, and no, we hadn't exactly completed the act, but accidents happen. And this was a joyful accident.

We were cautious at first. We had reason to be. But the months passed and everything seemed fine. It's supposed to be the happiest time of our life, especially for us. We didn't suffer a third miscarriage. This time, the baby is healthy and normal.

Or so I was told.

I didn't go with her to the last ultrasound. I'd promised Dale I'd help him build a wheelchair ramp to his porch. He needs it to get around in more and more these days. He's grown a lot older in the last six months.

I helped him with it and missed the doctor's appointment. Tara went by herself. She promised that she'd bring home a picture of the baby, so that I could see it too. When she got back, she seemed quiet and distant. She said that they couldn't determine the sex, and that the machine hadn't been working right. She told me there was no picture. Then, complaining of a headache, she'd gone to bed and slept till the next morning.

The distance between us started then, and we've continued to grow apart ever since. Now I know why. This morning, when I was putting away the laundry, I found a piece of paper crumpled up and stuffed into her underwear drawer. It was from the ultrasound. A picture of our baby.

The baby. . .

The baby has horns. And what appears to be cloven feet.

And it's definitely a boy. Judging from the size, it takes after its father.

Tara is upstairs crying again. I confronted her with the picture, and I guess I said some things I shouldn't have. Accused her of remembering more than she'd let on. Mentioned an abortion. Hell, I demanded one. She was furious with me. Accused me of wanting to kill the baby. She ran up into the attic and locked the door.

I've sat here all afternoon, reading through LeHorn's books, trying to figure out what to do. She's stayed in the attic. Occasionally, I hear her crying, but she's been quiet for the most part. I think I found something, a certain potion and spell to stop this from happening. All she has to do is drink it, and that should take care of the baby. I'm going up to the attic and try to talk with her. I love my wife. I want a family. But not like this. I want things to be normal again. Everything I have to do now, I'm doing for her. If I can make her see that, then maybe we can get through this. Maybe we can still have a child of our own.

I want her to love me the way she used to.

I'll write more later on. I'm going to save this file and then burn it onto disc, and hide it with LeHorn's books, so that it stays safe.

I'm going up to the attic now, and I will do what I must to make things right.

It's funny. I've been up in that attic a million times, but those stairs have never seemed steeper than they do right now.

I am very tired.

BRIAN KEENE is the author of over twenty-five books, including *Darkness on the Edge of Town, Urban Gothic, Castaways, Kill Whitey, Dark Hollow, Dead Sea, Ghoul* and *The Rising*. He also writes comic books such as *The Last Zombie, Doom Patrol* and *Dead of Night: Devil Slayer*. His work has been translated into German, Spanish, Polish, Italian, French and Taiwanese. Several of his novels and stories have been developed for film, including *Ghoul* and *The Ties That Bind*. In addition to writing, Keene also oversees Maelstrom, his own small press publishing imprint specializing in collectible limited editions, via Thunderstorm Books. Keene's work has been praised in such diverse places as *The New York Times*, The History Channel, The Howard Stern Show, CNN.com, *Publisher's Weekly*, Media Bistro, *Fangoria Magazine,* and *Rue Morgue Magazine.* Keene lives in Pennsylvania. You can communicate with him online at www.briankeene.com or on Twitter at @BrianKeene

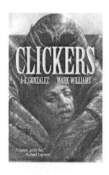

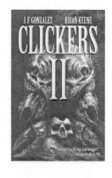

"The Haunter of the Threshold" Edward Lee - There is something very wrong with this backwater town. Suicide notes, magic gems, and haunted cabins await her. Plus the woods are filled with monsters, both human and otherworldly. And then there are the horrible tentacles . . . Soon Hazel is thrown into a battle for her life that will test her sanity and sex drive. The sequel to H.P. Lovecraft's The Haunter of the Dark is Edward Lee's most pornographic novel to date!

"The Innswich Horror" Edward Lee - In July, 1939, antiquarian and H.P. Lovecraft aficionado, Foster Morley, takes a scenic bus tour through northern Massachusetts and finds Innswich Point. There far too many similarities between this fishing village and the fictional town of Lovecraft's masterpiece, The Shadow Over Innsmouth. Join splatter king Edward Lee for a private tour of Innswich Point - a town founded on perversion, torture, and abominations from the sea.

"Highways to Hell" Bryan Smith - The road to hell is paved with angels and demons. Brain worms and dead prostitutes. Serial killers and frustrated writers. Zombies and Rock 'n Roll. And once you start down this path, there is no going back. Collecting thirteen tales of shock and terror from Bryan Smith, Highways to Hell is a non-stop road-trip of cruelty, pain, and death. Grab a seat, Smith has such sights to show you.

"Apeshit" Carlton Mellick III - Friday the 13th meets Visitor Q. Six hipster teens go to a cabin in the woods inhabited by a deformed killer. An incredibly fucked-up parody of B-horror movies with a bizarro slant

"*The new gold standard in unstoppable fetus-fucking kill-freakomania . . . Genuine all-meat hardcore horror meets unadulterated Bizarro brainwarp strangeness. The results are beyond jaw-dropping, and fill me with pure, unforgivable joy.*" - John Skipp

AVAILABLE FROM AMAZON.COM

CPSIA information can be obtained at www.ICGtesting.com
Printed in the USA
BVOW02s1150060616

450381BV00019B/118/P

9 781621 050308